THE LITTLE COFFEE SHOP OF HORRORS ANTHOLOGY 2

PAUL CARRO & JOSEPH CARRO

Tether Falls Press

Contents

INTRODUCTION

W HAT CAN WE GET you this evening? How do you like yours? Straight up, dark as night? Maybe you prefer a sweeter concoction, one that leans red? Oh, we have milk and sweeteners, but you don't want to water things down do you? That's not why you are here. You are here to caffeinate until you shake. We understand. It's okay, we'll keep your secrets here.

You might have noticed this is no regular coffee shop. There are no warm inviting couches dropped into too many coffee establishments copying the vibe of *Central Perk* on *Friends* oh so many years ago. Nor is it designed to seat people comfortably in such a manner that they face one another, forcing them to be social.

Because we understand. You want a place to hide, to be your weird self, to people watch, but not be seen yourself. You're that person that beelines for the corner seat, the one in the shadows. Like a vampire, light is not your friend, only something to tolerate. While you sip and soak in the caffeine, you watch, you spy, you wonder how is it all these people came to be in the same spot as you, and how is it none are as strange as you? How can they be so... normal?

That is where you are wrong. Somewhere under the façade of monotony lies another person, the truest version of who they really are. That impeccably dressed businesswoman trying to impress her equally well-dressed boss while they await their order? Is that the hint of a tattoo riding up along the back of her neck? She scratches at it, as if aware, and her breath hitches at the touch, a lingering excitement from whoever she allowed to see it the night before. She raises her collar to better hide it and turns the smile back onto her coffee partner.

There is another couple, males, both wearing wedding rings. Both wearing suits themselves (aren't they always at this hour clinging to the daily ritual of formal wear?) Except when you look closer at the gap between polished shoes and hem of pants, you notice the one is not wearing dress socks, he is wearing fishnet stockings. Does the other know? They do not appear intimate. Their interactions are formal. Fake.

They do not notice you of course. No one ever does. That is your superpower. Invisible in all circumstances. The proverbial fly on the wall.

I understand. Make that, we understand. The authors, Joseph, and I, traveled to various coffee shops around the country. We sat in a corner the way you do, and we watched. We watched the people come and go, trying to hide their true selves, trying to mask their shame in waves of black warm liquid, or frozen treats laden with sugar and desperation. Extra whip? Someone had been extra bad the night before.

We watched people independently, because together patrons would notice us. No, Joe and I needed to remain invisible just like you. We set up in corners of our own and watched. We used what we observed to create short horror stories, single sourced ones, inspired by the environment, the location, or the people.

Like you, we saw through the fake skins that people wore (as if they were video game avatars). We recognized the hidden realities within the hustle and bustle as coffee's aroma hid stenches of guilt that customers wore like perfume. You hold in your hands the result. A volume two for those who survived volume one. Twelve tales designed to induce tremors in those who have developed too strong a tolerance for caffeine.

But I forgot, this is about you. You can use our book then, in your corner of the coffee shop where you sit. Use it as a shield to cover your face. Your face is easy to read, it bleeds desperation as you hungrily search the public sphere hoping to find one of your kind. You long to find that other freak, that other corner person, the other shadow people in your midst.

You read while waiting and watching. Then it happens. He enters (or she enters, I don't know your life) and you think, this could be the one. They do not hide their true selves. They wear their skin appropriately. On the outside. Their tattoos are on full display, the individual's clothing covers as little as possible but enough to avoid arrest. They desire to show off their skin. Want you to see their flesh for their exposed skin tells a story as much as the ones in the book that you hold.

Every tat has meaning, each colorful splash of ink penetrated skin speaks to who they are. The colors are designed to entice, to draw the attention of the right person. The peacock effect. It works on you. Already warm from your cup of coffee, you flush with heat. Is this individual worth emerging from the shadows for?

Light reflects off the piercings of their shrapnel style chin, nose, and ears. They are an individual unafraid of puncturing their flesh. Their body entices you. Many bodies do. That is part of the people watching. But the body in question is designed to send a signal. That they seek you. That they desire you. They yearn for you.

Are they dangerous? You know the answer, yet you refuse to look away. Can you become part of the patchwork of ink on their body? Can you become part of them? To do so they must consume you in some fashion. No influencer of social media are you. You simply want to be that person's next ink. Or the next scar on their heart were you ever to leave their orbit after time spent together.

You want to make an impression. But you are shadow people. It takes a certain type of person to notice shadow people. Their drink arrives. You listen for the name written on the cup. When it is announced it makes you smile. Fake. You assume it's a fake name and if it is not, it is wonderful. Something one might read from the Necronomicon.

But now they have their drink. They are about to leave. You are shadow people. They cannot see you. Except they do not turn toward the door. They turn toward you. They can see you. Your superpower does not work on them. You are no longer invisible. They see you. The real you. And they are unafraid. They smile with hungry teeth.

You shiver. Happy. Excited. Scared. They approach and look at the blood covered clown on the cover of your book. With a nod, you understand you have found one of your people. They complement your choice of reading material.

This book is for all the shadow people. Used properly, we will provide the introductions. The rest? Well, that is up to you...

ESTATE COFFEE, SANTA MONICA

E STATE COFFEE IS EXACTLY as it sounds, a coffee shop in a realtor's complex in a beautiful stretch of Santa Monica. The environment, as one might expect, provides a pleasant atmosphere with great service for all the realtors looking to meet with clients or close deals. As a coffee shop, this place is excellent. Staff is friendly and quick with the drinks, and the immense space is relaxing and comfortable.

A diverse group of people occupy an equally diverse array of seating options, ranging from tables to booths, to stand up counters, cushioned chairs, and couches. The customer base is bright and cheery and it's hard to spot anyone ordering to rid themselves of a hangover.

Yet in a window on the way to an office is a sign that reads, '*always be closing*.' Therein lies the rub, does it not? Like a model home in a housing complex, the space presents the surroundings in the best light, even if that light is fake. Like a ring light for influencers making social media videos, sometimes the secret is all in the lighting. But reality dictates that where there is light, there must be shadow.

This little tale came to me as I looked at all the homes on display in pictures all around. They promised a new life, a new start, an escape from life's drudgery. If only one buys that house, that specific house, then life would be great.

The costliest places advertised were water-adjacent homes. Ocean mostly in Santa Monica. But it got me thinking about where I grew up. Water was plentiful. Yet rivers ran through some of the most impoverished neighborhoods. Why were some areas considered subprime despite their proximity to a riverbed?

Maybe because the phrase body of water is so close to the phrase body IN water. Water is essential to all life, yet it is also so frequently used to hide the dead from prying eyes. Locals understand the secrets that are hidden below the pristine surface of waterways where they live. No one speaks of them, no one dares whisper what they know, for surely the river always has room for one more.

This little tale is a reminder that some rivers run cold, but revenge runs colder.

COFFEE RECOMMENDATION: An ice-cold drink is a must on this one, and Halloween comes to mind. Therefore, I suggest a pumpkin spiced ice latte.

.

CUTTING BAIT

Paul Carro

S OME DAYS, TOMMY HATED the crick. The correct term was creek, but Tommy did not know any better. To him, it was always crick, because that was what all the locals called it, so that is what he called it. At seven-years-old, the crick meant the world to Tommy. Swimming during humid, hot summers (which required a leach search party after stepping out of the mulch bottoms) and fishing for food when there was seldom any back home. Most of all, it served as a peaceful escape while his dad slept off the boozing.

Tommy's dad had an old lawnmower that all but spoke to the dead in the graveyards down by the four churches. (The churches anchored all four directions of the town, so they got you coming or going.) That lawn mower which could wake the dead was a close second to the volume of his father's snoring after a bender. Tommy's daddy was a mighty angry drunk. Somehow, it was Tommy's fault that their mother up and left years ago. Tommy tried to remember her sometimes, but it got harder every day. The easiest place to recollect was along the peaceful shore of the crick, where never a lawnmower was heard.

That was the crick's major draw. The quiet. Old Man Felton, the local barber and notary, once talked about the crick with Tommy, though the old man used the word creek, a rarity from townsfolk. Tommy took the barber for wise, the way he used words and the way he could clip Tommy's hair to the tightest of buzzes. Tommy liked the man. The two laughed when Old Man Felton told Tommy that cutting Burt's hair (the barber used the name Burt instead of dad) was like shaving a bobcat. The two laughed a good while over that.

Whenever the laughter died, Old Man Felton snarled like a bobcat, and it started Tommy giggling all over again. In one of Tommy's laughing jags, he leaned too far to one side, leaning into Old Man Felton's blind spot, resulting in a snip on Tommy's ear. A battle scar. Everyone in town had one from the barber. While a good haircutter, Felton's eyesight was about as useless as a screen door on a submarine, or at least that was how Tommy heard the adults tell it in the shop each time the old man slipped.

Yes, the crick was the center of Tommy's universe, but as much as he visited it for escape, it disappointed him when fishing came up dry. Many suggested the crick was all fished out, but others said the fish learned to hide where fishermen did not go. Brambles, burrs, and fallen trees lined much of the banks of the crick. Impenetrable was how he heard it called. Certain sections of the waterway were beyond easy reach.

The crick eventually fed into a larger waterway the next town over, one with nice beaches that brought enough people out that hot dog vendors set up shop on the weekends. His dad took him there occasionally, but the only time he ever got hot dogs was if he visited with the families of school friends. Some relative in the bunch would take pity on him and his swim trunks of cut off denim and buy him one or sometimes two with all the fixings. Dang, those dogs were good.

Fish was even better than hotdogs when cooked fresh. The only time Tommy got to feel wealthy was when his father melted that butter in the pan and cooked the fish just so. It was the one thing Tommy could count on his father for, cooking the catch to perfection. Yet lately the crick denied him of even a nibble.

The spot Tommy fished from opened into a minor bank, mostly obstruction free in a section where neighborhood kids sometimes swam once they overcame their fear of leeches. Heat usually removed such fears. It was a cool day, though, so Tommy found himself alone. His guts churned with hunger. The stale bread at home was useless because they had nothing to add to it. Not even peanut butter or the government cheese that came in an enormous block and could bend any knife daring to cut into the orange chunk. He desperately wished for a catch.

Reeling his line back in, Tommy cursed at the sight of a worm still wriggling on the hook. Then he sensed he was not alone. He turned and leaped in fright. A boy in a ghost mask sat on a boulder at his rear. The boy, black, based on his arms wrapped around his knees, sat there watching. The mask was a cheap drug store style that wasn't Casper, but darn close. Besides the mask, the boy wore jeans and a short-sleeved striped tee. His feet were bare, which Tommy thought odd given how rough the area was.

Tommy's dad did not like Tommy speaking with any black kids in town, but his father never gave a good reason why. For that reason, Tommy looked around to make sure he was alone before finally speaking to the kid.

"Cool mask," Tommy said.

"Thanks," the boy replied through the face covering.

"Did they move up Halloween?"

Tommy was confused. He was off school for the summer but could have messed up the months. His father never would have noticed when it was time to go back to school. The boy in the mask remained still, sitting there staring through the cheap mask.

"It's always Halloween where I'm from," the boy replied.

"Neat!" Tommy was excited.

Was that why his father did not want him talking to black kids? Because they lived in a much cooler place than he did? Did his dad consider it unfair some got to live in a place with year-round Halloween while others did not?

"Ain't no fish there, you're wasting yer' time," the boy said.

"How do you know that?"

"I can see them."

"The fish?" Tommy asked.

Casper nodded in silence. Tommy liked the kid already. Always Halloween and then the ability to see fish. Tommy wished his life was that exciting.

"What's your name?" Tommy asked.

"Chris," the boy replied.

"Nice to meet you, Chris," Tommy said.

Tommy turned and gathered his supplies. Despite being poor, Tommy had a legit tackle box, ten cents at a yard sale. One that even came with a few lures, though worms worked best. It disappointed Tommy when he turned and found the boy gone from the rock. Tommy turned back to the water and leaped again. Chris stood right in front of him, the mask in full view.

Chris pointed downstream. "If you desire the biggest catch, I can show you where to go."

Tommy scrunched his face and shook his head. "Ain't no getting downstream. Too many pricker bushes," Tommy said.

"There's a path just over yonder that will lead you through," Chris said.

Tommy shook his head. Bad idea. A fortress of misery stood in their path. In some spots, pricker bushes at least had the decency to offer blackberries as a treat, but the ones looming ahead were like the razor wire around construction site fences in town. Tommy's stomach growled loud enough to sound over the running water.

"Won't be hungry any longer after the catch you'll make if you go to my secret spot," the boy said, his voice faintly muffled by the plastic mask.

The idea lit Tommy up. "Secret spot?"

Casper nodded. Tommy had yet to think of the boy as Chris. Tommy eyed the treacherous path ahead.

"How secret? Hoe many know about it?"

"Me and one other," Chris said.

"Wow! Why are you telling me?" Tommy asked.

"Because I feel you could make the catch of a lifetime and I'd like to be there to see it."

"Do I have to share what I catch?" Tommy asked, looking for a catch in what he might catch.

"You do as you please with whatever you get," Chris said.

"I don't know," Tommy said. He was hungry, but his dad did not like him speaking to strangers or black people and he was doing both.

The boy saw his hesitancy. "You can have my mask."

"Casper?"

"Dapper. Dapper the ghost is the official name. I couldn't afford a real Casper. But yes, the Dapper mask is all yours if you visit my secret spot."

"Well, lead the way," Tommy said.

Immediately, Tommy regretted the agreement. Despite using the tackle box to push away the branches with long sharp prickers on them, the plants bit him plenty, drawing blood in various tender spots. Tommy yelped and cried out as the sharp foliage tore at his clothes and flesh. The branches also grabbed at his fishing pole and tried to pull it from his hands several times. On one occasion it tangled with something so tight it almost yanked the entire pole from his grip, as if he had a fish on the line.

Tears formed in Tommy's eyes, and he wished he had never entered the mass of painful, twisted branches, but he looked behind himself and noticed the way back looked further than the opening ahead, so he kept going. Chris seemed to move with little effort. The mask was the secret. It protected the boy's face. That mask would be Tommy's on the return trip, so maybe it was all worth it.

Tommy noticed various strips of cloth along the way, caught on the pricker bushes. The sight gave him hope. Chris thought he was the only one who knew about the place, but there had to be others based on the torn clothing along the path. If that many people dared make the trip through, then it would be worth the while.

Once or twice, Tommy thought he heard something moving through the same bush, but when he stopped, the noise stopped. No, only he and Chriss were foolish enough to make the trip. It was mighty painful, and Tommy fought not to sob in front of his new companion.

Tommy wondered if they missed the opportunity to go around the bushes. In the distance beyond the brush rose a steep loam filled hill leading into thick forest. To get downstream without a car, and Tommy did not have one, would have required a significant climb to get above the ridge. That was if one could make the climb. The loam leading up was so steep and slick, it would likely knock one's feet out from under them, sending them tumbling back down. No, too much work and effort. The prickers sucked, but were less work, and Tommy was a hungry boy.

A raft. If Tommy had a raft, it also would have been easier. But he could barely afford the fishing pole. A raft was not in his future. Chris fell silent on the trip through the punishing flora. The boy never complained which made Tommy feel bad about his own struggles. Tommy continued through the painful brush and cried out in relief when they emerged on a small, weed-choked path.

"Wow! This looks great," Tommy said.

Chris shrugged. Probably had seen it a hundred times. But the area was unfamiliar to Tommy, and the water widened along the stretch. It looked even deeper than the other parts of the crick. The ground descended gently into the water, leaving plenty of space to fish from without fear of falling in. And because the area was open, there were likely fewer leaves to turn into mulch, so the area would likely be better for a swim than where he normally went in. Tommy figured a swim was in order if he failed to make a catch.

There were no rocks for Chris to sit on, so the boy stood on shore while Tommy eagerly baited his hook. Tommy was skilled, so avoided puncturing himself while he squished the worm onto the hook. He checked to make sure his new friend was in the clear and then Tommy cast far out into the crick. The open space with no trees overhead to tangle his line allowed Tommy to cast further than normal.

The current drew his bobber downstream, but the current was gentle. Almost immediately, Tommy felt a tug. He yelped in glee and gently tugged the line. He needed to be careful as he often got too excited and tugged before the fish had a good bite. Another tug.

Something sounded behind Tommy. It sounded like footsteps in the distance, or the snapping of twigs. He turned to look even while the activity on his line continued playing out.

"Did you hear that?" Tommy asked.

Chriss simply shook his head. Then a tug, a real one. Tommy yanked. The absence of trees that allowed him to cast so far also gave him freedom to yank hard without fear of tree entanglement. His line pulled free from whatever nibbled below.

"Dang!" Tommy said, and reeled the line in. The worm was half gone. A fish had outsmarted him and got a free meal. "Double dang!"

Tommy pulled the coffee can from the tackle box and dumped out the dirt contents onto the crick bank. The pile of rich earth came to life with squirming worms. Chris leaped back at the sight.

"What? It's just worms."

"I don't like that," Chris said.

"You only use lures, then?" Then it dawned on Tommy. "Hey, where is your fishing gear?"

"I don't like fish," Chriss said.

"But you know where they are?"

Chris nodded and then pointed to a spot further downstream. Tommy added another worm to his hook and prepared to cast. He followed the direction of his new friend and cast out to where the boy pointed. It had been a long time since Tommy had a nibble so quickly after a cast, so he trusted Chris. Tommy aimed for the spot mid-crick and cast as hard as he could.

There was no immediate nibble. That was normal, but after his first cast, it was a bit of a letdown. He considered reeling the line back in and recasting, but his friend seemed to read his mind.

"Give it time. You are close," Chris said.

Then Tommy heard something again. He looked back and swore someone was crunching through the pricker bushes. He was about to ask Chris, but the boy was gone. Tommy looked all around, suddenly nervous at being alone and noticing the sun had lowered in the sky so it would be dark soon.

"Chris? Where did you go? Is that you in the bushes?"

It had to be. There was no one else around, and no one was foolish enough to make the trip. But why would his friend leave? Tommy started reeling in the line when he felt a tug. Massive. Something pulled on the line. Tommy yanked and whatever it was, he had it!

Tommy wound the slack until the pole's tip reached hard for the water, bending like he had never seen before. He had a catch all right. A big one! He yanked again, hoping to force the fish to break the surface, but it did not. Whatever it was, it remained submerged. He would have to do the hard work of bringing it to shore.

The bushes crunched behind him, and he excitedly called out. "Chris, come back. I've got one! A big one. And you owe me your mask!"

The thought of getting a big catch and a cool mask delighted Tommy. Why his father wanted him to stay away from such people made no sense. His new friend had led him to the ultimate fishing spot and if he kept his word, there would be a mask in his future as well. Tommy figured Chris just stepped away to pee, but the pricker bushes seemed a dangerous place to do so.

He would worry about that after he landed his prize. Tommy pulled with all his might and felt the catch moving closer to shore. He was reeling it in! It was only as the catch drew closer to shore that he finally saw it bob toward the surface. The sun was going down; the world was fading to gray, leaving him to wonder whether he was seeing things wrong.

The fish did not flip or flop, but simply rode the line to shore. He could barely make out the form and squinted because its shape made no sense. Not trout, the colors were off. What fish was as white as that which floated on the surface? As it drew closer, it became clear the thing was not a fish. It was far too big to start. Tommy stepped back in disbelief, almost running from the shoreline.

In his fear, he kept hold of the pole, which only drew the catch closer to shore. Tommy scrambled back, fell on his ass, and dropped the fishing rod. He landed a catch alright, one now resting on the crick bank in full view. Tommy rose on legs of rubber.

Tommy forgot about his pole. He stopped thinking about his tackle box, suddenly not caring about any of it. He simply walked forward toward the shore to examine the unbelievable thing attached to the fishing line.

The Dapper mask stared up at him from the shore! It was Chris but covered in crick slime, his body rotted partly away. The bloated body looked so small and sad on the shore. Tommy glimpsed movement and leaned in closer. Could Chris be alive? When had he fallen in? Worms different from those of his own bait lashed out through eyeholes of the Dapper mask. They were black and thick, reaching as if for fresh flesh. Leeches.

Tommy leaned back and covered his mouth, trying to hold in the scream and the puke, both of which built inside of him. Suddenly, a loud snap drew his attention. Tommy turned, already frightened beyond what he thought possible, until he saw what emerged from the pricker bushes.

Old Man Felton! The man wore jeans and black dress shoes shining enough to see a reflection in the spots not covered in mud. He wore black dress pants and a white button down with the sleeves rolled up to his elbows. Not immune to the prickers, lacerations covered his body. Thin slices of red bled through the crisp white shirt.

In the barbershop the man never seemed imposing, stood in a stoop even, his greasy hair a testament to his age but now the man who emerged from the brush stood tall, his forearms thick with muscle, the grin on his face that of a much younger or at least virile man.

Normally, Tommy would have yelled for help from an adult. He would have explained his catch, and how the boy stood on the shore moments earlier, so if he just now drowned, maybe they could revive him. Except there was something in the old man's eyes which gleamed as brightly as the large razorblade in his grip.

Tommy watched the man shave adults before, his arm pulling at the person's head until exposing a throat just so. Then the man would scrape the long-edged blade across the person's neck. Like the barber did with kids, Felton occasionally nicked an adult, and they would scream like squealing pigs. Little did Tommy know then that it was practice. For as Tommy stepped back and toward the water, he noticed Chris' throat slit wide open.

The wound no longer bled, the sliced flesh gleamed white along the cut, bleached into translucence by time in the water. (How long had it been?) Tommy looked from the boy to the man and hoped the sight of a dead body would revert the oncoming attacker into responsible adulthood. Tommy hoped the barber would ask him what happened, and demand Tommy exit the scene, because surely the sight was something no child should see. Instead, the old man spoke in a baritone Tommy did not know Old Man Felton to possess.

"What have we here?"

Tommy tried to speak, tried to form words, but the old man waved the blade in arcs, signaling his intentions. All those haircuts and the snip along Tommy's ear was a warmup to slice more flesh. Tommy stepped closer to the water and searched for the best direction to run.

"Found my secret place, did you, boy? I arrived for something else and thought I saw you wandering where you should not. While not my normal type you will do," Felton said.

Tommy was not sure what the old man was talking about, but it did not sound good. Tommy's legs did not seem to work. He wanted to run but wasn't sure which way to go. The best escape route was at his back. The water. He stepped into the crick, which felt cold, but Tommy did not care.

"Big mistake. Think you can out-swim me?" Felton asked as he approached the shore.

"Leave me alone!" Tommy yelled.

He knew he could not out-swim the old man, as he could barely swim. His father never taught him how, only threw Tommy into the water, so he learned to splash and paddle and survive, but a swimmer he was not. Somehow, he thought the old man would not follow him through the water, but the man placed the blade in his mouth and waded in.

The man charged fast, not needing to swim because he touched the bottom, while Tommy, moving backward, was soon up to his neck. The man was six-foot-three which meant he would still walk long after Tommy started treading water.

Tommy felt trapped in the crick and worried he might soon see fishes the same way Chris did. Tommy started sobbing, tears blurred his vision. Treading water exhausted him. He tried to swim away but only splashed in a wild panic. He never moved while the man drew closer, smiling despite the blade in his teeth.

With a sudden strike, the man grabbed Tommy's shirt. Tommy tried to pull away, but his feet were off the ground, making it easy for the man to pull Tommy closer. The man might not have had a pole, but Tommy was the catch.

Old Man Felton kept a grip on Tommy's shirt with one hand, then raised the blade with the other. The man was about to swing the blade home when suddenly a loud splash distracted him.

What happened next made no sense. The Dapper mask appeared over the old man's shoulder. A look of surprise crossed the man's face, and he released Tommy. The man reached for his back, trying to dislodge what had leaped onto him.

It was Chris! The boy rode the old man in a piggyback. Chris seemed agile in the water, hanging on tight while the barber tried unsuccessfully to shake the child off his back. The man sliced the blade over his shoulder only to yelp in pain after accidentally slicing his own shoulder. Blood flowed into the water, forming a red sheen.

The cut caused the barber to cease swinging the blade. A mistake. Chris stole the blade away from the man and, with one quick slice, opened Felton's neck at the front. A geyser erupted from the man's neck and immediately turned his white shirt red, which soon bled into a lighter pink as the water cleaned away some of the blood. The old man grabbed at his throat, but the blood flowed all around the man's fingers. The cut was as deep as when Tommy used to clean his fish.

Felton lost his footing and tilted forward. Tommy thought the man would splash right into him, but the man just missed. Felton's eyes met Tommy's as he fell. The old man splashed into the water face first and Chris rode him like a bridled horse. The two vanished beneath the water as the blood dispersed through the crick.

Tommy splashed for the surface, swimming as best he could until finding his footing. Then he trudged toward the shore and dragged himself up and out of the water. He coughed out water taken in during his screams.

Too fearful to close his eyes, Tommy rested on the bank, splayed out on the wet ground, staring at the darkening sky. He waited until his strength returned and then he rose, looking for any signs that the old man found his way out of the water. The barber did not. The water remained calm.

Tommy left his pole and tackle and started toward the pricker bushes. He wanted nothing more than to escape. To return home, even though his father was often cruel. The warmth of his own bed beckoned. But before he entered the brush, he looked back and saw something on the ground. The Dapper mask sat on the edge of the water along the shore. As promised, Chris had given him the mask.

Picking it up, Tommy put it on and walked through the prickers. He felt no punctures as he was too numb, too tired, too scared. Tommy simply walked through, allowing the weeds to instill whatever damage they pleased. At least the mask kept his face protected.

When Tommy broke into the open at the spot that he knew so well, he noticed a van parked in the distance near the edge of a forest path. The barber's white van. The business name *Felton's Cuts* covered the sliding door of the van. Tommy heard muffled cries inside.

When Tommy slid the door open, a hogtied boy of Chris' age and color thrashed. But then the boy noticed the mask and saw that Tommy was not his captor. There were many blades in the van. Tommy used one to cut the boy free.

The two walked in silence back to town. Neither speaking along the way. It was only when they reached the sheriff's office that the freed boy turned to Tommy and spoke.

"Are we dead?"

"I know I am not. I hope you aren't," Tommy said.

"Me too. I'm Horace," Horace said.

"Tommy."

"Cool mask."

"Thanks. I got it from a friend. It's always Halloween where he is from."

"That must be nice," Horace said.

"It is now, I think."

Then the boys paid a visit to the sheriff.

SERDA'S COFFEE COMPANY, MOBILE ALABAMA

S ERDA'S COFFEE COMPANY IS a bustling cafe in busy downtown Mobile, Alabama. Situated at a crossroads of local commerce, it's within walking distance of my favorite bar, The Haberdasher, as well as my favorite local bookshop, The Haunted Bookshop. It's also within walking distance to the park featured in this story, known as Mardi Gras Park, where I would spend hours sitting and thinking. The coffee shop serves lattes, soups, sandwiches, and even gelato. Its interior is cool and during Mardi Gras, Serda's is smack dab in the middle of the parade route. The trees outside remain covered in Mardi Gras beads year round.

One day while drinking my white mocha latte, looking down toward Fort Conde, I crafted this story in my head and wrote several pages there. There's a notorious (and hilarious) local legend called the Crichton Leprechaun, which Serda named a drink after. Look it up on YouTube. Long before I had any intention of setting foot in Alabama, I heard about the Crichton Leprechaun and so this story emerged partly because of the sensation surrounding that, but also because of my shared love of cryptid creatures and crypto zoological oddities. Shadowy demons are present in every culture, and when I learned that the Choctaw Indians had a similar spirit that called southern Alabama home, I knew Shuck was a natural fit since the English had at one point colonized and controlled the south as well.

I combined all of that with a vivid dream I had one night about an old church being dug up by archaeologists, some cursed colonial silver, and of course a massive black dog/lion hybrid which chased me.

Much like the main character of this story, I haven't been able to rid myself of the image of those fierce predatory eyes staring back at me from the darkness.

COFFEE RECOMMENDATION: It's hot out in Mobile most of the time, and this story will make you want something to cool off with, so I'd suggest something icy and sweet. My recommendation would be an iced white mocha latte, preferably from Serda if you can get it because theirs is the best.

THE CARPETBAGGER

Joseph Carro

WHEN I LEFT MOBILE, Alabama and returned north, I did so with my tail between my legs and with a profound sense of sadness, regret, and guilt which will forever remain with me. I fled the South after an 'Urban Legend' proved itself more real than my friends and I bargained for. I'll always wish I'd never seen that dig site. The following is my account of events surrounding Mobile's annual Mardi Gras celebration up to my terrifying encounter with an entity known locally as 'Black Shuck'. Many will say that Black Shuck isn't real, that the massive shaggy dog with feline features and glowing red eyes is simply a story created to frighten the young and naïve. I would have said the same until I saw it with my own eyes. Black Shuck is real, and sometimes when I close my eyes... Black Shuck is all I can see.

-Dustin Harding Stowe, Vermont 2020

I met my friend Luke Weller at the Stonecoast MFA Program in southern Maine years back. His real name was Lucas, but because he leaned *Star Trek* and I leaned *Star Wars*, I called him Luke to annoy him. It stuck, so our entire circle of friends called him Luke. He and I were as different as two Americans could be from one another on paper. He was a good old southern boy, born and raised in Mobile, Alabama. I grew up in Lewiston, Maine, surrounded by derelict mill complexes and canals. I poked fun at Luke's southern drawl, and he called me a "genuine, macaroni-eating Yankee."

Despite being on opposite ends of the map, Maine and Alabama have some interesting similarities. Maine has rednecks with regional accents who love country music and go '*muddin'* in four wheelers or pickups. Alabama has similar good ol' boys driving their jalopies through flooded swamplands while antagonizing water moccasins and gators.

Maine's state dessert is the Whoopie Pie, but Mobile is famous for Mardi Gras celebrations where people throw boxes of Moon Pies to onlookers. Being from the North, I still prefer my Whoopie Pies, but I won't begrudge '*Mobilians'* their love of the marshmallow treats known as Moon Pies because they grew on me during my stay. Nothing beats a glass bottle of Coke and a trusty Moon Pie under the heat of the Alabama sun.

Finally, just like any great state in the country, both Maine and Alabama share a fair number of ghost stories, urban legends, and folktales. Maine is the home of author Stephen King, so tales of ghosts, apparitions, and evil demons lingered for as long as King has been writing. And boy, does he write *a lot*. But aside from King's influence on Maine's worldview, the state has been the home of many grisly murders, mysterious disappearances, and unexplainable phenomenon.

Not to be outdone, violence and mystery reign in Alabama, so it's only natural each state laid claims to their own unique spooky tales. Maine has *The Legend of Wessie*, a variant of the Loch Ness Monster, as well as the Beast of Turner. The latter made national news when a photograph surfaced of what later turned out to be some sort of canine with mange. There's also the *Pocomoonshine Lake Monster*, *The Haunting of Wood Islands Lighthouse*, *Bigfoot*, and my favorite: *the Legend of Colonel Buck's Tomb*. Yep, Maine is freaky-deaky.

Alabama offers *Cry Baby Hollow* in Hartselle, the *Witch in the Woods* over in Gadsden, and the *Dead Children's Playground* in Huntsville. But Alabama has something Maine (and the rest of America) doesn't have, and that's the Legend of Black Shuck.

The day I learned of Black Shuck was the last day of Mardi Gras 2020. COVID was still in its infancy. We wouldn't quarantine until months later. (Oh, how I wish now I was in lockdown sooner. Maybe none of this would have happened.) I arrived in Mobile in November 2019 planning to visit for a few months and escape some drama I left behind in Maine. My wife cheated on me, and our marriage fell apart. I was ready for comfortable friends and comfort food.

Luke and his own wife, Carolina, invited me to stay with them while I sorted out my life. I bussed from Maine to New York City and stayed for a night trying to drink away my sorrows. From there, I hopped on an Amtrak train which clicked and clacked all the way from Manhattan to Mississippi, where Luke and Carolina picked me up.

The trip allowed me time to process the end of my marriage, but I was going through so many emotions that the memories of the journey faded like a dream by the time I hooked up with my friends. The Wellers introduced me to my first southern food immediately upon arrival. My welcome included collard greens, fried okra, and possibly the best barbecue I'd ever had in my life.

From Mississippi, we drove two hours to Mobile, Alabama. When we arrived in the city it was dark, but I perked up in the back seat, eager to get the lay of the land. I sheepishly admitted how I had not expected Mobile to be so... Advanced? I'd expected people living in shacks, wearing suspenders, and sitting on porches in rocking chairs, drinking sweet tea. This was the power of television and movies. Luke relayed his similar biases when he visited Maine for the Stonecoast writing program where we met. Touché!

Luke explained, "It is a major metropolitan center. We have universities. I work in one, remember?"

They laughed at me while I stared, open-mouthed, at the scenery. There were three lanes of traffic, sometimes four. There were copious amounts of chain restaurants, strip malls, and chicken shacks. With increasing amusement, I also noted the sheer number of Dollar General stores and mentioned each one as we drove by.

"I'd never really noticed just how many there were," Luke said, laughing.

I guess when you live somewhere; you take things for granted in your own backyard and the nuances get lost in daily commutes. Too much time sitting in vehicles processing the day or daydreaming about the future or regretting the past. I'd done a lot of regretting recently, lamenting the loss of a woman I'd never really known. How do you mourn someone who turned out to be a total stranger?

We arrived at my friend's home; a cozy ranch-style house located in a cozy suburban neighborhood. Carolina explained as they helped me into my room with my things that the house was once owned by a famous local author named Sanders Anne Laubenthal, who authored a book set in Mobile called *Excalibur*. It was a Southern take on the Arthurian legend. There was a copy of the book on the nightstand by my bed. I dropped my luggage, settled in, and flipped through a couple chapters of *Excalibur* before experiencing the best sleep I'd had in weeks, untroubled by ghosts of happiness.

I planned Mobile as a brief stopover, so for the first week after my arrival, Luke or Carolina remained in a tourist mode with me, showing me around Mobile and the surrounding towns of Daphne, Fairhope, Spanish Fort, and places further away like New Orleans, and Gulf Shores in Alabama which was two hours away. There I experienced white sand beaches for the first time in my life. Luke and his wife were very kind hosts and very generous. They let me use a small red pickup truck so I could drive myself around without waiting for them to do things after work. True Southern hospitality at work.

"Give it a name," Luke told me. "You can't drive it without a name."

I called it *Mater* because it was red like a *tomater*. The vehicle had no discernible bells or whistles and reminded me of the beat-up southern accent truck in the movie *Cars*. The unfanciful ride provided me the freedom to explore Mobile and the surrounding areas by myself while Luke and Carolina worked.

Often, I would visit a coffee shop called Serda's, where I would write until they closed for the night. Luke sometimes joined me. We were both drafting novels. We acted as one another's equivalent of a gym workout buddy pushing the other to bench press at least 1,000 words per day. It was one of the more enjoyable things I will remember about my time in Mobile, and about Luke. Two writers, hitting the coffee shop and getting words down on the page, both rooting for one another's success.

Okay, enough color. I understand I've made a promise to share the awful thing. But I needed time to process it all. Mardi Gras was about to start and that is where all the shit hit the shit. And as for the guilt, well, I wanted to make certain people reading this understand how wonderful my host family was. But first, Mardi Gras.

Mardi Gras originated in Mobile, Alabama in 1830. New Orleans adopted Mardi Gras in 1856, so Mobile did it first. Some suggest Mobile's even went as far back as 1711. The first Mystic Society appeared in 1830, and that year they hosted a parade featuring a papier mâché canine of some sort which struck fear into the hearts of locals. In those early days, Black Shuck was not an urban legend to people, but something tangible and worthy of fear.

Black Shuck would, over time, fade into the stuff of urban legend, even being adopted by future generations as a mascot. Nothing to be feared, only celebrated.

(If they only knew!) But early settlers were properly fearful of the dark beast and its oft mentioned *"strange and terrible wonder."*

Little did I know I would come to sympathize with those early settlers. Despite the modern age and the luxuries afforded citizens today, evil remains evil, and when it casts its shadow upon the unsuspecting, tragedy surely follows. In my case, the lesson came on the last day of Mardi Gras.

The last day of Mardi Gras—Fat Tuesday—I'd just woken up while Luke and Carolina were at work. After showering in the green and white painted guest room and dressing in a long sleeve shirt, jeans, and my black pea coat, I rubbed my eyes and jumped into Mater and headed downtown. I remember that the sun felt warm on my face, and to my northern sensibilities, it felt strange how February so easily cast off its winter coat. In my old home, people would be fearful of a groundhog promising six more weeks of winter. I rolled the window down and felt the fresh air brush through my whiskers.

I pulled Mater toward the Temple Downtown, which was a mysterious pyramid standing out among all the other buildings in Mobile. It was once home to the Free Masons and their order. Two sphinxes guarded the entrance, carved out of stone, with male faces and massive stone bosoms. My friends introduced the location to me on New Year's Eve where I'd had so much to drink, I ended up christening the steps with vomit. I later joked that I'd cursed humanity with my actions by vomiting on holy ground. We all laughed (and they said they were never drinking with me again).

The reason I parked in the Temple's lot for my current outing was because I'm a creature of habit. That New Year's Eve, the lot became a familiar landmark to me in a land of unfamiliarity, so I parked there from then on. It was only about a ten-minute walk into downtown, past the many shops and bars and restaurants of downtown Mobile.

Once there, people were already pouring in for the evening, trying to secure their spot on the parade route for the night's festivities. Intricate floats would soon roll down the street while people wearing masks and costumes would toss boxes of Moon Pies or ramen noodles at the thousands of onlookers. Vendors were already peddling boiled peanuts as they drove by in carts. I heard '*Sweet Home Alabama*' blasting from a nearby speaker, a pox tune to locals. I laughed at the song, then entered Serda's Coffee and ordered.

From there, I walked with my drink, enjoying the sights and sounds of the festivities. They had stationed some floats along some side streets, and I glimpsed one of Black Shuck, unaware that soon I would not dare cast my eyes upon it. Happy to enjoy the night, I strolled toward Fort Condé with my camera, taking some photos to post for my blog. History was a hobby for me, and I explored as many forts as I could up and down the east coast.

Knowing this, my hosts explained to me early on about the fort and the historical nature of the area. Fort Condé was just a reproduction (still old, though). The original stood opposite the street from the current version, or at least the remnants of it did.

What remained of the original fort was a smattering of old cement and brick, surrounded by a commemorative wall and iron fence. The weathered rock foundation had seen its share of floods and hurricanes, and who knew what else. I snapped photos, having finished my latte, and I'd lost track of time when I stumbled upon a dig site.

It abutted the property containing the original old Fort Conde site and comprised a small makeshift shack surrounded by blue tarps. I was not unfamiliar with the dig. It was in the news and was a big deal for locals. Apparently, the University of South Alabama had discovered the exact location of a historic church. The First Holy Trinity Church, long ago destroyed in a violent storm. They believed it to have fallen roughly during the English occupation of Mobile in 1763.

The English occupiers brought with them a legend about a fierce spirit of a shaggy dog called Old Shuck or Black Shuck which haunted the fields and forests of Britain, and which Sir Arthur Conan Doyle based his Hounds of the Baskerville on.

Luke was a big fan of Sherlock Holmes, so had regaled me soon after my arrival with the lore behind the Hound while his wife rounded out other bits of the church's history. Apparently, the Choctaw tribe of Native Americans believed a massive shadow creature crept into one's subconscious if they partook of evil thoughts or fell under the thrall of depression.

I joked at the time about being a prime candidate, what with the marriage crumbling as thoroughly as the ancient church itself. They were patronizing me, trying to help me forget my own miseries. They were great people. I scoffed at the idea of Black Shuck but played along and asked if either of them had ever seen the demon hound in person.

"No," Luke replied, laughing. "You wouldn't want to see it, either."

"Why?" I asked.

"It's an omen of death," Carolina said, taking on a serious face.

My eyes widened with interest and incredulity, causing her to chuckle and wave a hand at me to let me know she was just joking.

"It's just a Southern superstition," she said. "Sort of like how we don't do laundry on New Year's Day because it's bad luck."

"I thought it was because everyone was hungover," I said, laughing.

They showed me that night an old newspaper account. Saved under their favorites online. Creepy much? It talked about how Black Shuck famously attacked the church before it fell. They showed me the article and gave me time to read it. (I saved it under my favorites as well, because why not?)

The article was from a 1763 newspaper and reported on the first-hand account of parishioner William Tunbridge at the 1st Holy Trinity Church in what is now present-day Mobile, Alabama. The article reads as follows (spelling modernized):

During a most terrible storm, an ungodly clap of thunder shook the church, and the doors crashed open upon our service of prayer. The congregation stood transfixed by the Devil Hound, who gazed at us with fiery red eyes. Its footfalls made no sound as it stalked us and leapt upon the rafters. Then it ran all along down the body of the church with great swiftness and incredible haste among the people, a strange and terrible wonder. It passed between a young boy and his father, as they were kneeling upon their knees, and occupied in prayer. With wicked jaws, it wrung the necks of them both at one instant and they died in horror. The black Shuck then pounced upon the Reverend at the pulpit. The beast's howls chilled the blood and his wicked paws set aflame the pulpit. We fled, leaving the bodies of our fellows in fear. The steeple crashed down upon the pulpit with a second clap of thunder, and the church collapsed in a fiery pyre. The Dog's tracks remained fixed upon the earth, and the church lay in ruins. We will not go back, for it is now cursed ground and marked by the Devil.

Eventually, the location of the historic church became lost to time. Until shortly before my arrival. A dig for a town modernization project (read gentrification) unearthed unique timber frames and a few old coins, enough to warrant a study. The University stepped in and announced they had identified the location of the First Holy Trinity Church. They also discovered some old colonial-era silver and religious relics.

I pushed the legend of Black Shuck to the back of my mind that night and had mostly forgotten about it until wandering into Mardi Gras Park for my picture taking. The park comprised a large green space with benches surrounding the perimeter, flanked by the History Museum of Mobile, Fort Conde, and Mardi Gras related statues.

And of course, the dig. The sight of it immediately intrigued me. Maybe it was the signage, warning people away. I approached the nearest sign, which read:

ARCHAEOLOGICAL DIG UNDER WAY

– NO TRESPASSING –

UNIVERSITY OF SOUTH ALABAMA

The small door on which the sign hung swung open and closed with the breeze coming in off the water. When the door swung open fully every few seconds, I caught sight of something silver flashing in the light. I glanced around to search for any people moving within. No sound emanated from the small workspace inside, which seemed like a hastily erected room made of thin wood and rudimentary equipment designed for light excavations.

Barely any pedestrians were nearby. The few I could see followed an invisible arrow directing them to the festivities I had already walked away from. Police had blocked off many side streets for the parade, so even traffic was light in the immediate area. Most of the fun things going on were on Dauphin Street or North Royal Street, blocks away.

I called out a greeting to anyone who might be around, as the small excavation shack seemed vulnerable and open. Silver coins gleamed at me from inside the doorway, and loose papers flittered around and onto the floor inside. It looked like whoever was originally there had fled in a hurry. A cup of coffee lay spilled on its side near one of the small tables. The brown contents had long since dribbled through the makeshift floorboards.

I heard whispering in response, so I called out again while poking my head inside the shack. Upon doing so, I glimpsed a portion of the old church's timber frame sticking out from the earth in a dug-up section of the floor. The wood looked old and fragile and seemed to be scorched. Below it, I could just make out a stone foundation of sorts.

In another corner sat carefully labeled and protected glass vials, which looked ancient, no doubt taken from the dig. On one table rested a batch of colonial-era silver coins, looking far too shiny and new to be from the colonial era. I realized, with my eyes widening, that they were New England shillings.

History is a hobby as I mentioned, and I collected as many old things as I could. A small part of my brain told me to scoop up the silver and take it with me as a souvenir. I checked the date on one coin. 1652! My brain worked in overtime as I remembered my grandfather's coin collecting and my historical collecting converging when he told me about rare New England shillings which were worth hundreds of thousands of dollars a coin.

Before the gravity of that thought hit me, something else did. With a loud pop, something shocked my finger like electricity. I groaned in pain and shook my head.

Then a generator switched on with a bang, taking my breath away. I had just started catching my breath when the lights inside the shack grew brighter and brighter under an intensifying cacophony of the generator.

In my pocket, my phone grew uncomfortably warm against my right thigh, increasing to such a high temperature I yanked it out. Smoke rose from within its protective Otterbox case, and soon the case itself grew too hot to handle. With a curse, I dropped my phone to the ground, where it caught fire. Lights exploded around me in glass shards, and everything went black as I lost consciousness and hit the floor.

When I dreamed, I dreamed of two red eyes peering at me from the darkness. They felt far away and extremely close at the same time. The two eyes over time merged into one all-seeing red eye that burst into flame and hovered over me as I screamed, the flames rending my flesh from my bones and igniting my hair and clothing to ash until eventually even my screams turned to dust and I choked on them.

I woke up dazed, feverish, and drenched in sweat. Confused at first, I thought I was back in the guest room at Luke's house and dreamed everything about the red eyes and the archaeological dig. But soon, I realized I was sitting on the front steps of the Temple Downtown, clutching a handful of colonial silver. With dawning horror, I realized that somehow, I took coins from the archaeological dig, and walked all the way to the Temple. My body ached worse the more fully I woke from whatever stupor had overtaken me.

My confusion increased when I noticed it was dark out. What had happened? How'd I reach the Temple Downtown? How long was I passed out? I had so many questions. I looked to the sphinx guardians on either side of me for answers and found none, so I stood on two shaky legs and reached for the phone inside my pocket, but it wasn't there. Then, in a flash of memory, I remembered how it had caught fire somehow in my pocket and then how I'd dropped it right before passing out inside South's excavation shack.

I looked down at my jeans and noticed the singed denim where my phone had been. A couple passed by me on the sidewalk, and I approached them to ask them the time. They gave me side glances, hurrying along. I must have looked so disheveled, that they thought I was homeless. I walked across the parking lot toward Mater, shoving the colonial silver into my pocket.

I had the distinct and unsettling feeling that I was being watched, and as I neared Mater, I felt isolated, thinking I should head back to Luke's house. But they planned to meet me in town. With no phone, they wouldn't be able to reach me. Then the whispering from the shack earlier came back. When I turned toward the whispering, I saw it.

Black Shuck!

There, glowing in the darkness, were two bright red eyes belonging to the biggest, most muscular wolf I had ever seen in my life. It watched me from a crouched, predatory stance. I froze in fear, instinctually not wanting to move. The beast rippled with musculature culminating in immense broad-shoulders and a thick neck cloaked in what looked to be a lion's mane. Its fur was shaggy, seemingly coarse, and jet black in appearance. Though perfectly designed to blend into the night, the light emanating from its own eyes betrayed its stealth. More a lion/wolf hybrid than pure canine, it adapted the deadliest features of both. If it stood on its hind legs, my head would likely only reach its chest.

I inched away ever so slightly. A feeling of icy dread washed through my limbs, making my mouth go dry. I forgot where I was, and I forgot what I was doing. All that mattered were the two blazing red eyes fiercely locked onto me. That's when the beast bolted forward!

I turned around, hauling ass through the parking lot as fast as I could run. I knew my life was at stake. The worst part of it was that I couldn't hear the beast running unless I weaved in between parked cars. Only then did it make a sound, jostling as it crashed into the vehicles. Car alarms blared so that soon I could not even hear its stumbles.

Twice I scrambled and almost fell. While stumbling another frightening element of the pursuit came into play. Shuck's teeth snapped shut just behind me! Heat emanated from where his massive paws scorched the pavement.

Never looking back, for I dared not slow even that much, I made my way finally down past the Saddle Up Saloon, vaguely aware that people were gawking at me. A couple of women even let out small shrieks of fear. I wasn't completely sure anyone could see Black Shuck. If they could, wouldn't they too all flee?

Their relative calm in my storm meant I was probably going insane, and who could blame me? I'd suffered through exile from friends and family because of the actions of my ex-wife and was trying to figure out my next stage in life. The pressure was enough to get to anyone.

When I finally reached the more populated Dauphin Street, I risked a look back. Old Shuck was gone, but there was the proof I was not entirely crazy. A trail of sizzling and smoking spots on the road stretched down the sidewalk behind me, leading to the Temple's parking lot. All around me, people gave me a wide berth. I ignored them and made my way toward North Royal Street once again.

I reached North Royal Street without further incident and encountered a Mardi Gras parade. I'd gone to a few earlier in the season and filmed myself catching a football thrown from one float. This was the last parade, though, so onlookers desperately shouted and screamed for the Krewes to toss them some parade goodies. I ignored the food vendors, the screaming onlookers, the parade floats, and made my way past the now-packed Serda's Coffee Company heading back toward the archaeology site.

There I saw the two burning red eyes once again, blocking my path toward Mardi Gras Park. My heart froze as I realized the beast looked even bigger, dwarfing the pickup truck driving in front of it. I involuntarily backed into some onlookers who made threats against me for being a douche.

I did not care. Something frightened me more than drunken locals. I stared at Black Shuck while it slowly lumbered toward me. I understood I was going to die. Somehow, I had taken the silver from the dig, and this was my punishment. Black Shuck was about to pounce. It was so close! Why wasn't anyone else afraid?

Then something struck my face. A Moon Pie. As fast and as hard as it smacked my cheek, it hit the ground and someone from the crowd grabbed it. I looked up with clear eyes. People surrounded Black Shuck, and they tossed boxes of Moon Pies and even tee-shirts. I caught my breath again and put my hands on my knees and laughed. As the fear dissipated, I realized that this Black Shuck was only a Mardi Gras float.

I continued toward Mardi Gras Park and skirted around the edge, once again encountering the archaeological dig. This time, there was a chain and padlock across the door and the lights were all off. Someone had been there since I left. I wondered whether to leave the coins there in the dirt. But no doubt someone would take them, and then what? They would have been off my hands, that's for sure, but what if someone saw me take them? What then? Maybe the person who locked the place up knew I was the culprit. The thief.

I couldn't just explain that I'd blacked out before waking and being chased by Black Shuck. Black Shuck, primarily known as an English apparition, is not even supposed to be in America. I felt the weight of the coins in my pocket, and they grew warm. I spun around and was again face to face with Black Shuck. Its fur bristled and it let out a low growl that made my hair stand on end. This was no float. And this thing did not appear to care it belonged over the pond, as they say. It was here, growling at me, in Mobile. I was out of gas for running.

"What do you want?" I asked it.

Black Shuck's growling intensified. Inside the shack, the generator leaped to life and spotlights erupted all around the dig site, momentarily blinding Black Shuck. It snarled and drew back, and I used the opportunity to run for my life.

With the second wind, I let out a low wail and ran past the museum and back toward North Royal, toward the floats and the revelry. A howl behind me turned my blood to ice. My legs felt like stone. I was so tired of running. I risked a glance back, and Black Shuck was gone. At least for now.

I'd been so concerned about escaping from Black Shuck that I walked right into a couple of people and almost bowled them over. I gave an exasperated apology, but I heard Luke's voice and my vision centered on him and his wife Carolina. It was they who I ran into. They knew where I parked so were out looking for me. Told you they're the best.

I apologized to them and attempted to give a sort of unconcerned apology, but what erupted from my throat was a smattering of words concerning stolen colonial silver, dreams of fiery eyes, and of course the chase and how I'd escaped Black Shuck. The couple didn't want to or didn't have time to interject. Smiles vanished from their faces as they realized I was being serious. They glanced repeatedly at one another, growing more concerned by the minute.

"Are you okay, man?" Luke finally said.

"I don't know," I replied. "Maybe I'm crazy."

Luke said that he and Carolina were going to call it a night anyway and that maybe we should all head back to their place. We had all originally planned on grabbing drinks at Boo Radley's Bar, but Luke gently suggested that maybe he should drive me back in Mater since I didn't seem to be in a fit state of mind.

Carolina agreed and said she'd drive the sedan home. Despite the circumstances, I felt a flush in my cheeks. So embarrassed. A northerner, visiting the south, spooked beyond belief by a silly southern urban legend and becoming unraveled in front of his good friends and respected academics.

Impulsively, I withdrew the old colonial silver coins from my pocket and showed it to Luke as Carolina walked away, hoping that maybe somehow by showing him, it would validate my story in his eyes, and he'd understand what

I'd gone through and that I wasn't insane. Instead, the opposite to happened. A look of surprise and disapproval registered on his face as he realized I stole some of the archaeological find for myself. And why wouldn't I, in his eyes? Wasn't I the history buff into historical collectibles?

"Dustin, are those real?" He asked, already knowing the answer.

I explained to him about how I'd seen the silver flashing at me from within the dig site, how I'd wandered inside once I didn't see anyone around. How my phone had caught fire, and the generator had jumped to life, and how I'd become unconscious and came to on the steps of the Temple Downtown with the silver in my hand. And then, how Black Shuck had appeared in the Temple's parking lot next to Mater.

It's not that Luke didn't believe me; I could tell he really wanted to, but the entire ordeal was far too outlandish with each additional detail I added. I eventually just stopped talking, letting him absorb the information. Just naturally, we'd begun walking up Dauphin Street toward the Temple, moving our way through the trash-covered sidewalks, through the drunk revelers.

The silver jingled in my pocket and felt extremely heavy. I kept thinking I should dump it somewhere, but each time I thought about doing it, I just imagined I might still get in trouble for accidentally taking it in the first place. If I ditched it I would be unable to return it to show my innocence. Maybe if I brought it back the next day, there wouldn't be much of a punishment.

We passed Boo Radley's on the right, and I could smell the alcohol-soaked floor and see the people gyrating against one another, unaware of my plight. Luke and I walked in silence and took the next right toward the temple.

"That demon left some paw prints on the ground," I said, pointing to several of the scorch marks on the pavement as we passed the Saddle Up Saloon. "Look, I'm not crazy."

I crouched down. Luke obliged me and used the flashlight from his phone to illuminate what indeed looked like a massive paw print scorched into the asphalt. Not only one. The asphalt melted in several spots coming from the direction of the Temple where we now headed. Luke looked over at me, finally considering whether I was telling the truth.

Luke took some photos with his phone and then we both stood and continued toward the Temple. When we turned the corner, we noticed flashing lights from a police car in the lot. Two Mobile police officers talked on radios, shining flashlights at a few cars in the lots alongside them.

I recognized the vehicles I'd run between while fleeing from Black Shuck. I could see the Shuck inflicted damaged from when it pursued me. There were dents and places where the metal slagged upon the touch of Shuck's paws. My heart pounded in my chest. I didn't bother relaying this information to Luke. I'd already told him about it earlier and the police presence confirmed I had told some version of the truth, since something damaged the vehicles.

We both slid into Mater and drove home in silence. Luke finally spoke before we went inside his house.

"We should take those coins back tomorrow."

I nodded.

When I dreamed, I dreamed of the eye. It was much larger than I remembered. It hovered over me, an undeniable menace vibrating through the surrounding air. I waited for the conflagration, and I closed my eyes as the air became thick and humid and then super-heated. But it did not burn me up as it should have. I tried to open my eyes and found that I could not. In growing panic, I reached for my sealed eyes with shaking fingers. Silver colonial coins covered each of my eyelids. I knew the eye was right in front of my face. I felt the coins ignite, and the pain made me scream. The silver turned to liquid metal and burned into my sockets.

I woke with a start in Luke's guest room where I'd been staying. My sheets and clothes were drenched in sweat. I lay on the floor with the sheets wrapped around my body. Gasping for air, I coughed in a fit until finally calming down. I turned on the bedside lamp and saw the coins in a small pile shining back at me in the yellow artificial light. I knew what I had to do.

I changed my shirt and grabbed the keys for Mater, which Luke had left on the kitchen counter. I slipped as quietly as I could outside, coins in a small shopping bag on which I scribbled a note:

THESE ARE YOUR MISSING COINS. SORRY. DIDN'T MEAN TO TAKE THEM.

I wasn't sure the note or even returning the coins would absolve me of my "crime," but I figured I had to try something. My plan was to drive downtown and return the coins, even if I had to pry open the door to do so. I jumped into Mater, put it into second gear and hauled out from the driveway toward downtown Mobile.

The early morning was peaceful enough. The air was chilly at only about forty degrees. Spring Hill Avenue was completely empty save a few random vehicles running up and down the side roads. It was nearly three in the morning.

I passed by the Starbucks on Spring Hill Ave, where I sometimes got work done. It was so early even the baristas weren't up yet. I'd befriended a few of them there as well as the store manager, who were all extremely nice, putting up with my extended stays as I worked on my novel when Luke couldn't get in a writing session with me at Serda's. The sight brought back some sense of normalcy.

Driving further downtown, I encountered fewer and fewer vehicles. I made my way past several partially torn down barricades and parked at the Temple Downtown. The sphinx guardians were there as always, but there were only three cars in the lot, including mine. The coins felt heavy inside the shopping bag, and I didn't allow for any slack in the handle lest I make jingling sounds all the way down Dauphin Street.

There were a few homeless men scattered on doorsteps throughout downtown and especially on the wrought iron benches in Bienville Square with its live oaks and aggressive squirrels. None of the men moved as I walked toward North Royal Street seeking redemption.

When I finally made it to Mardi Gras Park, I noticed the trees littered with strands of Mardi Gras beads. It saddened me to miss the last night of Mardi Gras, but I was glad I'd made it to several of the other parades in the weeks leading up to it. I'd even made it to the Mardi Gras Museum to round out my knowledge of the event, although I still didn't understand most of it.

The dig spot was still closed and padlocked. I flattened the coins as best I could and shoved the entire bag of them through a crack between the door and the floor of the makeshift shack. I felt an immense sense of relief as I made my way back to 'Mater. Before long, the sun would be fully up. I texted Luke and told him I'd dropped off the coins and I'd probably head home soon and not to worry. I revved up Mater's engine and headed back up Spring Hill Ave.

The morning air was pleasant, and the sun was just about to make an appearance. I was humming to myself when Black Shuck appeared in the road straight ahead of me!

He charged headlong at the truck. I screamed and slammed on the brakes, causing Mater's front-heavy body to slide sideways in the middle of the road. What would have been a head on collision turned into a T-Bone on the passenger side. Mater rolled over. After the first two spins, I lost consciousness as my face took the glass.

When I dreamed, I dreamed of Luke and Carolina. Two sweet faces and good friends. Their smiles faded and behind them, the Eye appeared and burst into flames, hiding the features of my friends in shadow, and causing me to cry out in alarm as the flames licked at them ever closer until they morphed into two separate fiery eyes. The eyes of Black Shuck. I didn't know why, but I felt a great pang of sadness in my chest, and I began to cry. But the tears sizzled and evaporated, consumed by the heat of Black Shuck's stare.

I woke in the hospital and the Mobile police department promptly questioned me regarding my accident. They asked if they performed an alcohol blood test how did I think the results would come out? I shook my head, but only because I figured they already knew the answer. I was uncertain how long I had been out, but it could tell time had passed, enough time for every bone in my body to have stiffened after lying in bed for over a day at least. Maybe more.

I waited for them to ask if I was okay. That would have been nice. Or even asked me why I was out so early. Normal questions, but no, they were dancing around something. They remained strangely quiet and watched me with great interest.

The coins. They must have known about the coins. Before I could plead guilty and explain the dog in the road to boot, I noticed something. Or rather, the absence of something. I asked them where my friends were.

A passing nurse stuck his head in, concerned about my overwhelming cry of grief that reached the furthest hallways. The cops gestured all was okay and the man scrammed. Nothing was okay! I tried to rise, tried to run, tried to be anywhere but there. Tried to find my way out of a nightmare. I could not so I screamed again. Everything hurt, every inch of my body, but mostly my heart.

Without giving me time to absorb what they had told me, they asked if I knew anything about the fire that tore through the Weller family home the same morning as the crash. I shook my head. I couldn't find my breath, couldn't find any words.

I'd lost my friends, so nothing mattered to me anymore, and I endured question after question. It took me some time before I realized they were going somewhere with the questions. Someone from the University of South Alabama had checked cameras, which caught me coming back to return the coins. Local papers dubbed me 'The Carpetbagger.' So named because I was from the north.

Apparently, when I'd visited the site, an amateur archaeologist had spilled coffee on a relic, and left for just a few minutes in a hurry and had forgotten to lock the door. However, the footage inadvertently cleared me of the suspicion because it was time-stamped. A neighbor confirmed what time the fire started at the Weller home, and they had the time from when that neighbor called 911. I was returning stolen goods when the flames took my friends.

I was afraid to ask if authorities found any unexplained burnt footprints at the scene, from something resembling a beast. (Did Black Shuck search for me there first before he found me on the road? Had his footprints sealed the fate of my wonderful hosts and friends?) In the end, I did not ask the officers about burning footprints. If I said anything, it would surely make the papers and add crazy to carpet bagger.

When I finally healed physically and the police couldn't pin me with anything (the school decided not to press charges since I returned the stolen coins) I left Mobile by bus, traveling to Hattiesburg, Mississippi. Then I hopped on an Amtrak train to Vermont, where I've been ever since. I've never looked back.

My days are unhappy and full of tormented nightmares of Shuck. I understand it's just a matter of time before the old dog comes to claim me as well. I'll never fully understand what transpired at that archaeological dig, and never understand how I ended up on the steps of the Temple with a pocket full of extremely rare New England Shillings, covered in sweat.

The only thing I am certain of. The one thing I know is that sometimes urban legends are real. Someone said life finds a way. I no longer believe that sentiment. What I believe, what I know for certain, is that evil finds a way. I also know that I wish that I'd never laid eyes on that demon. I wish Shuck had taken me in place of my friends.

GOODBOYBOB'S SANTA MONICA

T<small>HIS COFFEE SHOP IS</small> a personal favorite. Located in an art, media, and tech startup complex, it has a truly unique vibe. Inside is intimate with couch-oriented seating but not centralized in the cliched Friends TV show manner. It has its own feel, with one wall covered in pictures of every imaginable public figure drinking coffee. Boris Karloff as Frankenstein, Anthony Perkins, Marilyn Monroe and many more. The pictures are as intimate as the location.

More seating stretches out into the parking lot. In the relatively tight confines, one must know how best to navigate in order not to spill their drink or bump others and spill theirs. Except everyone here knows the shorthand. Outsiders are welcome and would quickly learn the lay of the land, but it is a place of regulars. All as pleasant as the staff.

The music played is top-notch, matching the quality of their drinks. The food offering while limited hit the spot and are quite delicious. I always suggest tipping, but this place makes it a simple decision. The staff is so knowledgeable and friendly that it makes opening a wallet less painful.

With the place being so great, it would be difficult to find a horror story in there, would it not? Wrong! The clientele is so friendly, so perky, so nice that there must be more below the surface. There must be demons. Everyone has their own, no matter how tamed they may be. One wonders how well hidden such demons are in this special place.

Maybe the good boy is not as good as they profess. Maybe there is a bad boy in there. It was this play on the name that got me thinking about what hides within the kindest of people. And seeing the pictures on the wall of so many public figures over the globe, I imagined some of the very people on the wall (those still living) might very well have passed through the doors of this unique coffee shop.

And each of those people were possibly hiding their true selves, their true impulses. How many passed through while hiding the depths of their worst impulses? I imagine there were many. Because there will always be someone passing through...

COFFEE RECCOMENDATION: Because this is about passing through, one should not order their usual. Something unique is the way to go. I suggest something not frequently ordered, a red eye.

PASSING THROUGH

Paul Carro

S HERIFF LINDSEY BAKER SPOKE loudly into her cellphone over the omnipresent sound of a siren. Cars moved out of her way as she sped down the freeway. Normally she would have road raged at drivers slow to pull over, but the phone conversation held her attention. The loud siren made it difficult to hear clearly. She refused to raise her voice to compensate because the conversation already bordered on an argument.

"No, honey, I don't have time to cook ribs tonight. They take too long and I'm on the job."

She shook her head as her husband Glenn argued his case on the other end. *Blah, but I want ribs tonight. Blah, and you never cook anymore. Blah, ribs, I want ribs.*

And I want you to get off your duff and order your own damn food. If you can call me then you can call a restaurant, Lindsey thought. "Honey, if I have time, I will pick up some ribs. How about that?" Compromise struck. She did not need to buy any wine for the meal. Her husband was supplying plenty.

The object of the initial service call finally made an appearance in the form of a head looming over a car which had pulled over to allow the sheriff to pass. Lindsey's internal siren went off louder than the one atop her city vehicle. Walking along the side of the freeway, was one of the largest men she had ever seen.

The tall man strode along the interstate highway. Not walked, not jogged, but strode, was how Linsey thought of his gait. Tall was an understatement. She had several 'big fellas' on her team, but this stranger was taller. Six-five minimum and at least two fifty.

"Honey, you ever read them Lee Child Jack Reacher novels? Because I think I just ran into his much larger cousin," Baker said as much to herself as her husband.

Glenn's response was swift and infantile. The sheriff pulled her phone away and looked at the screen, incredulous. Were they face-timing, she would have flipped him the bird. She stuck her tongue out at the phone just to preserve some sanity before pulling it back to her ear and continuing the conversation.

"You're asking if I find him cute? A man who could put me in the ground? First, the word would be handsome or even hot. Someone that size is not cute, never cute. Good ole Lennie wasn't cute when he crushed that poor puppy, or rabbit, depending on which version one reads," she said. The utter silence on the other end prompted a response. "*Of Mice and Men*, honey. Sorry, I guess that reference was like bringing a knife to a gunfight with you," she said.

Glenn took to cursing loud enough to be heard over the siren. Lindsey declared her love to her frustrated hubby and hung up. She killed the siren and drove closer to the roadside stranger. The man appeared oblivious to her presence.

At least he appeared to be heading out of town, and she considered allowing him to go on his merry way, but there was the possibility of him becoming a road flapjack. Big guy or not, a semi did not discriminate. It was also against the law, walking on the interstate like that.

She lit him up, but the man kept moving, never looking back. At the speed vehicles raced past, she could not safely make a traffic break with a single cruiser, so she pulled onto the breakdown lane behind him.

Bloop!

Baker single blipped the siren, but the man just kept on keeping on. Baker was five-ten and gym fit. She could handle herself in most cases and where she could not, she had the great equalizer at her hip. Still, the man was large, and better than gym fit. He was all kinds of muscle as best she could imagine, considering the oversized black duster and black sun hat he wore.

Being so tall, the man's sleeves fell short on his arms along with the coat's bottom which barely reached past his quads. Hefty forearms and calves suggested the man was muscle-packed everywhere. The muscles that were visible were not the glory ones, but were the ones routinely ignored by show boaters at the gym. That likely meant the man was big everywhere. As it was, the coat seemed in distress at having to cover such a massive form.

She pulled up closer behind him. The man moved at a brisk pace and continued his ignoring the law tour. Realizing her lights and blooping siren were slowing traffic in a looky-loo fashion, she killed both and life on the freeway went on.

Once a break in traffic occurred naturally, it was Maine after all, (if *one does not like weather or traffic wait a minute)* she pulled alongside the man. The sheriff gestured for the pedestrian to move further from the traffic lanes. The stranger looked her way and tipped his hat. That was her last straw. She gunned it ahead of him and hit the brakes, storming out of the vehicle only to gasp in fright as a pickup blew past, honking at her for being too close to the road.

She stepped into the man's path, and to his credit, he stopped. *Shit, more mountain than man*, Baker thought, but did not let her unease show. She felt suddenly small. Man was a brick house. No coat could hide his proportions. She should have called backup, she thought.

"Stop right there, close enough," Baker said, hand on her weapon.

"I already stopped, sheriff, though it pains me to do so," he said in a voice like gravel in a blender.

"Why is that?"

"Because I'm just passing through," he said.

"Just passing through?" Baker asked.

"Yes, ma'am, and you're impeding progress," he said.

"Is that so?"

He nodded. She examined the stranger from a safe distance. An odor emanated from the man, but nothing unpleasant. Sweat, dirt, leather from the jacket, but no sign of alcohol, nor the sickening sweet smell of certain drugs.

"You don't need to call for backup," the man said.

"Why does that make me think I should?" Baker asked.

"I'm letting you know I will not hurt you unless..."

There it was. A threat. "Unless what, cowboy?"

"I mean no harm. I'm just passing through," he corrected himself.

"How about if I give you a lift?"

He lit up at the suggestion, which Baker found strange. She also got a better look at his eyes. She heard of gray eyes before but never met anyone who had them. He did, but when the brim of his hat blocked the sun, the eyes went dark, ink black. She jerked into a defensive posturing when he suddenly moved. Baker tightened her grip on the weapon.

"I'm just taking you up on the offer. Glad to get off my feet," he said and started toward her vehicle.

She raced ahead and opened the back door. He got in the rear seat with no problem, despite his immense size. Once inside, she breathed a sigh of relief and slammed the door. She retook the front seat and readjusted her rearview, which had never needed to be aimed so high.

"Looks like you have had practice getting into police vehicles," she said.

"Yes, ma'am."

Then it hit her. She met his gaze and felt a chill. His eyes were black for certain and colder than any she ever saw. While uncertain who she had in her backseat, she felt unsafe, despite his calm demeanor and her position of power over him.

"I'll ride as far as you will take me, but I think it would be best for all if I get to the town line," he said.

"Is that so?" She asked as he nodded in reply, eyes never blinking. "Well, we have one stop to make first, I'm afraid."

Baker tried to focus on the road, but she kept glancing in the rearview. The man's eyes remained focused on the same mirror, waiting for her to look back again. For a tourist passing through, he was uninterested in scenery. She leaped in surprise when a cell rang. Hers. Waylon Jennings professed his love to her through a ringtone. She always answered Waylon.

"Honey? Bad time. I know, I don't like leaving things where we did either, but one of us must work." Baker glanced in the rearview. Her passenger gazed with eyes shifting from that gray to black. *Damn those eyes*, she thought. "Honey, I love you, but I have to go."

She disconnected with her husband Glenn. The stranger watched her intently during the brief exchange, waiting for her to finish the call before speaking, his voice still like pebbles clacking together.

"Trouble at home?"

"Don't know that I would call it that," she said. "And none of your business."

"You really should let me pass through," he said.

With that, he finally looked to the street. Baker had already pulled off the interstate. Baker operated out of the nearby Monmouth station. There were holding cells there, but they would deliver anyone booked to the prison down south. Their county was massive, and the drive was substantial. It was not worth making the trip for such a minor infraction, but it was those eyes. Baker feared letting the man go only to discover him responsible for some atrocity along the way.

"What is your name?" Baker asked her passenger.

"Crevice," he answered.

"Crevice? What kind of name is that?"

"A name."

"And where are you from?"

"That I can't answer," he said.

"Well, ain't that convenient," she said.

"Not at all. It is a burden I carry. One of many," he said.

The man ceased speaking for the rest of the trip.

Crevice appeared disappointed when they arrived at the sheriff's station. Two of her big boy deputies that she had called ahead greeted her. Officers Nolan and Higgins, both good men that she would give her life for. They could not help but remark on the man's size.

"Dang, how much do you weigh?" Nolan asked.

"It fluctuates," the man answered.

"Something wrong with your throat?" Higgins asked.

"That's how he talks," Baker said.

Waylon crooned again. "Honey, please. Bad time right now. Yes, I still love you..."

Baker waved her deputies toward the station, and they led the big man inside, but not before Crevice called back to her.

"You really should let me go."

Baker finished the call with her husband and rushed inside. The office immediately opened into desks, no reception area to speak of. There were five total. An admin, off for the weekend, and four officer desks. Off to one side was a solo cramped office, hers, and then straight ahead and toward the back was a short hallway followed by four holding cells, two on either side.

The sheriff spoke to her deputies, forging a game plan. She eyed the hallway in the distance, unsettled by the mysterious prisoner. The deputies grilled their boss on one point.

"Any reason you did not cuff the man when you brought him in?" Higgins asked.

"Figured they would not fit, and if they did, he might break them and use them to knock me senseless," she said.

The deputies nodded, good point. She eyed the men. "Look, I've got shit to hold him on, but he gives me that bad feeling. Nolan, get him a water, then run prints off the bottle, ASAP. Higgins, you get on the horn and find out what our friend may have left in his wake. We should have heard by now if he did anything in our county, so start beyond our borders."

"Think he walked over from Canada?" Nolan asked.

"Worth a check."

The men split off while she walked to the holding cells. Crevice sat on his cot, looking straight ahead with the same disinterest he showed toward the scenery earlier.

"Walking on the interstate is a crime. While I am not formally placing you under arrest, I need to reach a judge to set a date for you to appear for the ticket."

"I'm disappointed. I was just passing through and took you at your word for a ride," the man said.

"And I will honor it once I figure out what is going on. If I need to hold you for the road violation in the meantime, I will," she said.

"At least you are honest," he said. "But please finish what you must before sundown. Though I fear it's already too late in the day."

"Why sundown? What is so important about that time frame?"

"Just best for you all. Best to let me..."

"Pass through. Got that. Don't tell me you turn into a werewolf or vampire or something after sundown?"

He smiled for once. It was not an unpleasant look. A hint of kindness behind the teeth. "Nothing so mundane," he said.

Baker eyed the man once more, deeming him as dangerous as he appeared kind. A walking contradiction, and one who liked to walk on interstate roadsides at that. She stepped away as her deputy arrived with the water bottle.

The sheriff stood by her cruiser at the front of the station. She watched the sun setting. The orange glow neared its last gasps as the horizon sought gray. She squinted after inadvertently looked directly at the last of the sun's rays. It would not be long now, whatever concerned the man. Her deputies walked out of the station.

"Dude knows we're printing him," Nolan said, flashing the empty water bottle.

"Why do you say that?" Baker asked.

"Because he said so. Offered to give prints straight up. Asked if he did so, would it expedite us letting him go."

"Thinks we will immediately let him go? Are we sitting on a spook? Is he going to come up as a government stooge?" Higgins asked.

"He's a spook alright. Got me worried. Something is off, and I can't put a finger on it," the sheriff said.

"It gets better. Guy says if he has prints on file…" Nolan started.

"If?" Higgins asked for both him and his boss.

Nolan nodded and continued. "Would not cop to having any on file. But, get this, said if they were, they would be the prints of a much thinner man."

"What? Thinner?" Higgins guffawed.

"Once upon a time before steroids? I don't think our guy understands how prints work. Lucky for us." Waylon crooned again. She answered. "Honey, can you hold? Have and to hold? Don't be so dramatic, hon. It's a marriage, we work things out. Listen, never mind holding, I need to call you back."

"Troubles at home again?" Nolan asked.

"You sound like my backseat passenger. I need to pick up some dinner for Glenn. It's getting late and I'm missing something here. Take Crevice up on his offer for prints. Ask one more time about his evening concern. It's officially sundown. That time frame seems important to him. No audible explosions, and no immediate emergency calls coming in. Maybe the guy is just off. Keep digging while I deliver some ribs to a hungry man who can't seem to order takeout on his own. Hoping the drive allows me to refocus, figure out what's wrong with this entire picture."

Higgins chimed in. "Still waiting to hear from Canadian Mounties. I also checked the local tow-yards. If this guy was walking because he broke down, maybe we can find something off a vehicle."

"Great idea. Hadn't thought of that," Baker said. "Nell is off for the weekend for her baby shower, so don't bother her, but Sandy is in the field. I will update her on the situation. Broad strokes at least. Call her if you need an extra set of eyes or ears."

"What?" Higgins asked, cupping his ear as if unable to hear. "What did you say?"

"Knock it off," Baker said.

"She's on lunch anyway, visiting her mom at the retirement home," Nolan said. "Won't hesitate to call if we need the help, but for now might as well let her be."

Nell was their admin. Sandy was a deputy, long in years (the oldest in the squad) but passionate and smart. Baker often straddled the line over how much to defend the older woman and how hard to suggest the woman push back against the testosterone in the office on her own.

Two family dramas to deal with. Work family and her husband. She left the deputies to their work and headed for her cruiser. She needed to attend to her husband. As usual, Glenn had bad timing. By the time Baker reached her cruiser, the sun had already set. Something big could go down soon, but she had a family issue to address.

Her husband, Glenn, was so whiny. It was a wonder she never jumped in bed with one of her coworkers the way her husband cried about such a scenario all the time. He was so jealous that she often considered giving him something to be jealous about by sleeping with someone for real. She loved Glenn, though. That was the thing. She didn't know how to get it through his thick head that she would remain monogamous for the right man.

There was one way to convince him. She would show him how much she loved him after picking up some ribs. Baker was glad she never used her cuffs on the stranger because she was sure going to use them on her husband. Suddenly she could not get home quick enough.

Damn, I'm horny, she thought, and hit the gas.

"Drop your weapons!" Sandy Walker shouted at the two men.

Unlike her fellow deputies, Sandy belonged to another generation. Petite and sixty, she was the oldest in their office by far. Normally Monmouth was a quiet town, but as Sandy finished visiting her mother, two of the nursing home's residents squared off. Sandy noticed the darkness outside the window, which meant sundown had passed and her dinner hour was up. She worked the night shift and considered herself back on the clock.

Mookie and Bitters were octogenarians who were formerly best friends. Now the two battled with canes, slashing at one another in a slow-motion sword fight.

"Take that, you son of a bitch!" Mookie yelled at Bitters.

"Stand down, Mooks and Bitts!" Sandy yelled, shortening the men's longer nicknames. The two were beyond listening. Whatever started the fight, the pair were interested in finishing it with bloodshed. A crowd of wheelchairs had gathered to watch, but the lone staffer was nowhere in sight. The two men ignored Sandy.

"Screw you and the horse you rode in on!" Bitters yelled.

"That horse was your mother!" Mookie yelled back.

The canes clacked with kinetic violence. What started as a slow-motion dance had escalated. The thick wooden sticks moved faster and harder than Sandy thought possible from the two white hairs. Like herself. White hair. That was what they called her around the office when they thought she wasn't listening. Thought she **couldn't** listen.

Sandy did not wish to work but had to. She never got the pay raises and promotions others got in previous workplaces. She came to the job later in life after a divorce that left her broken financially and mentally. So, what that she was forty when she started on the job? She hit her twenty-year mark recently, but the retirement benefits were for shit.

Now she was a white hair. Called that by her coworkers and the snot-nosed criminals around town. Every youth was a criminal, some just hid their deeds better than others. The odor of pot lingered around that entire generation. There was no stopping them, even though she was the law.

Sandy felt her blood pressure rise. Even the old farts in the home refused to listen to her. No one gave her any damn respect. A loud crack drew gasps from the crowd. Bitters screamed.

One of Bitters' arms went dead at his side, Mookie had broken it with an epic swing. Bitters wore a short-sleeved shirt which gave a clear view of the swelling arm. It filled with blood at the point of an obvious break.

Finally, the fight was over, Sandy thought. Except it was not. Bitters raised his cane with his good arm and smacked Mookie in the face. Mookie's nose exploded with a loud pop and splattered blood over the pristine white floor tiles. The two men shook off the injuries and clashed with the canes once again.

"Stop now!" Sandy yelled.

The crowd cheered on the fight. No one paid attention to Sandy. No one ever did. They ignored her at work, ignored her on the streets when she confronted criminals, ignored her at the bar when she tried to find a new husband, any new husband. She wasn't picky, except none picked her back. Bastards, the lot of them. *Especially these two*, she thought.

Sandy pulled her weapon and fired. Bitters made a weird sound, pissed himself, then dropped to the floor. Even landing on the broken arm did not faze the man. He was out.

"What did you do to my friend?" Mookie asked her.

"Are you kidding me?"

"He was mine to jack up. Pigs like you shouldn't be stepping in and messing things up," Mookie growled through the bloody, broken nose.

"Is that so?"

When Mookie replied in the affirmative, Walker released the taser cartridge, loaded another and fired. Mookie's eyes went comically wide as he shook and fell to the floor, smacking his head on the tile. The staffer finally appeared and rushed to the fallen men. The staffer, a college intern named George, hovered over Mookie with grave concern.

"He's not breathing. We need the defibrillator," George said.

"Oh please," Sandy said, and hit the juice again.

Mookie's body jerked on the floor. When she stopped pressing the juice, Sandy looked at George, who confirmed a heartbeat.

With a nod, deputy Walker left the home. There was a convenience store where some stoners always hung out. She figured it was long past the time to pay them a visit. She got in her cruiser and slammed the door.

"Fuck, that felt good," she said before hitting the siren and squealing out of the parking lot.

"Thanks for calling back," Higgins said, chatting with someone on the phone.

Nolan entered with the digital fingerprint reader and moved to the computer. He made a show of plugging in the device, making the task as loud as possible while Higgins tried to finish his conversation. Finally, Higgins hung up.

"Loud much?" Higgins asked.

"Sorry, did not know the kiss up was so fragile," Nolan said.

"What do you mean?"

"I heard the boss praise you for the tow truck idea. Next thing you know, you're my boss. What a delight that would be," Nolan said.

"You should be so lucky. Maybe you should work harder like I do," Higgins replied with a bite.

"Hey, I got the prints, didn't I?"

"Guy is your type," Higgins said.

"What did you say?" Nolan got in his face and pressed a hand to his weapon.

Higgins leaned back in his office chair and spread his arms. "Tell me the big guy isn't your type?"

"Fine!" Nolan backed off. "Let's run the prints. Figure this out."

"That call was with my Canadian connection. Canada had a thing a few months back. Timeline works out possibly. They asked us to send his picture their way. You want me to snap the picture or would you prefer to? I'm thinking maybe instead of the usual booking photo, you ask him to drop trousers for the shot? Get your thrill?" Higgins said more than asked.

"Not going to let you bother me with all this talk. It says more about you." Nolan grabbed the camera when a call came through.

Higgins answered the phone, mouthing to Nolan that it was a 911 transfer. Nolan waited as Higgins said "uh-huh" over and over. Higgins hung up.

"Altercation at Sid's Diner," Higgins said.

"I'll roll on the diner. You get the guy's picture and run the prints." Nolan stopped at the door. "As for our fight, if you **do** get him to drop his pants, all will be forgiven."

Nolan handed over the camera with a smirk then exited. Higgins smiled. Despite Nolan calling him a kiss up, Higgins loved his buddy, gay or not. Still, Higgins felt he deserved a promotion. It was way past due. He should be running the shop, not a woman drowning in home life issues. Higgins realized he was angry at the wrong person. It was the sheriff who drew his ire.

Grabbing the camera, he decided to see what shot he could get to put on the wire, and what thirst trap photo he could get for his friend. But before he made it to the holding cells, the phone rang. Higgins answered with a hello.

Strange call. He assured the person on the other end that he was on the way. Higgins hung up and rushed to the door, but suddenly another call rang. He picked it up, then another line rang, and another. Soon, every line was ringing.

"Why didn't you call an ambulance, Dolores?" Nolan asked.

Dolores, a twenty-year-old goth waitress, stood defiantly next to Nolan. At some point, she served someone fresh coffee as the deputy dealt with the situation. Her waitress outfit was black and tight. Diners continued eating despite the drama. Many grumbled, though, about how the whole thing slowed the service.

Meanwhile, poor old Dean Anderson sat there with a fork jutting from his eyeball. He looked directly at Nolan with the good eye.

"Can't believe the bitch stabbed me," Dean said.

"Because you called me a bitch," Dolores answered back. "Besides, you're always leering at me, always. Sitting in the same spot seven days a week."

"I'm called a regular sweetheart, and I've seen plenty of asses better than yours," he said.

"Oh, so now you don't want this ass?"

"No, I still do," he said, almost resignedly. He was chipper for a forty-year-old married man with a fork for an eye.

"Shouldn't you lean your head back or something?" Nolan asked.

"So that I can blind my good eye by staring at a light? Good thing you're not a doctor. My wife is on her way. She's packing, so she'll take care of my friend here for me."

"That's what you think. Wait until you see what I can do with a spoon!" Dolores yelled.

"We're not waiting for anyone. This is assault. Sorry, Dolores, I need to take you in," Nolan said.

"What? He started it!"

Nolan pulled the cuffs out, and Dolores swung at him with the carafe. Nolan dodged and corralled her. She fought even while he cuffed her. The place smelled like spilled coffee and eyeball juice. He was ready to leave.

"I'll check on you later," Nolan said to the man as he led Dolores to the door.

Harvey Wilhelm stepped in front of Nolan and got in the waitress' face. "Where are my ten cheeseburgers?"

"Sorry, Harvey, I'm off the clock," the handcuffed woman said.

"Not without my ten cheeseburgers, you're not," he said.

Harvey grabbed at Dolores' apron and tried to pull her away from the officer. Nolan pushed back, hard. Other diners growled in the distance, yelling about their food as well. Harvey charged again and Nolan stepped to the side. Dolores stuck a leg out and Harvey tripped. His face smashed into the side of the diner's counter. His jaw crunched audibly, and the man struggled to rise, holding a hand over a mouth flowing with blood.

He spit out some teeth and raged. "How am I supposed to eat my ten cheeseburgers with no teeth, you Jezebel?"

The diner filled with people screaming for their food. Nolan looked around. Those already served ate greedily. The Millers, a family of four, devoured their meal like pigs. Nolan thought he heard them oink. Tim, their six-year-old, looked at Nolan with fire in his eyes and French fries sticking out of both nostrils. He could have been a walrus. Nolan did not like where things were heading.

He pulled his service revolver and fired at the ceiling. Everyone froze long enough for him to leave with his arrestee. He would let the rest of the diner workers figure their stuff out. Nolan leaned Dolores up against the squad car and patted her down. She looked at him over her shoulder.

"Fancy a go?" she asked.

"What?"

"You know, throw me a little dicky wicky? What do you say?"

He spun her around until she faced him, their bodies pressed together. "I say you're not my type."

Nolan pulled her away from the door, opened it, and held her head until she got in the backseat. He took a moment to collect himself as he grabbed the driver's side door. He heard shouting inside and wondered whether it might be wise to go back in. Something was wrong. Something was off. He knew for certain because when the woman propositioned him, for a moment, a very brief one, he was ready to ravage her. He'd never been with a woman, never wanted to, but in that moment, he barely contained himself.

While driving out, an ambulance pulled in. Nolan wondered whether the emergency workers understood they were getting a twofer. Eyes and teeth were on the menu in that diner. And possibly a kid needing help to dislodge fries from his nasal cavity. Nolan drove the cruiser back toward the station.

Higgins drove down MainStreet while trying to reach his boss again. No answer. He threw his cell down in frustration. The mall appeared on his left. He received many calls and decided to take them in the order he got them regardless of the emergency level. He assumed some calls would soon reach the rest of the staff. No one around to coordinate the whole mess. The situation only strengthened his view that he would be a better sheriff than his boss, but she was in the seat for now.

With the number of calls coming in, Higgins figured he could gain a leg up on the competition by setting a record for most calls caught in a single night. Calls in town were always goofy shit so he could clear each one quick and move on, becoming a bigger stud and legend with each case cleared. The initial emergency call came from the mall's movie theater.

There was one problem arising as he caught his reflection in the rearview mirror. *Damn, I'm a mite fine specimen of manhood*, he thought and believed.

Then a new concerning issue came to mind. "What if during my quest to clear the most cases, some hot chick decides she wants to bob on my nightstick? I'm impossible to resist. It's bound to happen," he said aloud, worried about the possibilities.

He slapped his face with great force then grinned at his reflection. "Oh yeah, like that! Daddy likes it when you're rough. Harder!" Slipping into a feminine voice Higgins said, "Oh, you like it rough officer?"

Higgins punched himself. His nose popped. He jerked the wheel, swerving toward another car that blared despite his vehicle being a cop car. Higgins looked at his reflection and his new bloody nose.

"Yeah! Man, that felt good! But I better not run into any of the ladies tonight, I've got a job to do. Most cases cleared ever. I am Supercop!'

He turned on the radio. Nine Inch Nails blasted. Higgins figured they would blur the part about doing something like an animal, but the station left the f-bombs in. Higgins cranked it up, wondering who was running the station. Theirs was a conservative town, so maybe Boston bought out the station. He dug it. He kept driving, destination mall.

The mall sat on a square mile of property. The parking lot around the place was immense. He entered off the freeway side and crossed the mostly empty parking lot when he saw it. Two cars parked alongside one another, with two men fighting nearby. Or one was fighting. The other was raising arms to fend off the attack.

Both were sizeable men with sizeable vehicles. Higgins hit the gas and charged at the two men. He stopped the car just short, leaving high beams aimed on the two. The battered and bloody man appeared relieved to see law enforcement. The other guy spit at the ground in frustration, but kept his fists raised.

Higgins exited his vehicle and stepped out of the car. He drew his gun and waved it between the two men.

"Officer, thank God," the bloodied man said.

"Mind telling me what's going on?" Higgins asked, surprised he knew neither of the men.

"Officer. I park my vehicle all the way out here because I just had a wash. Also, the truck is my baby, so I don't want any dings. I'm about a quarter mile away, a long walk," the one delivering the beating said.

"Agreed, but how does that end in you two being jackasses?"

"Because he parked next to me! All the way out here. Therefore, I kicked in his window, dragged him out and beat the ever-loving stuffing out of him."

Higgins looked at the immense space surrounding the vehicles and the distance to the mall. He walked over to the other driver's car and noticed the broken driver's side window. Then he looked at how close the cars were parked.

He stepped up to the man on the ground, who whimpered in relief at his protector. Higgins scrunched his face and shot his gun arm toward the mall. "What were you thinking?"

"Officer?" the bloody man asked.

"He's parked all the way out here and you park next to him? Who does that?"

Higgins walked back to his vehicle, upset that such a foolish thing was keeping him from his actual call. Both men stood silently, waiting for instructions.

"Proceed," Higgins said.

The larger man growled and began beating the one on the ground with abandon. The man begged for help as Higgins got in his cruiser, hit the lights, and raced toward the mall.

Lindsey pulled up to Johnny Red's Barbecue Blitz. The shack of a restaurant had a small screen door front porch. Beyond that was a small storefront to order from and then nothing but counter and kitchen past that. Diners could eat on one of the many picnic tables or at wooden counters lining the sides of the building. Multiple families were eating when Lindsey pulled up and got out.

Her phone rang. "Yes, honey, dang, I'm getting the ribs, even though I should be at work! I swear. Why can't you order and go do the pickup? Because you work from home? Is that what you call it? Remote? How much porn have you ingested today during your 'workday'?"

Lindsey stopped short of entering the establishment despite signs of an argument inside. The shouts were loud, but she was too shocked by her husband mentioning how he was currently watching porn. He normally hid his proclivities from her as if she was law enforcement in the home and outside it.

"You're watching porn now? Since when did you get so confessional? You know I was thinking about something earlier. Maybe I come home right now, and we have some fun," Lindsey said, feeling flush.

A customer barged past, bumping her hard enough she almost fell off the front steps. The collision left her chest smeared red as if blood-soaked.

"Excuse you!" Lindsey shouted, realizing her husband remained on the line. "No, not you, honey."

The man continued toward his distant truck, Lindsey called out to him again and the man threw the bird over his shoulder before tossing a bag of food into the truck. When the man turned to get into his truck, Lindsey noticed how he appeared bloody head to toe. The sheriff slipped into work mode, hanging up on her husband. She ignored his immediate return call.

"Eldon Mulch? Are you okay?" Lindsey asked.

Suddenly, the screen door burst open, and Johnny rushed out baseball bat in hand. Johnny wore sauce as well. The sheriff tried to figure out what was going on when she sniffed the red smears across her own chest. She licked it. Barbecue sauce.

Eldon peeled out, leaving a gigantic dust cloud in his midst. The sheriff thought the behavior was odd, as the fleeing man was seventy years old. Could have fooled her based on how Eldon body slammed her on the way out. Johnny growled and eyed the sheriff while climbing back up the steps. She followed. He gave her a sour look.

"Where were you five minutes ago?"

Before she answered, he let the screen door slam in her face. She threw it open, aggravated and confused. Once inside, she gained clarity. Red splattered the entire entrance to the restaurant and shards of glass covered the floor. A display rack of barbecue sauce sat mostly empty. Broken bottles lined the floor where they were smashed like sweet smelling bombs. One had been smashed against a nearby wall. Lindsey figured someone could throw a frame around it and call it art. The thought made her snort with laughter.

A worker swept up the mess while Johnny wheeled out a mop and bucket. Despite the obvious chaos, smoke filled the air. Grills were going. The place normally smelled wonderful, but the odor of the thick red on her outfit overwhelmed her. Her husband kept ringing her phone. She ignored it.

"What happened?"

"Regular customer always gripes about more sauce. Then today he would not stop. We gave him extra even though we normally charge. He said that wasn't enough. Opened a bottle and gulped the damn thing down. Then he smashed the bottle. He grabbed another and did the same," Johnny said.

"He drank all these?"

"Nah. Did the two and then started smashing them all, cursing us all out. That's when I went for the bat. Why didn't you arrest him?"

"Because I just now found out. I know where he lives. I'll pick him up."

"You wouldn't need to if you got him just now! Lazy cop. All of you lazy cops. How many times we get robbed before you catch someone?"

"Is that your way of asking for help?"

"Nah. It's my way of telling you how full of crap you are," Johnny said. "Maybe I should chase you out with the bat as well. Make sure you get some pep in your step. Get after the goon who made Johnny Red's red!"

Johnny went for the bat, raising it. Lindsey placed her hand on her weapon and backed away. The worker with the broom raised it and got in line behind Johnny. The cook stepped out from behind the counter and grabbed the mop as a weapon. It made no sense. She knew them all, but the men were rage filled. She stepped back and out the door even as the trio followed.

"I understand you are upset but drop the damn weapons or things will get ugly," the sheriff said.

Off to one side of the establishment, families at picnic tables stared at her with rage filled faces though they continued eating even while watching her. They gorged on massive amounts of food, their faces smeared red like her chest. The sight unsettled her, but she had bigger fish to fry.

Her husband's ringtone blared again, which gave the advancing trio a new target. Somehow, the ringtone set the men off further. Johnny placed the bat over his shoulder and kept approaching.

"You going to get that?" he snarled.

"Yeah, you going to get that?" the cook asked before spitting into the dirt.

"Answer the damn phone!" Johnny rushed forward, swinging.

Lindsey drew her gun too late. She ducked to avoid the blow and came back up, swinging. She hit Johnny in the side of the head with her gun. He tumbled to the ground, dropping the bat. She trapped it underfoot before picking it up. Johnny's hand came away from his head caked in blood, though it was hard to tell with all the sauce.

"Gee, what did you do that for?" he asked the sheriff.

"Yeah, why'd you do that?" The cook asked as the two workers checked on their downed boss.

Lindsey holstered her weapon and climbed into her car. Her night was becoming one big paperwork mess. The phone rang again, and she tossed it out the window. She needed to get to the station to talk with her new friend and find out what was going on.

Hitting the sirens, she peeled out of the lot. She sped down the street and noticed all the calls coming in through her laptop. She turned that off as well. The station, she needed to get to the big man in the station.

She slowed at the nearest intersection despite her flashing lights. She briefly closed her eyes and decided on something. One more stop. One more stop and **then** she would visit her strange prisoner at the station. Blooping the siren in a burst, she U-turned and sped off.

Sandy sat in the shadows. After driving around town looking for the little snots to no avail, she decided they would eventually show at the Fast Stop. They always did. Shoplifting beers, then harassing customers. Moments earlier, a customer argued inside the store with the clerk, and things got heated. The customer was Maude Plotkin, a pastor's wife. The clerk that night was Greasy Nick. People called him that because his face resembled a pizza.

Maude gave plenty good, dropping F-bombs about something or another. Maude knocked over every rack she could find that would move. The pastor and his wife were notorious stick in the butt types, so it pleased Sandy to see the woman loosen up a little. By the time Maude finished, she left the establishment empty-handed, but looked like she had partaken of a religious experience. Maude fanned herself and blew her sweaty bangs out of her face before getting in her minivan and peeling out.

Greasy Nick locked the front doors to the shop and placed a sign up that read, *Clozed for Kleaning*. A whizz that kid. While leaving the rest home, the sheriff had called Sandy. Lindsey mentioned something about a big man in their holding cell and that they needed all hands on him.

Sandy made a sexual joke that her boss laughed at which surprised Sandy. Lindsey also mentioned something about sundown but that was where the information train ended. Lindsey had a call come in from her nagging husband and hung up.

The sheriff never called back but Sandy was not going to go to the station either way. She had a stop to make and planned to wait all night if necessary. But she did not wait long. The snot-nosed skateboarders rolled up. She heard them from a mile away, the annoying clop of wheels on asphalt.

The trio of kids approached the front of the store and cursed a storm about the locked door. They pounded while Greasy Nick flipped them the bird. That was all it took to set them off. One of the three began kicking the door. The glass withstood such an attack. Still, she did not want them to get lucky and crack it, so Sandy stepped out from the shadows.

"Hello, boys."

The smallest in the group tapped the kicker on the shoulder. "Hey, Justin, po-po."

Justin looked over at Sandy and smirked. "Yeah? What's she gonna do?" He kicked at the glass again.

Sandy pulled her gun and aimed it at the two who were not fighting the door. They raised their hands, and she drew a finger over her lips in a shush motion. She waved the gun, prompting them to step to the side. They did. Sandy moved forward and as soon as Justin kicked again, she swept his anchored leg out from under him, resulting in his falling to the ground while one leg remained stuck on the metal rail of the door.

Justin screamed in pain over the forced split that ripped his pants down the center. He could not dislodge the leg trapped on the door push bar. "Tug! Dan! Help me, man!" Justin pleaded.

"She's got a gun," Tug said.

"Nah, I'm not a cop tonight. I'm a concerned citizen who is tired of the disrespect that certain ignorant teens show their elders."

Sandy ejected the clip from her weapon and tossed it. She ejected the chambered bullet and placed the gun in her holster and snapped the holster closed.

"Wrong move!" Tug, a lanky, tall goober, yelled.

He rushed Sandy and kicked her hard between the legs. He smiled, waiting for her to fall, except she matched his grin with a wider one. Tug eyed her crotch.

"Honey, I have felt nothing down there since the nineties. Remember how I said I wasn't a cop tonight?"

She removed the badge from her outfit and placed the needle end through the fingers of her fist and stabbed forward. Tug screamed and grabbed at his head.

The badge stood out on his forehead with the pin stuck deep in his skin. Red poured down into one eye.

Dan helped Justin free his leg. Justin went fetal, grabbing his groin. Dan looked around and saw his two buddies nursing wounds. He stood alone. Sandy bent down and picked up one of their skateboards. She spun a wheel.

"You know what wheels represent?" Sandy asked.

"What?" Dan said.

"Freedom. Wheels allow you to travel. They give you freedom to move, but also freedom from harassing innocent people. The freedom not to terrorize people who simply desire a large soda and some gas. Freedom from bullying other teens. Freedom from being total and utter assholes!"

"We're just having fun," Dan said.

"And how old are you guys?"

"Eighteen."

"Good, good to know, so I don't pull any punches if you were minors, not that I would care much," Sandy said.

Tug finally yanked the badge from his head and ran toward the woman, fist raised, roaring in his approach. Sandy swung big with the skateboard. It cracked along the underside of Tug's jaw with an epic pop. The teen immediately crumpled to the ground, where he fell into a twitching fit. Dan stood there wide eyed, horrified. He started toward his downed friend, but Sandy waved him off with the skateboard.

The kid eyed his own skateboard near his feet and grabbed it. He raised it threatening. Sandy nodded and the teen charged. He swung, and she held hers up. The impact caused both to drop the weapons and shake out their hands.

Dan saw his chance and punched Sandy in the gut. She wheezed and grabbed her stomach but smiled through the pain and stood. The kid looked surprised.

"See? You don't understand we were all young once. All had our time in the sun, but time does its thing. We're like cookie batter, being baked into shapes. Some thick, some thin, some big, some small," Sandy said and gestured to Dan's friends, highlighting the difference, and emphasizing the word small.

Dan punched her in the face. Her lip split and gushed blood. She smiled again. "That dough? It's not formed yet when you're young. And it's a delicate process. Squeeze it too hard, abuse it, and it becomes the worst cookie in the bunch. Turns into something inedible, something untouchable, something no one wants. Burnt maybe. Is that what you really want? You know it's a matter of time before you bake into the person you will be. So, if you don't want to be the worst in the bunch, you can start by respecting your damn elders!"

Dan struck again, punching her in the face. She immediately punched back, smacking him in the face. He looked surprised and raised a fist again. She nodded.

"One for one? Show me yours and I'll show you mine. Let's go."

She stood tall. Dan went for the gut again. She took the hit even though a rib cracked with a loud snap. Dan then stood in place, and Sandy punched him in the gut. He fell to his knees gasping, but quickly rose. He punched her in the chest. She yelped loudly.

"Ah! Boob shot. Bastard."

She wiped the smile from his face by striking his chest hard enough to knock him back while he massaged out the pain. He went for her lip again. She reciprocated, drawing blood.

Then, with a loud cry, Justin charged her on shaky legs, skateboard held high, aiming for Sandy's skull. Acting as one, Dan and Sandy both punched Justin's face. He crumpled, unconscious. Then Dan and Sandy faced off again without missing a beat, ready to keep going.

Nolan locked Dolores in the cell across from Crevice. Nolan glanced over and noticed something odd. The man sat on the cot, leaning forward, the brim of the hat covering most of the man's face. But something seemed different. The clothes appeared to fit the man better than when they first brought him in. A trick of the light, surely. The phones in the squad room were ringing off the hook when he arrived with his prisoner. The entire way to the station she vacillated between propositioning him and threatening to bash his skull in.

The man in the cell was Nolan's type, mysterious, large. But also, creepy. There was that. Now, the man appeared off. Nolan could not place it despite being a student of the male form. He did not wish to look too long lest he become creepy himself. Without looking up, the prisoner somehow knew he was being watched.

"Should have let me go. A little busy, are you?" Crevice asked.

"You know something about that?' Nolan asked, wondering what the man knew.

"I know the phones haven't stopped ringing."

Nolan shook his head. Of course, the man knew how busy they were; they locked in him with all the phones. Nothing mysterious there. The guy simply heard call after call. The prisoner lifted his head and Nolan spotted his eyes. Were they blue? He did not remember them being blue on the way in. The man's face seemed more relaxed than earlier.

The phones kept ringing. Nolan wondered what all the calls were about. Nell directed them when she was on the job, but she had friends in town for a baby shower, so was off. Absent an admin, the phones transcribed the calls and sent them to their laptops in their cruisers. Nolan left the prisoners and headed toward a desk when his own cell rang.

"Nell? Wait, what?"

"Told you that you should have let me go," the man said from his holding cell, but Nolan was already gone. Then the man looked at the woman sitting on the cot opposite him. "What are you in for?"

"Botched eye surgery," Dolores said.

Nolan rushed to his car and sped down chaotic streets. Everywhere he looked, there were issues, fights, fires. Emergency vehicles sped past in various directions. Nolan watched calls scroll by on his laptop but ignored them all. Nell needed his help.

Nell was frantic on the call, saying something about stealing a phone out of someone's back pocket, but she was struggling to work the phone. She called him first and said she would hang up and try 911. Nothing Nell said made sense and he avoided telling her dialing the emergency line would be pointless.

He blasted his sirens until a block away. He did not wish to alert anyone inside to his presence. But they might have heard him drive up onto the front lawn, tearing grass without an afterthought. Nell needed help and her driveway was full. There were multiple cars there. What was going on? Wasn't it baby shower night? Nolan drew his weapon and stormed into her two-story home.

Signs of both a bridal shower and a struggle filled the living room. Bloody smears covered the floor. He heard a thump overhead. Voices sounded from somewhere in the large home, but he could not identify where or who they belonged to.

He climbed the stairs, gun pointed. Nolan knew the place well, was friends with Nell. She was his go to in the office for talking about hot guys. Her baby daddy was one, a cop from Boston she met at a convention. He was married, so she was doing the single mom thing.

The thump seemed to have come from the bedroom, but he also heard movement in the kitchen, but that was down a corridor and off to the right, so he went up first. He did not call out because he did not wish to alert any intruders to his presence. Stealth was required until he located her.

There were two bedrooms at the top of the stairs. A small bedroom, a separate bathroom, then the master bedroom which anchored the hallway. The door was open in the master bedroom through which he glimpsed the feet of someone on a bed kicking against bonds. Nell!

Nolan cleared the two rooms on the way before rushing into the master bedroom. Nell was nude and tied to the bed with duct tape. The tape over her mouth was loosened, allowing her to talk and make the emergency call. One hand was also free but the cell phone she had used to call Nolan had fallen to the floor alongside the bed. She was lucky she got a call through.

"Thank God!" Nell yelled. "Where are the others? I didn't hear shots? Did you kill them? They've gone crazy."

"Who, Nell? What's going on?"

He struggled to untie her. The tape refused to cooperate. He bit at the tape which secured one foot to a bedpost. It caused a rip that he exploited, tearing it away. Nell nearly kicked him out of instinct when her foot came loose. He dodged, ignoring the gynecological view of the fully nude woman on the bed.

Blood covered her still tethered foot (responsible for the smudges downstairs?). Nell noticed his concern.

"It's not my blood. I kicked Felicia in the nose."

"Felicia? Your best friend, Felicia?"

"Yeah, cracked the bitch's nose. If you didn't encounter them, then they are around here somewhere."

Behind him, footsteps sounded in the hall. Heavy. Nolan looked over his shoulder and could not fully understand. Felicia stood in the doorway. Felicia was a large woman, three hundred pounds at least, and well known as one of the town superstars for the annual chili cookoffs. Normally gregarious and full of joy, the woman wore a scowl bordering on homicidal. She waved the chef's knife in her hand like a scolding finger.

"Tsk, tsk, tsk, Nolan. We cannot have you release her."

We referred to two other heads barely viewable over Felicia's shoulder. Felicia was Nell's best friend from high school. The other two were likely friends as well. All assembled for a pre-baby shower before the bigger party that would include her family and work friends. Felicia blocked the entire doorway. There would be no getting past her without force, but Nolan was hesitant to draw his weapon, as nothing made sense.

"We're Nell's best friends and have collectively decided we are going to deliver this baby tonight. What better way to celebrate our friend's pregnancy than by ending it? Poor thing carrying around so much weight."

Kettle calling a kettle a kettle, Nolan thought and finally unclipped the weapon strap. He would figure out later what was going on, but for now, he needed to protect his friend. Before he could unholster the gun, Felicia charged, knife raised over her head.

Nolan froze. Nell screamed. Then something snapped violently. Felicia's ankle. She fell face first as her other leg gave out, face-planting with a loud '*schnick.*' The woman landed on the upturned blade which stabbed through the bottom of her jaw. The tip made a blood-covered appearance through her right eye. She twitched and gurgled as blood coated the floor.

"What did you do to Felicia?" Kristen yelled

He identified the two women once he could see them. Kristen and Julia, both mothers and friends of Nell. They charged knives raised high. Nolan pulled his gun, but Kristen slipped in the pooling blood and fell, laying still, trying to breathe after having the wind knocked out of her.

Julia came on next, mindful of the blood. Nolan braced himself against the bed and kicked her. Julia flew backward against the wall and crumpled to the ground. She growled, but the fight had mostly gone out of her. Nolan approached Kristen and kicked her face, knocking her unconscious. He took the unconscious woman's blade and cut Nell free.

"You back-stabbing bitch!" Nell yelled and charged Julia.

Julia dropped the knife and looked up apologetically to her friend, but Nell was not having it. Nell kicked Julia's face causing the woman's head to bounce against the wall and back. Though bloodied at the nose and lip, Julia remained conscious. Nell kicked again. Repeat. Nell's bare foot did not provide the extra oomph that Nolan's work boot did.

Julia laughed through the blood pooling in her mouth. She spit a red, pink spittle as she raged at her friend. "Think you're the shit having a baby? Anyone can have a baby. Look at me! Look at me! I'm the number one greatest mom. I have a stupid ass coffee mug that says so! Look at me!"

Nolan corralled Nell and led her down the stairs. Nell led the way outside to the driveway. She was still completely nude and did not care what the neighbors saw. Nolan dialed the sheriff on the way but got no answer.

"We need to get you to the hospital," Nolan said.

"I can drive myself," she said, getting into her car and peeling out without so much as a thank you.

Nolan turned to the house and wondered where to begin. He dialed emergency services for an ambulance but got only a busy signal for his troubles. He had enough. Nolan decided it was time for a change. He was nothing but a dam holding back a flood of crazy, and structural failure was imminent. There was nothing more he could do.

He got in his car, turned off the laptop pinging emergencies, and drove toward his house to collect his things. The town could screw itself. Life in the woods sounded pretty good.

Higgins loved everything he was hearing. All around him, people dealt with issues and sleights with fisticuffs. None bothered asking for his help. Higgins continued toward his destination, the business that made the call which brought him to the mall in the first place.

He approached the movie theater premiering a hot new movie starring a hot new starlet and a famous actor. Higgins planned to watch it eventually but figured no time like the present. Signs on the doors of the business said they were closed. A male teen worker about nineteen waited at the doors and unlocked it when Higgins appeared.

The officer stepped inside and noticed a second female worker of the same age staring towards a closed viewing room door. Higgins approached her. Voices cried out inside.

"What happened to your face?" the male asked. "Should I see the other guy?"

"I am the other guy," Higgins said.

The kid furrowed his brow, confused. Higgins approached the stunned young woman. She pointed to the closed theater door. The sounds inside were clear.

"You left the movie playing?" Higgins asked.

"Yes. Do you want us to stop it?"

Higgins shook his head. "And the other theaters?"

"Empty. We evacuated and called it in," the other kid said.

"Adults only?" Higgins asked.

"Yeah, rated R. We card. And we know everyone in town," the guy said.

"I used to babysit for the Langdon's. They are both in there. And not with each other," the girl said.

"Look. This may take some time with the amount of people involved. I suggest you all lock up and go home. Unless you want to go in with me?" Higgins asked.

The two could not escape fast enough. They raced for the door. Higgins watched them lock the business from the outside. Higgins opened the door to screening room three and stepped inside. The voices from the seats drowned out the screen's soundtrack. Up on the big screen, the starlet engaged in simulated sex while down in the theater the entire audience engaged in actual sex.

The teens were right. Higgins knew many of the people in the theater as well. Many were married and those folks had split off to engage in sex with others. Every position and combination available happened under the lights of the silver screen.

Higgins stepped further inside and waited for his eyes to adjust. Once they did, he stripped off all his clothes. His initial worries at being interrupted so that he would be unable to solve the most cases ever came true. He was not going anywhere. Let people figure their stuff out he thought.

Tonight, he was not a cop; he was simply home.

Sandy sat against the wall of the Fast Stop and lit a cigarette. Smoke poured out of her crooked nose. Bruises and abrasions covered her face. She handed the cigarette to Dan, who occupied a part of the wall right next to her. He sported a deep black eye, one that would not heal quickly. He nodded and took a drag.

"Thanks," Dan said.

"Any idea when your friends vanished?" Sandy asked.

"Nah, I was too busy getting my ass kicked to notice," Dan said.

"Hey, don't sell yourself short. My kidney is killing me. I expect I'll be pissing blood for a few days," she said.

"Really? Gee, that's nice of you to say," Dan said. "I'm the runt, so they always pick on me."

"Yeah, well, not anymore when you tell them how you beat up a cop."

"After I get out of jail. Am I under arrest?"

"Hell no. I started it. I just wanted some respect out of you turds."

"You got it, props."

He handed the cigarette back. The kid from inside appeared and handed off two bags of frozen peas. Sirens roared in the distance. Sandy and Dan nodded thanks and applied the bags to different wounds, wincing as they did so.

"Strange night, huh?" the clerk asked. "What do you think is causing it?"

"Not a what. A who."

Sandy remembered the weird conversation with her boss. Sandy figured it was worth checking in on their prison guest as soon as she could find her feet again. While she felt like absolute crap, she also felt more alive than she had in years.

The sheriff drove toward the station, lights flashing. She ignored all the street craziness while speeding toward the source of the town's ills. Once there, she walked straight to Crevice. She ignored Dolores sitting in the adjacent holding cell. Dolores raced to the bars.

"What happened to you?" Dolores asked, eyeing the red liquid covering the sheriff's body.

Lindsey ignored the woman and looked inside the other cell. The man's clothes fit perfectly now, but only because the man had shrunk. He looked to be about five-foot-seven, and thin, lanky even. Petite, the sheriff thought.

He looked up at the sheriff. "Rough night?"

"You knew it would be,"

He nodded. His voice matched the image of the man. The voice was almost comically high, like a kid in puberty. The sheriff did not question the change. She simply unlocked the cell.

"Let's go," she said.

Crevice rose without question and joined the sheriff. She did not cuff him, only gestured to the front of the station. Crevice exited while Dolores sniffed the sheriff and backed away from the bars.

Lindsey led Crevice to her vehicle. The man stopped short, awaiting instructions. She came around and opened the front passenger door.

"Guess you better sit in the front seat," she said.

He nodded and got in. No trouble at all since he was so petite. They drove in silence for some time before Lindsey spoke.

"How does it work?" she asked.

"You know those water purifiers? The charcoal filters?"

"Takes all the garbage out?"

"Exactly. Think of it like that. But I must keep moving. When I do, I scoop up all the garbage that a location harbors."

"But when you stop? Like when a cop forces you to stop?"

"It's time to change the filter. I've given up trying to explain to law enforcement in advance. Would you have believed me?"

"Never."

"Exactly. If I am not moving or sleeping by sundown, it all comes out. Everything I scooped out of your town, and everything else cleansed from other towns along the way. I tried to nap in the cell, I did. But sadly, my cycle is off. Could not work up a snore. Therefore, at sundown it all came out."

"All the evil?"

"I prefer to think of it as impulses. But it's all semantics. Come sundown when I'm not moving or sleeping as I mentioned, then whoomp there it is."

"The things people do in such a case. It reveals their true nature?"

Crevice nodded and looked in the rearview mirror, finally taking in some scenery. The sheriff checked the mirror as well to see what the man was looking at. He turned back to her. The warm smile version.

Lindsey flushed. She longed for a romp with the stranger. Clearly, she remained under the influence of the voodoo garbage charcoal-filter man brought with him. She wondered about her own true nature.

"There's a chance your town was innocent and is only experiencing the fruits of my journey. I have passed through many a place."

"Including Ledgerton?" the sheriff asked about a notoriously decadent town up north. "Place is one big strip club and drug factory."

"And might contain some of the most decent people. Urges acted on sometimes cleanse the soul. Allowed to build up, and well, I grow large. It's a heavy burden to carry. I'm the size I need to be to support the weight of darkness on my back. I started at my current size when heading into the Bible belt once and popped a button before I made it to the town border."

They arrived at Lindsey's town border. A large wooden sign wished visitors a fond goodbye. The sheriff considered just such an action. She pulled her weapon and placed her finger on the trigger.

"And if I shoot you, it stops?"

"No. Things get worse. Much worse."

"Worse than all this?"

She trusted his grey eyes when he locked them on her own and nodded. She released her grip on the gun. He tried the door. Locked. He waited for her to release him. The sheriff tilted the rear-view mirror and looked at the back seat.

"I truly loved him," she said.

"I'm sure you did," Crevice answered.

Lindsey stared at her husband, Glenn, in the rear seat. His eyes were open wide, a single bullet hole in the center of his head drooled blood in a straight line down the man's face. The shot was merciful compared to his other injury.

A thick rectangular cut of flesh rested in the man's lap. Blood drooled from the large piece of flesh. Like a puzzle piece, the skin chunk would have fit exactly in the spot where someone sliced it away from the man's torso. Placed properly, the fleshy puzzle piece would fit into the gaping wound in the man's side. The opening in the man's side exposed a rib cage.

The slick red liquid covering the sheriff's uniform was from more than barbecue sauce. Before heading back to the station, she visited her husband for rough sex, but he whined too much. (Asking for ribs while she rode him? Really?) She decided if he wanted ribs, she was going to give him ribs.

He was already handcuffed to the bed, so she exposed his rib cage with relative ease, surprised at how the carving came out in one piece. While pleased with her work, her husband's screams brought her to her senses long enough for her to unlock him, place him in the car and head toward the hospital.

But oh, how he continued whining. Worse than over the phone, the way he carried on. His cries went from wanting ribs to screaming about how he could see his own. There was no pleasing the man. The single gunshot made things right, brought peace to her world.

She explained the entire scenario to Crevice, but the man appeared unmoved by her plight. She supposed he had seen it all. The sheriff pushed the button to unlock the passenger door. The man got out and walked off into the night. A man just passing through.

TATTE BAKERY & CAFÉ, BOSTON, MASSACHUSETTS

B OSTON IS A SPECIAL place for me. Every year, multiple times per year, I travel to Boston to see historical landmarks from the American Revolutionary War. One of my repeat spots, no matter how often I travel back to Boston, is the Bunker Hill Monument in Charlestown, Massachusetts, which is pretty much still in Boston.

Only about a five-minute walk from the Monument is a lovely little café called Tatte Bakery & Café. They serve sandwiches, pastries, salads, and even Shakshuka. I spent many a time there, especially after Covid waned, thinking about the Battle of Bunker Hill after visiting the Monument and the nearby museum. It's where I first got the idea for this story.

I live in Woodford, Vermont right now. In nearby Bennington, there is a very similar monument erected honoring the Battle of Bennington, which also happened during the American Revolution. No matter where you are in New England, there is a reminder of the Revolution and the ghosts it produced. But Bunker Hill is pretty much where it all began.

COFFEE RECOMMENDATION: The American Revolution was spurred along by tea, so why not have yourself a nice London Fog Latte, sometimes known as an Earl Grey Tea Latte. It's smoky, it's sweet, and it's just the thing for fall.

BLOOD BROTHERS

Joseph Carro

MY NAME IS NATHAN Blood, and I am dead.

It was morning. June seventeenth, 1775. The smell of the sea from Boston Harbor filled my nostrils with salt. The sun rose, seemingly from the water itself, casting its warmth in long bands across my neck and cheeks. It was a welcome balm. I lifted the cap off my head and wiped the night's sweat and grit from my brow with callused hands. Farmer's hands. Eternal partners fog and darkness burned off the top of the Charles, revealing English ships in its waters. Three by my count, the one closest to us in the Harbor being called the *Lively*.

I suffered through much jostling at the hands of toiling men. Groans and grunts accompanied their movements as they bustled around me. There was much work still to be done on the earthen redoubt and breastwork we began building during the night under cover of darkness. But it did not appear we had enough time to put the finishing touches on it. The English meant to occupy Charles Town, but *we* meant to stop them at whatever cost necessary. We knew in our hearts they would fight us tooth and nail to make an example of us to others of like minds and dispositions.

Men moved past, carrying ammunition and supplies down the line of former farmers and fishermen who had turned into soldiers overnight, leaving their homes and families to protect their future and their pockets. I saw among the men plentiful faces from town. Elias Wheeler was one, a farmer who lived down the road and someone who'd shared supper with us before Mother died. He was a kind man who sometimes brought us vegetables without asking for barter, though Father would often give him something in return, most often an invitation to the dinner table. Elias loved mother's cooking, as we all did. Turning my head, I saw a boy my age, Jonathan Wright, toiling alongside his own father as I had done with mine. We nodded to one another, then I shifted my gaze back to my group.

I stood with my brother Francis and our father, Ebenezer. I looked at father as he packed shovels full of earth and rock and tall grass onto the redoubt. He felt my gaze upon his back and turned. His body steamed just like the top of the Charles and his broad shoulders worked just as hard all these hours later as they had since the night before. They were shoulders which seemed to carry the weight of the world. They also carried the weight of our dead mother. We locked eyes, and he smiled, with a hint of pride in his countenance. He gave me a slight nod. I nodded back before returning to my work, the wood shovel handle renewing its bite into my dirty palms. I returned to my previous pace, grunting with each shovel full of dirt I dumped next to Francis, intent on not being outdone by my father.

Francis, the youngest of us, stared nervously toward the Charles. He was barely a man, too young to be there with us on Breed's pasture among those ready to die, but we needed all the souls we could muster, and we could muster but few. I, with my dark eyes and sharp features, looked just like father. Francis looked more like our mother. His eyes were green, his features more rounded and innocent—like a cherub in a painting. I was tall and sturdy, the oldest, and grew in spurts the past two years. Francis remained small, not yet grown to his full measure. He worried he never would, and I mentioned how I'd once felt the same. I urged him to give it time.

I lost myself in my work, appreciating the morning sun on my back, the redoubt growing to great heights with each shovel full of the earth from our collective efforts. Time seemed to pass in years rather than minutes, and still I waited for the English volley of cannon fire to rain from the sky at any moment and fling us all from our mortal coil. There was an urgency in the air that I could feel in my bones, like when lightning threatens to strike. But the redoubt would be our only shelter from the cannon fire which would no doubt erupt soon from the British ships.

"They are moving on us," I heard Father say. He had a voice like two soap stones grinding together. It was a voice that commanded respect. He'd stopped shoveling momentarily, apparently having seen something we had not, his eyes focused beyond the redoubt and on the ships in the Charles.

Indeed, the *Lively* and the other two ships moved into formation. Small red specks of men darted back and forth on the decks of the ships. Though harder to see, there were flashes of movement in the bellies of the ships as well. I imagined them readying cannons to fire on us. The wind carried the sounds of their ship commanders shouting orders.

"Are the redcoats going to storm the hill now?" Asked young Francis. "Will we join Mother in Heaven?"

Father looked stricken, his gaze resting for a moment on the clouds above us, before placing his hands on our shoulders and drawing us together in a circle. His hands could easily crush our skulls if he so wished, yet I always marveled at his genuine wisdom and gentle nature.

"They'll come up this hill soon enough. I love you boys. I love you both. When they march on us, I want you to aim for their red coats. I want you to be brave. We will all stand together, and we will all go home, God willing."

I hope we can all return home, I thought, looking with a sort of regret over the lip of the redoubt. Though I was an excellent shot with a musket, I'd only ever fired at game and small birds and squirrels. I'd never shot a man. The thought turned my stomach, and I wished the lobsterbacks would just leave and then we wouldn't have to engage in violence and bloodshed against our own cousins and brothers.

Other men nearby chattered amongst themselves and pointed into the harbor with shaking fingers. We left the huddle and crowded around the safety of the redoubt to see what transpired in the waters. The earth felt cool and welcome against my stinging hands as I leaned into our construct, and the smell of the damp earth replaced the salt in my nostrils from the Charles. I looked again to the ships and watched men in uniform rushing around the deck of the *Lively*.

Echoes of English voices bounced off the rocks and water in the harbor. They'd seen what we had been up to during the night and had finally seen fit to do something about it. Men ran to places of concealment and safety within the breastwork along the redoubt, reaching for their muskets as casually as they reached for psalms on Sunday mornings. I wished to join them. From the look on my father's face, I could tell that he was worried, despite his earlier brave words to Francis.

Boom-boom-boom-boom-boom.

The thunderous sound caused me to catch my breath. Men shouted, taking cover all around us. The ships fired on us. I crouched in the breastwork and traded my shovel for my nearby musket, bracing myself. My brother and father followed suit, each of us occupied by our own dark thoughts.

"Oh lord, our God," Father began, grabbing us close. "Our young patriots, in thine image, go forth to battle. Please protect us and give us aid as we fight for justice. We ask you, He who is the source of love, to guide us, and may you have mercy on all the souls certain to be lost here. May we forever fight the tyranny and oppression of our cousins. Amen."

"Amen," me and Francis said.

We endured the cannon fire for some time in a collective fear and anxiety before we realized the guns couldn't reach as far as the English hoped, leaving us relatively safe for the moment. My fingers shook regardless, and my legs felt like hollow reeds. Scouts reported the cannon fire wasn't yet reaching the redoubt, but in time the English would maneuver into a better position. With the redoubt all but finished, we set to work fortifying a rail fence to the left of Breed's pasture, strewing hay across the ground behind it for our men to lie on. We worked swiftly, for we all knew what was coming.

The day grew hotter as we worked, and I had to seek shade where I could find it. Francis had already done so, his youthful energy waning. The ships' firing ceased after a time and we learned that in the chaos of building the redoubt and rail fence, an errant cannon ball had ricocheted and killed a man, striking him down in a grisly display. A warning of the violence yet to come.

I took a break from my work and went to see the body. It was a young man by the name of Samuel Brooks, from Exeter, New Hampshire. Though I hadn't known him, it steeled my heart against any fear I may have felt before and turned it to righteous anger. The tyranny of England had gone on long enough. They had drawn first blood this day, but we would see it through to the end, I was sure. I thought about Samuel the rest of the day, his unseeing eyes looking toward Heaven where my mother was.

During that time, we rested when we could, ate when we could, still waiting for a direct attack from the redcoats. Their cannon fire had done little to dissuade us from the nest we'd made on Breed's Pasture, though some men had fled in fear after the bombardment killed the young man, dropping their shovels and desire to fight in the dirt on that hill where so many later died. Since then, there had been many false alarms.

During a lull, our father reached into a sack he'd brought with him and fetched three pears, one for each of us, and some bread. I snatched mine out of the air as he tossed it and quickly brought it to my nose before taking an indulgent bite. It was soft, fragrant, and sweet, and brought much needed moisture to my lips and throat. The bread was dry but tasted fine and would help fill our bellies.

"Are you scared?" Francis asked me, chewing his own pear while awaiting my response.

"I suppose I am," I said, thoughtfully. "I'm scared that we'll die for nothing. Like Samuel."

"Who is Samuel?" Francis asked. Obviously, father had shielded him from the death for the time being.

I paused. It would do no good to scare him. "Nobody."

Father ate in silence and sat down for a moment in the dirt, right next to us but distanced all the same. He had always been like that.

"Do you think we'll die?" Francis asked, his voice shaky.

"No," I said. "We are fighting for our homes. I think once they see they cannot move us, the British will turn around and go back to where they came from."

"They are fat and drunk," said Father, spitting out the stem after biting the top of his pear off. "They think us sheep and that they need only herd us from this hill, but that won't happen. Once they understand they cannot move us, they will turn around."

Francis seemed content to leave things at that and continue eating his pear in silence. I tousled his hair and gave him a smile.

Later renewed firing from the English man-o-war ships in the bay began. Some also fired from Boston on top of Copp's Hill. While still wary of the potential threat from the cannon fire, we'd seen little in the way of damage on our side from the constant bombardment, so we continued our work with caution. We prepared the fortifications as best as our motley crew could manage, and now we waited for the English to retreat or to land their attack parties and come for our blood. Hope arose with Colonel William Prescott's arrival.

His silver-lined voice called out. "Hold fast, my boys!"

We all turned on our heels to see him striding, unsheathed cutlass in hand, toward us from Charles Town with a dozen men. One I recognized as Doctor Joseph Warren, behind whom walked several black men. Prescott's calico coat lifted with grace, caught in the arms of the breeze. The bill of his three-cornered hat ruffled ever so slightly, cocked to one side. Mud and sand covered his boots and clothing, while his skin held a sheen of sweat. Doctor Joseph Warren walked at an equal gait, both taking confident steps.

"The English mean to drive us from this hill, but by God, we'll give them Hell and more," said Prescott, lifting his saber for emphasis. Cheers of agreement from the lot of us, myself included. We lifted our hats into the sky.

"If they want the hill, they can have it at a high price," he continued. More cheers. "We will sell it to them dearly, rock by rock, root by root, and we will let them see what sort of mettle we're made of. We are one thousand strong!"

I found myself caught up in a wave of hysteria that we all seemed to share. We, the Bloods, hurled our hats into the sky. Prescott raised his saber and screamed, spit flying from his mouth in an arc.

"When the redcoats come for us, and come for us, they will, do not fire until I tell you! Do not fire until you see the whites of their eyes. The whites of their eyes!"

More cheering from the men and then Doctor Joseph Warren, who bore an uncanny resemblance to Washington, came to Prescott's side, clapping him hard on the back. The two men locked forearms, which stirred my spirit along with the others in our vicinity. We felt invincible, like demigods, with these two men directing us. Prescott climbed atop the redoubt and walked back and forth along its length, checking its durability.

Boom-boom-boom-boom-boom.

Boom-boom-boom-boom-boom.

Boom-boom-boom-boom-boom.

I heard the cannon balls slam into the ground beyond the redoubt and heard others still crash into stones and some, though rarely, hit the redoubt itself. I stood and chanced a look over the lip, my legs shaking.

Smoke filled the harbor and covered the Charles in an artificial fog. Despite the bombardment, I could see Prescott still standing on the redoubt, directing us, his men, to stay calm. He was unflinching. Fear left me momentarily while watching Prescott stand so brave above us in harm's way, though sand and debris washed over the lip of the redoubt like sea spray during a storm, making it hard to see and filling my mouth with grit which cracked between my teeth and spread on my lips.

"Sit tight, lads," said our father. "This wall should hold well enough."

Boom-boom-boom-boom-boom-boom-boom-boom-boom-boom.

After a time, there was a migration of British soldiers flocking from the other side of the harbor and disembarking from the man-o-wars in small ships meant for landing parties. They were coming, finally. We saw them floating across the waters, almost as if they were enjoying the summer day at their leisure. Then, there was a commotion from the southwest, near Charles Town. Smoke rose, originating from the town's direction where great licks of flame reached up to tear down steeples and the dwellings of many of our countrymen in fiery, crackling heaps of lumber.

"They've set Charles Town ablaze to smoke us out, I'd warrant," said my father. His eyes were grim with a gleam of panic and anger in them. "It will take much more than that to move us."

It confirmed his theory when some sentries reported several landing boats on Moreton's Point, close to Charles Town. The *Lively* fired some more on the town, no doubt targeting the many snipers in our ranks perched in the buildings, waiting to fire on any redcoats approaching.

We lined up at our fence and we settled ourselves there. Score after score of Englishmen lined up at the water's edge below us, at the base of the hill. Soon, it became a sea of red. Screams of anguish and anger rose from the men on our side as the ash and soot from Charles Town filled our nostrils and lungs.

I shivered, despite the summer heat on my back, my blood turning to ice. Francis laid next to me on my right while my father took a spot to my left. We were shoulder to shoulder, arm to arm.

The British played their drums and began a slow march up the hill, toward our redoubt.

"Shouldn't we fire on them now?" Francis said, licking his lips in nervousness. "They are so many, and we are so few!"

"You heard Prescott," I said, looking down the barrel of my musket, though my finger ached to fire the round I loaded into the gun earlier. I moved the mechanism into place so that it was no longer half-cocked, and I waited with my finger hovering over the trigger.

"THE WHITES OF THEIR EYES!" yelled Prescott.

Several commanders across the line repeated the cry from the redoubt to the rail fence we waited behind. Smoke wafted from burning Charles Town, stinging our eyes, and filling our breath with soot. Still, we held our fire.

We heard the commands of the English officers as they marched their army up the hill, over stone walls, and waist-high tall grass. I was shaking but held my finger at bay. Sweat crawled over my body and my heart pounded along with the English drums.

"THE WHITES OF THEIR EYES!" Again, the cry came across the line.

"They're getting too close," Francis said. "They're almost upon us!"

"Hold, son," said our father. "Remember, aim for the red. If they reach us, run, run as fast as your legs will carry you. Do not look back! Do not tarry!"

I could just make out the features of two British soldiers marching toward us, through the smoke, in the front line of the brigade. One looked to be a boy, not much older than Francis. Their uniforms were neat and handsome, unlike our own simple, dirt-stained clothes. They were rigid in their march, but they wore uncertainty stitched across their faces like badges on a uniform. Their commanders marched alongside the ranks, waving their cutlasses or sabers into the air, shouting commands. They walked on and on, marching directly toward the fence where we lay with our guns.

"FIRE!"

The call came down the line and there erupted a brilliant display of gunfire and gunpowder smoke. I pulled the trigger, screaming, aiming somewhere into the crowd of red-clothed soldiers. Gunpowder flashed in front of my face, obscuring my view and stinging my eyes, but I heard the screams of the men as the balls from our muskets tore through flesh and ended their lives. Francis fired his weapon with a look of fear and disgust on his face. He shook after firing, every muscle in his body protesting the death and carnage surrounding him. We coughed, inhaling the smoke from our guns and the nearby burning town.

"RELOAD!"

The call came down the line again. We all set upon stuffing our powder and ball down the barrel with the ramrod before slipping the rod back into place.

"FIRE!"

We heard the call from the English commanders followed by a great thunder of guns. I pulled Francis down with me to make ourselves small as musket balls whizzed by our heads and ears like angry bees disturbed from a hive. Francis screamed, which stopped my heart, but he was not hit. The fence and a few other men were not so lucky. One of our own howled in pain, clutching at a bloody wound on his left shoulder where the ball passed through him. Red seeped between his fingers as he fell and pressed his back against the fence.

I brought my gun to bear again and then, to my astonishment, there was a great cheer. The British were fleeing down the side of the hill, running back toward their boats, leaving their dead and wounded behind.

"HOLD YOUR FIRE!" Came the cry down the line. "THE WHITES OF THEIR EYES!"

Did we defeat them? It doesn't seem possible!

My father stood and howled, waving his hat around in the air. Francis still looked down the barrel of his gun. I wiped the sweat from my hands and waited and watched.

The ground before us sat littered with corpses and wounded English attackers. Some screamed, calling out for their comrades or their families during their death throes. Others hobbled away as fast as they could from where our cheering lines of men made their stand. I saw the young English boy I noticed earlier. The youth was dead, eyes open to the summer sky. I wondered if I had been the one to end his life. My stomach turned when I acknowledged to myself that I'd aimed for him. I patted Francis on the back, reveling in seeing him draw breath. But the British boy's face stayed with me.

On the shore below us, the British officers and commanders screamed and leaped around, brandishing their swords at the fleeing regulars, and desperately tried to rally them into formation for another attack. Some men tried to flee regardless, and I could see them struck by the officers and nearby soldiers with fist and foot, then re-directed into the brigade.

Another attack! God help us all.

"Here they come again!" screamed our father, returning to his spot on the hay below the fence.

And again, the British regulars ascended the hill, this time at a faster pace. Once they drew close enough, we didn't need the command, but someone shouted it anyway.

"FIRE!"

I searched for one of their field commanders and fired in his direction. He was a short man, with thick eyebrows who spun after I pulled the trigger, falling out of view, blood spraying the grass red. Shots rang out all around me, obscuring us with powder smoke. I reloaded, again pushing powder and ball into my barrel, and stuffing it all in, good and tight, with the ramrod, as fast as my trembling hands would allow.

Again, the English commanders screamed for their men to fire, and a white wall of gun smoke exploded from their muskets, temporarily muting the wails of the wounded, and dying. I dropped as far as I could. Musket balls tore into the wooden fence as I pulled Francis down with me. One ball grazed my shoulder, tearing open my shirt along my back. Not a mortal wound, just a scratch, but I felt the heat of the ball. Panicking, I rose and fired, aiming for any bit of red cloth visible through the smoke. I couldn't tell if I hit anyone.

No time to think about that, now. Just load and fire. Load and fire.

Screaming on both sides was deafening. My fellow soldiers fired one more volley and dropped scores more of the redcoats, causing the front lines of their force to retreat again down the hill in a rushing red wave. Bodies twisted in agony, some dragging their torn limbs behind them in long, bloody trails.

"Boys, boys, we did it again!" My father hollered, hooting and again waving his hat into the air before reloading. I turned to look at Francis and saw him focused on a group of dead men to our left. They lay in a twisted heap, some slung over the fence, some lying on the ground behind us. Others in our ranks carried them off as fresh reserves bolstered our lines.

Down below, once again, the redcoats attempted to get into boats, but surviving officers shoved and beat them back into formation. The *Lively* swung into view and fired its guns toward our location anew. The British regulars stormed up the hill with a rabid ferocity and a cannon that they must have forded across the harbor. They fired on our redoubt from the bottom of the hill.

Prescott charged up and down the line. "HOLD, MEN! THIS IS THE LAST PUSH! STAND YOUR GROUND! STAND YOUR GROUND!"

We fired as fast and fierce as we could, despite scarce ammunition. Some of the British threw bombs into our redoubt, causing explosions which killed many, sending pieces of our brothers scattering across our ranks. They made a charge toward our fence, and they fought fiercely, firing multiple rounds in the time we fired one or two each.

Panicked, Francis forgot to remove his ramrod from the musket barrel after reloading. When he fired, the ramrod rocketed through the air like a spear and impaled a young soldier's neck. The enemy soldier scrabbled on the ground, grasping at the ramrod, as a fountain of red erupted from his wound. But being unable to reload his weapon left Francis vulnerable.

"Run, Francis!" I shouted, reloading. Musket balls thunked all around me, hitting the ground and the wooden fence. "We will find you later!"

"No, I can't leave you!" He shouted, searching corpses around us for a usable ramrod. He found one and attempted to reload again. I fired my musket, this time, into a group of soldiers all aiming toward our father. I hit one of them in the face, and he went down, knocking over one of his comrades with the force of his death. His teeth and eyes erupted from his skull in shards. In retaliation, they turned in my direction. I shoved Francis out of the way before the crack of musket fire pierced the air. As I fell on top of Francis, I felt a twinge of cold in my left thigh and another on my left calf. Then, the cold erupted into horrible and sickening pain that exploded through my body. They had shot me. Probably more than once.

I hauled Francis up from under me and shoved him forward. "NOW, FRANCIS! GO!"

Francis, tears in his eyes, ran. I turned back to the battle at hand. We were losing. Men fled the redoubt amidst explosions from cannon and hand-thrown bombs delivered with renewed vigor from the British soldiers. We were not well-equipped and were running out of ammo. I had two shots left.

Redcoats swarmed toward the fence. I again looked at my father and met his gaze. We knew what was about to happen, but we went into the fray. We had no bayonets, so I turned my musket around and held it by the barrel so I could use it like a club, swinging the butt-end toward any attackers who might come near.

A screaming soldier in red came toward me with great haste. I favored one leg but waited until my enemy drew closer. He lunged at me with a bayonet. I stepped to the side, grabbing his musket with the loop of my arm, and punching his jaw with my balled fist. He screamed in desperation and bit me, and all I could think to do was to pull him to the ground.

We landed in a heap where I choked him with as much force as I could muster before Father came to my aid and smashed him in the head with a musket. My attacker fell still, his brains pouring from the cup that was his open skull. My father then waded into the sea of redcoats, swinging his guns in short arcs to connect with the bodies or heads of his enemies.

I hobbled out to join him. To my right, I saw Doctor Warren fall to the earth after being run through with a cutlass, followed by several bayonets, the blades experiencing only slight resistance while passing through flesh and bone. A soldier trying to stop the doctor's slaughter was cut down alongside him.

I charged onward, swinging my gun-club against the bodies of any redcoat I found along the way, sweat rolling down my brow and neck. I turned to make sure Francis had escaped the melee. When I did, a young Englishman with fear and anger in his own countenance brought the sharp blade of his bayonet down onto my chest. I felt pressure, then a supreme sort of pain I'd never encountered before. It felt as if I were trying to breathe underwater and my vision grew dim. I fell to my knees and saw Francis in the distance being pursued by redcoats. Blood poured from my lips as everything went dark.

It shocked me to watch myself being run through by the Englishman just a short distance in front of me. At first, I assumed I regained consciousness in time to see my father being run through in an identical manner as myself. There was the resemblance, after all. But it was unmistakably me, my body, my own death!

Somehow, I stood outside of myself and watched the white orbs of my eyes as they rolled back into my head. Blood poured like a fountain from my chest as the British Regular twisted and maneuvered the bayonet to finish the job.

Yet I also stood off to the side, a witness to my very own death. I could not determine what form I existed in. I tried to look at my hands but saw only fog, or smoke from the battlefield. English soldiers pursued Francis near the top of the hill. Whatever was happening to me, I still had control of my consciousness. I needed to act.

I needed a weapon.

Without thinking, I surged forward, screaming with rage, causing the English soldier to flinch. As I grabbed hold of him, I screamed again. The force of my bellow blew his wig off. I was uncertain which of us was more surprised but likely him. His eyes opened so wide they appeared they might fall out, then he screamed in pure terror as whatever I had become choked him. Then everything went dark.

Opening my eyes, I gasped for air, as if I'd just been underwater and drowning. I clutched at my chest. There was a chest. I could see my body once again; except I was caked in blood. Then I felt my chest and scrunched my face in confusion. It was not the red of blood but the muddy red of an English uniform. Remembering Francis' peril, I scrambled over the ground, across my dead body. It brought great discomfort to see my eyes rolled back into my head with fresh blood spattered on my lips; lips that had recently tasted the vitality of a juicy pear.

I somehow found the weapon needed to help my brother, I wore the skin of a Brit. But I would need more. Grabbing a tomahawk discarded by a fleeing soldier, I raced up the hill, all while shouting for Francis to run. My cries drew the attention of the pursuing English soldiers. They turned fearful of the enemy only to find one of their own. Confusion overtook their faces. Two halted, while one continued chasing Francis.

The closest examined my face and called me by a name I did not recognize. "William, what's wrong with your eyes?"

The redcoat was tall and muscular. I screamed with an unfamiliar voice and charged into him, swinging the tomahawk with a ferocity and strength previously unknown to me. The blade sunk several times into his throat before lodging into his collarbone. I yanked it free with a sickening crack, bringing with it a torrential splash of blood. The soldier behind him screamed in terror and fired his musket at me.

The ball penetrated my flesh, but I felt disconnected from the pain. The redcoat grabbed the dropped musket of his fallen friend and fired once more. Again, the shot penetrated my borrowed body. It did not stop me. I launched myself at the shorter, more rounded soldier, sinking the tomahawk into his skull with a sickening slap. His body stiffened, and he fell forward and rolled a short distance before becoming entangled in his convulsing limbs.

Next, I unsheathed a knife from my waist and turned on the third who had gained distance on Francis. I pumped my legs as fast as they would carry me. Blood ran freely from musket wounds, and I felt my connection to the body severing, as if I were waking from a deep sleep and deeper dream. When I reached the third soldier, he had Francis by the collar and tugged him backward. I tackled the soldier before strangling him, as I'd done the first time.

"William! William! Snap out of it, man! Snap out of it!"

"My name is not William!" I shouted in a stranger's voice. One that had an English rhythm and cadence to it much different from my own. "I am Nathan Blood, and I am your death!"

At the sound of my name, Francis recovered, looking at me in alarm. As I choked the life out of the soldier, I felt myself dropping out of the body I possessed. In a blink, I was gazing into the lifeless eyes of the Englishman my spirit had just occupied. The man they called William.

The dead man had hold of my neck, but nothing left in his grip. I shoved him off and turned to face Francis, who looked at me as if I were the devil himself. For had not the one redcoat just strangled the other? Wasn't I, the one rising from the ground, already dead at the hands of his mad comrade?

"Francis," I said, in a new stranger's voice, this one reedy and firm. I crawled to my feet. "You must flee. I'm dead."

"You're not Nathan," he said, tears rolling down his boyish face. He was dirty and covered in black stains from the battle.

Cannon fire and muskets erupted near us. Men screamed, fighting in close quarters for their very lives.

"I am not Nathan, at least not anymore," I said. "Yet I also am. Maybe only in spirit. I'm not sure what magic is at work here, but I've saved you one last time. Now you must run."

Francis backed away slowly. "You're not Nathan," he sputtered.

From behind me arose shouts of anger. "There's one! FIRE!"

I turned to spot a group of redcoats clambering up the hill toward where Francis and I stood. They looked at me, and for a moment I forgot I inhabited an English body and so I braced myself for another death until I realized they were targeting Francis.

"He's just a boy," I shouted.

"Move out of the way you bloody oaf," said the officer.

I turned one last time toward Francis. "RUN FRANCIS! I LOVE YOU! I'LL TELL MOTHER YOU SEND YOUR LOVE!"

At this, young Francis faltered. A tear rolled down his cheek, but he did as I commanded and ran. I turned my attention to the red garbed soldiers in front of me and a fury filled my spirit. "You'll not have him," I shouted, hurling myself at them with my hatchet raised high.

Musket balls ripped through my body, momentarily slowing me down. I felt the life force dissipating, but I still held sway over the English soldier's body, fully committed to its bloody end. Swinging with all my might, I brought the hatchet to bear on the first soldier, splitting his forehead open in a horrible gash, spraying myself with blood. The second squealed as I hacked away at his chest. The third ran down the hill, but I gave chase and sunk the hatchet into his back, bringing him to the ground as he pleaded for his life and coughed up blood.

"Why?" was all he managed before I sunk the hatchet into his face over, and over, and over again.

"For Francis," I said, in a voice not my own, before everything went black.

Time passed in what felt like years before I saw Francis again. Things were different, as if I were reduced to a shadow. I felt cold and lonely, and the carnage brought to bear by my own hands replayed in my mind repeatedly. Each memory brought with it something approximating pain, an icy jab in the spot that used to be my heart. The look of abject horror on the English soldiers' faces played over in my head and I could not clear the images from my mind, no matter what I did.

Francis looked older. I wanted to cry, seeing my young brother become a man in what seemed to be such a small window of time. But it confirmed what I'd suspected; that I was merely a spirit. But I completed my mission. I'd protected

Francis. I'd saved him. Francis knelt in prayer. I moved toward him silently and attempted to place a hand on his shoulder. He shivered at my touch and opened his eyes.

"Nathan?"

I tried to speak but failed. I'd forgotten the sound of my own voice.

"Thank you for saving me all those years ago. If you are her. I think I can feel you. I wish for the day I can rejoin you, father, and mother."

Then do not commit violence, I longed to tell him, for I had not seen either of our parents. There was no reunion to be had, as I wore chains of memory anchored by the blood I shed. I felt my current reunion slipping away. Francis began fading, and so too did my former earthly concerns, until all that remained was my never-ending battle with the British men that I'd killed in life.

SUNRISE BREW, MALIBU CA

T HIS COFFEE SHOP IS a tiny Airstream RV set up in a parking lot steps from the beach. The place is idyllic and gives off a great surfing in Malibu vibe. If one visited the area, they would be hard-pressed to find a more relaxing spot. The menu is simple enough to fit on a free-standing chalkboard. The menu options are California healthy, and the drinks are good. But sometimes things are too perfect.

Sometimes the world is not as it seems. While I drank my wonderful, iced concoction, two people sitting nearby loudly spoke the way two old friends catching up do. One of the pair was a long time LA transplant and the visiting friend lived in their original small town. Despite the enthusiastic greeting and brief raving over the wonderful scenery, things soon took a turn.

The visitor took a call, and the conversation grew heated. The host grew increasingly uncomfortable as his 'friend' engaged in highly aggressive and rude conversation with the person on the phone. The host appeared embarrassed and eyed the nearby tables to see who might be offended by the awkward call.

It led me to believe how sometimes we do not know people as well as we thought we did. At the least, we might be unaware of how people changed over time if we were not there to see the gradual shifts in character. Before the conversation was over, the visitor demanded the woman on the phone take her contagious disease not only onto a plane but to a wedding, (despite the obvious protests on the other end of the line about giving it to the wedding party). The host looked like he wished to be anywhere else.

Finish the cup of coffee and run. That was the feeling I got from the man who saw his friend in a new, distasteful light. Except, sometimes one cannot run. Sometimes, one does not realize the situation until things are too late.

COFFEE RECOMMENDATION: For this I recommend the type of drink that likely upsets small town residents, a very LA based drink in honor of this distressed host. An espresso shot over ice. Don't be snobby. Try it. If you can also get avocado toast all the better!

THE REPLACEMENT

Paul Carro

"THERE IS A UNICORN in the yard, you can see it, if you try very hard," Troy Gelb read in a high-pitched voice.

"I don't see it daddy," little munchkin Julia said.

Julia's words came out garbled because she pressed her face too tight against the window, searching the large backyard. Troy smiled, not just because of his daughter's attempt to spot a unicorn, but over the thought of owning a yard to begin with. Sometimes it took a children's book to remind him of how good he had it. And how shitty things used to be.

"Maybe you're not looking hard enough, munches. The book suggests you must look very hard."

"Keep reading daddy, I'll keep searching," Julia said, squinting like a warrior. She would find one if she had her way.

"Enough reading, the both of you," Tessa said from the doorway, caressing her baby bump.

Troy closed the book and set it next to the stuffed unicorn that came with the children's book. *Unicorn In the Yard* was Julia's *most favoritis*t book in her significant library. The adults in the room preferred their books digital, but Julia was all about the paper. And unicorns, she loved them despite never having spotted one yet, even after reading the book about a zillion times. Could be less. Troy lost count after twenty.

"You heard the general. Sleep is upon us!"

"The general," Julia giggled and looked away from the window.

An imprint of the child's face remained on the glass, along with voluminous amounts of fingerprints. The book should have also come with some glass cleaner, Troy thought.

"Can I kiss my brother goodnight?" Julia asked.

The little girl was already smooching the pregnant belly in the doorway before Tessa could finish nodding.

"Wow, that's a lot of kisses," Tessa said. "Aren't you going to save any for after he is born?"

"No, because then he will be gross. I won't want to kiss Snotty Booger Head once he is a real live boy."

"That is not his name," Tessa said.

"It is until you name him something else," she said and scrambled to her bed.

Troy tucked her in. "Snotty Booger Head has a nice ring to it."

"I know, right?"

"You two," Tessa said, and exited the room.

"Oh, oh, the general is mad," Julia said, giggling.

"Yeah, I better go see what I can do to repair the damage your top-notch naming skills have caused. Maybe if we call your brother Nathan, she might be happy?"

"I don't think so," she said, rolling her eyes.

"I'll work on it." He kissed her on the forehead. "Love you munches."

"Love you, daddy."

Troy turned off her light, left the door open a crack, just how she liked it, for the tiny sliver of light, and stepped into the hall. He knew he was in trouble when he saw his wife waiting in the hallway.

"The general, really?"

"It was a spur-of-the-moment thing."

"If it sticks, I will need of a new family. I refuse to be known as the general."

Troy blinked. He could not understand how he got so lucky. Even eight months pregnant, his wife stunned him with her beauty. She would call herself a hot mess, hair everywhere, hell, belly everywhere. Still, she was the most beautiful thing he ever saw, except for the munchkin in the other room. Troy moved in on his wife as she leaned into the hallway wall, batting her eyes.

"What would you prefer to be known as?"

"Lucky," she said then kissed him.

He slid a hand into her gown, caressing one of her breasts. They both glanced at the nearby master bedroom at the end of the hall. She motioned her head toward its open door.

"You love those pregnancy boobs, don't you?"

"You have no idea," he said.

"We better take this to our room, because I plan to get loud,"

"I thought women did not get so excited this far along," he said.

"Well, I'm not just any pregnant woman," she said and kissed him again, rubbing him through his pajamas.

"No, you're not."

She led him down the hall, and they shut the door behind them. Troy loved seeing his wife's naked pregnant body. While it turned him on, it also promised a bigger family on the way. A second child now, but eventually more. Three was his fantasy ideal but he was unopposed to four or five. Dreaming of a family sometimes felt strange coming from a man who once upon a time never dreamed about anything positive.

The couple kissed like teenagers until neither could take anymore. They skipped any other foreplay. He slid inside her, and she lived up to the promise of being loud.

The sex was wonderful, almost too good. Troy battled the sleep demon. He normally dozed immediately after such satisfaction, but he worried whether their child overheard anything, so he checked on her. Out, like the little angel she was. He performed the check because Tessa mercifully fell asleep. She struggled with sleeping during pregnancy, so he hesitated to return to their bed too soon. Besides, if he woke her, he would want to go for round two and was not sure either would survive it.

Ridiculous, the two of them. Walter loved how physical they remained, even after years of marriage, but occasionally they discussed when they thought their collective libidos might chill out a bit. It did not appear to be on the horizon. Maybe after a second child tired them out enough. Their first was a handful, but not two handfuls. Divide and conquer. The couple managed just fine with their little beauty.

While he waited for his wife to fall deeper, he explored the refrigerator. Orange juice called to him. He needed to replace some electrolytes. Once upon a time he would have grabbed a beer, but he and Tessa left alcohol behind years ago. Their lives improved almost immediately after the change, though it also changed their friend circle. The newly abstained couple found themselves surrounded by people who pushed them to be the best versions of themselves. It took time for them to realize how much certain people could drag you down and how helpful it was to have people around who lifted others up.

After emptying the alcohol in their house, and adjusting their lifestyle, they felt better and found a replacement for booze. Sex. Not long after getting sober, they had their first child.

Troy took the orange juice from the refrigerator and, though tempted to sip from the carton, did the responsible thing and pulled out a glass. A juice glass! He laughed. There was no such thing when he grew up, a glass just for juice. Hell, there was never juice, not even Hi-C, just a cheap knockoff. Usually, a raspberry flavor that was always blue instead of red.

He placed the carton in the fridge and lifted the glass. It was small. Too much sugar in such drinks, so they designed juice glasses for moderation, not chug-athons. Troy lifted the drink with steady hands. A pleasant side effect of his lifestyle change. He drank alcohol from an early age, mostly to escape the world he lived in. For years, he suffered hand tremors from low-level alcohol dependency.

What an awful life. Living in a terrible place under terrible circumstances. School was his outlet, his portal to a better world, but he had to make it through graduation first and feared he never would. There was only one bright spot back then, his best friend Ricky. But even that ended when Ricky suddenly vanished when they were both eighteen.

Troy pulled the glass away from his lips. He hated thinking about his lost friend because it made him want to add vodka to the juice. Ricky's disappearance was the one thing that still haunted Troy. How many years had it been?

A long time. A lifetime ago, a much different lifetime. Ricky's parents couldn't be bothered to wonder what became of their child because he was eighteen when it happened. Troy checked in with the police over the years. Their five-year class reunion came and went. Troy did not attend, happy to have broken the cycle of poverty from living in that neighborhood. Now with the ten-year anniversary approaching. Troy considered attending so he could ask around about Ricky to see if anyone knew anything.

A sound shattered the night's quiet, and his glass shattered on the floor as a result. Their only corded phone, a dinosaur of a device which came with the house hung alongside the fridge. Previous homeowners had painted the kitchen so many times that the phones edges provided a history of the kitchen's color schemes.

The phone rang relentlessly, as if daring Troy to answer. Their house was large enough the noise would not disturb the upstairs sleepers, but the intense volume so late in the kitchen felt ominous. None of their friends would ever be up at such an hour. Troy understood nothing good could come from answering the phone, but he did anyway.

"Hello?" Heavy breathing greeted him. "Sorry, I already have a sex partner." He moved the phone back towards its cradle when a voice called out on the line.

"Troy?"

Troy pulled the phone back to his ear. "This is Troy," he admitted and immediately regretted it.

"I'm back," the voice on the phone said.

"Who is this? You know it's three-thirty in the morning, right?" There was a long pause after Troy's question.

"Oh, yeah, I guess this is inappropriate, huh?"

The phone went dead, and Troy went cold. The words *I'm back* echoed in his brain. Just two words, but they carried the weight of a world. Who was back? He struggled with the voice; it was familiar enough to make his flesh goose pimple but not familiar enough to remember clearly. His memory teetered just on this side of recognition like a sneeze that failed to arrive without the aid of sunlight.

Then it hit him. Could it be? He had just thought about his old friend. Ricky's voice was so high when younger. The person on the phone sounded different. Tired, nervous. Something. But there was no way to know if it was his friend.

A bead of sweat splashed into his eye, and he realized he was gripping the phone so hard his veins were bulging. He looked around the kitchen and felt a deep sense of dread, as if everything he ever built, all the poverty he escaped, could vanish with one simple phone call.

It made no sense. He loved his friend even if they trafficked in misery together back in the day. The two longed for an end to their troubles back then. Collectively, they fought to find a way out of their dismal circumstances but escape always felt impossible. Life was hard and would only get harder. Surely if Ricky had stayed around, he too would have would have found his own way, made it into the big leagues like Troy did. Tessa had many single friends and sometimes Troy envisioned introducing one of them to Ricky (if he were around) so that he could join their friend circle.

There was one way to know for sure. Star sixty-nine. A number he and Ricky would have giggled for hours over. Why was Troy afraid it might be his friend who called? Why was troy not excited at the thought? It made no sense. He hung up the receiver to ensure the connection was reset, then lifted it again. He was about to dial when a hand fell on his shoulder.

"Honey, it's time. Our baby wants to come out," Tessa stated matter of fact.

"Huh? Now?"

Tessa smiled briefly between contractions. "Sorry for the inconvenience."

There was a strange sense of calm in the air, unlike their first hospital trip. The early morning arrival of their Julia created a show that would have made Barnum and Bailey proud. Back then, at his wife's first scream, Troy leaped out of bed at near the speed of sound, but the only sonic boom was his face-planting because of sheet wrapped feet.

Troy quickly rose bloody lipped from the floor and spun, frantically attempting to release himself, but mid-spin, he smacked one hand into the dresser with such a loud crack that he should have known immediately he broke something. It would be hours later, after his adrenaline wore off and an alarmed delivery nurse spotted the swelling, that his condition became apparent.

Things worked out, though. They made it to the hospital, and Tessa was a superwoman throughout the delivery. That Three Stooges night was the last time chaos reigned in Casa De Gelb. This time Tessa walked to the car on her own, tears free, while Troy carried an overnight bag and a sleeping daughter in two unbroken hands. They encountered no traffic because of the late hour. Upon arriving at the hospital, they encountered a friendly and efficient staff at the hospital. Everything went as well as his life had been going. Except it was a false alarm.

Troy rubbed eyes and yawned, setting off a chain reaction of the same across the floor of his workspace. It was at such times he wished there were walls at the startup he worked at, but walls designated individuality, and the company believed in everyone being equal. Troy never considered himself an equal on the job, even though he was a supervisor. Troy did not know shit nor shinola about computers, but his life experience combined with some management experience (hey the Shoe Barn counted) made him the boss of a roomful of rich, too smart for their own good twenty-somethings.

Those echoing his yawn instinctively reached for cans of energy drinks. Metal pops, each followed by a loud fsshh, rose above the sound of tapping keys. Troy regretted his show of fatigue because he had something to prove to the employees, all of them younger than he. Despite his being up all night for a false alarm, he needed to put on airs that he was not an old fart.

At other companies he once worked for, there would have been a camaraderie around his baggy eyes, an understanding that wrecked would be his look du jour for weeks leading up to the birth. And for months afterward. But no, those in his sight were curiously free of children, and in most cases, spouses as well.

Someone please notify the Surgeon General. I've discovered the best form of birth control ever. A computer screen, Troy thought. Troy figured the reason he kept popping out kids was because of his priorities. *Computers bad—sex good.* Those around him acted the opposite but seemed okay. They were good kids. Wow! He thought of those in their twenties as kids. When did he become a man?

Troy smiled, knowing that any day now, his cell would ring with Tess announcing labor for real. The previous night's dry run went so smooth that he and his wife were ready for the inevitable. And excited. Troy wasn't sure how excited Tess was for a boy, but his own Y chromosome was singing to the heavens with joy. If genes skipped a generation as often reported, his son was bound to be a star athlete as Troy was anything but.

As if on cue, his cell phone rang. Troy grew excited until noticing the ringtone. His wife's number rang Wagner's *Ride of the Valkyries*. Instead, it rang Motley Crue, a holdover from his younger years, and a tune reserved only for unknown numbers. Probably a robo-call checking up on his car warranty.

In all the craziness, he forgot about the call in the kitchen. The chill from the previous evening returned. He answered.

"Troy?" the voice asked.

Troy was not so quick to give information now that he was awake. "Who is this?"

"I'm sorry, this is daytime, right? This is more appropriate?"

Troy still could not place the voice, but it felt familiar. "How did you get my number?"

"He gave it to me."

"Who?"

"He has many resources and ordered me to contact you," the voice offered.

"Well, tell him you did your job, and he can screw off now!"

The level of anger in his own voice surprised Troy and the surrounding employees. The workers twisted as if they had ants in their pants, unaccustomed to conflict. But the caller matched the anger.

"Do not talk about Him like that! Jesus, you haven't changed a bit!"

Troy froze. Did this person know him? What did the voice mean? Troy changed drastically since his youth. On days he felt religious, he thanked God. On days when he didn't, he thanked his lucky stars. All Troy knew was life exceeded all expectations. Anyone reminding him of his past was a very unwelcome guest.

"Who is this?"

"I'm sorry. I thought you knew. It's me Troy boy."

"Ricky?"

"How are you doing, Troy?"

"I need a frame of reference to answer that. You've been gone, what? A decade now?"

"I guess. Time doesn't really mean anything to me."

"Where did you go? And why are you calling now?"

"I owe you a drink," Ricky said.

"You don't owe me anything. You were never there for me to thank, but despite our top-notch degeneracy, you always pushed me toward college. Not sure I would have made the leap if it weren't for your nudging. It turned my life around, made everything perfect."

"No, don't say that!" Ricky screamed through the phone before falling silent. He continued softly. "It's important you don't say that."

Troy looked around his surroundings. A group of young people with so much money and so much ability all wishing they were in his seat. Not as a boss, but as a family man, or one who had a life. One who went out for more than happy hours. One who banged hot chicks. Or chick. One very special pregnant chick. With the voice from the past on one end of the phone and the activity going on around him on the other, his head spun.

Troy once read Time Machine by H. G. Wells and suddenly felt like a character in that novel. Trapped between two time periods—the future and the past. He loved where he was now, but he held a longing to hear from the voice on the phone. Ricky's presence in the present felt unnatural.

"Okay, so if I'm not supposed to say my life is great, then what do I say?" Troy asked.

"Say you'll meet me for a drink."

Troy used his GPS to navigate to the address Ricky provided. The location was a coffee shop, not a bar. Ricky's choice of venue gave Troy hope. The pair never much hung out unless alcohol was involved, so it meant Ricky too had found a way to clarity. Maybe he, too, was in a good place. Maybe he had a wife and family.

Troy asked as much over the phone, but Ricky was elusive and promised to catch up in person.

The ride unnerved him though as Troy was unfamiliar with the downtown area; him being a Westside guy. A large green sign caught his eye. It read, *Not Starbucks*! Based on the name of the establishment, he assumed his usual Venti Mocha Frap was out of the question. Besides, Troy only drank those in front of the younger workers to appear younger himself. Troy parked in the lot behind the establishment and entered.

The place was dark. Troy stopped in the doorway to allow himself to adjust to the change in lighting. He had not been somewhere so dark since he and Ricky used to frequent strip clubs. Music blasted, and he wondered if that was the true nature of the business. It was strip club dark, with layers upon layers of shadows cast by flickering candles at every table.

A perfect place for vampires to spend their daylight hours, Troy thought. Murmurs alerted him to the presence of other patrons, but they were difficult to see, blended as they were into the shadows. Troy felt his way to a table near the back, as Ricky had suggested. Away from the coffee bar so they could speak without the loud frothing of milk in the background. A large man sat at one table, might as well been a wall how big the guy was. Troy wondered for a moment if the man was Ricky but decided not to perform the awkward ask. Troy would sit and wait for his friend to approach. He had a million questions chambered.

Troy tried to refocus on the excitement of seeing his old friend again. Troy's college friends attended his wedding, but he missed his childhood friend. Despite everything, he would have chosen Ricky as his best man. That never happened because Ricky simply vanished. Troy was relieved to discover his friend was apparently okay. Not only okay, but local.

While hopeful about the reunion, the dark surroundings, combined with the recent bout of exhaustion, brought Troy to the edge of dread. Breathing. He worked to slow it. Meditation was a staple in their office, a coping mechanism for all the young workers with little to be stressed about. Troy breathed deep, only to exhale in a yelp when a bony hand clasped onto his shoulder. Troy rose from his seat and found himself face to face with his old buddy, his old pal.

"Ricky? Rick?"

There was a reason Troy thought the mountain man at a nearby table might be his old friend. Ricky was always a jock. While his friend did not possess the discipline to train and compete, he always had the jock body, already six feet in high school. Ricky wrestled only one very successful season in high school but decided being yelled at by a coach wasn't for him.

Ricky dropped out of school senior year. It was not long after that his friend disappeared altogether. When Troy tried to convince police to look for his friend, he realized how little he knew about Ricky's day-to-day activities during normal school hours. The life Ricky led once he dropped out of school was a mystery.

Understanding how muscular his friend used to be, it caught Troy off guard to see the gaunt figure standing before him. Flickering candlelight highlighted every sharp angle on the man's frame where bone met pale skin. Troy was relieved they met indoors because, if outside, a wind might have carried Ricky's skin away like so much paper. Though impossible, Ricky seemed shorter than before. His hair, once jet black, was now snow white.

Besides the thinner appearance, the once upon a time conservative guy sported piercings. Multiple. Ear, chin, eyebrow. Large loops filled his stretched earlobes. The only thing that matched the memory of his friend was the grin. Ricky's grin always drew in women like bugs to a zapper. Ricky spread his arms wide to show off his new look.

"So, what do you think of the new me?"

The feelings hit Troy in a wave. He felt immensely relieved. Despite the strange changes, his friend was alive. Troy had long since assumed Ricky dead. Now, there he was, no matter how different. Troy hugged the man.

Through the embrace, Ricky trembled, subtly at first, then progressively more violent until squirming like a landed fish. Ricky broke free from the embrace with a yell.

"No!"

Troy was less surprised by Ricky's actions than by how powerful someone so fragile could be. He eyed his friend, who quickly composed himself. Ricky found his grin and raised his hands apologetically.

"I'm sorry. I just thought we should get coffee before getting lovey-dovey. We've got some catching up to do."

"No shit," was all Troy could come up with.

"Black?" Ricky asked. Troy nodded and sat. "I'll be right back."

As Ricky went for drinks, Troy examined the dark spot. His eyes had since adjusted, and he could make out shadow people all around. Many were hipsters, tattooed, pierced. Maybe this was how Ricky lived his life now. Maybe these were his people. At least there was no alcohol in the mix.

Ricky plopped into the opposing seat and handed off a coffee. Troy sipped immediately, grateful for something to occupy his hands. The two smiled at one another for an uncomfortable amount of time. Despite Ricky appearing a few breaths away from death, there was a surprising amount of life in his sparkling eyes.

"Ricky, what's going on? Are you sick? What is it? Cancer, AIDS, anorexia?"

Ricky leaned in. "I'm going to let you in on a secret. I've never been better, never been more alive."

"Okay, good. Then where the hell have you been?"

"Uh-uh-uh. I bought the coffee—I name the topic. Let's reminisce first. You remember your dog you had when we were kids?"

"Of course."

"His name was Tippy, right?"

"Yeah, Tippy, we had him thirteen years."

"Thirteen years, I knew it!" Ricky laughed and tapped a finger against his temple. "My memory used to be for shit."

"Yes, it was. Whenever you owed me money, you forgot."

They both laughed and relaxed a little.

"No more Troy. My memory is flawless. When Tippy was five, you threw a Penn number three tennis-ball into the street…"

"Yeah, I threw a tennis ball and Tippy got hit by a car and lost a leg. Come on Ricky, if we're going to stroll down memory lane together, let's turn a corner right here."

"I rode to the vet with you guys. You remember how he wouldn't let go of the ball the whole time?"

"Come on, Ricky."

"He lost his right leg."

"No, his left."

Ricky's hands shook. "No, it was his right leg."

"He was my dog. I don't think so."

"Come on, think. Details are very important."

Troy wanted to say, "screw this, I'm out of here," but he saw a strange need in his friend's eyes. A few more minutes wouldn't hurt, he thought and sipped from his coffee. Caffeine was his last vice, the only carryover from his past life. The one he shared with the friend who he no longer knew who now sat opposite him.

"Okay, yeah, you're right. It was his right leg now that I think about it," Troy said.

Ricky slapped his thigh and laughed loudly. He shoved Troy playfully in the shoulder. Troy cracked a smile. It wasn't just the voice that was thirteen. Ricky was still as playful as he was back then.

"When Tippy got back from the vet and kept falling on his face, you joked about how he finally earned his name. You wouldn't even pet your own dog, the dog you crippled. Do you remember Tippy's eyes? I do. No longer petting him hurt the poor thing more than his leg ever did..."

Troy had enough and stood up quickly, too quickly. He was dizzy from a blood rush, so grabbed the table in support and anger. If the room wasn't spinning, he would have been out of there. He used the time he needed to recover to lash out.

"Screw you, Ricky. All these years of feeling guilt about what happened to you and now you add more to the pile? I'm relieved you're not pushing up daisies, I'm ecstatic that you've never been better, but I've got a life to get back to. One where people don't make me feel like shit, at least not on purpose!"

Troy turned to walk away and hoped that he wouldn't fall, as he was still somewhat dizzy. He wanted to look strong before his friend, like he had to in the office every day. Yes, he was living the best life he ever had, but there were hidden truths still.

While he had to take the office garbage, he did not have to take it from a part of a past he was happy to escape. It was time to move on. Troy took a step and almost stumbled. The dark did not help combined with the blood rush of standing so quick. He spun into the tumble to make it look planned. Ricky asked a question before Troy could leave.

"My mom?"

Troy returned and sat down with a sigh. The move was a save. Troy sat upright, looking like a virile young man, not an old fart. He would stand more slowly next time. Troy wasn't as young as he used to be—hell, his second child was on the way. He looked at Ricky and a thought sunk in. Troy was about to have a boy and that's what Ricky still was. Ricky apparently never grew up. Troy felt the moment was the perfect opportunity to test his parenting skills. He settled in to give bad news.

"She's dead Ricky. We buried her four years ago. We tried to find you."

"How was she killed?"

"It was an accident, a hit and run."

"It wasn't an accident, not at all. While I am fully aware of the circumstances of her death, I did not have the ability to attend her funeral."

Didn't have the ability? What was this cryptic bastard talking about? Troy wondered and found the strength had returned to his legs. He was ready to use them.

"Look Ricky..."

"Hey, here's to old friends."

Ricky raised his cup and Troy joined in. They clinked paper and drank. Troy slammed his empty cup down hard to send a message. *I'm about done with this shindig.*

"You remember how often we used to get injured when we were kids?"

Troy rolled his eyes. "How could I forget? You're the reason my health insurance premiums are so high today."

"Sorry about that. But you know, the thing is, we went about it all wrong. We didn't need to feel the pain. And not just the scrapes and bruises."

"Don't forget the broken bones and gashes."

"Oh, I can't forget those, but I'm talking about the emotional scars too. Those are what you make of them. Notice you informed me of mother, and it did not phase me."

"Well, you mentioned you already knew. It has been years. You have had time to mourn."

"Good point. Another test then," Ricky said and grabbed a candle from an empty adjoining table.

He placed the candle alongside the one already on their table. Ricky arced his hand over the flame closer to himself and gestured to the second candle. Then he winked. Something about the wink unnerved Troy. Maybe it was the way Ricky's eye twitched when he did so.

"Come on, I dare you!" Ricky shouted, but the place was so loud no one heard anything beyond their table.

"What are you talking about? We're not in fifth grade anymore," Troy said.

"Come on! Double dare."

"You learned some trick about pain. Fine, tell me about it. We're adults now. It's not show and tell anymore. Life is just told."

"Wrong. There are some things that must be shown, or experienced."

Troy grew sweaty. The place was stuffy and hot, Troy thought, but as uncomfortable as the place was, his friend amplified the discomfort by holding on to childish pranks that were not fun, even as children.

This was my role model? *This is the guy who taught me about life*? Troy shook his head in disgust and in response.

"I'm not doing it Ricky."

"Look, I can tell by the way this is going that I will never see you again. So, give me one last dare. Come on!"

Finally, something making sense came out of his mouth. Ricky was correct. There would be no more meetings, only the occasional Christmas card. Troy locked eyes with Ricky. Mistake. That was how Ricky always got him. Those eyes were so damned innocent one would believe that, okay, maybe this time things won't turn out badly. Troy rolled up his sleeve and grinned despite himself.

They both waved their hands over the flame. Troy moved his hand around to keep it from getting too hot, but Ricky held his directly over the burning wick.

"Ow!" Troy pulled his hand away. "Okay, you win, amigo."

"Not yet, Troy boy."

Ricky lowered his hand directly into the flame which spread. Acrid smoke rose, but Ricky kept going. His hand blackened with his pinky-finger taking the worst of it.

"Okay, cool trick, but it's getting old."

"It's no trick."

Suddenly, the hand burst into flames! Ricky's skin burned and popped as he lifted it into the air until the hand supplied more illumination than the candle itself. The burning hand lit Ricky's face, giving him a demonic glow. Instead of appearing in pain, the man looked as though he verged on ecstasy.

Troy grabbed Ricky's unfinished coffee and doused the fire. Ricky's skin sizzled under the liquid. The flames went out. But the smell lingered. A horrific odor of burned skin and flesh. Troy looked around, hoping for witnesses to share in the shock of what had just happened, but no one looked in their direction.

There was too much noise, too much darkness. Too many strange people. Even a burning hand failed to draw attention inside a shop where most of the patrons had tattoos of flames all over their bodies. Except this was no tattoo. His friend had caught fire and might still be burning had not Troy acted.

"No pain, Troy boy, no more pain ever. Only something…" He clenched his blistered fist and shivered. "… better."

Troy had enough. He rose, stumbled, banging into the table, knocking over his empty coffee cup. He fell back into his seat, gasping for air. Where was all the air?

He was uncertain when it happened, but his hair stuck to his forehead, soaked through with sweat.

He attempted to wipe himself dry, but his limbs felt like lead. He breathed deep, trying to calm himself. Ricky's strange new look already had Troy on edge, and then the hand thing. No wonder he felt so ill. Troy needed to get out of there.

Except he couldn't.

Troy struggled to rise, as his muscles strained to do something, anything, but in the end he remained still. Even his voice fell silent as he found himself unable to speak. In his mind, Troy screamed for help. Screamed and screamed and screamed, but nothing came out. He wished he could be as loud as the espresso machine somewhere in the distance.

At least his ears still worked, and his eyes. He turned the eyes on Ricky, pleading. Surely his friend would notice something was wrong. Ricky would help his old friend. Ricky appeared to understand what was happening. Ricky spoke soothingly to his old friend.

"Don't worry, Troy-boy, it's all good buddy. Imagine no pain ever again, only different degrees of pleasure. No more worries, no more fears."

Troy couldn't imagine such a thing, not at all. He was too terrified. What was happening to him? Why did he agree to the meeting in the first place? Troy thought of his wife and prayed that she would hear him. *Help me Tessa, please!*

But she didn't know where he was. No one did. Not even the young computer zombies at work. It would have been too hard to explain to anyone that he was going to meet someone who everyone assumed had long since died. Troy informed no one about the meeting with his old friend. No one knew where he was. Now he sat alone with his past.

"The last time you and I were together, we used fake IDs to get into Mahoney's bar where we got stinking drunk. The more you drank, the more you cried, wishing to die because Heidi broke up with you," Ricky said.

"*That was then. This is now, asshole! I'm long past wanting to die,*" Troy played out in his mind.

"I mean, you sobbed Troy, right there in the bar. In front of everyone. How ridiculous was that? I felt for you, man. You've always been my best friend and there you sat weeping. It broke my heart. I couldn't take away your pain then, but I can now. You'll never wish to die again. Well, you will every moment at first..."

"At first? What the hell did he mean? Oh God, please let me move. There are other people here. Why can't they see what's going on?"

"You know what your problem was, Troy? You were too worried about pleasing women, you were always seeking their pleasure. I can't blame you. They're a worthwhile distraction. I'll partake of that fruit again at some point. Sooner than you will, I guarantee."

"No, you're wrong. My wife is going to have our boy any day now and then I'm going to hold my wife so close and make love to her again and again until we have our third and complete our family. I won't let you take that away, you freak!"

"See, the thing is, there are so many other pleasures. When the ones we know of run out, we wonder what's left to live for. But there is so much more. Normal people don't think in the bigger picture. But He does. Oh yes, He does. You won't appreciate His wisdom at first. Appreciation comes with time because that is how we are wired. I mean, why would we invent wine-coolers when we have fine wines available?"

Wine coolers? What decade are you living in? Troy thought, his mind racing, moving so fast, as fast as he wished his feet could move, but they couldn't. They were like lead.

Ricky continued. "After four or five years of wishing to be removed from existence, your mind will finally be open to the possibilities, to pleasures never dreamed."

"Four or five years? What are you talking about? I have a child on the way. I have a baby girl!" Troy's thoughts came out as drool at the corners of his mouth.

"I'll let you in on a secret. You know which pleasure I am especially fond of? The one that gets me hard the fastest?" He whispered in Troy's ear. "Needles deep under my fingernails. When they hit the spots just right..."

Troy heard Ricky lick his lips and felt breath on his paralyzed skin. Troy renewed his struggle, using every ounce of strength to at least make a sound, to cry out for help, but came up with nothing to show for his efforts.

In his mind, Troy laughed. This was comical. No way was Ricky talking about needles this and needles that. Maybe Ricky wasn't even there. The man disappeared a little more than a decade ago, so the whole thing had to be a dream. Soon Troy would wake next to his wife.

Ricky slapped Troy's face. It was a playful slap from Ricky, but the violence carried so much weight. The slap should have woken Troy if he was dreaming, right? *Why wasn't he waking*? Ricky sat back down, looking pleased with himself. His tapeworm style self. A stick figure of a man.

"You know what else I like besides the fingernail thing? No, I can't say. I don't want to ruin the surprise. You will thank me—eventually. You'll curse me for a year or two, but then you'll forget I exist at all. Hell, you'll forget who you are. You'll forget everything except pleasure and pain and eventually the two will become the same and at some point, you will reach a moment of clarity where every second of your life returns to you because He demands it. You'll see things in a new light, you'll be reborn. I'm doing this because I love you, buddy. And because I have to. He ordered me to."

"I already have been reborn years ago when I met my wife. You weren't there. You missed it. Please, let me go. My son doesn't have a name yet. He'll share yours, I promise, if you just let me go!"

"You see, the only way He lets you leave is when you give Him someone else. But not just anyone. Someone you know intimately so you can feed Him all the details of that individual. I had to tell Him all I knew. He knows everything about you now, every detail, every moment of pain. When your mom fucked Charlie from our senior class? He knows all about it. When you and I masturbated while watching Sarah Harper through the window? He knows all about it. He knows all and, I must say, He's very excited to work with you."

Ricky breathed deep and gathered himself.

"I'm jealous if you must know. Though if I still experienced guilt, I would feel it over this as I remember how traumatic the procedure is at first. I mentioned I knew the circumstances of my mother's death? I killed her. He demanded it of me to ensure I was ready to move on. Driving a car at that speed, don't you see? Pleasure! I also said I lacked the ability to attend the funeral, well, that was because it was our scheduled foot binding day. He follows a tight schedule, and I would never deviate from what He says, no, nope, no way."

Despite the paralysis, Troy felt his insides burn much like Ricky's hand over the candle had. He cramped, his muscles tightened, and he could not move to alleviate them. *Why could he not move? What did Ricky put in the drink?*

Ricky tilted his head which made his charming smile go crooked. "Difficult to choose who to become one's replacement. I thought, who better to hand off than someone who hated life more than I did? You know you used to be a miserable little turd, don't you?"

"*Was, was! You don't know me, you don't understand. Julia, oh my little munchkin, what are you doing right now, sweetie? Daddy's in trouble, but he's trying to get to you. He's trying for you, sweetie. Daddy loves you, baby.*"

Suddenly, Ricky stood, and Troy could only stare at the man's obscenely skinny waist while Ricky bid adieu. "Goodbye buddy. We'll meet again for coffee sometime so you can thank me when He's done with you. He figures eight or nine years is how long it will take to rebirth you."

Troy was uncertain because of the paralysis, but he thought he was wetting himself. Ricky stepped away from Troy's limited view and that's when Troy spotted "him." The man sat at a distant table. It was the man who was the size of a wall! The one Troy noticed upon first entering the place.

The man smiled wider than Ricky ever had. He was massive, beefy, and greying at the temples, but the man reeked of confidence. The man studied Troy from a distance for what seemed like hours. Troy could not even blink.

Then the most terrifying sound filled his ears. Troy's phone chirped out the Ride of the Valkyries. Tess. She was having the baby! The man rose from the table and walked over to Troy. His body was too big, too large, an imposing individual.

The stranger reached a massive hand into Troy's jacket pocket and pulled out the phone.

Without saying a word, the man showed the text that appeared after the call went to voice mail. The text read, *it's time*. Tears filled Troy's eyes and he could not blink them away.

"*My boy, my baby. Tessa, please take pictures of our son, honey. I'm going to need those memories. I promise if you wait for me, I'll do my best to wait for you. Please, I promise I will try to remember you...*"

The phone rang again, and the man switched it off before slipping it into his own pocket. Once Troy's phone had rung with the birth announcement, he no longer heard background noise from the coffee shop. No conversations, no music, no footsteps of people roaming to order drinks. For a moment, all was silent except for beating hearts.

STARBUCK'S UNIVERSAL CITY WALK

T HIS IS NOT JUST another Starbucks. Sometimes location is everything, and this one is in a sweet spot. Here it is impossible to have a bad day. Universal City walk is a stretch of retail, restaurants, arcades, and bars leading into the famed theme park. While I love Disneyland, I have never bought an annual pass there but have done so many times at Universal Studios.

As a screenwriter, I had many a meeting with producers in the bungalows, some of which fall within view of the trams giving studio tours. If one wished to mess with those riding past on the trams, one could put on sunglasses, pull a ball cap down low and shy away from the passing vehicle. The amount of cell phones snapping pics of the 'celebrity' was amusing. (Not that I ever did that several times.)

When visiting the park as a writer, one might pass Stephen Spielberg's offices, which are behind a Jurassic Park style gate with guards as big as dinosaurs out front. I love it there, everything about it, whether going for a possible writing job or as a passenger on the trams.

One of the first ever red-carpet premieres I attended was there. As someone who dreamed of a life in Hollywood, Universal Studios is a treasure. The Starbucks is midway along the City Walk and has prime outside seating for people watching, which is fun in such a bustling environment.

It was here that I birthed a story about someone committing an unspeakable murder. The victim? The Big Guy. I don't want to say much more other than I can't imagine I ever would have thought up this story had I not visited this treasure of a place.

COFFEE RECCOMENDATION: Since the locale is sunny, and fosters a good mood, I chose something light. Rather than even the density of a cold brew, I suggest when reading this one you order an iced Americano.

THE BIG GUY

Paul Carro

I DIDN'T NEED A badge to navigate the police tape. The assembled officers were expecting me. Most did not like me. That's fine, I'm not a fan of myself either. Still, I had a job to do, and I was good at what I did. Very good. Too good sometimes. My doggedness drove many a person from my life, usually those of the female persuasion. There was one I missed more than others. Unlike some others who I angered along the way, I understood Amy would not be coming back any time soon.

Amy was a simple name for a complicated woman. Things began badly between her and me and ended worse. Despite my desire to make things work, she made clear her intention to never see me again. Circumstances worked in her favor. The fact I was thinking about Amy instead of whatever I was walking into shows how routine murders had become in the city. Sad but more of the same.

Until I saw the crime scene. Amy vanished from my thoughts along with other women whose names I could not remember to begin with. This murder was big. Literally. Though I'd been a PI for half my lifetime, I understood this would be no ordinary case. The evidence before me differed from any I had ever seen. Starting with the color of chalk on the ground.

"Blue?" I asked, referring to the outline of the deceased on the pavement.

"Right out of white we were. My partner Toomie had blue carpenter chalk in her trunk, so we went with that," Hector said.

Hector was a good bloke. I call him bloke because he speaks with a British accent. He is Latino but suffered through a nasty car accident a few years back and came out talking that way. He made up plenty of words as well, but coworkers and friends never corrected the mistakes. We mostly figured out what he was trying to say. He was great at what he did, though. Like I said, a good bloke. Hector shook his head at the scene.

"Blimey," Hector said.

"Blimey indeed," I repeated. "Took a lot of chalk for this one. Big guy."

"The biggest," Hector said.

I circled the spot where they found the body, which they had already removed. "Strange spot for an ambush of a guy so large," I mused.

Hector nodded in agreement. "Took six right toughers to get him in the coroner's van."

While circling the outline, I noticed damage to a brick wall in the alley. A shopkeeper looked out through the fresh hole in his establishment, watching the ruckus. I waved at the weasel of a man. Who says I'm not nice? The shopkeeper twiddled his fingers back at me. There were no bricks on the outside of the hole, meaning they all fell inward.

"What do you suppose caused the damage?" I asked Hector.

"The noggin' I suppose."

"Speaking of. Did you run out of chalk?"

"No, Toomie did not run out. Her outline is right exact it is."

I let go a long overdue harrumph. That was curious. The chalk outline rounded closed atop the massively broad shoulders, meaning someone made off with the big guy's head. There was no mistaking the outline. I never even asked who the victim was. Only one guy that size around town and everyone knew him. Love or hate the big guy (and most hated him) there was no mistaking that someone had just offed Frankenstein's Monster.

And they did it by means other than fire and pitchfork brigade. No matter how it went down, the big guy tumbled, and his head struck the wall, breaking through. From there he bounced back and landed lengthwise in the alley, otherwise he might not have even fit. The kicker was that someone made off with his head.

There were plenty who would have liked to off the big lug after that whole thing with the young girl some years back. Say what you will. The guy did his time. He had been a mostly solid citizen since his release from prison. But why take the head?

Solve that and I'd solve the case. I knew it wouldn't be easy, though. These things rarely were. Something crunched underfoot. I looked down and spotted some broken glass. There would be plenty of that in an alley. I needed to look for things that did not belong in an alley to learn what happened. A cursory glance revealed nothing telling. No smoking guns. When I got a minute, I would check what business was behind the non-damaged alley wall. I hadn't noticed when I drove in.

From what I could see through the hole in the wall, the damaged business was a bookstore. The worker was a potential witness. I threw a thumb toward the shopkeeper. "Whole thing must have caused a ruckus. Did our guy over here hear anything?"

"Nutter," Hector said.

"Nothing?" I asked, assuming Hector had misused the word.

"No. Nutter," Hector reiterated by waving a finger around his temple. "Says he was unlocking his shop after lunch when he heard the noise. By the time he got inside and looked through the hole, someone was racing down the alley. Says it was an alien."

"An alien? Like from space?"

"Aye."

It was Hector that started it. He snickered, and that got me started and soon we were grabbing our sides laughing so much. Never in my life had I heard anything as ridiculous as aliens. My eyes were tearing up from the type of laughter that you can't stop once it starts. Something hit me mid-guffaw, though.

"Maybe he saw a werewolf?" I asked through a gale of laughter.

"No. Says some of his customers are werewolves. Knows them right well he does. No, this here fella is seeing aliens. Little green men," Hector answered, wiping his eyes.

I laughed some more, thinking about little green men while looking at the blue chalk outline of the former big guy. The laughter finally died as sure as the victim did.

"Is Frankenstein's Monster the name on the death certificate?" I asked.

"Toomie!" Hector waved his partner over.

Toomie was a pro body builder when she wasn't busy being a cop. She was whip smart and would soon be in the role of detective. She was quick to take to me, figuring we'd work together someday. Her biggest muscle was her heart, though. She cared a lot about people. Maybe too much.

"Hello, Dalton," she said.

"Toomie."

"What did they tag him as?" Hector asked.

"Frank Jr." Toomie kicked the ground.

Rocks flew, plural. The woman would have given the big guy a run for his money where few others could. But someone else managed the rare feat. Taking off with the head as a trophy, no less.

"Frank Jr. it is," I said.

"Shame what happened to that little girl," Toomie said, looking straight into my eyes since she matched my six-one height.

"My thoughts exactly," I replied.

That made her smile, which I liked plenty. That warm heart showed through whenever she flashed those teeth. Word was, she had a thing for werewolves, both his and hers, but I did not traffic in rumor. And if that was her thing, they were lucky to have her. Get this woman her detective badge. By mentioning the little girl, Toomie forecast who I should investigate first and she was right.

"I'll be in touch. See ya Toomie, Hector."

Toomie nodded.

"Cheerio," Hector said.

I tipped an imaginary cap and went in search of my Mustang, parked somewhere outside the perimeter of the police tape. It was time to find out what happened to the sometimes-gentle giant. Originally born of dead bodies, Frank Jr. was dead again, and it was my job to find the monster who did it. Human or otherwise.

After a short drive, I arrived at the city outskirts. The sky went from dark grey to less grey. Skyscrapers vanished, giving way to scattered homes which grew sparser where forest met water. The little thatch-roofed hut sat a short distance from the bank of the river. Technically, the area was more marsh than river, comprising still water. Weeds rose from the waters in tight clots of green.

Braving the waters was a fool's errand. It was easy to get tangled and pulled under. That very concept came to play in the big guy's trial. There was no driveway on the premises, only browned grass where it appeared other vehicles occasionally drove onto. I pulled up and honked my horn.

The place was small enough that it would be easy to learn whether the owner was home. I stepped out of the car and flashed my smile in case he was watching. A quick glance toward the water, and I noticed a tuft of daisies. The sight caused my smile to falter. When I looked back, the old man was staring through the window, curtain raised.

I approached, cautiously. At the very least, based on the trial, I knew the guy to have a pitchfork. I had a gun but did not yet feel the need to make it known to the man. I approached the window. He spoke through the glass.

"Are you with the press?"

"No."

He looked past me, searching the grounds. "Worse than vampires, those folks. Suck more than blood out of you. How dare they try to rehabilitate the image of such a monster?"

There it was. Motive. "You know I can agree with you much better if it's not through glass."

He looked at me as if considering, then dropped the curtain back into place. The front door opened into a cramped home with a low ceiling. I ducked initially out of instinct, worried I might hit my head, but I ended up with about an inch to spare. The man got around just fine. He was already in the tiny kitchen.

I sat in one of two chairs while he finished setting himself up with tea.

"Fancy a cup?" He held up the one he already made.

Not a fan of being poisoned on the job, I always declined liquids from strangers. I nodded him off and leaned back in the chair. The kitchen was so small the tip took me partially back into the living room. Water closet and a tiny bedroom. Someone had covered the couch in bedding, and it looked slept in. Something odd about that for one who lived alone.

"What brings you to my house, mister?"

"I wanted to ask you about what happened all those years ago." Suddenly, I noticed daisies in a vase by the sink.

Leaning back in the chair again, I noticed a shrine on a mantle near what appeared to be an old black-and-white TV. At the least, it was a tuber, but seemed old enough to be monochrome. I couldn't know for certain without turning it on. I'm not that good a PI.

The man made a sign of the cross from head to chest and sighed. His sigh was the wheeze of someone on their way out. Ironically, a certain doctor could probably save him with a lung transplant, but no way was I going to bring that up.

"Aye. Marilyn. She threw a daisy into the water and the monster wished to throw something as equally beautiful in. So, he lifted..." The man choked on his words, squeezed the tablecloth. "The big goliath lifted my most beautiful Marilyn and threw her in the water!"

He stood and waved his hands in a tossing motion, reliving a scene that he surely had to live with every day. The man did not stand for long. Reliving the events buckled his knees. He fell onto his ass in the chair. I watched him grow small before me. But too small to get revenge?

"Anyway, the lawyer, an Invisible Man of all things, tried to muddy the waters with a different story. Oh, how I hated the man. I think there were days where that man was not even in the courtroom. How would we ever know?"

For a moment, I wondered if I needed to check on the Invisible Man's status. If he was deceased along with the Big Guy, we maybe had a serial murderer. Though I suppose if someone killed the Invisible Man, no one would ever find the body. Maybe there was such a thing as the perfect crime.

"That ruthless, horrible, invisible lawyer suggested my Marilyn threw the flower in and went to retrieve it, only to get tangled and drown. That's not how it happened!"

The man pounded the table with renewed vigor before remembering he had tea. He sipped. There was rage in the man and he had a motive. Maybe Toomie was right. Maybe the most obvious suspect was the killer. There remained the how of it all. I had nothing to lose by sharing some information to watch how he reacted.

"Somebody offed the big guy."

The man spit his tea back into the cup. It was as gross as it sounds. His eyes lit up wide and he yanked his head back so fast I wondered whether maybe he burned his tongue on the liquid. No, that wasn't it. Man was glad was all.

"Hot diggity dog!"

The man set the cup down and started dancing a jig right there in the kitchen. The floor shook as he bounced around. Never a happier man did I see.

"Marilyn, we're free!"

A tiny voice sounded from down the hall from behind the bedroom door I noticed earlier.

"Pa-pa?"

The man rushed past me. I rose to my feet and watched as he bent down on one knee with a grunt and stretched his arms toward the bedroom door.

"Who is that?" a tiny set of eyes asked through the cracked door.

"A friend. My new BEST friend!" The father looked up at me, reaching with those same outstretched arms. "I would hug you my friend if I could stand back up? Do you wish to lower yourself into my arms?"

I declined the generous offer. Then the door opened and the cutest little girl, maybe seven years old, stepped into the hall. Through the door, I saw the accoutrements of a pre-teen in the room. So, Daddy slept on the couch. I was unsure of what the mother situation was.

"Pa-pa?"

"Marilyn Two!"

"You named her Marilyn Two?" I asked.

He nodded from the floor. "Aye. Too many painful memories to call her simply Marilyn," he said.

"Couldn't have gone with Harriett, or Cora, or any other common names?"

"She will always be my Marilyn Two." He waved his hands.

The girl remained in the hall, seemingly unsure. "Is it safe?"

"Now and for always, my love. You needn't hide from the monster anymore."

"We can go outside?"

"Yes, baby, there are no more threats in the world to hurt my little girl."

"Pa-pa!"

She raced into his embrace. I didn't want to bring up all the vampires and werewolves and a certain gill man I thought I saw moving in the marsh when I arrived. No point bringing all that up. The two were quite happy.

I finally left, but not before learning the two had never left the house since the girl's birth. Various gig workers delivered meals and essentials to their door. He refused to leave her side. No way the man would leave the girl alone long enough to go to an alley and off the big guy. This guy was not who I was looking for. It was back to square one.

Next stop? The spouse.

The immense mansion made an impression. I had visited once before for a different reason and understood my return would be unwelcomed. The Bride and I had a history, a tragic one at that. I was loath to return, but if the father of the dead girl was not the killer, then I needed to look at Frank Jr.'s spouse.

The Bride had done some modelling in her early days when she wore another body. I preferred her current one, but who was I to say? Her visible stitches were a big hit, and the pictures became ubiquitous. She invested her earnings wisely, started a business and voila! A mansion in the hills.

I called ahead, so the guard at the gate gave me no grief. I drove into the palatial estate and up the immense driveway, quite a difference from the previous home. Licking my hand, I slicked back my hair and straightened my tie. It went crooked again as soon as I released it. Stupid, trying to put on a show for a past that was never coming back.

The front doors were immense, designed to accommodate the big guy's size. The door buzzed open while I stood there looking like a tool. Above the door hung an obvious camera. She would watch me the entire time I was on her property. Smart woman. When I entered, a metallic voice spoke through the tiny box alongside the door.

"Make your way to the bedroom," the voice said, sounding sexy despite all the tin.

I ascended an ornate staircase, the trimmings of which looked to exceed my annual income. I never paid attention when I was here before, as there were other things on my mind back then. It took all I had not to focus on that memory as I climbed.

Upon reaching the top of the stairs, an open door at the furthest end of the hall greeted me. It appeared the woman was waiting, and here I thought she never wanted to see me again. Then my phone chimed.

A text from Toomie appeared on my screen informing me they already called the Bride about the murder. That was a relief. I did not want to be the one to break the news. There was also a text from Hector asking if I wished to join him for some fish and chips later? I declined the invitation. I still had plenty of work to do.

Walking down the hall, I felt my bowels clench. I wasn't sure I was ready to face her again so soon after—well, all that happened before. Finally, I stepped into her room without even a knock. The woman lay propped up on an elegant, oversized bed, one that could accommodate her large body. And oh, what a body it was!

The woman wore a sheer nightgown, leaving little to the imagination. Scars and stitches showed through the material, along with other things. There was more to look at than just her body. The woman was striking from head to toe.

Not only was the bride's body stunning, (and familiar) but her face was worthy of an artist's attention. Luxurious black hair stretched into a pyramid atop her head, with dancing white lines running the lengths of both sides like smoke trails. (Legend had it that the white resulted from the shock of first spotting her future husband.)

The corpse-like pallor of her face only emphasized the plush red lines of eminently kissable lips. Her eyes were pools of grey that slipped into different colors depending on the environment.

Yes, there was plenty to look at, but my gaze kept returning to her body. Her positioning (propped up against an insane number of pillows) caused her chest to extend prominently forward. I tried to pretend not to notice. She noticed my predicament and smiled while dabbing the edge of a massive beach towel on her hair.

"You must excuse me. I am fresh from the shower," the Bride said and puffed her insanely high hair with the terrycloth fabric.

The same towel covered a huge portion of the pillows and one of her shoulders. She let the end go, and I found it odd that her hair appeared totally dry. Had she really showered or was this for show? Was she trying to seduce me? And so soon after learning of her husband's death? Did she only pretend to take a shower to excuse her evening wear being worn in the middle of the day?

A scent floated in the air. A familiar one which left me dizzy with emotions. I held it all in check. I am a professional. The scent did a good job of hiding the musk of dead skin though.

"Wish I could say it was nice to see you again, Dalton. Still upset about our last encounter?"

"No. It's all good," I lied.

"Excuse me if I do not believe that. What brings you here? Questions about my husband or something... else?"

She traced a hand along that stunning body. Something stirred inside me. She stared directly at me. Part of her beauty I never considered until now was that since her hair always remained high and tight, it left her eyes eternally exposed. Her smoldering eyes were almost as beautiful as certain other parts of her anatomy. I gave up on trying not to stare. She knew better, anyway. Why try to hide it?

I glanced around the room. High-end everything. Soft lighting filled the room, almost as subtle as candles, but there would be no open flame around. Not in the house of Frankenstein. I was uncertain what it was I searched for, maybe signs of a woman in mourning. I found none. She did not seem upset at losing Frank Jr. Was that a tell, or was she too busy enticing me for me to notice her sadness?

"This is business. I do have questions," I said.

"And in your profession, you make it a habit of undressing your clients with your eyes?"

She twisted provocatively without moving off her elevated perch, while somehow showing off her body even more. Everything pressed up against the silk.

"You are not a client. You are a suspect."

"Am I now?"

I nodded and tried to look for something out of place. The beach towel. It did not fit in with the décor of the room, which was what I would term modern goth. Lots of black and red around the room. Then I spotted something interesting. Very.

A set of knee-high green leather boots with black laces and buckles running the entire length stood alongside a chair clipped together at the top, so they stood as if filled by legs. Long ones. They were tree trunk high. I tried not to imagine what they might look worn by her and failed. The image stirred me up some more.

That wasn't all either. Draped over the chair was a glossy green rubber body stocking of some sort. I could see enough of the outfit to understand it would show off one's assets in as enticing a way as possible. A sexy outfit for a fun-filled night. I wondered if Frank Jr. enjoyed the benefits of the outfit or if she wore it for someone else. Someone who might have helped kill the big guy.

I should never have noticed the boots or the beach towel. But it all meant my mind was picking up on something. A clue of sorts. But the meaning behind the items eluded me. Something was off, but I did not know what it was. I got to the point behind my visit.

"Do you kill your husband?"

"No. I did not," she said.

She ran her hand down her torso again, like a person showing off prizes on a game show. She was never the flirtatious type, was always loyal to her husband as far as I knew. That meant the show was for me. I needed to cut to the quick and get out of there.

"Suspect is almost always the spouse and no offense; you don't seem too broken up."

She laughed, which always threw me. Her mouth opened slack-jawed wide. She threw her head back as a cry of laughter somehow emitted. Her mouth never moved through the laughter or scream once she opened it. I saw her scream once before, but I didn't mean to make it happen. I lost my cool back then.

Maybe it was the recently wet hair, but something kept her from guffawing all the way back. Her head did not tilt as far as I was used to seeing it when she laughed. She finally brought her head back down and licked her lips.

"Do you know Frank Jr. did everything rough?"

She touched a breast while saying it and I went red with anger, not excitement. I was losing it like the last time I visited her bedroom. Frank Jr. intercepted me that day when I had stormed in. He roughed me up before tossing me out the nearby window, which I noticed they had since repaired. I never pressed charges; I would have done the same as the big guy. Despite the window toss, I wanted to find Frank Jr.'s killer.

"Stop," I said.

She did not. "Everything rough. Think of those massive hands of his. If I asked Frank to open a jar of pickles, he did. But do you know how?"

"You can't open you own jar of pickles?" I asked, trying to change the direction of the conversation.

"Sure, I can. I have superhuman strength. That's not the point. I can control it. I can screw off the top of a jar of pickles or screw... other things without damaging them."

She wasn't wrong. The woman had tossed me into Frank's hands that night. She could have launched me through the window as well as he, but Frank was so angry at finding me in the bedroom with his wife that he did the honors. As for the Bride, she continued her line of thought.

"Think about it. He takes the jar of pickles in one hand and the lid in the other. Then before he can twist the top, the glass explodes into shards, and we have pickle juice all over the floor. He doesn't mean to. He never means too, but he went his whole life never being able to control his own strength. "

I nodded despite myself. That must have been a bummer. At least she had brought it back from a sexual direction. Until she started up again.

"Sometimes I wondered if the problem was in his brain, but I don't think so. I always loved that part of him. Such a sweet talker, that guy. And funny. So funny!"

"Like when he threw me out the window?"

She did the creepy laugh thing again before settling her head back into place. (Why was she elevated so high on the pillows?) I could not put a finger on why it bothered me. She showed a mouthful of teeth, enjoying the memory of my two-story fall.

"That was funny, yes. Perfect example. Frank Jr. laid a claim on what was his that night. All night thanks to you. You got him worked up, and he enjoyed every minute with all my body parts."

"Enough," I said, working my way up to getting thrown out a window again.

"Imagine him getting excited. I know how to work this body. I'm going to make sure me and Frank have an enjoyable time. Even under normal circumstances, Frank Jr. might get rough by default. But imagine him with a little extra gas in the tank. We have had plenty of unfortunate accidents in the past that have damaged either him or me. That is why I require upgrades from time to time."

That one hurt. She waved both hands over her torso now, tracing down her neck and along the side of the breasts. Then she made it worse.

"You know why I don't feel so bad about Frank Jr.? Maybe because each of these limbs I own still feels what its previous owner feels. So, this torso? These breasts? This heart? It longs for you Dalton. I still feel Amy's love for you."

There it was. Just her saying Amy's name brought me near tears. But if what the Bride said was true, then Amy was still in there somewhere, stitched in the puzzle of a woman before me. I longed to touch Amy again. Even though I understood it could not be real, I wanted to believe the Bride could channel Amy since she was wearing part of Amy's body.

"Really?" I asked.

Then the Bride did the laugh thing again. Once. Twice. Three times. Normally, it was creepy, but this time only infuriated me. She came out of the haw-haw-haw of a laugh and looked at me with contempt.

"No! I cannot feel her presence. That isn't how it works. Oh, the look on your face when I suggested such a thing. You are pathetic. Both for believing and for allowing her to die. I mean, a zombie bite? Really? You let her get bitten by a zombie? They are so slow. They ramble so leisurely they could be walking backwards in time. Thankfully, you had your gun."

That night flashed through my mind. We were street side dining. The walking dead came out of nowhere. Slow, yes, but Amy became trapped behind the guardrail after running the wrong way before the staff could scuttle the thing away with the promise of a spoiled steak. It got her arm, and I had no choice. No choice. Amy and I said our goodbyes on the sidewalk of my favorite restaurant. I have never returned since. I can't chance they could not wash the blood off the sidewalk. The Bride's taunting brought me back out of the memory, which was fine. That was not a place I wished to linger.

"Lucky for me the virus had not spread, and you wife was an organ donor, so her body remained viable. Nice of her. So now? These boobs are mine, Dalton! You understand? Mine! You used to have access to them, but no longer. No boob for you. Only me. I touch them all I want!"

She did just that, grabbing them while I exited the room. My previous visit to the same room was when I showed up and demanded Amy's body back so I could bury her. Frank did a number on me for my troubles. It was wrong how I stormed their castle. I understand now, but the Bride's cruelty had me reaching for my gun that day. Not to use on the Bride as I could never shoot Amy a second time. But I was worried I might use it on myself.

Now, after returning and trying to find the truth, the Bride worked me up too much for me to determine if she killed her husband. Something about her behavior bothered me as well, but the nature of what disturbed me failed to materialize in my current state. Thinking about it later with a clear head was the best remedy. Until then, I needed a drink. And I knew right where to go.

The bar, to put it kindly, was a dive. Dark during day or night, I did not want to know what it was hiding. It drew a large crowd because of the cheap drinks and proximity to a local college. None of the young ladies looked my way when I walked in, as it should be. *Stay with your own age kiddos*, I thought as I dropped into a seat next to the only other guy as old as me in the room.

The bartender, young himself, looked over from where he was buffing a glass. I thought that only happened in the movies. Who knew? I asked for a whiskey and a tequila shot. He nodded and slapped the bar rag over his shoulder then dropped the drinks in front of me.

"We don't want no trouble here," the bartender said.

"He talking to me, or to you?" I asked the guy sitting next to me. The man was a handsome fella with striking features and eyes that glared brightly despite their underlying darkness. He wore a wide-brimmed hat that seemed designed to hide his presence. It did not work with me.

"Both, I imagine," the man said and turned around on his stool to face the crowd.

Young men and women did their thing, grinding on the floor, playing pool, fighting the vomit comet, and draping themselves over one another. That did not help with my Amy memories. I gulped the shot before treating the glass of whiskey in the same fashion. I raised a finger for round two. The bartender seemed miffed.

A group of women came in hot. They were young, stunning, and dressed in bridal party accoutrements. Even in a loud packed bar, they stood out as obnoxious. Maybe after another round, I might think about getting over Amy. My adjacent barstool friend seemed to take a liking to them as well.

"Allow me to introduce myself," I began.

"No need, Dalton. I know who you are," the man said.

"So, Van Helsing really does know everything."

"Your face was in the papers when the whole thing with your wife went down," he said.

"Fiancé. That's why I had no say in what happened to the body in the end," I said. The bartender delivered round two just in time. I reached behind me for the shot and chugged.

"I have seen the Bride. She looks good," Van Helsing said.

I couldn't tell if he was ribbing me, so I let it go. "I am here because someone offed the big guy."

"And you assumed I did it?"

"I know you could have based on your reputation. But you would have been tidier with the cleanup. No, what I really need is to see who else had the means or skills. You traffic in those sorts of folks."

"No recent full moon," he said, paying a lot of attention to the bridal party.

The women in their twenties settled into a table yelling and shrieking, having a grand old time. They arrived already drunk, as no one had them yet. Like sharks, young men began circling. The bridal party would not have to buy their own all night. Van Helsing spun his barstool back around and started on his beer. I turned around as well since he had not yet turned down an offer to help.

"And no scat at the scene and major tasty organs intact. I already ruled out werewolves. Witness on the scene said it was aliens," I said.

Van Helsing, who had gone back to his beer, almost spit it out. He swallowed and chuckled. "Aliens? How absurd. Look, I'd like to help, but you are messing up my stakeout."

"Don't you mean stake in? Isn't that what you do?"

Van Helsing stared ahead where the bottles lined against the bar back mirror seemed to double. The guy was the serious type. Never cracked a smile at my little joke. He looked at me in the mirror, though.

"The answer will always come in the small things. The tiny things that you overlook are the same things that people involved in the crime overlook. That is where you will find your answers. Witnesses know more than you think they do. They only need to be asked the correct questions. And above all else, always trust your gut. Now hold this, will you?"

He reached beneath his cloak and handed me a wooden stake. I examined it, confused. It was quite light, and I wondered how something so trifle could do the type of damage it was known for. Van Helsing read my face.

"Pound those in the ground and they hold down a circus tent in inclement weather. Trust me. I'd take the certainty of my grip over a weapon that can jam any day."

I couldn't argue, but I also couldn't understand. I spun in my seat, searching the bar for a threat. Two of the ladies in the bridal party had pulled out compacts and were touching up their makeup. Beyond that, nothing else had changed since I last looked. I spun back to face the bar with my new friend.

Van Helsing gestured to the mirror. And I'll be damned (which is a given) if the compacts the women were holding were not floating in the air. The brides themselves were nowhere to be seen. Van Helsing finally smiled.

"Their form of camouflage. Pretend to adjust themselves in mirrors, so no one assumes they are vamps."

Van Helsing swept his arms and his cloak fluttered into the air while he launched himself from his seat. The man was too cool for school as he emerged from the spin with dual stakes in hands. Under the flutter of fabric, I noticed a band of wooden stakes strapped to his chest like a beauty sash. Extra ammo.

The women immediately revealed their true colors. The "bride" in the party (my second bride of the day) grew fangs and ripped into the throat of a young college stud. She drank while the guy spasmed in place. Having drank her fill, she ripped a chunk of his throat out and the guy timbered right there. A geyser of blood shooting into the air from the wound.

The bride grew talons and an attitude. It appeared the drink did her body good. Muscles rippled and ripped, showing one tough monkey. I think even Toomie might have had a rough time with this one. I leaped off my seat and followed my new drinking buddy.

Like obedient soldiers, the vamps on the periphery (there were seven in the party) launched themselves at us. Van Helsing jabbed the stake in one woman mid-flight. Ash danced in the air. Unaccustomed to such battles, I blinked, and the muscled vamp was on me. Never had I witnessed something move so fast.

My instincts kicked in and I stabbed the stake into her chest. Big mistake. Stabbing the woman was like pounding through steak. Quite gross, nowhere as clean as a knife. I'd had plenty of knife fights before. It took a substantial effort to drive the stick home. But when the woman bopped into ash, the result was like a tug-o-war where the other team let go of the rope. Except in reverse.

Once the resistance disappeared, I fell forward and smashed my face on the bar floor. I smelled the sour odor of years of spilled drinks until my nose popped and filled with blood. Despite hurting like hell, I rose to my feet. The next vamp did my work for me. She spotted the blood all over my face and could not help herself.

With a hunger not to be denied, she growled and launched herself at me, destination bloody face. I saw her jaws open wide and thought that was it until she hit the stake in my hand and puffed into ash. I was breathing through my mouth since my nose was out of commission. My mouth filled with ash, and I had to spit. The taste was foul, like eating evil itself.

Another college kid ran past me, hands around his bleeding neck. There was no stopping the flow. The kid continued a few feet and dropped onto the floor next to me. One more vamp leaped onto that kid's back, seeking dinner. The kid didn't put up a fight, but I did, stabbing the vamp through her back. She exploded into ash. I stayed on my feet that time.

The bartender yelled for everyone to cool it even while people stampeded to the exit. I reached out toward the bartender, and he got the point. He tossed a bar rag my way. After blowing into it to clear my nose, I gripped the cartilage and twisted. I'd felt worse and was on adrenaline, so I managed.

Next, I wiped as much blood off as possible to minimize myself as a target. I'd already learned vamps could not control themselves. Their human part must vanish over time, the animal side of the bat taking over. If they could feed, they would feed.

Despite Van Helsing's experience, he still had two left. He spun when one flew at him. The man's cloak spun like the skirt of folk dancers I once saw in Mexico.

He came out of the spin below the vamp who landed. It surprised her to discover she failed to behead the man with her claws. Van Helsing tossed a stake, and the vamp went to dust. There was one woman left. The bride. She hissed as her face went full bat. Her eyes gleamed red and her mouth opened, revealing drool covered teeth stretching the length of her jaw.

"Thosssse were merely my minions. Do you think you are fast enough to defeat me?"

Spittle flew as the vamp postured before the man. Van Helsing spun the blades in his hand. The vamp watched with great interest as he tossed them away. Then he postured, facing her, and raised his cloak. He was empty-handed, all his stakes sheathed.

This time, I did not have time to blink. She was on him as if always there. I never saw her move. She had hands on either side of his head, the two locked in an embrace. Time froze as the pair stood in a silence.

She had not dusted, which meant he was gone. I gripped my stake, not sure what I could do against one so powerful. Then the funniest thing happened. Van Helsing stepped back. The vamp remained in place, hands reaching out as if she still cradled the man's head.

The vamp looked down at her chest as surprised as I was. "Three? How did you manage three?"

Thunk. Thunk. Thunk. The stakes dropped to the ground as the vamp finally turned to dust. How had he managed three? Van Helsing approached the bar and dropped some money. The bartender lit up over the amount. Then the man tipped his wide brim hat to me.

"Thanks for the assist. Remember, it is the little things."

Then he headed toward the back. Either to the restroom or the back door. I wasn't about to stick around and find out. I headed toward the exit even as more college kids started pouring in, oblivious to the carnage on the floor. Maybe the place was too dark.

"Hey, wait, you are a witness," the bartender cried out.

"Sorry, I have another murder to deal with and I need to get somewhere before dark."

I floored my mustang, driving the winding roads up into the hills where the rich and famous lived. My mustang stood out every time I passed a Lexus or BMW. I didn't care. I was moving too fast. My muscle car did just fine, thank you. Still, I bet many of the drivers I passed called back to their homes to alert security someone was casing the neighborhood.

Not a single Tesla passed by. Spotting one would have felt ironic based on my destination. The place came into view. On a hill of wealthy people, this one place stood out, rising high at the top of the hill. It appeared gloomy and under threat of a storm. Lightning flashed in the distance. Trouble was heading our way.

There was one man bigger than the big guy and I needed to speak to him. The uber wealthy liked their privacy, so lived in gated communities overflowing with security cameras. Stealth was not an option for me. They already had my plates.

I reached the top. Ornate metal gates surrounded the property. The metal twisted into various ominous shapes. The foreboding nature of the fencing would not be enough to keep out certain people, but it likely kept tourists and looky-loos away. Atop the perimeter of the fencing were the all-important spikes to make certain only those chancing a ball sac tear would dare climb over. It surprised me to see the gates open on their own for me.

Stone stairs as old as the castle greeted me when I stepped from my car. A hunchback wearing a valet vest took my keys. The man had trouble trying to get into my front seat. Rather than wait, I rushed up the stairs. I felt for the gun at my waist. If I needed it anywhere today, it would be here.

A plaque at the front door read The Institute for Reconstructive Surgery. After the fiasco with the big guy killing the girl, a certain doctor went about rehabilitating his image. He started by offering free reconstructive services to prominent politicians and their spouses.

Soon the well to do were walking around as if they had no cares in the world since the treatments removed their ability to frown. The doctor sculpted their faces into someone's version of perfection. Those who went under the procedures trended on media and stars were born from nothing more than daring to trust the mad dude running the place.

Unlike the castle's dreary exterior, the interior was sterile upon entry. The place looked like a modern-day hospital. They dedicated most floors to surgical services for the wealthy clients. A starlet of some acclaim talked with a receptionist at the front desk.

"The Phantom? Get out!"

The Starlet gripped the desk and leaned into the perfect beauty behind the counter. They could have been twins. The counter lady smiled back.

"Yes. He is having a procedure as we speak. His fifth one. The Phantom still wears the mask because of insecurity, but he is ridiculous hot now."

I coughed, ensuring my presence as a buzzkill. "I am here to see the doctor."

"I should think so with that face." The receptionist waved her hand around her own nose instead of mine.

In all the action of the day, I had forgotten about my nose. The starlet scoffed and rolled her eyes at the receptionist. The woman tried to snicker, but her face kept getting stuck, so it all came out as a half snort.

"Might want to have that looked at," I said.

The starlet took offense. "I could say the same. You really believe the doctor will see you? He has a staff of dozens. Any of them would see what they could do with that horrible mess on your face. But THE doctor seeing you?"

"How about you call the man upstairs and tell him Dalton is here to speak to him?"

The receptionist shared a devious look with the starlet and picked up the phone. The receptionist's brow furrowed. Time for more Botox. She pointed to the end of the hall, past a bank of elevators, to one at the very end of the hall.

"The last one goes to the top. He is expecting you."

"Want my autograph?" I asked the starlet, walking away before she could answer.

The elevator door opened soon after I pressed the button. Another hunchback stepped out wearing a security guard outfit. He had a hand on a taser.

"Going to need to relieve you of your gun, friend," the man said.

"Sure," I said.

I pulled it out of my waist and smashed him in the nose with it. He went down, hard. The women in the distance screamed. I relieved the man of his taser and entered the elevator. As I suspected, it went straight to the top with no stops in between. I kept the gun and taser ready, no sense hiding them now.

The elevator dinged and opened. I was unsurprised to see the man himself standing in wait. Victor was a tall man, dashing, with deep-set eyes approximating burning coal. I refused to look away, unwilling to give him the satisfaction of knowing I felt uneasy. The man wore a white outfit that looked more appropriate to a butcher than a doctor. It covered him from neck to toe.

His jet-black hair, coifed like a movie star, came unraveled at the part. Strands hung down his face on one side in search of an eye to cover. I would not have minded had the strands succeeded. One less eye for him to probe me with. He was calculating my weaknesses as sure as I was standing too long inside an open elevator. I stepped out into another century.

Unlike the state-of-the-art facility of the lower levels, the top floor remained as it was when the castle was first built. That meant torches on the walls, moss-covered stones for hallways and an omnipresent chill. A black and white tube TV hung near the elevator. On it, the doctor joined me in watching his security guard recover.

"Was all that necessary?" Victor asked.

"He wished to take my gun," I replied.

"Following orders, he was. Now I will have to fix his injuries on my dime. Looks as if you could use my services as well."

"No thanks. It adds character. It will heal just fine."

The man squinted, and I feared firing out of nervousness. It was unlike me, but I heard stories about the man. Brilliant in all the wrong ways. I loosened my figure on the trigger to avoid a misfire. He seemed uninterested in the weapon in my hand.

"Do you know why I am here?" I asked.

"To determine if I had anything to do with Frank Jr.'s death. But beyond that, you also seek DNA samples of my daughter's various body parts to see if she was involved."

The man was good. He was right on the money. "Don't you mean daughter-in-law?"

"Frank Jr. is my son, but the Bride is technically my daughter. Yes, I consider her my daughter-in-law. I try not to think about the whole thing. It borders on creepy."

"You traffic in corpses, and you think their relationship designation is creepy?"

"Yes. I find corpses beautiful. Walk with me."

I would have preferred not to, but he was already marching along the corridor. An open window revealed lightning was imminent. A gray cloud headed right for us. Raindrops pattered against the stone walls of the castle.

We marched along and the kind doctor was good enough to keep his hands behind his back as he walked, knowing it would put me at ease.

"I cannot talk for long. The forthcoming electricity in the air will be part of an experiment tonight. I am trying something new, something different."

"You intend to create something other than a massive child-killer monster?"

The man turned, leaning into my face with only his pointing finger in between. Victor spit as he yelled. "He is a good boy my son! How dare you come into my house and accuse me of such a thing? He is not a monster. Frank is as alive as you and me!"

"Or was," I said, glad to have rattled the doctor the same way he did me. Now he understood. I could be a handful too and he had better watch himself.

Maybe I couldn't get off three shots like Van Helsing did with stakes, but I could easily fire one bullet. There was always the taser, but maybe this guy took one too many lightning strikes. For all I knew, the taser would simply tickle the man. He squinted again.

"You meant to rile me, throw me off my game."

"I just want answers."

"Then answers you shall have."

He threw open a large wooden door, and we entered the inner sanctum. Tesla coils rose high in various spots throughout the room. Electricity crackled and buzzed. An orb of unparalleled brightness hung near one section of the ceiling, hovering over a large medical table tilted such that I could not see what lay atop it. Black fabric (garbage bags?) stretched out along both sides of the table. Cables ran from tesla coils down to the table's upper edge. The angle of the metal slab was such that anyone on it would be nearly standing.

Circling around, I spotted another medical table, one empty but showing signs of recent surgery. Blood-soaked cloths filled a bucket alongside the cold metal slab. Not a cleanup crew in sight. The man had appalling sanitary standards, or he had performed surgery recently.

Victor watched with interest as I swept around to get a look at the table under the blinding orb. What I discovered rattled me. A hideous creature lay strapped to the surgical table. I stifled a cry.

The creature was an amalgamation of various species. The head was a werewolf, but the torso was that of a nude man, albeit one heavy with musculature. What I thought to be garbage bags were massive bat wings spread out from underside each shoulder. The legs resembled those of the Gill Man or one of his kind from the Black Lagoon at least. Victor had pinned the tip of each wing to end tables on either side of the trapped creature.

"What in the hell is this?" I gasped.

"Hell is nearly correct. A Helloceraptor is the term."

"How are you keeping the werewolf in form?"

"Artificial moon."

He pointed to the orb. "This is a special breed that resorts back to an actual wolf, not a man. So, it will remain a killing machine, full moon or not. The wings are from a standard vampire transitioned to bat, but cultivated in the lab to be larger, stronger."

"Why? Why make something so horrible?"

"As a weapon, of course. Government funding. We are on the cutting edge of the most efficient soldiers ever."

He hit some switches, and a skylight opened. The storm was in full swing. Large levers surrounded his workstation. He pulled one and twin tesla coils rose into the sky. That flop of hair made the rounds of his face as sweat built from his efforts. He ran back and forth, connecting cables and hitting more levers.

Lightning struck. Rain poured into the lab. Thunder rumbled as if announcing the end of a world or a beginning. Victor cranked a turret on the side of the table, repositioning the beast toward the storm. The wires that ran from the tesla coils merged into a metal skull cap which he affixed atop the werewolf's head. The man, to his credit, continued talking as he worked, still oblivious to my gun.

"To answer the questions that you have not asked yet. No, I did not kill my son. And no, my daughter did not kill my son. Here are my daughter-in-law's current DNA profiles. I believe you know at least one of them intimately."

The doctor winked as he handed over a flash drive. Victor knew what buttons to push. The comment tempted me to repeat with him what I did to the guard downstairs, but I worried the good doctor might like it. Despite the jab, everything felt too easy. Was I missing something?

I had what I came for, despite sensing the man held something back. Then I looked at the abomination on the table and decided circumstances led me here for a reason. Someone had to stop the madness. I aimed the gun at Victor. If he could read me as well as I knew he could, he would understand I meant business.

"I am afraid I cannot allow you to do this, doctor. It goes against the laws of nature."

"Precisely. It is life. New life. But people like you will still call it a monster!"

Before I could pull the trigger, he pulled a lever. A metal drum wrapped in a copper coil spun with an overwhelming hum. My gun hand trembled. Before I could identify what was happening, the gun yanked free of my hand. My borrowed taser followed right behind. The weapons flew across the room, along with a few medical tools adjacent the empty surgical table. Each item clanged onto the surface of the spinning drum.

"Magnet. I have antimagnetic fields surrounding most of my equipment. Forgot I left some of my sculpting tools out. No matter. I insist at this point that you leave."

Three hunchbacks, including the one I had hit, rushed into the room. Their own guns ripped free and joined the magnetic party. The same thing that disarmed me disarmed them, but there were three of them, and this was not my mission as much as I wanted to stop him.

"You got lucky this time," I said, setting up the idea of becoming a gadfly in Victor's life.

"Yes, I did. I expected you here, and you delivered by giving me everything I needed."

"What are you talking about?" I was confused.

He spun to face me. The spin allowed his hair to find one eye, covering it, giving the lone one extra caveat.

"You and all the small-minded town folk always claimed my boy was a monster. But now, the very fact you are investigating a murder means you believe something about my boy that I always knew. He's alive! ALIVE!"

Lightning cracked and hit the twin coils. Electricity danced down a string of wires connected to the metal bowl atop the creature's head. The creature danced and writhed in place as the hunchbacks escorted me out.

They ungraciously tossed me to the curb alongside my car, which remained where I parked it. The valet was still trying to get in the front seat. He gave up and handed me the keys. More lightning struck the coils, causing sparks to fly down onto the lawn.

Something horrific screeched and roared and cried out from the top of the tower. Through open turret windows lining the upper chamber I saw shadows where the massive creature rose, swinging its wings wildly, flapping them about. The exaggerated shadows played out like a puppet show as I got in my Mustang and hit the gas.

Victor was right. It took a murder for anyone to consider Frank Jr. alive. But the man unknowingly gave me everything I needed. I hit the gas with a specific destination in mind. I finally figured out what happened to Frank Jr.

Rain followed me from the castle as I pulled back up to the scene of the crime. I hoped the storm did not wash away what I was looking for. As I pulled up, I finally noted the business on the other side of the alley. I had forgotten to check originally. The revisit proved informative.

Someone had torn down most of the police tape. Likely locals taking pictures for their socials and all. The wind caused the loose ends of flagging tape to flutter about. I walked to the spot where I had stepped on the glass originally. It remained in place, so small against the backdrop. No one had swept the area.

Rain made the chalk bleed a dazzling blue. Someone taped up the business' damaged wall from inside with cardboard. It sagged with wetness from the rain. I went inside to speak to the shop keep. He had one last bit of information I needed.

"It's you," the man behind the counter said.

A spin rack of pulps spun next to the counter. The man had been filling the rack when I entered.

"Funny how many people greet me that way," I said.

I stopped the rack from spinning. It rested on an angle that belonged in a carnival ride. Facing me where I stopped it, a gumshoe with a gun took aim at me from a twenty-five-cent cover. Shame I had no change on me.

"Sorry. I don't know you, but I saw you outside that day. With the police," the man said.

I finger waved again to remind him. He waved back, same as before. Looking around, I spotted what I was looking for. A science-fiction section. More pulps there. I grabbed one and brought it to the counter.

"You a fan of science fiction?"

"I am a fan of all written works. When one thinks about books, it is amazing stories ever come to be at all. A person is born, then they spend a lifetime watching TV, meeting people, experiencing family, friends, life events, tragedies. Then some of those people take time to write the words down."

He stopped suddenly, likely used to people poo-poohing his verbal treatises. I was not a poo-pooer, rather someone who needed info. And he had it. I remained silent to suggest he continue. He seemed excited when I did not stop him.

"These authors, each one, took different parts of what formed them. All their baked in things."

"Like raspberry?" I was trying to be helpful.

"No. Real ingredients. Pain, sorrow, joy. A gamut of emotions and they sit, and they type, and no two people would ever produce the same work. So remarkable. Every book in this place is a miracle."

By the time he was done, he had me believing the pulps were worth a quarter. I waved the science fiction volume, which had a little green man on the cover. Pure fantasy.

"You told police you thought aliens killed him? Do you really believe in aliens?"

"No. Please. I am not crazy. But the person was unlike any I had seen before. The legs were too long and strange. And their color..."

"You don't have to say it. I know what color they were."

I returned to the science fiction rack and spun it until I found what I was looking for. I brought the book to the shopkeeper and showed him the cover. He pointed excitedly.

"Yes. The head was just like that! That's why I mentioned aliens."

The cover revealed heads of humans collected in formaldehyde jars, watched over by a tentacled alien hovering above them. The heads appeared alive and unhappy to be in such a predicament.

I had everything I needed. After placing the books back, I exited the shop and jumped in my Mustang. I didn't let the rain slow me down.

I entered the mansion expecting to see her positioned the same as earlier. I was not wrong. She feigned interest, but I glimpsed an underlying weariness in her over seeing me reappear.

"Two visits in one day? To what do I owe the displeasure?"

She made no move to rise and greet me or show me the exit. It did not surprise me when she refused to move. She was in the perfect position to entice, which was her greatest weapon against someone like me. One who could not take his eyes off his former fiancé.

The Bride could have any man she chose. Though in the end there was only one man that meant everything to her. And for that, Frank Jr. had to die.

"You overplayed your hand earlier," I said.

"How so?" She seemed genuinely intrigued.

"Earlier you suggested your body parts synched up, that you could feel Amy's desires."

She ran her hands along her body again, trying to rattle me. I refused to admit she did so the moment I walked into the room. There was something captivating about the Bride beyond the Amy part of the equation.

"There is some truth to that, as I am sure you know. So, I reached my mind out to Amy, asked her to tell me about what happened, and you know what she told me?"

The Bride started to sit up but caught herself. The Bride had not even moved enough to stir the beach towel which remained incongruous, wrapped alongside her like a hand-me-down quilt.

She fell back into position, stretched enough for me to focus on the parts that were hard not to focus on. (Had her nightgown gotten shorter?) She flashed those pearly whites and batted those baby doe eyes. She wished to regain control, but I had it now.

"Impossible, but I will humor you. What did she say through this mystical connection?"

"That you have been a very bad. She believes you are solely responsible for the fate of Frank Jr."

"By what rights do you accuse me?"

"By following the evidence. And in a twist of fate, a confession from your father."

"He would never turn on me," she said.

"Not knowingly, but then you would never knowingly leave evidence behind, and yet you did."

I let it hang there for a moment, relieved she had not risen and relieved me of my head. That was a possibility ever since I set foot in the room. I had to lay the cards down just so to keep her interested, otherwise she might resort to taking her wrath out on me.

"You told me about your husband's inability to open jars. In that, you confessed to the crime."

"You're crazy," she said.

"Amy sometimes thought so. Is that you speaking or her? Either way, you did confess. I returned to the scene of the crime and what did I find? An apothecary!"

Her nervousness faded into a chuckle. That was not the evidence she expected. It was time to inform her I was aware of the entire plot.

"Throw a nickel and you hit an apothecary. They are everywhere," she said.

"Throw a nickel, or throw a child in a lake?"

She jerked up, anger crossing her face. The tearing of my limbs appeared imminent until she forced herself back into her sit. The damn beach towel almost fell away, but not quite. I could not help but focus on it. So out of place.

"Your father's company runs this one, which supplies his practice up in the hills. Daddy's daughter stops by for a visit, well she has full access now, doesn't she? Including many poisons."

"Enough. I did not kill my husband!"

"I already checked with the staff at the shop. I am aware of what you purchased, and that you were indeed there. It was not only poison you bought that day. No, you purchased something else you needed to complete your plan."

"If you know all this, then where are the police? Shouldn't they be here by now?"

"Maybe because I wanted time to rub it in your face the way you rubbed my fiancé's body in mine. You procured a small test tube of the liquid. That was as much as you required, despite the big man's size. A friend told me to look for the small things. That was the broken glass."

"What glass?" The Bride asked, jerking forward once again, as if gathering the strength to rise and toss me out the window.

I held renewed confidence that she would not move, at least until she discovered how much I knew. "The broken glass in the alley from the same test tube. You left the apothecary and met your husband in the alley. There you handed him the vial, forcing him to drink. When we spoke earlier, you unwittingly supplied me with another clue. The jar of pickles? Well, he did the same to the test tube after drinking from it, did he not?"

Her face went a lighter shade of corpse blue. She locked eyes with me and gripped the edge of the towel. I was getting a rise out of her literally. She was preparing to rise to her feet. I could only hope she gave me time to put the nails in the coffins of her various body parts.

"No need to answer. Frank Jr. answered by smashing his head through the neighboring business when the toxin took him down. He bounced against the wall, head breaking through the brick, then his body fell back into the alley. But you had more to do, didn't you?"

"It is time for you to leave. You are not the police; I do not have to stand for this. Leave now or I will toss you out myself," the Bride said.

"I'm sorry. Am I making you uncomfortable? I don't think you will do anything of the sort. Allow me to finish with a backtrack. Earlier in the day, before you poisoned your husband in the alley, you gave him one last go in this very bedroom. And not just any. You wanted it to be special. Exciting. You wore the knee highs and leather outfit."

I pointed to the green boots and the sexy leather bodice draped over the chair. She did not look to where I pointed, kept her gaze locked with mine. If I did not know better, I think she may have blushed but hard to tell what with her skin being dead and all.

"How do you know that? Did you have cameras planted here?"

"Maybe Amy told me." I could not help but get the dig in, make her doubt her own body after suggesting such a thing to me earlier. "You then relieved Frank Jr. of his head. And used the other item you bought from your father's shop. You placed Frank Jr.'s head in a nitrogen tube. The shopkeeper thought he saw an alien running away, but it was the long green boots and a metal canister containing a head and emitting ice crystals that prompted the shopkeeper to imagine the scene was from a sci-fi magazine."

The Bride's body jerked wildly, as if not under her own control. Yet she remained in place, struggling not to move. She grunted, which I took as a sign to continue.

"You then went to your father's lab. I saw the remnants of the work. At first, I thought it was part of his current experiment, but once I put it all together, I understood what type of surgery he had performed. And one more small thing. When he talked of Frank Jr. he used present tense, not past. As your father said, he's ALIVE!"

I stormed forward. Either a theory I had would prove correct or she would rip off my own arms and beat me with them. I yanked the towel away. Someone growled at me, but it was not the Bride.

Frank Jr. looked up at me!

Stitched to the bride's shoulder was one angry monster. He roared his disapproval over my presence. As for the Bride, she was now a two-headed being. The stitches of thick black cord held his lower neck to the upper portion of her shoulder. Yellow liquid ran from the contact point like dried iodine. Frank Jr. formed a garbled word which I could not make out.

"He says fuck you," the Bride offered.

Sounds about right. Her body shook again, more violently now as he fought for control, eager to set me free of my consciousness. All the attempts the Bride made to rise earlier were what I thought they were. Frank Jr. trying to rip me a new one.

"Yeah. I gathered that. I knew you would not throw me out because you can't move. You are recuperating. I came to confirm the results of my finding. You did not kill your husband."

"I would never think of such a thing. I love Frank Jr., but he was too much of a brute. Oh, he tried to change his ways, tried to be gentle. You can take the man out of the monster, but not the monster out of the man. Yes, we had one last wild ride together in his old form, like you suggested."

"Me love boots," the Big Guy murmured.

Poor guy appeared to be relearning how to talk. The Bride smiled and reached up with her hand on the same side as his head and stroked his hair. The big guy grinned at the petting session.

"But that broken test tube in the alley. That was your body every time he touched you?" I asked.

She nodded sadly, the Big Guy's head mimicking the move. The two would have to learn how to tango together.

"I have always loved him for his brain. Now this way we can share it, and be together without him hurting anyone any longer," she said.

What do you know? A part of Amy had found true love. I found it once with Amy and doubted I ever would discover it again. These two appeared willing to do anything for one another. I would like to think Amy loved me as much as I loved her, but I would never know for certain.

The only thing certain was that Amy now belonged to one of the truest loves I had ever witnessed. My work was done. It was time to leave the lovebirds alone.

"Will you tell the police? We wanted people to think he was dead so they would finally leave him alone," the Bride said.

"If you get weird impulses to throw children in a lake, do you promise to call me?" I asked.

"Certainly," the Bride said.

"Then we are done. No one needs to know. I doubt you can keep it secret forever, but the news won't come from me."

"What will you tell the police?" she asked.

"Oh. I'll make up something. Maybe say it was zombies that took out the big guy. I will not suggest it was a beauty that killed the beast."

I smiled for the first time since the case started and took my leave. I felt as green as her boots but because of envy. The two had found true love in a crazy world. But if even monsters could find love, it gave me hope that maybe some of us humans could do the same.

WOODFORD GENERAL STORE, WOODFORD, VERMONT

I RECENTLY MOVED TO Woodford, Vermont from Mobile, Alabama, and when I first arrived, I had never heard of The Bennington Triangle, which Woodford is a part of. The Woodford General Store is located atop a mountain eight miles from the town of Bennington, but not that far from where I moved to. This resulted in me walking from the house I'm staying in to the general store to get supplies here and there rather than go all the way to Bennington.

The people are super friendly who work there, and they serve delicious pressed lunch sandwiches, breakfast sandwiches, maple syrup ice cream, mac & cheese, soup, and they've even got a small selection of local produce. Oh, and of course they've got coffee. They usually keep a pot on for weary travelers or local commuters. I've walked there a few times in the mornings, and I've sat on the front porch eating a pulled pork with Vermont cheddar and washing it down with delicious coffee in the chill mountain air.

When I heard about the disappearances of people in the Bennington Triangle, the kind folks who work at the general store engaged me in conversation about it and filled me in on their theories and their own suspicions. I was immediately at my laptop writing my theory about the disappearances, albeit a fictional one. The area in the Bennington Triangle comprises some of the most beautiful landscapes you've ever seen, so it's too bad so many folks went missing there.

If you're in the area, you should definitely stop in at the General Store. The folks are friendly; the food is good, and the scenery outside is beautiful. Just maybe don't wear red...

COFFEE RECOMMENDATION: I'd suggest, if you can find it, a nice hot maple latte in honor of this Vermont tale. If you can't find one, you can use maple syrup as sweetener in a normal hot coffee or latte and that will give you a little Vermont pizzaz.

BENNINGTON TRIANGLE

Joseph Carro

A MONTH AFTER HEARING of the ghost town Somerset, Alex Venderbeck rode a Greyhound from Portland, Maine, to Vermont. The bus ride was seven hours, so he occupied his time fiddling with his camera and looking out the window as stunning scenery unfurled before his eyes in a green and hill covered tapestry. Occasionally, he dozed off, using his hoodie as a makeshift pillow against the cool glass of the bus window. The constant thrumming of the engine and changes in gears became white noise in the background of his mind. The bus was mostly empty.

His camera was nothing fancy. A Canon PowerShot point-and-shoot model, but with adjustable settings and a 50x zoom which captured incredible shots of the moon. Alex liked to fiddle with the settings and experiment but considered himself less of a photographer and more of a scenic opportunist. The beauty was already there out in the world and seldom needed artistic alterations. He knew what to look for to compose a great shot and capture it. His background in painting and sketching helped him with composition, and that strength became his most relevant skill with photography.

Recently, a professional photographer's exhibit inspired Alex. The collected photos were of ghost towns across Texas. Something about a building or town abandoned a hundred years or more commanded attention. They represented where lives had been *lived* and stories played out. Births and birthdays, weddings, funerals, passionate sex, vanilla sex, intense fights, murders, and the doldrums of everyday life all took place within the walls or on the surrounding streets. Focused properly, the lens of a camera could capture the essence of all those things.

Alex had photographed old forts and bunkers, like the one on Peaks Island in Portland, but never expected to find a *genuine* ghost town so close to home. Most ghost towns were out west where entire towns sprung up around the prospect of, well, prospecting in the 1800s.

A chance encounter with another guest at the photo exhibit alerted Alex to the ghost town in his own relative backyard. Nearby Vermont had its own rush of coal and timber at around the same time as the gold rush. Somerset was once a bustling commerce area. But after most Vermont forests had been clear cut, the cash flow for the towns dried up and everyone left. Traveling to Vermont was cheaper than heading west so hopped a bus.

The bus stopped in a quaint mountain town called Bennington. Alex stepped off a bus into what felt like a Christmas movie for the Hallmark Channel. Trees were alight in orange and red hues, and the hills were ablaze with the same beautiful autumnal colors. People dressed in jackets and jeans sipped coffee while strolling the streets. Alex shouldered his bag and sought out the nearest pub. He chanced upon a squat building with a green façade reading MADISON BREWING CO. PUB & RESTAURANT.

The pub was mostly empty when he entered so he took a stool at the bar. A portrait of a family from the 1800s hung on the wall and a football game played on the television. A short man with a chiseled jaw and a bald head approached. Alex gingerly placed his backpack on the floor by his chair.

"Can I get you anything to drink?" the bartender asked, leaning forward with the order pad, and handing over a menu.

"Yes, exactly why I'm here," Alex said, licking his lips and perusing the choices, of which there were many. He'd wanted a beer as soon as he pulled into town and hoped to get information about Somerset at the same time. Two birds with one stone. Three, if you counted the food he was about to order. "I'll take the cream ale on tap."

"Great choice," the bartender said, writing it down. "Any food?"

"I'll take the cottage pie. It looks amazing."

"Excellent choices. I'll put that in for you now. Be right back with the beer."

"Awesome."

Within minutes, the bartender brought an ice-cold beer in a glass, with just the right amount of foamy head. Alex took a swig and felt the beer rush down into his insides. He let out an appreciative sigh. The bartender looked on and smiled.

Two female servers appeared briefly at the bartender's side to put away silverware or punch something into the computer. One was a cute brunette who flashed Alex a smile before disappearing around the corner.

"You from around here?" the bartender asked.

"Nah, I'm from Maine."

"Ah, Maine is nice. What brings you here?"

"Photography."

"Oh, are you a leaf peeper? Don't they have foliage in Maine, too?"

"I'm not here for leaves. I'm looking for the town of Somerset."

The bartender's smile faded. He stopped drying the glass and leaned in close.

"Hoo-boy, the stories about that place," he said in almost a whisper, looking around. "You're not going there by yourself, are you?"

Alex chuckled at the man's seriousness and sudden interest. "Yeah, I am. I'm staying in a little motel in Woodford. Then biking to Somerset."

"Hang on," he said, and went about filling more drinks and taking orders from a cheerful-looking couple who'd just come inside and sat at the other end of the bar.

Alex sipped his beer and grinned. An air of mystery already surfacing around the ghost town made the trip to Bennington even more worthwhile. If he posted the images one at a time on Instagram, he could make an entire series out of them. Perhaps rack up more followers. He was already over 2,000 and could hopefully reach 3,000 by the end of the year.

The bartender returned about ten minutes later with a steaming cottage pie. The flaky crust was orange-yellow, and bits of mushroom and gravy oozed out of the top. Alex's stomach rumbled as the aroma reached his nostrils.

"Here you go," the bartender said. "Careful, the plate is super-hot."

Alex nodded, breaking open the top of the pie and inhaling a forkful of tender beef and vegetables.

"Now, what I was saying…" The bartender paused to make sure other patrons did not need him. "There are some things you don't want to do around here and what you said you're about to do is pretty much all of them."

"How so?" Alex mumbled through a full mouth. The food was excellent and just the type of savory, down home cooking Alex expected from a mountain pub. He washed the gravy and meat down with beer, let out a small belch, and wiped his mouth with a napkin.

"Right now, you're in what's known as The Bennington Triangle."

Alex chuckled. "What, is that like the Bermuda Triangle?"

"Exactly. Except instead of planes and boats vanishing it is people. Lots of them go into the woods and never come back out. There are three rules about the Triangle, which includes Somerset. Don't stay the night. Don't go alone. And most of all, don't wear red."

I followed his gaze to my hoodie. Yep. Red. I asked the obvious question. "Why red?"

"Simple. Most people who disappeared wore red. They've only ever found one body, and she seemed to be crushed. The rest vanished, never to be seen again."

"How many missing?" Alex asked, sipping at his beer, curiosity engaged.

"Nobody knows how many. But even the native Americans said Glastenbury Mountain is cursed, and that's at the center of the Bennington Triangle."

"What do you know about Somerset?"

"Somerset is just a bunch of bricks now, but at one point, was a small town. Everybody left because of the Bennington Beast."

Alex couldn't help but chuckle again. "Bennington has a beast, too? Dang, this place has everything."

"Nah, it's not seen around here. They named it for Bennington because we're the biggest town around, but it's seen more toward Somerset. Those who witnessed it and survived gave it conflicting descriptions."

"As in, made it up. A thing is a thing. Wouldn't their descriptions match?"

"Maybe. But buddy, I don't think you'd want to run into it yourself, no matter what."

"I'll keep that in mind," Alex said. "Can I get my check?"

"Absolutely," the bartender said. "Good luck out there, brother."

Alex paid, finished his beer, shouldered his bag, and waved goodbye to the bartender. Once outside he started walking along Route Nine.

The walk from Bennington to the motel was a straight shot of about eight miles. Alex contemplated everything the bartender had shared. Willingly. Too willingly. Alex figured small towns thrived on their lore, it would bring in suckers like himself, those hoping to spot the elusive Bennington Beast. What a goof.

Even his red hoodie came into play. Alex was certain the bartender would have warned him off blue if that was the color he wore. Nice guy but Alex felt played. Besides, wasn't a ghost town enough of a draw? The bartender had minimized that, calling it a crumbling piece of history. Alex wanted to see for himself. He was eager to take photos of the place.

The motel he booked rented out bicycles for guests, so once there, he could reach Somerset in under two hours. But first, the long slog to the hotel. An hour into his trek, a jovial man wearing glasses in an SUV pulled up with his windows down. The man wore green flannel and had his sleeves rolled up to his elbows.

"Need a ride?" the man asked.

"Well," Alex said, "that depends on if you want to drop me off at a motel in Woodford?"

"No problem. I live up there near the ski resort. I pass by that motel every morning on the way to work, and every night on the way home. It's right next to a neat little general store. Hop in," the man said, smiling.

The ride only took about fifteen minutes to roll up the mountain. Alex's ears popped several times as the man-made small talk. His name was Shane, and he was a talker. He mentioned how there were many hikers in the area, so he was used to giving rides to folks. Alex thought it best to not disclose his eventual destination of Somerset. Shane asked Alex what brought him to Woodford. Alex replied he wished to get away from city life in Portland and that he'd always loved the mountains and hills of Vermont.

"Yes, I love it here." Shane said, pulling up to the blue and white painted motel that looked put together with clapboards. "Nice meeting you," he said, as Alex opened the door to step out.

"Same to you," Alex replied, shutting the door and waving. "Thanks for the ride."

"Oh, and a word of advice," Shane said, grinning. "I wouldn't wear red around here. It's bad luck!"

"Thanks," Alex mumbled as the SUV pulled out onto the road and out of sight.

That was the second warning about red. Maybe there was something to the whole thing, but it was the only hoodie Alex brought, and while the weather wasn't exactly freezing, it was chilly. As he entered the main lobby, he saw a handful of worn-looking bicycles chained to a metal pole just outside the front door. Judging by the poor maintenance, he wondered if any would even get him to Somerset. He continued into the lobby and paid the kind old woman at the front counter. After entering his room, he set the alarm on his phone and went to sleep.

Alex woke before his alarm. He'd set it for six in the morning but was up by 5:45. He made sure he'd plugged his camera batteries into chargers the night before. They all registered green lights. Good to go. The antiquated motel room was severely outdated. It looked to Alex like Stanley Kubrick had sex with the 1980s. Wood paneling surrounded a shag carpet and an old heater. The bed was lumpy but comfortable, and the old musty smelling blanket had kept him warm through the night.

The shower ran for some time before hot water made an appearance. The water felt nice in juxtaposition to the chill morning air, and Alex looked forward to the morning ride. By the time he showered, dressed, checked his camera, and packed his bag, it was eight AM. Much later than he'd wanted to start out, but it was only a two-hour ride, so he'd be there before noon and still have plenty of time to shoot before the sun set.

Alex got the key from the old woman at the front desk for the bike and unlocked a Schwinn. He rolled down the slope of the motel driveway, noticing for the first time the Woodford General Store down the road from where he'd come the night before. A flag hoisted above the main entrance read *Open*. The rustic general store had a cozy looking front porch. If he had more time, he might have enjoyed his coffee in one of the rocking chairs on the porch.

Alex put the kickstand up on the bike and went inside. The interior was as equally cozy as the exterior. There were plenty of items for sale, knick-knacks, Vermont maple syrup and cheese, and camping staples such as instant potatoes and canned goods. Alex looked around and found the coffee. A friendly-looking man sat behind the counter reading a book.

"Morning," the man said, cordially, smiling but not looking up from the page very long. "Anything I can help you with?"

"No thanks," Alex said. "Just found what I was looking for. I need some coffee."

"Oh, yeah, we just made it," the man said. "You get the first cup."

Alex poured his coffee into the largest size cup and poured in a little cream, stirring it with a wooden stick. He reached into his pocket for some cash and put the money on the counter. He sipped and declared it good.

"What're you up to around here?" The man asked, raising an eyebrow as he took in Alex's appearance and processed the sale.

"Just doing some photography," Alex said, sipping more coffee. "Speaking of, should I be worried about bears out there?"

"Oh, yeah, I mean, the black bears are out. We had to lock up our dumpster out back because the damned things kept getting into it and strewing trash everywhere. There's a rhyme about what you should do with bears."

"Yeah?"

"If it's black, fight back. If it's brown, lay down."

"If it's white, say goodnight?" Alex finished questioning if he had it right. He heard the rhyme somewhere before.

"And if it's in transition, you should be pissing," the man said with a sudden gulp of seriousness.

Alex tilted his head. He'd never heard that part before. What did transition mean? How could an animal be in transition? Then it hit him. Hibernation. If a bear woke from hibernation, they were hungry and dangerous. Alex assumed that was what the man meant and probed no further. The grim look on the proprietor's face faded and his warm smile returned.

"Last part comes from the native Americans. All superstitious gobbledygook, I'm sure." Then he raised his eyebrows further and pointed at Alex's hoodie. "Although if you're going out dressed like that, you might have more problems than just bears around here."

"Oh, yeah, everyone keeps telling me that. Is it really that serious? Or is it more like don't walk under any ladders and don't step on any cracks?"

"All I can tell you, son, is that a whole mess of folks went missing around here."

"What happened to them?"

"Well, nobody really knows. They only found one. Looked like something massive squeezed the humanity out of her. Had to identify her by dental records because she had no *face*."

"Damn," Alex said, a little unnerved but remembering how superstitious and gossipy small towns were.

When he'd traveled to Madawaska in northern Maine years back in college, there had been a motorcycle accident and a fatality shortly before he arrived. The man driving the motorcycle had died. Everyone Alex spoke to in town had a different variation on the story. There was the decapitation version, the body hanging out of a car windshield version, and the body sliced clean in half version. That one was a twofer, sliced vertically in one, and horizontally in another.

Some towns encouraged mysteries, because it drew in curious tourists and those tourists usually came and spent money at hotels, restaurants, and gift shops. Alex felt it from the bartender and now from a proprietor. Hard to know what to believe.

"I guess I'll have to be careful," Alex said. He downed the rest of the coffee, remembered to buy a bottle of water, and before he knew it, he was cycling through Woodford on his way to Somerset.

Alex had never ventured so deep into Vermont before, especially not on a bike, but his jaw literally dropped as he cycled down route nine. Rolling hills and mountains surrounded him, and at points, a lazy fog hung over the forest canopy. Even if Somerset somehow turned out to be a wash, the trip had already been worth it for the beauty alone. Occasionally, the incline turned steep, forcing him to walk the bike or stand up and struggle to peddle. Following each challenging stretch was a sharp drop where he cruised swiftly down a road wonderfully devoid of vehicles.

At one point, Alex thought he'd somehow gotten turned around or had taken a turn somewhere he wasn't supposed to. The ride felt longer than it looked on the map. But just when he questioned his path, he encountered a sign reading *Somerset Road.* His heart soared. As soon as he turned onto Somerset Road, the pavement gave way to a packed dirt and gravel roadway. A sign in some bushes read *National Forest.* As he picked up the pace and careened down the path on the Schwinn, he heard a roaring in his right ear. Through the trees he saw the Deerfield River, which he recognized from the map. He grinned and pedaled forward. He was almost there.

Knowing he was close made the remaining part of the ride fly by quickly and soon enough, Alex pulled up to the one-room schoolhouse in the forest, right off the beaten path. Though exhausted, he'd finally reached Somerset. Or what remained. The online research he did before the trip seemed misleading. Though he stood in front of an old schoolhouse built in 1850, calling Somerset a town was a bit of a stretch. He'd passed various modern homes along the way, tucked into the trees with signs reading "NO TRESPASSING" and "PRIVATE PROPERTY" but there were no signs of an abandoned town besides the lonely schoolhouse.

The school was white with blue shutters and sat abandoned. A lone school-house was hardly worth all the time and effort he'd taken to reach the place, but as he hauled out his camera and looked through the lens at the old building, he saw its character shine through. It might not be a town, but it was the closest thing Alex was going to get to a ghost town until taking a trip out west. He photographed the building with the same energy he would have if there had been an actual skeleton of a town in place.

He shot while walking around the perimeter, using different angles and lenses. He had no reception on his phone but wanted to nab some video and phone pics for his social media followers. He took some selfies and recorded brief videos which he planned to narrate over later. Using video drained his battery quick so he was careful not to shoot too long. When he felt as if he'd shot as much as he could, he sat down, hauled out the sandwich he'd packed along with the water and looked over photos as he ate.

Alex scrolled through his selfies and spotted something in an image that made him inhale a piece of sandwich and choke. He coughed it out, but frantically stood up and backed away from the schoolhouse.

He looked at the selfie again. Just beyond his smiling face, near the rear of the old building, was a shadowy figure. The figure vacillated between black and gray, but any facial features remained elusive. Alex's heart hammered in his chest.

"Hello?! Anyone there? I hope I'm not trespassing! If I am, it wasn't on purpose!"

There was no answer. The silence only increased his nervousness. Then he heard a woman's muffled cry. She called out from somewhere in the trees beyond the schoolhouse.

"Help!"

He barely heard it. But heard it, he did. "Hello?!" Alex shouted, cautiously moving toward the back of the building where he discovered a well-worn path. With the Appalachian Trail nearby, it was probably a trailhead.

"Help, please!"

Alex moved forward, pushing away tree branches from his face and line of sight. The voice sounded clearer, but he couldn't tell where it originated from. What if it was a kid lost in the woods or something? The crying voice was warbly, as if shaking with fear. What he initially thought to be a woman's voice changed again until sounding more like that of a toddler.

Alex made his way cautiously through the brush, emerging into a clearing with old train tracks overrun by dead leaves and grass. The tracks led off into the distance. Alex thought he spotted movement so called out and continued walking.

"Are you lost? I can get you help if you need it! There are bears out here!"

Alex cringed as he mentioned the bears. He didn't want to scare whoever it was, although chances were that the child was more versed in outdoor life than he was. Back home, people labeled Alex a "flatlander," someone who lived in the city rather than the forests and hills of Maine. As Alex was about to call out again, he noticed a conspicuous absence of sound.

Birds stopped chirping, and the cries stopped. He saw no further movement ahead. The train tracks stretched into the distance where they vanished into a tunnel. He raised his camera instinctively and took a photo. The tunnel looked like something out of a postcard. The hills were alive with autumnal foliage, and the tunnel looked to be an otherworldly portal into a different realm. He took his phone out to get video footage, but the battery was dead.

"Shit," he muttered, and then sighed. It wasn't like he was getting service out there, anyway. He slipped his phone back into his pocket and was about to take a couple more photos of the tunnel when he had the sudden and very distinct feeling of being watched.

But from where? From inside the tunnel? Why not? The beauty of it all, the postcard scenery, initially kept him from even imagining something might be inside the structure's looming darkness. But it was the perfect place for something wild to watch from.

Except that was not where it came from. He sensed it came from somewhere else as a chill traveled down his neck as he trembled, feeling his DNA slipping into flight or fright. That's why the birds went silent. There was a predator! A bear? Black fight back. Except Alex wished not to fight at all. And besides, he had seen nothing.

Yet.

Alex turned and his heart stopped. The two biggest, most fearsome wolves he'd ever seen stalked him from behind, their heads low to the ground. They were about a half mile away on the tracks in the distance. His mind and heart raced.

My god. I was worried about bears, and there were wolves. Think quick.

Alex made a mental calculation as he walked hurriedly toward the tunnel, figuring if he could reach it, he could maneuver himself into a better position. maybe climb to the top ledge of the tunnel, giving him higher ground than the dangerous-looking beasts.

He fast walked and longed to break into a run, but he understood it would only cause them to do the same. Besides, he might trip because he could not help but look behind himself the entire time. Clutching his camera tight, he decided he needed to run at some point but needed to catch them off guard. He turned back fully around to get one last good look on their position and froze.

Alex blinked, trying to clear his vision, for he had to be seeing things wrong. His fear causing hallucinations. What he saw initially bordered on the impossible and then stepped several feet past that border. No longer were they a pair of wolves, but two massive grey humanoids scaling along the train tracks like spiders.

Hair still covered portions of their bodies, but much of it vanished and continued vanishing still, almost melting off. They were becoming more humanoid by the second, almost as if they were... *shapeshifting.*

They crawled toward him, fast, impossibly fast, and stared at him with featureless faces. Their wiry musculature rippled, and their gangly limbs grew longer and culminated in massive, hooked claws. As terrifying as they were as wolves, their twisting, mutating forms that changed with every step threatened to take Alex's knees out from under him.

He staggered and almost fell. His camera smacked the metal rail of the tracks, but he did not care. Break it, sacrifice it, but he had to get away! The abhorrent creatures were too close already. And getting closer!

A horrendous sound accompanied their herky-jerky movements. A mix of claws clanging on the tracks, and shifting, growing bones cracking like timbering trees. Such sounds normally made one run, but Alex found his feet planted in place, too terrified to move. Meanwhile, the beasts sped toward him like the missing freight train from the tracks.

Their speed made Alex finally move. He turned and ran the fastest he ever had in his life. When the creatures' bones settled onto a semblance of a form (what were they? Their shapes made no sense!) they cried out, squealing like a toddler's expression of delight.

The tunnel loomed in the near distance. Realizing there was no time to scramble up the hill to the top of the tunnel he aimed for the safety of darkness. Except was it safe? Were there more inside waiting? Locals told him about the Bennington Beast, but they were wrong. It was beasts, plural. At least two. Could they see him if he ran far enough into the darkness?

He thought of the old man in the store and desperately wished he had never come alone. He also thought of the rhyme. *If they're transitioning, you're pissing*. Well, he was. Or had. He did so upon first spotting the beasts. Now they had a scent to lock onto.

A truck hit him full force. For it had to be a truck. What else hit that hard? But no, it was **one** swipe. One swipe from barbed claws sliced easily through his jeans and hooked the back of his legs. The strike gave him momentum, tossing him through the air ahead of his captors. But he was not in control of the flight. By the time Alex hit the ground, he was already screaming.

He turned to look up at the beasts as they slowly approached. One still had no facial features, but the one who hooked him did. The humanoid face slowly mirrored his own, but in a creepy, AI generated way that looked slightly off, an uncanny valley of a face. Another hooked appendage pierced Alex's shoulder.

"HELP ME!" Alex wailed.

"Help me!" it repeated, mimicking its prey.

Alex continued screaming while the beasts stripped the skin from his body. As Alex faded from consciousness, he heard his own voice echoing back at him from the mouths of the two monstrosities. Once something inside him snapped with a twang, he could no longer see, but heard wet sounds of meat being torn from bone. As even his hearing faded along with his heartbeat, the last thing he heard was the creatures chanting a desperate refrain.

"Help me! Help me! Help me! Help me! Help me!"

LA MONARCA BAKERY & CAFÉ, SANTA MONICA

I HAD A TERRIBLE experience which led to the following story. But before I get to that, let me discuss this very special place as it is unrelated to the unpleasant experience. La Monarca offers authentic flavors from Mexico with a Monarch butterfly theme. The interior is very simple, with very few decorative flourishes. Chairs, tables, done. Slightly crooked legs on each? Yes. The dining space is narrow, and it is a tight squeeze when someone walks past a table to use the restroom. It is no frills décor.

But only because it does not need it. This place is all about the flavors. It is impossible not to partake of the various food items available even if one innocently goes in simply for a cup of coffee. The first thing one might notice is the intensity of the flavors in their brews. Every drink is vibrant and flavorful.

Once one considers how good the drink is, they cannot help but notice the tall glass cabinets lining the wall at the entrance. You know, the cabinets with various croissants, and other bakes goods inside? There are trays on standby, along with tongs, for one to select the different goodies they wish to purchase. From chocolate to cheese to guava options, it is impossible to choose only one which is why the trays are so large. Yes, this is an amazing taste of Mexico in a quaint space.

What about the unpleasant experience I mentioned? Before going to this shop to imagine a story, I stopped for lunch at a sandwich shop across the street. This was strategic, so I would not load up on too many of the amazing choices at this bakery.

The moment I walked into the sandwich shop; a man was screaming at a very petite, small woman who was the lone worker at the place. The man was being outrageous and there was nothing that could have elicited such a response from the man, so I was uninterested in finding out what it was. Everything changed the moment I walked in.

The moment he saw me, he shut up. I took it upon myself to ask if he was leaving or if he needed an escort. He left, mumbling under his breath. So, a real-life Ken. That was the experience. I apologized to the woman for having to endure that and she was very grateful I ordered, ate, and then went to the amazing shop across the street. But of course, that man remained in my mind.

There are some individuals who are simply intolerable. This is a story about one such man.

COFFEE RECCOMENDATION: Based on where I conceived of this, I would like to suggest an authentic Mexican drink, but I know they are not readily available. The one style of drink I occasionally see in some coffee shops is a Mexican chocolate option. so, if possible, order a Mexican chocolate latte.

THE KAREN

Paul Carro

M Y NAME IS HUCK, not Huckleberry, and I guess it all started at the Snack Mart where I fueled up on Cool Ranch Doritos and Mountain Dew. Not gas. Who can afford that? It was looking like an overnighter, so I needed life's essentials. I was not happy about the man I was about to meet with. I love ghost hunting. It's a blast man, but the guy I was about to work for was a real douche canoe.

Ghost hunting is sexy, but it does not pay many bills. My day job is at the supermarket, the regular one, not the fancy one. I bring the day job up because it is relevant. Revenant? Relevant? One's a movie and the other means it relates to my story. Anyway. At my job we get all kinds of Karens making life miserable, which then makes employees want to quit. The Karens complain about the lack of service they created by making people leave and the cycle repeats.

People have lost their minds since the pandemic and that train has permanently left the station. Those brains had one-way tickets. They ain't coming back. It will take a new generation to breed civility back into this world. Except young people aren't screwing because they are all dysfunctional and stuff from all the internet craziness.

I'm part of that generation. I just graduated from high school and decided college isn't for me. Every girl I meet asks why I am not in college, then they ditch before I get anywhere. Guess I should tell them I'm a part-time ghost host. Except I'm never on camera, I'm behind it. As in the camera, and that is where my current situation kicked in.

Here in town, we have one of the most famous haunted houses in America, the old McKendry place. While there were no confirmed murders there, there was a confirmed vanishing. Mom, pop, two girls and a boy. The whole family simply disappeared and left everything they owned behind, along with some crazy satanic drawings in many rooms in the house. Place ranks high on my spook-o-meter, and I've investigated plenty of places on my own. I have my own YouTube channel. It's just that I haven't got above twenty followers yet, but it's a start.

Since I don't date, I spend all my money on ghost hunting equipment and cameras. My videos on YouTube are professional and it led to lots of reality ghost hunting shows hiring me to tag along on their shoots. Most people live far from Maine, so production companies would fly talent in. By talent I mean the hosts. No crew. I am the crew at that point.

If it costs them less to hire me than fly in an extra person, do the math. I am paid less than a plane ticket. The hosts get stipends to eat, but I don't. Rather than hungrily watch them eat during a break in shooting, I now bring snacks along. Some hosts from the paranormal shows are cool and share their food.

Shauntelle for one. She is a new paranormal face on the scene who is as nice as she is stunning. That chick is super-hot! I could barely speak when I met her. Wait, chick is bad, right? I meant woman. Only early twenties, though, in my age range, except I can't get into bars yet.

The reason I bring Shauntelle up is to contrast her with the splooge I am about to talk about. It also ties into why I mentioned Karens earlier. Every person named Karen I know is super cool, so it bums me that somehow people settled on that name. But it is what it is. Karen's come in all shapes and sizes, except—no offense—most are old. There was a guy at my day job who had about twenty bags and asked for a carryout, but threw a fit when I started pushing the shopping cart. He demanded we leave it behind as he did not want it to scratch his car.

Twenty bags! He didn't help! He made me carry all twenty. My arms hurt for a week and the plastic cut into my hands and the guy is a... What is a male Karen called? Ken? Let's go with Ken. It's perfect because that was the name of the guy I was going to meet after the Snack Mart.

Everyone knows the guy is a tool. He's about forty and full of himself. I know some girls. I'm sorry, women, who say he is hot when they see him on TV. Editing can do wonders. They cut out a lot of this guy's bullshit.

Ken Lantern, shedding a light on the supernatural! Gag, dude. Fake name, fake teeth, fake everything. He'd have fake boobs if he could. I worked with him once before. He came for a one-day shoot for color. That's where you shoot backgrounds of the state where the haunting is. I shot him interacting with fans who were excited to see the guy from TV. But when the people left, Ken griped about how annoying the locals were. Hey, I'm one of them, pal!

He even ate a massive lobster and fried clam dinner and gave me nothing. Made me film him there at the picnic table overlooking the ocean, all while complaining about the seating. I was starving. I would have eaten the green guts stuff. You know lobsters are just sea spiders, right? It would be cool if they could shoot webs, though. Oh, and get this. Producers forbid me from talking to him. That was in the contract! He griped all he wanted but me? Could not say a word. Only from behind the camera was I allowed to speak because it was necessary for the job. Other than that, shut up!

After that day, he went on his way. I did several jobs for other ghost hosts in the meantime. (Have I mentioned I'm hard crushing on Shauntelle?) Whenever I mentioned Ken to other paranormal teams, they groaned, and shared stories of their own. Ken is not a good guy. Eventually, I got the call that Ken was returning for the actual ghost hunt. That is why I loaded up on snacks. Knew I wouldn't get a crumb from this dude, and he planned an overnight shoot.

After I got my food, I set out on the road. It was raining hard, which makes for good footage for ghost shows. Outsiders are not so great on driving on the country roads in Maine when it rains, but I'm a local, so I hauled ass. I needed to get to the house before Ken to enact my plan.

Most reality paranormal hosts are on the up and up. They want to believe, but they won't fake stuff. Not entirely at least. One show once suggested a demon was present on audio. Except I knew, from visiting the place that it was a neighbor's dog who incessantly barked. That got picked up on the audio track and the show ran with it as if a demon made itself known. I guess they need to hook viewers in the promos. But industry insiders knew Ken faked all kinds of shit. My plan was to help him along with that.

I arrived earlier than our scheduled meet time by twenty minutes, but it was already dark. Place is creepy for sure, but in all the times filming there, I never encountered anything out of the ordinary. Whoever owned the place (they did not live there though) made money off shoots such as ours. The owner kept the place intact from when the family vanished. And it remained relatively unscathed. Gives you an idea of how creepy the place is that people never looted the place.

It was the dishes left behind that were part of my plan. I felt kind of bad. It meant breaking some. What's the saying? To make progress, sometimes one must break a few eggs. Or if in the Mafia, then break a few legs? Point is you sometimes must break stuff. I planned to.

The house was remote and set deep off the road, nestled into a thick forest, as many Maine homes were. You could not see the house from the street. There was a long dirt driveway (muddy in the rain) that weaved up to the house, which made no sense. Why not make it a straight line? I never understood that part. But I pulled up. There was a carport off to one side that had partially collapsed. One side of the roof kissed the concrete inside.

There was plenty of parking in the driveway because it opened into a wide-open dirt space fronting the home. Almost like an undisciplined cul-de-sac. The house was large, but normal for the area. Two stories and an attic that was halfway there. Again, why not just add a third level at that point? It has a basement. How much storage does one family need?

The house was a yellow box of little imagination. Front door, window on either side of the front door, then one, two, three windows lining up directly overhead on the second story. Rising above even that was a pitched asphalt shingle roof with two attic windows jutting out like eyeballs watching for enemies at the gate. (Except there was no gate.)

A short porch fronted the home. Warped clapboard siding suffered peeling paint that was once white but leaned yellow in places where aged grey wood did not show through. Ken had yet to arrive. His rental car was nowhere to be seen. Out of courtesy, I always offered talent a ride from the airport, but heaven forbid that Ken ride with a peasant.

His last rental was a BMW. I expected no less this time. My banged-up Ford with the plastic wrapped broken back window was fine for me. (But also limited my dating options. Sorry, I keep bringing it up, I'm a lonely guy.)

Point was, I arrived before he did, which was perfect. Being a crew of one, I kept my equipment packed into a manageable size. My main camera had its own cushioned case. But I stashed everything else in one massive duffle bag from LL Bean. It was waterproof, snow proof, everything proof. That would come into play later. It certainly caused quite an argument with Ken, I will say that, but I'm getting ahead of myself.

I grabbed my duffle and my camera and raced inside. The way the place worked was the foyer bled straight into a stairwell leading to the second floor. To the right was the living room and to the left was a massive dining room which had its own door leading to the kitchen behind it. The kitchen looked out into the backyard. Oh, and there was no electricity. The owners figured it was better to scare overnight guests.

Entering a place alone is not my favorite thing, but I needed to set something up. First, I started with the nanny cams. The small motion activated cameras that housewives place in teddy bears to ensure the babysitters are not killing the kids and to spy on whether the husband is screwing the babysitter. The husband is always screwing the babysitter if they're eighteen or older.

Using one of my flashlights, I navigated through the house, setting up the cams in the most active rooms on the second floor. The light on my camera was much brighter than my flashlight, but I needed to save the charge until we were filming. Despite my having visited multiple times, the upstairs remained creepy, with kid toys littered everywhere and beds still perfectly made.

Timing was crucial because Ken would arrive shortly. His lateness, while inconsiderate, proved fortuitous. Despite my own agenda for the evening, I performed the part of the job they paid me for first. The cams were set. Infrared images would record to the cloud if activated by motion. With that out of the way, I scrambled downstairs to enact my insidious plan.

The fancy pants dining room housed a massive China cabinet. The homeowners did not stack the dishes; they stood them upright on transparent holders like displays at a department store. They looked expensive, and I felt bad I was going to ruin them. I admit to vandalism. I'm not proud, but I wanted to bust Ken's balls. Besides, it was Shauntelle's idea. When we shot together, she mentioned how funny it would be for me to prank Ken. She was aware of my upcoming shoot with the man.

I set my bag down and went to work. The China cabinet had a simple tiny metal hook that latched from one door onto a small nub on the opposite door. Not a hook like on fences, just a simple lift. One could flick it with a finger, and it would open. The doors were heavy enough they would not open on their own, so the lock was mostly just for show.

But the doors opening on 'their own' was my plan. I needed to help them along when the time was right. I always liked those weird metal door stops at high school. They were metal and curved into a wedge strong enough to keep heavy crash bar doors open. I stole one. Yes, I stole one. I am not perfect. And I used the stolen good to commit vandalism.

There were no legs on the China cabinet, as it had a solid bottom base. The darn thing was heavy. I put the flashlight in my mouth, then pulled the cabinet away from the wall. It was heavy, so I hurried, dropping the doorstop to the ground, then shoved it with my foot along the gap between the wall and the cabinet. Once it reached the midway point, I let the sucker go and it fell back into place, except at a lean. Not far enough to tip, but far enough that if the doors opened, the dishes would fall out.

That was the plan. The doors held but pressed against the little hook which bulged, holding back the tide of fine China that had shifted up against the glass. In the dark, the tilt was unnoticeable. My only worry was that it might crash prematurely. Next, I grabbed a spool of fishing line. I carefully tied one end around the tiny latch. The metal was so thin I would not need an upward pull. I wasn't trying to unlatch it; I was planning to snap the thing right off.

I ran the other end of the line out and cut it off at a certain length. I tied that end around a wooden handled corkscrew. It would work as a handle that I could easily find in the dark. I set the corkscrew down on the floor just inside the door. From there, I went to the foyer to wait.

Normally I would wait outside for the host, but it was pouring, so I waited inside. He would see my car and know I was there. On top of all the man's other charms, he was late. I was trying to reserve the charge on my phone's battery because sometimes I used its camera as a backup on shoots.

I grew tired of standing in the foyer, so stepped into the living room and sat on a dusty couch. It smelled rank but was soft. That's all my butt needed. I left my duffle bag on a table running the length of the wall in the foyer. Once upon a time, it would have had a dish for keys. Maybe people would have also taken off their shoes and staged them underneath the table. Now it was bare, so I put the bag on it before sitting in the living room. I left the camera case there as well. The camera I kept with me, ready to go.

Finally, the door opened. It was dark so I could not see the man, only knew he had to be there, but he did not even bring a flashlight. Like I said, douche canoe! Can't even bring his own light. I called out.

"Don't be frightened. I'm here," I said before remembering the rule. No speaking unless behind the camera.

I went into work mode, shouldering my cam. I looked through the viewfinder and turned it on. Yikes! Dude's eyes went wide and white in the camera, like a deer crossing the road at night. There was plenty of that around these parts. I switched the light on, and he raised a hand to block the light. Once he lowered the arm, I knew it was going to be a long, pretentious night.

Butt-munch wore an ascot! An honest to goodness ascot. Who wore those? It was bright red with an odd pattern, likely paisley. I kept the camera mounted on my shoulder so I could talk with his highness.

"Welcome Ken. I already set up two motion cameras upstairs. They work by remote control and send the feeds to my phone if anything moves. They are in the most haunted areas of the house. Do you want to start there?"

The man nodded. From a distance his head bobbed weird, like crooked. I chalked it up to the annoying ascot. Then the guy climbed the stairs in the dark. Idiot! No light. Dude stomped upstairs without a flashlight. He did not wait for me, so I had to rush to catch up. I noticed he was soaking wet from the rain, so that provided me with some joy. I assumed he was in location scouting mode, because there was no way he would appear on camera in such a state. I filmed anyway, figuring I could share the drippy McGee look of his with other paranormal hosts. My filming would remain loose until he was ready or until I led him to the dining room. Whichever came first.

I noticed he did not even have an EMF reader on him. So annoying. Did he expect to borrow mine? That was rude and presumptuous of him. My services included equipment rental. The price the producers paid only covered the camera, and two remote ones. If they wanted other stuff, they needed to say so in advance. I did not want to get stiffed. Yes, I had my EMF and other normal paranormal equipment in my bag, but that was a phone call and the promise of a payment away. Unless Ken had his own package ready to go in his rental car, then it was going to be a boring shoot.

The equipment was necessary for paranormal shows. The flashing lights and active meters provided a visual stimulus for viewers in the absence of any genuine ghosts caught on camera. No way was I going to cough up my personal stash for free.

We reached the hallway at the top, and suddenly I felt a chill. Like a real one. Strange. I felt no such chill when I set up the motion cameras. Then it hit me. I never heard Ken close the door when he came in. Maybe I would have noticed if I wasn't running to catch up to the reckless guy, to make sure he did not fall. I was not a fan but didn't want him to break his neck or anything.

Ken looked both ways. His head bobbled again, and I felt suddenly bad. He moved like a great aunt of mine who suffered from Parkinson's. Shaking off my feeling bad for the guy vibes, I steeled myself to continue with my plan.

We bypassed the middle room and went to the best-known hot spot in the place—the girls' room. Two sisters shared that room. The parents lived in the center room and a boy lived in the room to the right, another hot spot. He walked straight toward the louvered sliding closet doors, staring straight at them.

The air was frigid. I wondered if he acted high and mighty because he possessed some actual spiritual juju. He knew exactly where to go and already found a cold spot. Shame he was a dick. Because the vibe felt weird, I tightened my shot to capture any creepiness that might pop out. He had two hands, I had one, so another annoying factor from the dude. Leave it to the peon to open the doors.

I opened the closet door, sliding one side open, then the other. A Parchesi board game sat perilously on the top shelf, various clothes dangled in a mess on wire hangers, no plastic ones in sight. A creepy doll or two occupied the bottom of the closet, along with a few stuffed animals.

It felt creepy, which was weird. It felt fine when I placed the nanny cam. Dude never said a word, just turned to leave the room. Tool! I followed as he went to the boy's room. We repeated the earlier interaction, except this time the boy's closet was a single solid door and the items inside were of the toy truck and sports varieties. A baseball cap fell from a peg when I threw the door open. It scared the crap out of me, but I tried not to show it to good old Ken.

The man stood there and stared into the closet. Weird. I wondered if he was trying to pull off a con of his own with me. No. I was going to get him first. From the safety of my camera, I aimed the light right at his face to get his attention and stated my case.

"Before you got here, I sensed some strange stuff in the dining room. Do you want to go check it out?"

"Yes," he said simply, and led the way.

He headed down the stairs and I realized he had not dried himself off yet and it was cold. I felt for the guy and was going to ask if he wanted to break and take care of all that, except we were almost in the dining room. It was now or never.

I feel the need to clarify my plan. It was to make the guy drop a dookie right there. That was the goal. I wanted to see the look on the poser's face when all hell broke loose. However, it was more than that. Depending on how he responded, I could use it on my channel to gain followers. Nothing like a practical joke played on a famous paranormal host.

And on the more serious side of my occupation, I could note his response. If he tried to play it off for the cameras as a real supernatural event to raise his own stock, then I could nail him as a fraud. Not officially, I needed the jobs from the cable stations and streamers, but at least within the community. We could separate the frauds from the legit hunters.

He entered and moved to the center of the dining room, looking around confused. There was no closet to open, so he simply stood there like a tool. He scrunched his face as if trying to figure out why we were there. I aimed the light right back at him again, this time intentionally blinding him momentarily. That was all I needed. I bent and grabbed the corkscrew handle.

With a yank, the doors thrust open, and dishes poured out. They must have weighed a decent amount because they fell quickly, smashing to the floor. I leaped in fright at the noise, despite knowing it was about to happen bug kept my camera on the man the entire time.

He never flinched! Total dick move! Not only did I not capture the 'flying dishes' on camera because I filmed Ken, but he gave no reaction. None. Once the dust settled, Ken simply walked back toward the entrance, exiting out the door. I stepped aside and checked the floor, leaping when one more dish fell out and smashed.

I made a mess and had nothing to show for it. I felt bad. That was it. I had it with the guy. We had not even filmed the show yet, and he had not even told me the plans for the shoot. Then he ignored my ghostly flying dishes! Plus, I made a mess that would require an explanation to somebody. I was plenty angry at Ken, but mostly at myself. I did not even want to take the job, but I got greedy.

I charged into the foyer, already hot. What I witnessed made me even hotter. Dude was rummaging through my duffle bag! He was trying to get my EMF equipment, or flashlights, or whatever else he needed. I stepped up and zipped it closed.

"Back off! This is my stuff. You're so unprofessional. You know other ghost hunters hate you, right?"

"Yes," he said, the man of many words. Only then did I notice the strange cadence of his voice, but I ignored it, too angry at the attempted theft.

Then Ken started up the stairs. I immediately lost him in shadows. But I would not follow this time. I was done. He obviously took one of my flashlights because he ascended okay. All that I could see of Ken as he crested the stairs was his legs. I called out, careful to ensure he registered my anger.

"I'm out. And I expect to be paid. I'll come back for the nanny cams tomorrow. Your producer did pay for those, so they are yours for the night, but I'm out. You're creepier than any ghost, you know that?"

I was talking to the air. Cold air. The door **was** open. Idiot never closed it, but I slammed it as I trudged to the car in the rain. See? A lot of Karens in the world, or in this case a Ken. I dumped my stuff in the trunk, then got in the car and drove away without looking back.

Add speeding to my list of offenses. I was pissed, wondering whether I would get paid. I also worried about how much clout the guy had. Could he get me cancelled? Mostly, I was mad that he did not spook. Maybe Ken was the professional and did not scare because he knew the fix was in. Why did I try to scare the guy? It would have been great if it worked, but it did not. I was frustrated.

That is why I was speeding. Encountering cop cars in Maine was rare. Everything is too remote so chances of passing one are slim. Seeing three cruisers with lights flashing as I zoomed down the street caught me off guard. I hit the brakes and hydroplaned for a second before mercifully coming to a stop.

Something was wrong beyond my speeding. There were other lights. Red ones. Fire trucks, plural and an ambulance. A burning smell lingered in the air. I got out, something bad was going on. I wondered whether to grab the camera, but the next thing I knew, something blinded me. An officer aimed a beam at my face. I wondered if my eyes glowed white like deer. I threw an arm up. Great. Sympathy for Ken once I realized how sucky it was for me to light him up earlier.

"Hands!" the officer said.

I raised them, terrified of why the officer was asking. He moved closer and checked me out before identifying himself as Officer Bill Nelson. He had a partner, Samantha, nearby and called her over. They grilled me about what I was doing there and scolded me for going so fast. Once they realized I was an idiot local teen, they lost interest in me.

Samantha said I could go but do so carefully, as someone else had not been so lucky. The wreck had to be over the side of the road, down a steep embankment into the woods because a tow truck was pulling the car back up to the road.

They said I could go but not that I had to go, so I stepped closer to watch the show. The cable attached to a vehicle pulled slowly. An officer leaned over the ledge, guiding the cable up. Various people yelled occasionally, trying to communicate to get the vehicle up to street level. A flatbed tow truck separate from the one with the winch stood ready. It must have been an awful wreck if they needed the flatbed. Now I was curious.

Totaled. The black metal mess they pulled to street level was barely recognizable as a car. No way anyone could survive that. Samantha stood near me, and I asked her what happened to the occupants. She mentioned there was only one, but they already took him to the morgue. He was deceased. It took the jaws of life to free him.

Sad. It was still raining and there was nothing left to see, so I was about to return to my vehicle when something struck me. The wreck was barely a car anymore, but one detail emerged while being lifted onto the flatbed. A BMW insignia. What were the chances? I asked Samantha if it was a guy driving. She nodded. *Fifties*? She did not answer, but curiosity crossed her face. I couldn't believe I was asking if the deceased had an ascot.

"Did you know him?" she asked me.

I could not answer. It was impossible. He was still in the house, and I was speeding. No way he could have gotten past me. And if he did, there was no way that many emergency vehicles were already there. The accident had to have happened some time ago to be so far along in the recovery process. It had to be someone else.

"Don't know his age. The accident decapitated him. We still can't find his head." Samantha said. Then she looked past me toward my car. "Is that your bag?"

I turned. My duffle bag was on the street! My trunk remained closed. Impossible. Then the bag jerked! I was uncertain which of us jumped the highest.

"Why is it moving? Bill!" Samantha called to her partner.

"Is that yours, kid?" Bill asked, drawing his weapon, and advancing.

Samantha did the same. The bag jerked and twitched. Something was moving inside.

I could not find my legs, but I found my voice. "It shouldn't be there. It was in the trunk."

Samantha raised an arm to make sure I stayed behind them. No worry there. I finally found my legs and moved forward. Lightning struck, making me leap again. The rain suddenly felt oppressive. Bill leaned down, unzipped the bag, and jerked away in fright, firing his gun off into the woods. All the other officers drew their weapons and came running. Things got crazy. Someone threw me face down on the road, but it only gave me a better view of that which stuck partially out of the bag.

Ken's head! Eyes open wide in surprise.

Except what made me leap, and what made the officer shoot, was how Ken's closed eyes shot open when the officer unzipped the bag! I saw it as clear as day and would have shot my gun if I had one as well. The police cuffed me and took me to the police station.

Detective Mills set the written statement on the table. He was a serious looking black man well past retirement age who grew more serious the further along the statement he read. His salt and pepper hair offered as much gravitas as his crisp suit. His patent leather shoes reflected his frown. He looked at Hutch, who sat across the metal interrogation table.

"That's quite some story you wrote," Mills said.

"You said to be thorough," Hutch said.

"Could have done without your relationship woes," the detective said.

Hutch's leg bounced a mile a minute. "I need to pee."

"Third time since you got here," Mills said. "You nervous?"

"Hell yes! Didn't you read my statement?"

"Afraid of being found guilty?"

"No. I already admitted to stealing, speeding, and vandalism. I'm guilty."

"I know you are. I just cannot figure out how and when you got the head in the bag," Mills said, leaning in, looking into the kid's eyes.

Hutch met the man's gaze. "I didn't put it there. I could not put it there, especially because I did not even know it was missing."

"You know we looked at your tapes, right?"

Hutch bolted upright in his seat. No, he did not know. That was news. Mills reached down to a chair off to his side and produced a tablet and a flash drive. He made a show of injecting the drive into the tablet. He then tapped a few things and turned the tablet to face Hutch.

The screen showed Hutch clear as day touring the house, but no one was on camera! Every word Hutch said was audible, but there was no sign of Ken. The crash of dishes off-screen startled Hutch anew as they hit the ground. That was an important period of filming. Hutch kept Ken in his viewfinder, hoping for a money shot that never came. But now on the screen there was no Ken!

"Impossible!" Hutch said.

"As you keep saying."

"You think I caused his crash?" Hutch said.

"You admitted to hating the man."

"I did. I do. He's a splooge. But how did I do it? Run him off the road? No. He was a Karen, but I wanted to expose him, not kill him," Hutch said.

"Which is why that makes this all so tough," Mills said.

Hutch raised his hands, awaiting more information. He wondered what the detective meant. Hutch emphasized his hands once again.

Mills shook his head. "Ken's rental car has an emergency reporting system. It went off when he crashed. We know the exact time the accident occurred. It matches the footage of when you shopped in the Snack Mart. Also, there are brake marks on the road that line up to where deer tracks emerged from the roadside. Not to mention the deer carcass. Man hit a deer, plain and simple. Went off-road and hugged a tree. Upon impact, he acquainted himself with the windshield, which decapitated him. There are no other tire marks, no other signs of vehicles involved. It pains me to say you are not guilty."

"I have to pee," Hutch repeated.

"Still nervous even after I gave you your walking papers?"

"Yes. Because he was there, in the house. And since I wrote the pages you requested, and in the time that you read them, certain things came back to me. Some things made no sense. Ken was dripping wet, but I never slipped in his wake. He left no discernable trail of water behind. And he never dried himself. Ken is vain. Why keep the water-logged look? And his head, it moved weird. I thought it was Parkinson's."

"And you think it was what? A ghost? Given your occupation, I could see you trying to make something of this."

"The bag was moving. Your own officers saw it. The head opened its eyes!"

"I have their statement. The officers believe the rain could have caused the corpse's eyes to open if they were ever closed at all. The officers appear confused."

"Confused or frightened?" Hutch asked., receiving no response. "The bigger issue is when I caught Ken going into my bag, it wasn't to take something out. He was putting something in! I never saw his head. The man had his back to me and was leaning down. Then he went upstairs into the dark. Also, I never saw his car in the driveway. I didn't think to look for it, but now I remember it was not there, I basically did a donut getting out of there. No other car blocked my way, and the carport is damaged."

Mills' voice dropped to a whisper, maybe trying to avoid microphones. "The officers wisely realized they were confused. No way that bag was moving. What? A head was trying to chew its way out? Look. This paranormal host who died is a Hollywood type. That makes headlines. We already have a haunted house that draws looky-loos. How much heat do we want to bring down on our little town? Deer meets car. Simple. You walk. If something else gets in the mix, well, we need to hold someone responsible. Do you understand?"

Hutch did but did not. He nodded anyway, which resulted in an unlocking of cuffs. Just like that, Mills exited, but also left the door open. Hutch walked out into the hall. There were no other officers in sight. It was getting late. He kept walking until he found a front door. It was locked. He turned and his face instinctively found a camera.

A buzz sounded, and the door opened. He was free. He stepped out into the rain and discovered they had parked his car curbside at the front. The detective always planned to let him go, no matter what he had to say.

Hutch went to his car and threw up. It washed away into the gutter. He still had to pee but figured he could hold it until he got home. When he arrived home, Hutch jumped into the shower (peeing there) and tried to wash away the memories. He was done. He was never going back to the place. Screw his cameras.

Wait! His cameras were still there. Rushing naked from the shower, he stumbled to his desktop and fired it up. He pulled up the cams which fed into the cloud. There would only be files if something activated the cameras. There were files. He clicked on them. He watched himself enter the rooms, filming a man who was not there.

Just like on the tablet, there was nothing there. Ken walked around alone. Enough. It was all too much. He needed sleep. He turned to go to bed when he heard the ping. One camera started filming! But filming what and activated by what? He stared at the familiar angle of the girls' room.

Nothing at first, just motion near the edge of the frame, enough movement to start it up. Then Hutch thrust his hands over his mouth, stifling a scream. It was pointless. The scream caught in his throat. It would not come out, he could not move, could not fathom what he was witnessing. A girl appeared first, playful, racing into view of the camera before looking back off camera as if scolded. She reached out to a hand off screen.

Another hand reached into the frame and took hers. Then two girls holding hands entered the frame. The second girl held the hand of a grown man who walked into view, all in the sick-green of a night-cam. They kept walking across the girls' room until a boy came into view, holding the other hand of the adult. The man, who appeared minus a head, led the children into the closet. After a moment, the camera stopped. No more motion.

Hutch reached for the mouse with shaky hands. He dragged the file to the trash icon. The man was horrible as far as Hutch knew, was a real Karen. But then again, sometimes people are going through things that others don't realize. Maybe things aren't always as they seem.

As near as Hutch could tell, the man was leading the children somewhere safe. The last act of a horrible man, one who found kindness at least in death. The detective was correct. Was it fair to bring so many people to the old McKendry place just so they could haunt the dead?

Hutch clicked on the trashcan icon again and emptied it. With another click, he disabled the cameras. They would record no more. If the kids' parents were roaming the home looking for their children, Hutch wished not to see it. He hoped Ken was not a Karen and led the children to somewhere peaceful.

As for Hutch, his ghost hunting days were over. He planned to 'ghost' any producers reaching out to him and would not even follow up or explain. Like a climber who finally reached the world's tallest peak, Hutch had reached the zenith of his occupation but disliked what he found. Hutch was done. He would ghost hunt no more, for there was nothing left to prove.

Then he went to bed but did not go to sleep.

SPRING HILL STARBUCKS, MOBILE, ALABAMA

IN MOBILE, ALABAMA, THERE is a small neighborhood on the outskirts of downtown Mobile that is known as Spring Hill. It's a suburb, and it's only about twenty minutes from Spring Hill to get to downtown Mobile. Spring Hill Starbucks sits in a lot next to a chain restaurant I frequented called Hibachi, and right across the street is a strip mall containing a Waffle House, a Zaxby's Chicken Tender restaurant, and a massive car wash.

I worked at Starbucks when I first arrived in Mobile. I no longer work there and by the time you're reading this, I will have moved up to Vermont to stay for an indeterminate amount of time.

The inside of this particular Starbucks boasts a large central long table with power outlets on the underside of the actual table. The people are kind, and the employees and store manager are all very good at what they do, and some of the nicest people you could work with.

I spent a lot of my work breaks writing this story there. I had told this exact story to several of my co-workers, as a variation of this tale happened to me as a child up in Maine. Telling my co-workers reminded me of the horror surrounding that strange day picking apples and the weird men with the mechanical movements.

To this day, my siblings remember the same thing I do, and we're still not sure what happened. We probably never will.

COFFEE RECOMMENDATION: This story evokes images and sensory cues from fall, and especially deals with apples. May I suggest a hot caramel apple spice? It will pair well with this story.

SECRET TREES

Joseph Carro

PEOPLE OFTEN BELIEVE IN the craziest things regarding conspiracy theories. I'm not against wanting to believe in certain things myself, but there is a fine line between blind faith and being duped. One should also note how not all conspiracies are equal. Some are bonkers. Excuse me, patently absurd. Wouldn't want to offend the wackjob leaning folks out there. But many so-called theories can easily be disproven. Those should be called what they are. Lies.

Which fall into the untruthful category? Easy. That the earth is flat. (Hey, the 14th century called, and they want their schtick back.) How about those who say that one half of the remaining Beatles died decades ago? (Ironic if Paul is the last to go.) Or how about believing that fluoride in the water grows tentacles on one's forehead or something like that? (Even those who agree fluoride in the water is bad cannot agree on what it is doing to people.) The list of absurdities goes on forever. We haven't been on the moon? Sorry buddy, been there trashed that. False flags? False. There are not enough crisis actors in the world to fill the roles required for the obscene amount of national tragedies in recent years. Besides, actors are desperate. There is no way they would leave the gig off their resume. Actors would put their "scenes" on their socials for all the world to see.

And some conspiracies can prove harmful to society as a whole. An example is some individuals believing any celebrities or elected individuals are kings, or worse, gods. Politicians care about no one. Nobody! Even if they once upon a time did, (and they don't) the dark side of the force takes them one by one. But keep coughing up that cash to grifters. Just understand, they do not care. To them, people are nothing more than ATMs with no withdrawal limit. That is all. When folks are down on their luck, the anointed ones will not come to the rescue. Especially since they crafted the very policies which led to people's desperate situations.

Other conmen have learned what politicians understand, there is money in them there conspiracies! A growing industry of conspiracy theory peddlers is maddening to regular people who just want to make it through a hard workday and enjoy a sandwich and a beer. The embrace of such absurd concepts also confuses much of the population. The sheer zaniness is difficult for normal people to understand, especially logical thinkers who traffic in science and facts rather than speculation and make believe.

But like the broken clock that sometimes nails it, occasionally a conspiracy theory pans out. And once a theory (no matter how crazy it was) proves true, it gains a foothold in the public consciousness. Like a dam that breaks, a flood of curiosity will open many people's minds to other absurd possibilities. And as more former non-believers wade into the conspiracy theory waters, those who were already splashing around go even deeper. Once conspiracies go mainstream it forces some individuals to gravitate toward much wilder garbage.

Some conspiracy theories have gone mainstream if for no other reason than they are scientifically workable. Take cryptids. While many urban legends about such things are far-fetched, (the Mothman?) they remain at least biologically viable. More and more people have come around about the mostly bipedal beasties. And spirits? Get your spirits here! Ghosts have also gained a toehold in the collective consciousness. Throw a stick and one might hit a paranormal team filming a new TV show.

But one conspiracy reigns supreme over all others, and it is one I am familiar with. Many would say it has legs because it has crossed generations. The big one is UFO sightings. This one has it all: sightings of crafts moving in impossible ways, little grey (not green) men, abductions, cattle mutilations, and crop circles. (With some anal probing thrown in for good measure.) As recording devices have grown more ubiquitous, recordings of events once only talked about have amplified the possibilities that humans are not alone.

The government recently released a stunning report about the phenomenon, though renamed them UAPs (a turd of a name). As if a conspiracy itself, the world yawned when the government admitted (admitted!) the existence of UFOs. Maybe because of COVID and everything else, the report fell as flat as some believe the earth is. UFOs have gone so mainstream that many feel comfortable discussing them without fear of being handed a tinfoil hat.

There is, however, a separate conspiracy related to those who speak of having had UFO experiences. Many of the individuals who speak out about their terrifying encounters are subjected to a second round of visitation but not in the form of a ship. While the initial UFO encounters are spoken of widely in public, the second type of visit so frightens witnesses that they often clam up about their initial encounter. (And don't bother asking questions about the second visitation.) The creepy visitors appear in pairs and confront people when they are alone and at their most vulnerable. It only takes one visit from the mystery men to silence witnesses.

The silencers are at the forefront of their own conspiracy with people wondering whether they are terrestrial, or something extra. No one knows if they are from the government or from somewhere else. Because people are hesitant to talk, details remain sketchy regarding the creepy twin figures. The information gathered on the subject makes little sense as descriptions of the mysterious beings vary wildly. Like the inability of people to agree on what fluoride in water does, there appears to be no consensus on what the individuals look like other than one thing—the color of their clothes.

Black.

It is through the prism of such an encounter that I discovered the greatest conspiracy of all time. One that is more devastating and affects more people than all others combined. Though seldom discussed, my theory affects individuals constantly. Daily, weekly, monthly—their entire lives. It is a conspiracy theory that I firmly believe in because I have experienced it. There is no escaping it for many, no matter where people turn. What is it? Well, I'm getting ahead of myself. Let me tell you what led me to such a devastating discovery.

I witnessed a UFO when I was four. Ask anyone what they remember from such a young age, and most will remember nothing. At four, the cupcake of a brain still bakes in the muffin pan. Age five is where the good stuff begins. That I maintain a crystal-clear memory from such a young age signifies how spectacular the event was.

At the time, I lived in Lewiston, Maine, with my mother and my younger brother, Freddy. (Sis was on the way, but none of us knew it yet.) The fourth floor apartment offered a spectacular view of a local bread making company called Country Kitchen. As a bonus, a slight head turn from our dumpy place provided an epic view of the Lewiston Pawn Shop. The smell of baking bread haunted my dreams because we often went to bed hungry. My mother tried her best, but food was scarce and healthy calories were even scarcer.

One night, the smell woke me. The room felt warm, so I climbed out of bed, seeking the cool balm of the bedroom floor on the bottoms of my feet while placing my forehead against the equally cool glass window. Stars winked vividly in the distance. Among the sea of lights, one stood out. The star was too bright. And too close. Did it just move?

The light grew increasingly larger, careening erratically through the sky. It took time to understand how close it was because the angle was off. The backdrop of the night sky lulled me into thinking the object was one of its own, a twinkler that was part of a greater show. But soon, the object shifted in flight enough for me to glimpse a metal pod about as big as a car careening toward me.

For a moment I wondered whether I had sleepwalked onto railroad tracks. Was a train barreling down on me? For that was how fast it moved, and how bright its lights were. Except there was no honking horn warning me off the tracks. This object traveled in silence with great stealth. My room filled with a bright light, and I shrank back from its glow, terrified even at age four. The light blinded me. The world went white.

I woke with a start. The bakery had really kicked in, but the smell only soured my stomach. It was morning, and my mother cradled me. Eventually, I noticed the prize in my lap. An unhealthy amount of vomit for a four-year-old boy. I cannot say the sickness related to the sighting, but I could not discount it.

Kids are blabbers at that age, so I told everyone what I'd seen. As an adult, I can recognize the truth behind the sighting if for no other reason than I didn't even know what a UFO was at that age. I owned a plush ALF, but never thought of the toy in alien terms. He was simply a cat-chasing Muppet on that funny show I did not fully understand. My circle of people was small at four, so when I visited my grandmother, I spilled all the UFO tea.

"Oh, wow," my grandmother said, humoring me. "Just like ALF!"

In response, I pulled the string on my ALF plushie. The toy demanded we go check out the fridge. Grandma lit up.

"Great idea," she said.

We raced to the kitchen, where I opened the fridge and stared at the delicious contents. She'd look on and laugh. I sometimes wondered why we were eternally hungry when my grandma had so much. I wondered why she did not share the food, but later in life I learned it was for show. She stocked up for us grandkids when we visited at the expense of herself and her own food needs.

It also never struck me until later in life that she almost never ate around me. When I asked grandma why, she mentioned she wasn't hungry. I would later learn she ate whatever I left behind. The scraps of my unfinished meals. It also explained why us grandkids always visited one at a time. She could only afford so much.

While at the fridge with grandma, I bathed in the cool air, which helped ease the itching in my arm that arose every time I spoke about the UFO event.

The same morning after the UFO sighting, I discovered a bump just under my skin which itched immensely. Worse even than my childhood bouts with poison ivy exposure. It took years for my mother to finally catch on to how often I scratched my arm. Concerned, she checked my arm out when she caught me scratching more than normal. She declared it a cyst or a fatty deposit. (We limited doctor visits to near-death experiences; otherwise, we were on our own with home remedies.) Mom asked how much it hurt.

"It itches sometimes," I said. "Like mosquito bites." I downplayed the discomfort because I understood the fear in my mother's eyes. Anything more serious meant medical bills.

"Well, don't pick at it. I'm sure it'll go away on its own, but it won't if you keep irritating it."

"Okay."

Except it never went away. At least it never went away on its own.

Years later in the 1990s I decided to go exploring and took Freddy with me. We lived in an old farmhouse on the outskirts of Lewiston then. Our family had grown, I had a sister now, but as our family grew, our financial situation worsened. We lived in the sweet spot of grungy city and rural forests and backroads. Exploring our neighborhoods sometimes resulted in someone taking pity on us kids and giving us a snack.

Mom was single and tried to provide for us, but we were short on food a lot. My grandma brought things as often as she could, but she was getting older and having difficulties driving. Luckily, there was a farmer down the road named Tom who was tall, kind, and if he weren't so much older than my mother, she might have dated him. He made his interest in my mom known, and she made her disinterest known.

I liked him, anyway. Tom had a thick Maine accent and said he lived up near Calais most of his life, but inherited farmland where we lived. He sold produce at a Maine grocer called Blackie's. Tom was a kind man who would bring us paper bags full of seasonal vegetables. Sometimes, Mom would cook for him. On those nights I pretended, if only for an evening, that Tom was our dad (because I did not know who mine was) and we would all laugh and have a grand time. Because Tom had given up on dating mom, there was no awkwardness. He was merely happy to spend time with us all. We laughed a lot, like a real father and family would.

Tom undoubtedly felt bad for us *city folk,* with Mom not having a husband and us not having a father. Sometimes, he gifted us a little meat when things were extra lean. Mom would then make a dish that she referred to (even at our young ages) as 'shit on a shingle' which was canned chipped beef and gravy served over toasted bread. When things were even worse, and we didn't have the money for the chipped beef, she used canned peas and mixed it in with the gravy and called it 'crap on a board.'

In those days, we ate a lot of processed and canned foods, and so even to this day, me and my siblings prefer canned veggies over fresh. Low-quality snacks and cereals, too. Junk food is in our DNA. But there were a few fresh foods I couldn't resist. Some of my favorite gifts from Tom were fresh grown tomatoes as big as my fist. I drenched them in whatever dressing we had around the house. My favorite was ranch. Apples were another favorite treat when Tom had some to spare.

Imagine my delight that day when Freddy and I went on our adventure and stumbled upon an abandoned apple orchard about a quarter of a mile from our farmhouse. Better yet, it fronted a beautiful waterfall which normally would have drawn all our attention, but we were so hungry that all we saw was red. As in apples.

The orchard produced some of the brightest, reddest, juiciest apples I'd ever tasted. The trees looked somehow regal, with strong roots sinking deep into the earth. That day, Freddy and I ate as many as we could, relishing the satisfying crunch and tart sweetness that was better than any candy we'd ever had. Our bellies full, we rested under the trees, listening to the rush of the waterfall with apple cores strewn around us. Upon returning home, I made Freddy promise not to tell anyone.

They were our secret trees.

After a few weeks, I eventually worked up the courage to tell my mom about the orchard. I feared she would disapprove of my wandering so far, especially dragging my brother along. As I explained everything, I mentioned how they blew Tom's apples out of the water, handing her one from my last trip as proof. When she took a bite, her eyes grew wide and asked how I'd found them and if there were any buildings around or fences or signs.

"Are you sure it's not someone's property, Finn?"

"No, mom! I swear! It's hidden back from the road in the woods. There're no houses or anything, and there's, like, just a cliff with a waterfall."

"A waterfall?!"

She balked at that part, believing I exaggerated. Waterfalls were not unheard of in Maine, but the Androscoggin River, flowing between Lewiston and Auburn, only had one waterfall everyone knew of, and that was near the mills. The Lewiston side offered a cascade of brown-green frothy water. Our house was a few miles downstream where the water ceased to churn, instead rolling gently by while appearing less polluted than upriver.

"Well, just be careful," she finally said, looking me in the eye to make sure I understood. "Take some shopping bags and take your brother and sister and bring back what you can. We can certainly use the extra food."

"Okay, Mom," I said enthusiastically since I wasn't getting in trouble. "We'll get a bunch. There are still so many!"

"Well, don't ruin your appetite, either. Dinner's going to be ready in a couple of hours. We're doing beans and hot dogs tonight."

"Okay, Mom," I replied, half-listening. I was already running upstairs and yelling for Freddy. His full name was Frederick, but I enjoyed calling him Freddy instead. He liked it, too, because it reminded him of Freddy Krueger. He dressed up once as Freddy on Halloween, and the nickname stuck. At that age, Freddy Krueger was horrifying to us, but he was also cool, and we often bragged to the other kids at school that mom allowed us to watch *Nightmare on Elm Street*. That year, I was eleven years old. That made Freddy seven, and our sister, Krissy, was six.

I found Krissy in the living room watching *Darkwing Duck*. It was her favorite.

"Krissy," I said. "Do you want to pick some apples with me and Freddy?"

Krissy smiled from ear to ear with no hesitation and shouted, "yay!"

"I'll take that as a yes."

Even though she was my annoying little sister, her smile was infectious. I grinned at her excitement while feeling proud of myself for discovering the secret trees and the bounty of the apples. For once, we had something to call our own, something that could keep us from eternal hunger.

Even better, I was the one who discovered it. We had no father figures other than Tom in so long that I felt as if I graduated, taking on the role, if only partially. I was helping provide for the family where our biological father failed. Over the years, men came in and out of our lives (those who mom dated) but none ever stayed. Some were abusive, verbally, and physically. Tom was the exception. I treasured him and thought about how I might eventually share the secret trees with him.

I helped Krissy dress while Freddy put his coat and shoes on, running up and down the hallway in excitement. Though sunny, it was autumn, so once we finally dressed for the weather, I handed each of my siblings a large paper bag, and we marched up the road toward the orchard.

Freddy ran on ahead and then back to us again every so often, and Krissy skipped next to me, humming the *Darkwing Duck* theme song. We didn't see any cars. People had little reason to be out that way. I once walked six miles each way to bring formula from the grocery store for my mother when she unexpectedly ran out. It was a long walk for a boy, and lots could have gone wrong, but I eventually made it back with the formula, and I'd always felt a semblance of pride about it.

Not nearly as much pride as I felt thinking about how we were about to fill our empty bags with a juicy bounty.

About a half mile up the road, I made my siblings stop, and we stared up at the wall of trees. Birds flew from somewhere deep inside the forest and then off into the horizon. The forest seemed dark and impenetrable from where we stood. Had I not already been there, I never would have guessed there was an actual orchard nestled within. I wondered how often people went about their daily commutes without seeing hidden treasures just out of sight.

"The apples are just through these trees, okay?" I said, looking at my siblings, who nodded in reply.

"Let's get... dangerous," Krissy said, furrowing her brow. I laughed.

"Yes, let's get dangerous. Okay, we're going to jump over this ditch." Krissy and Freddy nodded again.

"I'm gonna' eat so many apples," Freddy said, licking his lips, no doubt reliving his last trip to the orchard.

"Yeah, but don't eat too much. Mom's making dinner."

Freddy said nothing and jumped over the ditch in response. Krissy couldn't jump very far, so I placed my hands under her armpits and lifted her over the ditch. Then, I jumped over it.

When we were all safely across, we took our time walking through the tree line before emerging into the magical clearing that reality seemed to have forgotten. Dozens of trees bristled with fresh red apples. The ethereal waterfall positioned directly behind the last wall of trees by the cliff's edge provided a soothing soundtrack to our adventure. The air was crisp and hinted at the coming winter. Krissy and Freddy ran forward, giggling and grabbed for the low hanging fruit.

"Don't pick up any rotten ones," I said. "There are plenty that are fresh. Rotten ones might have worms."

"Okay," they both muttered as they filled their bags.

I beelined toward a majestic-looking tree. The fading sunlight burst through the towering limbs in ribbons of golden color, intertwining to create a kaleidoscopic effect centered on the brilliant red, yellow, and orange leaves. I wished I had a camera.

I felt a tingle and assumed the beautiful scenery instigated goosebumps, but it soon became intense itching. It centered on the weird lump in my bicep. It only ever bothered me when I talked about the event from my youth.

A sudden sharp pain caused me to drop my bag. I grimaced but didn't want to alarm my siblings, so I let it pass before picking up the sack. Momentarily forgetting the pain, I busied myself by picking apples as fast as I could, letting let that consume my thoughts. Soon my bag was nearly full.

Krissy and Freddy had already ceased picking apples and sat in the cold grass beneath the trees, legs splayed out, munching contentedly on hard-won fruit. I smiled, seeing them eating and happy. Our family had been through a lot, and it was nice to have something finally. Such a feeling meant I was not yet a believer in the conspiracy theory that would soon guide my life's philosophy.

"All right, guys," I said, helping Krissy and Freddy to their feet. "It's time to go. We've got to get back for dinner."

The sun was setting, and soon it would be dark. I could picture a full plate of hot beans and steamed red hot dogs waiting for us back home. Maybe Mom would make an apple pie for dessert if we begged her. We bundled ourselves as best we could against the increasing cold and began the trek back to the house. When we reached the ditch, I felt something was wrong. I could not place what it was though.

Krissy and Freddy were singing a song they'd heard on Barney & Friends, and that's when I felt the thing in my arm sliding around under the skin. It hurt. Bad! I stifled a scream, but then felt something in my gut. Not illness, but an ominous feeling. Nervousness overtook me, reaching the recesses of my mouth until my fear tasted like a mouthful of pennies. The air sucked from my lungs, causing my body to tingle into pins and needles.

"SHUSH!" I said, dropping my bag of apples to the ground and grasping my right arm with my left hand.

The thing inside my skin moved. Krissy and Freddy had never seen me act so urgently, and when their big brother seemed frightened of something, they were, too. I craned my neck, peering down the road to where it curved, disappearing behind a small hill. There was enough daylight left, despite the setting sun, that nothing should have put me on edge. Scary things were only supposed to happen in the dark. But the bump in my arm now worked its way to the surface, literally.

We'd been giggling and picking apples minutes ago, yet terror overtook my limbs, making them quake. My legs wanted to run, to carry me away from the impending danger and to the waiting safety of home, but I couldn't leave my siblings. Krissy wouldn't be able to keep up, though Freddy might. If I left them behind, who knows what could happen? It was my duty as their big brother (and new father figure?) to protect them. The bump in my arm felt like it was going to rip out of my body, and I grunted in pain.

My eyes fell on the road by the hill. My vision narrowed, darkening at the edges as my heart rate and breathing increased. There was something there, something dark and terrible, that was hurtling toward us with malicious intent from down the road.

"Get down, now," I said to Krissy and Freddy. My voice trembled with fear. "Lay on your belly and don't move. Don't look up!"

They nodded and lay on the ground without hesitation, belly down, in the ditch. I stayed on my feet a moment longer, watching the road, though I felt like I should drop out of sight. On shaky legs, I clutched my arm and lowered myself as quickly as possible while keeping my eyes on the road. A sleek, black Lincoln Town Car with tinted windows rounded the corner by our house, heading in our direction. My breath left my body as I completely flattened myself.

Freddy and Krissy looked scared. I couldn't explain my concerns or why I asked them to drop, but I found myself on autopilot. They took the cues from me. I wasn't sure how I knew to do what I did, but the words flowed from my mouth on their own.

"Don't move. Don't talk. Stay still. Say it with me."

They joined in. "Don't move. Don't talk. Stay still."

"Good," I said. My arm increasingly hurt, but I didn't have time to worry about it.

I hoped the dark Lincoln would keep rolling by. To my horror, it didn't. The car stopped directly in front of us. It was unusually quiet. I don't know if it was just because I was so scared, but I didn't hear the rumblings of an engine. Ignoring my advice to my siblings, I lifted my eyes from the grass, chancing a look. The passenger and driver's doors both opened simultaneously.

Two men moved in synchronicity as they emerged from the vehicle. They simultaneously swung their legs out first, revealing black dress pants. Each wore black dress socks and shiny black dress shoes. They stood at the same time and timed the shutting of the doors so closely it sounded like one door closing rather than two. They wore black suit coats and dress shirts. I could only see a little past their waists. I dared not lift my gaze any higher, certain something terrible would happen if I did. And the repercussions would not spare my siblings.

When the two men moved, they reminded me of the stop motion animation from *Rudolph the Red-Nosed Reindeer*. In my head they became Clockwork Men. The Clockwork Men moved erratically toward us before coming to stand directly in front of my face, their feet evenly spaced apart. The tips of their shoes were only about a foot from my face while I shook as if freezing. I looked at my siblings. Freddy had his eyes closed tight, his mouth grimacing in discomfort and fear. Krissy searched my face. I blinked at her, and she blinked back.

The most chilling part of the Clockwork Men was not the machine-like move-ments, but their complete and utter silence. They could clearly see us. The pair stood over our prone, shaking forms and looked down at the backs of our heads. Three children lying next to sacks full of apples that had spilled everywhere. Three children who dared not look up. I grew increasingly concerned that Krissy or Freddy would become overwhelmed and start crying or acting out, but they seemed to understand deep down what was at stake.

Thinking back, I remember wondering if the Clockwork Men owned the orchard. Maybe they were security guards. The apples were the best I'd ever seen and tasted. Maybe we tripped a perimeter alarm on the property. Then it was less about what they were doing and more about what they were not doing.

They did not ask if we were okay.

They did not scream at us for being on private property.

They did not lure us to their vehicle.

They simply stood, mute, unmoving, directly in front of us. Their evenly spaced feet, *too* evenly spaced apart, showed my reflection in the intense glossy shine of their shoes. I listened for any semblance of humanity. Breathing or sighing. Anything. I found nothing. My heartbeat was all I heard.

After what seemed an eternity, a new intense pain rocked my arm. Then the world went bright with a hyper-intense flash of pain and light. Time felt as if it had passed, but I wasn't sure how long. When I came to, it was dark and old Tom shone a flashlight in my eyes as I vomited onto the grass. There was already a considerable pile of vomit in front of me. Krissy and Freddy were there with me, and they were throwing up as well.

"Your mother's been worried sick about you three. Saw some lights in the sky over this way and thought maybe you kids were out here playing flashlight tag or something."

I coughed, trying to understand what had happened. Without filling Tom in, I simply replied, "We don't have any flashlights."

Tom's farm was up the road a way. From where we were, we could see his house outlined against the night sky, porch light on. It looked cozy.

"Well, you about scared your mother to death. She came to me about an hour ago and said you'd gone to pick apples. She mentioned you found a secret orchard. I've been up and down these woods for the past fifteen years and never seen an orchard. She said you saw a waterfall. In the Androscoggin?"

"Yeah," I said. "It's right behind us in the woods. I swear. We've got the apples right here."

I stood up to point at where the apples were. Krissy and Freddy were not crying. They simply sat, docile, and stared out into the night. The apples were nowhere to be found.

A loud knock startled Tom and me. It originated from behind him. We both looked that way. Two shady figures stood motionless at his front door with an equally shady car parked in his driveway. I gasped and instinctively reached for my arm, expecting it to hurt, but when I reached for it, I noticed the bump was gone. I lifted my sleeve and saw what looked like a cauterized piece of skin, though I felt no pain.

"Those men are bad," I said. Krissy and Freddy started crying. I shushed them. "Be quiet. Please be quiet. Remember?"

They stopped crying; the fear taking over.

"HEY!" Tom yelled, ignoring us momentarily. "WHATEVER YOU'RE SELLING, I DON'T WANT IT!"

The men didn't move.

Tom threw his hands up in frustration and said, "ah, hell." He turned to me. "Listen, go back home. Let your mom know you're okay. I'll check on you kids in the morning. I've got to go see who they are. They look like cops. There's been some disappearances in the area, which is why your mom got so worked up. You kids are lucky you didn't become one of them. Now go on home."

"Mr. Tom," I said. "Don't go. They're bad. I can't explain it, but they're bad! Please, listen to me."

Tom waved me off with a shrug and shook his head, mumbling something under his breath. He wouldn't listen to me. I helped Krissy and Freddy to their feet. Their legs were as wobbly as mine. Within a few minutes, we were almost home. I risked a look back toward Tom's. He and the men were nowhere to be seen. In the sky, I saw what looked like four lights spinning through the air and in the time I blinked, they zoomed out of sight.

We moved about a week later. Mom had been worried sick about us and at first, she was crying, but then she got angry, especially when I tried to tell her about Tom and how I couldn't explain anything and didn't have any apples to show for it.

She fell into a depression when Tom disappeared. It turns out she liked him more than she let on. Nobody knew where he went. Some police officers questioned all of us. Krissy and Freddy couldn't remember anything about that night. Mom spoke to Tom before he went in search of us, but never saw him after that. Me and my siblings were were the last to see him. No one ever saw Tom again.

The government bought our house after declaring an ecological hazard on the property. Something about a sinkhole under the house and resources below which belonged to the state. Mom was happy about the money. They paid us more than the house was worth. We moved to downtown Lewiston, near Luigi's Pizza—home of the Fergie. The apartment was cheap, and we were closer to school, and Mom had a little more wiggle room with the money. (It wouldn't last though; it never does with three mouths to feed.)

I went back a few weeks later with some friends. We rode our bikes down River Road, but when we reached the spot where our house used to be, there was nothing but a barbed wire fence surrounding the property. They tore the home down. The fence extended all the way to where the Orchard had been. Signs along every few feet on the fence read:

"WARNING: RESTRICTED AREA – USE OF DEADLY FORCE AUTHORIZED – NO TRESPASSING"

We biked past under the scrutinizing gaze of gate guards posted out front wearing combat fatigues and holding military rifles. Huge vehicles carried trucks full of something covered by tarps. When we reached Tom's, they were demolishing his home. A man waved us down and told us to go the other way, go back home, that it wasn't a place for kids. He hauled out a walkie talkie, and we turned around and sped away, not wanting to be escorted from the area.

Every so often, I relive what happened that night, but I can never remember what happened where we lost several hours of time. My sister and brother remembered less than I did. Mom didn't like me to talk about it, so I stopped mentioning it altogether. I've eaten apples since, but they tasted bland and occasionally gave me panic attacks.

The orchard appears sometimes in my dreams, and I still carry the scar in my arm from where I believe they took out a device. I'll never be able to prove it, but it would explain the visit from the Clockwork Men. Also known as Men in Black. Like others before me, their presence was more terrifying than the UFO sighting itself.

No one knows if they work for the government, but I think they do not. Why? Because the government moved right into our little burg. The military built a facility where the orchard used to be, even creating a new road to divert traffic away from parts of Lewiston.

But in the massive parade of troops and contractors tearing up the place, I never saw a black car like the one I did that night. Nor did we ever see any workers wearing the mysterious black suits. The presence of the military in a small town gave rise to so many more conspiracy theories, which leads me to the biggest conspiracy of all time.

The one I promised to share (and ask you to do so on your socials) is simple. I believe those held down will always be held down. The biggest conspiracy on the planet is how society denies certain people the finer things: food, shelter, even stable family lives, like father figures. Did I say finer things? That is a victim of this conspiracy theory talking. No, these are the essentials of life denied to much of the world's citizens. That is the true conspiracy.

After the terrifying encounter with the Clockwork Men, we lost our apples, and we lost Tom. I will grieve him as a father because he sacrificed himself, confronting the Clockwork Men alone to spare us. We escaped, able to live another day, but is it living?

I'm older now and my entire family still struggles, remaining eternally hungry. I do not know what forces are at play, but they keep people down. Good food, good family? Not for us. Our family did not win that lottery. We are not the chosen ones. Our family struggles even though we work hard. We do what we can, but something still holds us back.

Mom is sick now. She cannot afford the medicine she needs, so I tell her it's no problem and buy it for her, even though it means I will not have enough money left over to eat.

I often think of that baking bread in the factory outside my room so long ago. Despite smelling the sweet odor, I could not partake of the food the bakery produced. I often wondered if the workers could afford the goods they made.

For so many of us, we work hard but get nowhere. That is the real conspiracy. Other conspiracy theories are terrifying, especially those involving the Clockwork Men, but the one that affects people the most is the conspiracy theory least talked about.

If the unchosen stumble upon relief, fall into an alternate dimension of comfort, something will take it away. (Look at lottery winners.) Some force will not allow good fortune to take hold for more than a moment. We are legion, those of us not allowed to have secret trees. Or fathers.

The orchard was a secret then, and it's even more of a secret now. We were not the ones meant to find it. That world was not for my struggling family. The gatekeepers raised their collective heads and cut our hopes off at the neck. But it is not enough to lose minor comforts. In this conspiracy, we punish the unworthy for even contemplating hope.

In a world of secret trees, some secrets carry a heavy price, and I believe Tom paid it for us.

STARBUCKS UNDER THE PIER

THIS COFFEE SHOP IS no longer open. It was in the news. I'm certain most people reading this saw it. Too dangerous, it must be closed! The thing was, I have lived near there for years and never knew it to exist. There is another Starbucks about two blocks away that I frequent all the time. That one is fine. Honestly, this was simply in a terrible location, hidden under a pier, beneath the feet of where thousands of people tread daily.

Yes, thousands. The Santa Monica Pier is a vibrant throwback to a simpler time. Besides the aquarium located across from the now closed Starbucks (the aquarium is still open) there is a stretch of restaurants, bars, an arcade, and more.

The **more** I mentioned takes the form of a year-round amusement park. Los Angeles has fairgrounds that open in the autumn every year like most places across the country, but here, one can enjoy the fairground environment all year round. There is the merry-go-round at the front of the pier, nestled in next to an ice cream shop. The Calliope plays incessantly as kids yell and scream at how fast the gentle ride turns.

For the older kids, the theme park picks up a few restaurants away, closer to the ocean. There, one can play all the games associated with a carnival. The basketball booth, the darts, and tossing the rings over bottle tops. Like most carnivals, never will any of the large prizes walk away. They remain the enticement tacked to the tops of game booths while workers hand out finger traps and goldfish.

Once someone passes the games section, the actual rides begin. The drop tower, the scrambler, and an enormous Ferris wheel known for elaborate lights shows playing out on both sides of the wheel. At the end of it all is the main attraction.

The roller coaster.

In all its glory. The one that makes the riders scream, tests their stomach, and makes them want to ride again immediately after getting off. It was this ride that inspired my story. I only visited this coffee shop because of the news of its impending closing. But while there, I visited the theme park.

And remembered the size of the crowds. Thousands per day. People packed in. In case I did not mention it, this entire fairground sits on a pier stretching out into the ocean. I thought of the roller coaster and how excited I was about them when younger. And then I thought, what a horrible place for an outbreak of any type.

And as we all know, some outbreaks are much worse than others...

COFFEE RECOMMENDATION: This story requires something as sweet as cotton candy. I suggest an ice blended caramel drink with extra whip cream and caramel drizzle on the top.

TITTY TWISTER

Paul Carro

"THE SECRET IS ALL in the puke catcher," Humphrey said, as the two twelve-year-olds followed shadows toward the chain-link fence.

"Puke catcher?" Nico asked, looking around frantically, afraid of getting sent to juvie for such a stunt.

The two kids stood in the shadow of what was billed as the largest roller coaster in New England and Old England. The Titty Twister was a double looper roller coaster named for what it did to people's titties during the ride. It twisted both his and hers. The ride did not discriminate. It also made people barf, which was why it was the only ride surrounded by a massive chain-link fence.

It was there at the puke catcher fence the boys dropped to the ground and looked for security clowns. The coaster was the star attraction at Clown Town, a traveling fair which visited Maine every fall. All the employees dressed as clowns. To local farmers, the fair was all about produce and livestock displays, but to everyone else it was an annual tradition centered around clowns, games of chance, deep-fried everything, and the Titty Twister.

Nico and Humphrey were too poor to attend. One could not simply walk in unnoticed. There was a ticket price for entry. Besides the puke catcher fence surrounding the coaster, a much larger chain-link encircled the fairgrounds to keep out others like them. The poor. The opposite of the statue of liberty. They were not welcome. Those who were welcome needed to navigate to the lone entrance on one side of the park and pay the per head fee.

Located, way in the boonies, even getting there was an issue. Luckily the boys had a connection. One Loogie Doug, known in their neighborhood for his spitting accuracy, was old enough to have a permit allowing him to drive to work. This was Doug's first year as a clown at the fair. He offered the boys a ride.

During the trip, a radio DJ spoke of people getting sick at the fairgrounds and mentioned how the fairground owners were unable to locate the source of infection. Doug turned off the radio when they parked.

Employee parking sat way out on the back side of the park, facing the backside of the Titty Twister. It was far enough away from the entrance that Doug and other late shift clowns rode a shuttle into the park. A shuttle driver clown wearing a limo driver's cap, pulled up to take Loogie Doug and others away.

The transport was clown only so Doug honked his nose and said goodbye to the kids figuring they would hoof it to the front. But the boys waited for him and the other clowns to depart. Each clown wore something or had props to represent the job they performed. Doug held a plunger as he was the porta-potty cleaner. (Gross!) One female clown wore an apron—food booth proprietor for sure. One clown held an oversized pencil and pad of paper, likely a front gate ticket taker.

After all the clowns got on board (exiting the vehicle endlessly at their destination!) it finally drove away along defeated field grass, a makeshift road designed for employees and emergency workers to get around without getting trapped in all the traffic leading into the park itself.

As soon as the boys cut the first link in the wire, an ambulance lit up the night in red, racing past on the same makeshift road. The boys watched it go, musing about how it was likely for some old guy's heart brought down by the grease from deep-fried something or other. It made the news every year.

Once the coast was clear, the boys had cut their way through a section of fence with wire cutters (thanks Humphrey's dad!) and raced to the puke cage around the ride's perimeter. Nico never would have gone along with his friend's plan to break and enter, except this was the first year that Nico was almost tall enough to ride the coaster. And he just had to ride it!

Humphrey was the same age as Nico, but wise beyond his years by a day or two and an inch taller, guaranteeing his ability to ride. Keeping true to the park's motif, a wooden clown with an outstretched arm holding a yellow balloon was positioned next to every adult ride. If one's head touched the clown's hand, they were tall enough to rock and roll.

Nico and Humphrey looked up the exact height requirement in advance and measured one another all summer, waiting for growth spurts. Humphrey got his. He was good to go. Nico did not. Destined to always be a runt, sadly. But the two hatched a plan to get around the issue. It all started with gaining entry, then securing enough cash to pay for ride tickets.

So, wire cutters it was. The fairgrounds remained fenced in year-round, but the puke catcher fence only went up after they built the coaster. The Titty Twister arrived a week earlier than the other rides because it required elaborate construction. They towed other rides in on trailers, unfurling each with minimal effort. Almost as simple as just add water and go. Though Nico imagined the swinging pirate ship probably took an advance degree to set up as well.

There was no lighting on the far side of the park, so only ambient light from the coaster lit the area where they were about to cut through the second fence. Spinning, twirling lights of varying colors covered the coaster, but the ride's massive structure also blocked much of the park lighting, giving the boys pools of shadows to hide in.

The ride towered over them from where they stood. Proximity to such a powerful and large ride made Nico's stomach flip. He wanted nothing more than to be riding in the car they heard zooming above, but the idea also scared him.

Then there was the matter of getting tickets. Five tickets per ride, a fortune. But Humphrey had a plan for that as well.

Humphrey grew animated as he cut the fencing and repeated much of their plan. Mostly trying to will it into being. "The puke cage catches everyone's sick when they hurl in the loops, but also catches anything that falls out of their pockets. Search every inch. I go right, you go left. Be fast before someone spots us. Meet back here with your spoils."

Nico ran and stumbled almost immediately. How powerful was the ride? It was the ground shaking that threw him off his feet. He fell onto his back and into a bright cone of light. Above, he glimpsed the carrier comprising five sections which rocketed by with riders in full scream. Their faces were a blur as the car left his field of vision. It vanished into the center of the ride, traveling through support beams that seemed way too low. Nico decided he would keep his head down when they got to that part of the ride. (If he got on the ride, there was still much to do.)

Nico rolled back into a shadow before rising to his feet. He did not want the sheriff's clowns to spot him out there in the field. His excitement grew while searching the ground, looking for fallen dollars. He studied the ride virtually online (while at school since he could not afford internet or a computer at home) and dreamed of riding it someday.

The reasons for his infatuation eluded him. But sometimes he thought maybe it was because everyone in school got to go to the fair except him. Many of the kids even went to Florida for Disney World. Meanwhile, he lived in squalor, melting in summer heat without air conditioning and freezing at night in the Fall and winter with no heat.

The roller coaster was the great equalizer. If he could only ride it, he would be—what? Free? Maybe. Just maybe. But freedom came at a price.

Tickets. They needed tickets. There were cigarette packages (empty), ice cream bar wrappers (also empty), and baseball caps galore. The ground had so much litter it appeared no one had cleaned the area since the park opened. Nico grabbed at the trash repeatedly, hoping each piece of paper was a ticket, but it was only garbage.

Tickets were blue, but it was hard to tell the color of paper in the pitch black of night. There was not as much debris in the lit areas around him, and where there was, he could tell it was only garbage. Nico grew frustrated. Where were the fallen tickets Humphrey promised? Maybe people who dropped theirs had someone retrieve them right away. Was there a clown retriever? One clown whose sole job was to get the fallen cellphones, tickets, and cash?

It appeared so. Nico came up empty-handed. He neared tears, thinking how everything was for nothing. Sure, they could wander the fair and have some fun, go see some cows and such since they were already in the park. But none of that involved riding on anything.

Then something in the distance drew his attention. A section of grass ahead of him fell into a strangely lit pattern. A pool of light followed by a slant of darkness, repeated several times in a row. On about the third shaft of light in the distance something odd stood out. Movement?

There was a substantial pile of something sitting there. (Again, why did it seem to move?) He dead legged toward it, nervous without reason. Hair at the back of his neck danced in a non-existent breeze. Screams of those in the coaster drew closer. With every step, the screams intensified, as if warning him off. But he kept going.

Shaft of light. Darkness. Shaft of light. Darkness. Until finally, he was close enough to see it. A mound of sick. Someone vomited, but the amount was abnormal. There was weight to the pile of spew, a thickness to it, and something worse. Blood? Whoever was responsible needed to see a doctor.

The smell was foul, the deep stew of rotten eggs, or his dad's sleep farts after passing out from drinking. Nico covered his nose and mouth but leaned in closer for a look. The movement crystalized. Maggots! Dozens, a swarm covering the already disgusting mess. How had he sensed movement from so far away? Maggots were small.

Then one leaped! It only reached a few inches into the air, but it had jumped from the pile (trying to reach him?). They grew animated in his presence, moving in spectacular fashion. As far as Nico knew, that was uncommon for maggots.

Chew straight down to the ground. Wasn't that their life philosophy? Nico needed to show Humphrey.

Then it happened. Nico turned around and his mouth dropped.

Humphrey stood holding a length of tickets. At least thirty! They would get two or three rides each! And to make life better, Humphrey held a fiver in his other hand.

Above them, the coaster went into one of its loops. The same screams that earlier unnerved Nico now sounded joyful. A soundtrack of parkgoers experiencing the best ride ever. Nico forgot all about maggots as the two boys ran back through the hole in the fence and blended into the fairgrounds.

"More towels. We didn't come this far for you not to get on," Humphrey said.

Nico grabbed wads of paper towels and folded them. He then slipped off his shoes and placed the wads inside. Putting the shoes back on, he was officially taller. Besides the new lifts, Nico earlier used all his sister's hair product to straighten his hair into a high crest. Combined, it would hopefully prove enough.

The boys then rushed off, eager to get to the coaster, but there were plenty of distractions along the way. Smells from so many food booths tempted them to spend the fiver on some fried dough, or funnel cake, or one of the many soft-serve ice cream spots that advertised with large sculptures of cones hanging atop their booths. The fake chocolate coating appeared real and scrumptious. A clown in a chef's apron stood center crowd with an arrow shaped sign advertising pizza slices. The clown spun it with great skill.

They passed the section of the park with the kiddy rides like the merry-go-round, teacups, and bumper cars. (Though they still loved the bumper cars.) Most of the clowns near the kiddie rides spent their time making balloon animals or balloon swords. The whoosh of air canisters sounded in all directions. It was pleasant.

Then there were the game booths. Something about a clown running a booth where people shot water streams into clown mouths until balloons popped above their heads felt ironic. A female clown in her twenties ran the booth and spoke through heavy static from the microphone in her hand. She cheered on a young girl while pile-driving insults at the other contestants, making them feel guilty if they let a child miss out on a prize. Nico stopped to watch, mesmerized by the energetic clown announcer, waiting to see the results. But Humphrey yanked him along.

Nearby was the similarly played horse race game, run by a clown with a white and green visor, looking like a bookie collecting a vig. (Besides drinking at home, Nico's dad drank at bars where bets were common. Sometimes his dad took Nico along for the day.) The basketball hoops game, where rumor had it, hoops were too small to accommodate the ball unless the angle was just so, and it could barely squeeze in.

And Nico's favorite, the darts game with massive stuffed animals lining the top of the booth. No one had ever seen a stuffed animal get off leash, so to speak. The routine prizes took the form of snake whistles or goldfish in a bag. Since no one knew where to buy fish tanks on short notice late at night, most of the poor fish took a fast flush trip to the ocean before the night was over.

The lights and sounds and smells were overwhelming to the two boys who travelled with awkward grace while moving and twirling and darting around handholding couples of various ages and groups of teens or large families enjoying the festivities. The boys shared an unspoken language, a GPS of sorts, that allowed them to sidestep in opposite directions and investigate other parts of the fair only to reconnect despite the crowd size surrounding them.

On one such diversion, Nico slowed, watching as two paramedics in dress blues walked frantically through the crowd with first aid bags in hand. The health workers followed a park medic, a clown wearing a surgical mask and comically oversized surgical gloves. He also wore a reflective visor atop his head over orange puffy hair.

The doctor clown looked highly upset and Nico did not find the fake smears of blood across the man's front remotely funny. Too far, that joke. A tap on the shoulder brought Nico back.

"This is it. You ready?" Humphrey asked.

Boy was he, though his stomach flip-flopped. A female clown with a cigarette stuck to her lipstick (painted wide over her mouth, stretching from chin to the underside of her nose) stood next to the *must be this tall* wooden clown. The woman instinctively frowned, not a good look on a smoking clown, and gestured with great aplomb for Nico to step up for height measurement.

"Don't get your hopes up, kid," she said in a voice that suggested it wasn't her first smoke of the day. Her oversized badge read Flo.

Humphrey leaped under the clown arm first, making a great show of being too tall to fit. The attendant rolled her eyes and waved him off. Nico stepped up, closed his eyes, then felt that which he longed for, a clown's caress of his hair. The extra product scrunching everything north worked. He was tall enough!

"What do you know?" Flo said, taking their tickets. She opened the gate and said, in a voice of bleeding apathy, "Once you step through the gate of death, your existence is no longer our concern. Have a great ride."

The cage around the ride was more than a vomit catcher. They used it as part of the ride itself serving two purposes. One was simply to feed the line of riders into a maze of fencing, keep them feeling like they were moving while waiting in an eternal line.

But the bigger reason was to mentally mess with riders, especially the younger ones. Make them think the thing is so dangerous it needs to be walled off, lest a dead body land in someone's slushie cup somewhere in the park. (Every year brought with it a new urban legend of a body flung from the infamous Titty Twister.)

Afterall, would not a double looper require a fence at the least? A second gate awaited riders at the end of the line. Speaking of which, Nico wondered where the line was. The friends zig zagged through waiting for the end of the line to appear and it never did which made no sense.

They arrived at the front to find only a few people waiting. Strange. Awesome!

"Sweet, we're getting right in, I think," Humphrey said.

"Five seats per car," Nico said, and the two took inventory of the people in front of them.

A teen couple of about seventeen fronted the short line, glued together in a making out session. Each had a solid square in a rear pocket. Cell phones. Unless people were taking pics, no one bothered with their cellphones at the fair. The grounds were in the boonies and there was no such thing as internet out there.

Behind the suck face couple stood an older couple with salt and pepper hair, both his and hers. They wore matching tie-dyes, well matching color schemes at least, the ink splotch designs were unique. The two were hippy thin and danced subtly to the yacht rock playing over the speakers.

Three more full-blown adults stood behind the hippies. They were each size-able adults and looked unable to fit as a threesome in one seat. (Three was the max.) The group comprised two men and a woman who laughed louder than any clown Nico ever saw. The woman, wearing a red, white, and blue American flag frock leaned into one of the heavyset men and kissed his cheek.

"Careful, Dotty, you will make third-wheel Louis jealous," the man said.

"Oh, Carl," Dotty said, and batted at her husband, laughing uproariously again.

The two were married and the other guy was a friend. Nico and Humphrey considered them a wild card. The three would not fit in a car together. They would have to split in some combination. Four cars filled for sure, but with room for at least an extra rider or two.

Next was a cowboy who stood out, both for being solo and for being a cowboy in Maine. Locals loved their country music, but most did not dress full cowboy. The man was roughly fifty, with a nicotine moustache and a full-blown ten-gallon hat and chaps. Maybe the man was waiting for someone. Hard to tell. He seemed to nap where he stood. Nico guessed the man had ice in his veins if the looming ride did not faze him.

The choice became whether to ride with one of the solo riders or wait for the next car. They agreed they would rather not wait; they were uncertain they could handle the suspense. But the rider had to be okay with them hitching. So just in case it played out, the boys played best two out of three rocks, paper, scissors. Humphrey won and immediately began suggesting how Nico could sit with Dotty and suck face during the ride. Dotty laughed grandly, as if she heard the joke. The boys lost their stuff, laughing along, which appeared to set Dotty off again.

A ride was imminent. They just needed to get through the last locked gate. Not truly locked but held closed with a U-clamp that the ride operator would soon lift. That clown (for weren't they all?) barely played the part.

The man was clearly a rebel, maybe eighteen, old enough to be missing a front tooth. He wore only the slightest semblance of a clown uniform along with a sleeveless Metallica tee, the same one that people could win at the basketball booth. He also wore skinny jeans and his long metal-band style hair sprouted out from under a baseball. A competing band that Nico never heard of fronted the baseball cap.

His obligatory name badge read Boosh. The teen stood on the same side of the gate as the line but worked from a raised platform on which rose an electrical stump culminating in oversized red and green buttons. Equally oversized letters labelled one stop and one go.

A large metal trash can took up space alongside the man, a last ditch spot for food wrappers and empty drink containers. Boosh leaned on the garbage can, speaking into a walkie-talkie. He appeared concerned.

"We shutting down, or not shutting down? Copy?" Boosh asked.

Static blared, followed by a squeal. *No, they can't shut it*, Nico thought. They were close. So close!

"They better not close it," someone shouted.

Nico nearly leaped out of his skin. He was so eager to ride, he never noticed more people show up in the line behind them. A high school kid wearing a Star Wars tee sucked through a straw getting nothing but air. He kept going, breaking away from the annoyingness only long enough to tell Boosh they better not close.

Behind the kid were two clowns. Nico could not tell if they worked for the park, thinking probably not. Their outfits leaned on the creepy clown side. They were vaping when they thought Boosh wasn't looking. They too were talking about a shutdown. Then they started to talk about something disturbing they saw in the park. It was too hard to hear so Nico turned to Humphrey.

"Why would they want to shut things down?" Nico asked.

"You saw the ambulance." Humphrey said. "It was on the news, a major flu or something going around. It's bigger than that, though. I saw lots of spooks on our way here."

"Spooks?" Nico asked, excited at whatever that was.

"Yeah. Government. Men in black types. Couldn't miss them, except I guess you did. You were too busy checking out the hot clown in the water cannon booth."

There Humphrey was, sounding smarter than Nico again. Nico went red, embarrassed. Yeah, the girl was pretty, but she reminded him of his mom who left so long ago. And he was so excited by everything that he never once saw a spook.

"That's okay. I'm looking out for us. I listened to what I could as we walked. GMOs or something like that. They had new foods this year, were testing some stuff, deep frying anything. Well, something did not sit well with the general populace, so a shorter line for us."

"If we get on."

The car arrived, but the screaming did not stop. People leaped from the cars, scrambling to escape. The starting point for the ride was the same as the stopping point. It was on a platform past the locked gate with two sets of stairs: one incoming, one outgoing. The riders used both to scramble away.

The fleeing group smashed into the fence, unsure of how to get out. Boosh lifted the U-clamp and asked what was going on, but the riders scrambled. There were three college-aged women left in the center seat. Two girls got out to help an apparently drunken friend.

The last girl, tee soaked with sickness, emerged and they escorted her through the gate. She did not smell good. Nico wasn't much for girls, but the woman was TV star pretty and her boobs were showing through her thin shirt because of how damp it was. It stirred something in him, but mostly worry that it would hasten a shutdown.

Her friends shrieked in concern. "Jess, oh my God, let's go. Let's get you to a bathroom," one of them said.

"I need a minute, going to be sick again," Jess of the smelly clothes said. Jess found the garbage barrel and leaned in, doing her best to fill it.

Nico recognized the smell. The mess in the puke cage. Was she responsible? It smelled like her. Most women her age (college aged) normally smelled of strawberry and cigarettes from Nico's experience, but this woman smelled different. She smelled like spoiled meat.

Boosh grabbed towels and a spray bottle, clearly used to cleaning after riding and went to the seat and cleaned up little specks of spew. There was mercifully little, so it cleaned up quick. The individual rider usually got covered but beyond that most people's sickness flung away into the night.

Once finished, Boosh gestured for the next round of riders to take their place while asking the girls to get their sick friend out of there. Boosh got two middle fingers for his trouble from the women circling their sick friend. The sick one still partook of the bucket. Her spasms were violent when she puked.

The boys watched with hopefulness as the next group of riders stepped up to the white lines on the platform leading to each seated section. Suck face teens lined up for the first seat, while the hippies took spot number two. Dotty split from the two guys who took the third car. She lined up for the fourth, leaving the cowboy in the final car. With practiced efficiency, Boosh whispered something to the cowboy, who nodded. Then Boosh waved the boys over to stand next to the old man. They made it! They would be in the last car.

"Don't worry, I don't bite," the man said in a voice deeper than Tether Falls Lake, which was near their home.

They all climbed in, with Nico as the middleman. He did not mind. The cowboy was cool and smelled better than the women who just stepped off. The presence of an adult for their maiden voyage made Nico feel more comfortable. Rounds two and three they could hopefully do on their own and sit closer to the front.

Once everyone got in, Boosh made the rounds and dropped the safety bars in place, checking each one. Dotty appeared concerned over the bar. To his credit, the teen put her at ease, said how the bar would not fail such a fine thing. The husband in the car in front of her yelled about the open flirting, but he could not rise because of the safety bar.

"Yo man, your bad. Should have ridden with the hottie, not the dude!"

"Yeah, Carl, you had your chance," the woman said, slapping her husband in the front.

"Very funny." Then he noticed his friend having a ball at the shenanigans. "What are you laughing at?"

"Marital problems," Louis said.

Carl fell into his seat defeated and glanced over his shoulder. "You are one sexy momma, honey."

"Now that's more like it. Preach!" Dotty winked at Metallica clown, who winked back.

Boosh finally approached the last car and grilled Nico. "How did you do it? Lifts?"

"Paper towels in the shoes," Humphrey said.

"Humphrey!" Nico protested.

"Flo down there can barely see through all the smoke. You fooled her but would not have gotten past me. But since they have promoted me to head ride monkey, I am no longer at the gate, and you are already in. Now hold on to your balls."

Boosh stepped through the gate and lowered the U-clamp. Behind him the women still helped their friend but asked the employee if he could get them an ambulance. Boosh called for Flo to come assist the women. It was clear he remained more annoyed than concerned.

With great aplomb, Boosh raised a single finger high into the air. Then he brought it down slowly, in a point and pressed the massive green go button as if he were a villain in a Saturday morning cartoon. The car jerked. Nico sat upright, nervous, then witnessed it.

The sickness.

Jess spewed all over Boosh. The mass of puke covered the ride operator's face and soaked his cool shirt. The woman's friends screamed until Jess turned and gushed over them as well. Soon everyone was screaming, but the car moved.

"Gross!" Humphrey said.

From atop the raised platform, Nico could see out into the park where people rushed past with their kids. Something was going on. People appeared frantic. Through it all, a clown caught Nico's attention. The traditionally dressed clown walked slowly along the fairway, dragging a handful of popped balloons on strings behind him. He moved as if drunk or sad. Or both.

The car sped up and ran along the tracks. They left the spewing group behind. Nico finally forgot it all. They were about to ride! This was it. Everything he longed for! He gripped the safety bar as if his life depended on it, even though they were merely navigating the initial straightaway.

Just as the car picked up speed, they jerked to a halt when they reached the first rise of the track. The cart clicked, clicked, clicked as it jerked along the lift. They were rising high into the air. The boys laughed nervously at first, then laughed wildly when the cart jerked extra hard. They kept rising high into the air.

Nico looked down, almost dizzy. They were getting so high into the air. Screams sounded out and Nico at first thought it was his fellow riders until realizing it came from below. Metallica clown yelled while fighting with the girls. Maybe angry about the puke. The man tried to put the electrical panel between himself and the others and hit a button in the process. The car jerked to a halt.

Now the riders did scream. What was going on? They stood frozen mid-rise, oh so high. The cowboy squinted, concerned but trying to hide it from the boys. Humphrey had the best view and leaned down.

"The girls are attacking the clown. They look angry. I think he hit the thing by mistake," Humphrey said.

Boosh hit another button in his struggle, and the cart jerked into motion. The force provoked a touch of whiplash, but Nico was happy to be moving again. When Nico glanced down, he swore it looked like the women had converged on the man and were biting him. Screams sounded from elsewhere in the park. Lots of screams.

Before they could identify what was going on, they were screaming themselves. The car crested the rise in the track, and then they were rocketing down the other side. Humphrey and Nico both yelled deliriously in between bouts of laughter. It was amazing! Nico held tight to the safety bar and leaned into it even as the force of the ride jostled him around the seat.

The drop left their stomach behind, but they went straight from a drop into another straightaway at incredible speed which fed into the structure of the ride itself. Support beams surrounded them on all sides, and then they went into their first turn.

Nico thought he might lose his lunch when the car leaned on its side while making a turn. The force caused Pops to slide toward the boys. Humphrey grunted at being crushed. Dotty screamed in gales of laughter in the car in front of them, loving every minute.

With a jolt, they came out of the sideways run and leveled out before hitting a smaller dip which dropped Nico's stomach out from under him. It was amazing! Humphrey and Nico screamed and hollered and held onto the safety bar for dear life. The cowboy remained silent.

The ride was a blur of speed and fun. Nico tried not to close his eyes but did so occasionally on the bigger turns when the jolts hurt his body, but then they fell into what felt like a free-fall as the car hit another straightaway.

Once upon a time Nico dreamed of raising his hands like the people in the movies, but he was hanging on for dear life. Besides, the support beams holding the structure together seemed so close he feared one might clip his product-raised hair. He screamed with joy.

The first loop approached. Nico thought he was ready. He was wrong. The ride had straightened out, allowing them to build speed as they emerged from the guts of the ride until they were moving across a straightaway at the peak height of the ride. So very high. The height was dizzying, and the car slowed, as if designed to highlight the view. Nico looked down, worried the car might tip if they breathed wrong, dumping them all over the side.

Known for a double loop, the Titty Twister did not have massive loops like the boys' Hot Wheels tracks. Instead, the loops just twisted the cars into a three-sixty spin in two different points along the track. The cars would turn upside down and keep running before eventually righting. That was the type of loop the ride offered. That is what the boys waited for.

"Here it comes boys, put on yer' big boy pants," Pops said.

The boys screamed from just the idea before falling into stunned silence as the car rocketed ahead, tilted, and twisted upside down! It was not a quick one and done spin; they continued riding upside down for what seemed an unreasonable amount of time.

The motion was incredible, but they could see the distant ground while upside down, and the force was greater than they expected. Humphrey mentioned the need to hurl but held it in check. Then they were upright once again and speeding on toward round two.

Right. Left. Jerk hard. Drop. Tilt sideways. It was impossible to keep track of it all. They burst into the guts again, surrounded by beams that felt like anything other than protection. Then they shot through it all, back into the open and shot up an abrupt rise, one not steep enough to slow them. A major drop waited on the other side.

The boys lost their collective shit and screamed. The drop was at rocket speed and looked as if they might hit the ground. They fell into the safety bar, the metal strap the only thing holding them in their seats. The cars roared as if about to smash into the ground below. Then a sudden sideways jerk and they were off to level ground and into loop number two.

Gravity took hold as they surged into the second round of upside-down flight. The motion was nearly too much for the boys to take. Their mouths opened into screams, but nothing came out. Soon they came out of the twist and rocketed upright where they went back into the belly of the beast.

The course became much more violent. Left. Right. Left. Drop. Rise as if to take off into orbit. Drop again. The boys lost track of their surroundings, but soon they shot out into the open again and saw the fencing off to one side. They were back on level ground. The car had slowed through the last round of turns. The violent motions at the end were surely part of the slowing toward the finish line.

Pops said as much. "Well, boys, you made it. What did you think?"

"It was awesome!" they cried in unison.

Finally able to let go of the bars as they slowed and came in for a landing, they high fived one another. Then those in the car's front seats screamed. It spread quick but was too loud. How could five seats of people produce such an enormous volume of fright?

It wasn't the riders. It was the park. The park screamed. Or people in the park, from every direction. Sirens screamed; people screamed. It could not have just begun. The ride had distracted them. Something was happening. Something bad, and it affected every section of the theme park.

The safety bars kept them from twisting too far hoping for a look. They did not need to look that far. As they rode toward the finish, a world in chaos came into view. Jess and the other girls fought with Boosh. Except it wasn't so much fighting as it was biting!

Jess gnawed on the man's shoulder blade. Blood spurted through the air in from a wound near the man's neck. Jess had the employee bent over the ride control panel. One of his legs hung limp while the other kicked repeatedly, as if trying to get away on its own, content to just hop on out of there. It did not need the rest of the body; it could do just fine on its own.

Loud gurgles confirmed the teen was alive through the ordeal, but he now spoke the language of the grunts. English had left the building. No more hard rock lyrics for that kid. His guitar solo was that of someone bleeding out in rockstar fashion.

There were a trio to start, but only one of the women appeared unafflicted, and she screamed while being snacked on. Jess and one of her friends looked checked out. Their eyes were blank, with nary a pupil in sight.

Nico often saw his after a bender, eyes bloodshot to the point it looked as though his eyes were bleeding. Two of the women's eyes were like that, bloodshot except with pitch black veins almost entirely covering the white. The dark lines all fed into where pupils used to be. Now the pupils looked like blood clots.

Jess' afflicted friend chewed through a spot in the non-afflicted friend's chest where a breast used to be. All that remained was a gaping hole below which dangled the woman's bra, shoved aside in the melee.

With a gurgling protest, the girl under attack went rigid as something inside her chest snapped. Her heart! Nico froze, gripping the safety bar. He was close enough to see the bloodshot girl bite her friend's heart out with her teeth! Blood sprayed everywhere.

The eaten girl dropped to the ground immediately, lifeless, no longer rigid or fighting the attack. She was a sack of flesh, nothing more. The hungry friend raised her head and gobbled the chunk of flesh with all the grace of a shark. Star Wars tee kid and Flo stood on the rider's side of the fence, their backs turned, watching the commotion on the other side. Likely they ran through earlier trying to escape the chaos. All of it happening in the time it took to ride the coaster once. Flo and the teen stood at ground level, below the platform.

"What? What is happening?" Humphrey cried out.

Not even the cowboy answered, too shocked to do so. Everyone was shocked. The occupants of the car remained silent after the initial screams. The cowboy finally murmured something as if an afterthought.

"We're about at the finish line," he said.

Little did he know. The ride slowed and approached the starting point. The arriving car made a clack. That drew the attention of the two on the inside of the fence. They turned around. Flo's cigarette still dangled in the heavy lipstick. It rose and fell in time with her snapping jaw.

She hissed upon spotting the riders and reached for them only to find them too far away. The car was on the platform. Flo kept trying to walk despite the obstruction. Nico thought how she looked like a video game avatar at the edge of a game world. Walking, walking, walking, but getting nowhere. Thankfully.

Star Wars kid also turned with eyes as black as Vader's. He hissed wildly, more energetic. (Hungrier?) The Star Wars kid leaped, trying to understand the nature of the platform. The hisses from the two on their side of the fence caught the attention of the others.

The girl eating her friend leaped at the fence, pressing her face against it, drooling around the chain-link, trying to get inside. The now heartless friend rose on unsteady feet and joined in. Guess the friend did not eat the entire thing, there must have been something still in her chest if she stood up Nico thought.

A twitching Boosh remained on the ground, while his detached arm covered the controls, his entire limb chewed off at the shoulder. Jess snacked on the employee, chewing a sizeable chunk of flesh from somewhere. She stood, slurped it up, then joined her friends at the fence. All hissed through the twisted wire holes, trying to get at the fresh buffet in the roller coaster car.

Boosh rose finally and stomped one foot, then another, planting them on the ground. Then he turned at the waist with a snap that sounded loud enough to break the spine. He stomped one foot forward, then another. Walking but as if for the first time. His legs faced forward, but his torso remained twisted to one side. The man moved straight ahead but facing sideways. The image frightened Nico more than anything else so far.

Nico wailed in a higher voice than he thought possible. His cries grew as unstoppable as the roller coaster car when in motion. Humphrey covered his ears. The cowboy leaned away. Nico fought the safety bar, trying to rise and run. The car had slowed enough, was about to land in the return slot. Except the bar held him in check.

And the car never stopped. It slowed, yes, but it rolled into the return spot before picking up speed and shooting forward. They were still riding. It failed to stop! Humphrey and Nico let go of the safety bar long enough to grab one another. They were physically shaking. In an environment designed for sensory overload, something had kicked everything into a higher gear. Humphrey reached his breaking point and fought against the restraints.

"We need to get out. Need to run. We need to get away!"

The cowboy yanked the kid back into the full seated position. "We need to figure out why we haven't stopped. I've ridden this plenty; we should have stopped."

Nico looked ahead, trying to see where they were heading. Then the Vader kid looked toward the front of the car as it passed. The kid opened his mouth wide and vomited a jet of thick, black spew.

All the riders in the cars instinctively jolted to opposite sides of their car to avoid the splatter and mess. Stuck in the middle, Nico was able to see through the sea of parting bodies. He witnessed the male half of the making out couple escape the spew while it bathed the female. Her scream faded into choking as she gargled the gross fluid swamping her face and mouth.

Frantic motions ensued as everyone tried to escape, only to find themselves strapped in. Then the car picked up speed. The ride was starting again! They sped up toward the initial rise. The car roughly connected to the lift and the click clack began as they climbed once again.

The female make-out queen had since cleared her face and screamed with an ear-piercing shriek, before falling into a moan that reached the back car. Her boyfriend yelled for her not to touch him, which brought her to tears. Alone, even in a shared car.

Jerking along slowly up the initial rise once again provided them all a clear view of what went on in the rest of the park. Clowns fed on people everywhere. There may have been other park goers doing some chowing down, but the clown outfits stood out. The movements of the afflicted were like those of Boosh. They moved quickly but with stunted stuttered steps and the legs of many did not match up to the positioning of the bodies themselves.

Pure chaos engulfed the park. People screamed and splashes of blood lined the concourse. Some living meals fought back. Then there were the crawlers. In spots all over the park were people partially eaten, their legs missing. Those afflicted dragged themselves along the ground, trying to catch up to fleeing food. For there were still some guests fleeing. Gunshots echoed. This was Maine, some people carried.

One man held a series of clowns at bay. It was hard to tell from so high what type of employees they were, but Nico thought he saw a security clown, a fast-food clown, and a garbage collector. That clown still held onto his pooper-scooper (what Nico and Humphrey called the small brush and waste collector basket on the end of a pole combo). The car tried to get the man's attention, hoping he might help with controls.

"Here! Up here!" One half of the tie-dye couple yelled from the middle car.

The gunman on the ground looked up. Big mistake! The brief distraction gave the clowns time to converge on the man. They leaped at him, with one sinking his teeth into the man's shoulder. The gunman shot wildly into the air and tried to pull away. He pulled free but came away minus an arm. One clown dropped to the ground feasting on the limb.

The other two clowns rushed toward the man. In shock, the man tried to reach out to stop them but did so with an arm he no longer had. He realized too late. The torn limb spurted blood in the clowns' faces and it caused them to shriek with joy before they tackled the man to the ground.

Nico focused elsewhere, where a trio of female jester dancers pirouetted in triangular formation. Each time they came out of the spin, they hissed and looked around for food. Then they advanced and spun again. Their movements showed how they were no longer among the living but had yet to let go of the practiced movements of their life.

Clowns everywhere. Too many. So many patrons dressed the same, happy to be part of the party. It was a thing. Nico would have done the same if he had money.

The coaster climbed. They fell into the ride again. The thing Nico once wanted most in the world, but now never wanted to experience again.

It was in the throes of the ride, as he and Humphrey grabbed the bar again, that Pops talked through it as best he could over the roar of the car and the cries from the park. Sirens sounded in the distance only to turn drunken, slow. Something had gone to work on the arriving emergency vehicles, or at least the rescuers in them. An explosion went off toward the parking lot.

"We need to find a way off!" Pops yelled over the noise.

They had already dropped and were roaring through the guts of the ride. They caught glimpses of chaos at every turn, with no portion of the park spared. A thought came to Humphrey.

"The spooks. That's why the spooks were here!" Humphrey yelled.

A ride that originally felt long was over quickly. The car slowed through the last turns and headed back toward the platform. Pops instructed the boys to search for anything related to finding a way off.

Nico focused on the arm resting on the controls. That was it. They were stuck in the go position. Cigarette woman was hungrier, hissing and screeching at the incoming crew, but the platform remained in her way. Meanwhile, the Vader kid had discovered stairs and with a grunt declared them good. He rose toward the platform.

Everything happened at once. In the front car, the male teen screamed. He visibly struggled against the safety bar.

"Amelia, no! What are you doing? What, oh God, no!"

The girlfriend's arms were everywhere at once, trying to get hold of her struggling date. Vader kid found his way to the platform, but the speed of the car confused him as it rolled past. Each rider cried out upon passing the grabby kid. Half of Star Wars guy's face was gone. Someone had bitten him, most likely Jess.

Flo looked intact but bathed in black. She probably approached the sick girls, tasked with escorting them out. Bites or puke. Either did the job of turning people into hungry bunnies. Nico broke out into a sweat when it was their turn to pass the Star Wars kid.

Vader kid's eyes were indeed gone from normalcy. Deep pools of bleeding black ink greeted the riders. The being looked their way but seemed to register nothing more than food. Black drool poured from his lips. Vader turned and stomped toward them on deadened legs.

The frantic kid in the front seat battled his girlfriend. Or former. With dark black eyes of her own, she sought to put an end to their relationship. She snapped at him but seemed confused by the safety harness. The boyfriend released the bar and leaped up in his seat. The bar rose into an open position above the couple's head. He was free, but so was she.

Making out kid leaped onto the platform, scrambling backward. Amelia rose in her seat but struggled with her positioning, unsure of how to step free of the car. She snapped and snarled and spun backward where she caught sight of the next car. The afflicted woman turned her attention from her former boyfriend to the hippy couple.

"How much did we take darlin'?" the older hippy asked his wife.

"Too much, too much! We need a guide; someone get us off here and help us land!"

The words meant little to Nico other than he could tell the adults in that second car were freaking out, as they should. But things were about to get worse. Much worse. Suck face teen scrambled and almost fell, dropping an arm to steady himself as he went into a run. He quickly rose and turned back as if to ensure his girlfriend was in fact a flesh hungry something or other. She was. The girl reached out for the hippies, but she remained rooted in place, her shoulder leaning into the lifted crash bar.

"There must be an emergency stop on this side of the fence. Help us stop, kid!" Pops yelled.

The teen searched for any sort of ride controls but when he looked back, Star Wars kid waited. Star Wars kid bit into the teen's neck with a loud crunch! A strange "urk" sounded from the teen and a surprised look overtook his face.

Blood shot like a geyser, spraying the tail end of the car as it passed. The riders screamed anew. They were soon climbing again, rattling up the huge rise in the track, one ready to push them off into something once thought of as fun. Nico's stomach churned. There was nothing fun about the ride any longer. He wanted off.

During the slow lift, a tremendous noise drew the attention of all the coaster riders. Masses of clowns climbed up the side of the Ferris wheel! Unlike the coaster, the giant wheel was stationary, already shut down by a quick-thinking employee on the ground. (Maybe one of the same clowns that now scaled the ride?)

Moving with startling speed and efficiency, the masses of clowns scaled the side to where riders sat trapped in buckets. Screams sounded as one by one the clown climbers chomped on passengers. Cries in each bucket died as quickly as they started. Some riders near the top leaped rather than face the oncoming mass of hungry clowns.

A thunderous rumble sounded along with the thwip of defeated safety cables anchoring the ride. Screams of twisting metal overshadowed the cries of riders as the enormous ride tilted and fell! It started slowly, but the weight took over and the ride tipped on its side in a massive cloud of debris.

The screams ceased. Only the moans of hungry clowns remained. Many of the clowns rose to their feet as if nothing had happened and went in search of food in the debris. They must have found something, for many grouped in one area and fed like hogs at a trough.

Then the coaster delivered them back into a freefall. Fast, so fast, once thrilling. "*The thrill is gone, baby,*" Nico's father once said to Nico's mother. A statement Nico felt was unnecessarily cruel, but then that was Nico's dad. Love them and leave them, except Nico figured the man never loved anyone at all.

Was his mother at the fair? Were other people he knew? Mrs. Hadley was a favorite teacher. Was she on the very wheel that collapsed? Nico was uncertain because he could not get out of the freaking car!

An enormous crack sounded, jerking Nico back into the real world. Amelia remained standing in the front car, pressed by gravity against the opened safety bar. Her shoulders leaned on it, but her head rose above it while her arms remained tangled in the bars, caught while reaching for the hippies who still talked about the worst acid trip ever.

It was a support beam that caught her head, lopping it off. The head rode in their direction, landing first in the laps of the hippies before bouncing along the car. The head paid a visit to the two men. They and Dotty had remained strangely silent during the ordeal. Screaming from time to time, but not articulating anything.

The decapitated head flew above the woman, heading right toward the center of the last car. Right toward Nico! It stopped short and hit the front edge of the last car, leaving a black smear, not red, and then spun directly over Nico. He looked up. It tumbled past as if the world had slowed to nothing, had become molasses, had forgotten that time existed.

As it spun past, Nico swore he saw the woman wink before the head vanished behind them. Time returned as the body in the front tilted. A trail of black gore shot from the neck and coated the screaming hippies. Liquid black goop choked their cries to a halt, their mouths filling with spew.

"What is happening?" Dotty finally found her voice.

Before anyone could answer the woman, they all screamed. Amelia's decapitated body tipped forward onto the track. The car ran over the body, causing the car to lift from the tracks, threatening to derail.

Dotty fell silent after her outburst, gripping the safety bar and praying. Briefly, she released her grip and made the sign of the cross before clamping down for safety once again.

"Dear Lord, keep this car on the tracks and please do not allow those clowns to eat anymore folks."

Humphrey snorted. The snort grew into a chuckle. The boy gripped the bar as tight as anyone else, but his mind was elsewhere as he verged on the edge of full-blown laughter.

"Don't eat folks? Who says that? Don't eat folks! Ha! Have you ever heard anything so ridiculous?" Humphrey said, bursting into an uncontrollable fit of laughter.

Nico heard it but considered it unfunny. Everything was unfunny. Especially clowns. But Humphrey kept laughing. Pops ignored their shared passenger, too busy scanning their surroundings, taking in what he could.

Meanwhile, Nico settled in for the ride. He tried to remember why he was there. He was finally big enough, tall enough to ride the adult ride. But then why did he feel so small? The hippies had cleared their mouths and screamed at one another as if their own partner was somehow responsible for the violation visited upon their faces. In their mouths.

The dark spew.

It was the spew that did it. And bites. Metallica teen was fine when they first started the ride. A super nice guy at that. But in the time that they circled around, Boosh was walking around minus a chewed off arm which kept the ride in the on position. A mishap that minus the cannibalistic clowns would have provoked great joy in Nico for the bout of good fortune. *Hey extra free rides everybody*!

The hippies were goners. Did they realize? Did they know? Earlier, they suggested they were tripping. Nico understood that as well. His father used what he could use when alcohol was in short supply, or maybe the alcohol when drugs were in short supply. And Humphrey, his best friend, was too busy cackling in the set next to him to be of any good. Nico turned to Pops.

"By the time we get down, make out kid will be..." Nico started.

"Waiting on the platform or even the tracks," Pops completed the sentence.

"And maybe cigarette clown if she figures out the stairs." Nico's stomach swooned, they did the dip signaling the next rise, bringing them higher, to solid ground, riding above it all for a short time before the next drop that would shoot them through the guts of the ride and send them back home.

"What's wrong with your friend?" Pops asked.

"Gone loco."

"Tell him to hang on."

"Humphrey, hang on!"

"What? Sure. Eating folks? Hilarious! Who says folks? Did you hear her?"

"Sure, Humphrey, sure."

Nico nodded to Pops once they were all settled in. Pops pushed up against the bar even as they approached the loop. The bar held despite the man's strain. The car rocketed down the drop into a loop. Nico thought the world looked better upside down. Once they emerged, the cars rocketed at a fast speed, but Pops went back into examination mode, studying the bar.

"I think I've found an emergency release. When we get down, we need to get out on the far side of the car. Can't stop them from getting anyone else necessarily, but we can try."

"But the car will keep moving. What do we do?"

"We get back in and ride again. Short-term solution, kid. Still thinking about the longer game. You good?"

Nico nodded. He turned to Humphrey, who laughed even harder upon hearing the plan. Nico worried but could not worry for too long. The end was near. Star Wars kid and make out kid were indeed both on the platform, each drooling, their mouths chewing as if waiting for someone to fill their maws with food. Awaiting a mama bird with mulched worms.

The twin terrors turned as one surprised at the appearance of a food train. The two afflicted men groaned with delight and reached toward the oncoming car, which slowed to a crawl. Each of the riders jerked away as far as they could in their seats.

Pops found a lever and pulled. The bar lifted, and they were free. Pops leaped out on the far side of the seat. That kept him on the opposite side of the platform that the zombies stood on, keeping the set of cars between them. Pops rushed over and attempted to help Dotty while yelling instructions to the men in front of her.

"The red lever, pull it, you can get out," Pops said.

"We can't get out, they'll eat us," Louis yelled.

"We need to get out! Help me, Carl!" Dotty yelled.

"Stay seated, Dotty. We're not getting out. We're going to keep riding until someone comes for us," Carl said.

Pops lifted Dotty's bar just in time. The car headed toward the afflicted. Nico leaped out and ran alongside Pops, tracking with the slow-moving ride. Then Nico noticed his friend was not with them.

"Humphrey! Humphrey!"

Star Wars kid moved quickly, approaching the youth who remained seated. Humphrey had his arms held in front of him as if holding the safety bar despite it being raised over his shoulders and above his head. Humphrey continued laughing.

"Humphrey!" Nico yelled and tried to get to his friend but found he could not move.

Pops had hold of Nico with one hand. Dotty got as far as far edge of her seat when the making out kid reached for her. She slid far enough away that the afflicted teen moved on to the closer meal. Carl. Carl fought with the oncoming teen. Dotty yelled to Pops for help.

"My legs are asleep. Get me out, I need to help my husband!"

"No, stay, pull the bar down as soon as we are clear," Pops said.

"Let me go!" Nico yelled, kicking as the big man held him in place.

"You know I can't do that."

Then Humphrey looked at the oncoming Star Wars kid. "Hey, did you hear the one about the folks that eat folks?" Humphrey asked.

Humphrey slapped his leg, proud of himself for repeating a variation of the word that he found so amusing. Nico noticed how a tear ran from Humphrey's eye. From laughter, or something else? With a crunch, the Star Wars kid bit the center of Humphrey's face coming away with a nose and its surrounding flesh. Humphrey twitched in his seat. A large black cavity occupied what remained of the boy's face. Humphrey blinked repeatedly, his mind trying to make sense of the sudden damage.

Star Wars kid wasted no time and grabbed the boy by the shirt like the biggest of bullies. He pulled Humphrey out of the car and then chomped a large section of neck. Humphrey fell immediately limp in the boy's grip, a thing now, no longer a person.

Nico's eyes filled with tears. He stopped fighting Pop's arms and instead gripped them like they were the safety bar on the ride. Groaning sounded nearby. The hippies! Their eyes were pools of deep black, matching the inkwells of those on the platform. The hippies reached out, searching for food. The safety bar kept them in check.

Louis scrambled for the far side of the car. Carl punched the kid in the mouth only for his hand to come back minus three fingers. Geysers of red gushed toward the sky in pulses timed to the man's heartbeat. Dotty noticed and screamed.

"Carl? Baby?"

Carl gripped his hand at the wrist. They were moving again, picking up speed as they passed the starting point. Nico looked toward the controls where the severed arm remained on the button. It was too far away. There were too many afflicted on the other side of the fence. Dozens had gathered and pressed against the wire, which somehow still held. They stuck tongues through the chain link like disgusting sexual deviants. Some chewed on the wire as if they might gnaw their way through to food.

Nico realized there could not be many people left unafflicted at the fair. If there were, then the clowns pressing their faces against the fencing would have been elsewhere, making meals of patrons. Dotty cried out again.

"Please. I can't get up; my legs are asleep!" Dottie cried.

"Stay where you are. We are moving again," Pops said and leaped back into the car. He reached for Nico and they both sat. He pulled the bar back down and they were off, heading toward the lift, the afflicted behind them occupied with poor Humphrey and Carl's fingers.

"My bar. My bar!" Dotty yelled.

"Pull it down. It comes right down," Pops yelled.

Dotty raised her arms but could not reach it. Nico and Pops reached toward her car as if they might will the bar down, but it was too far. Dotty kept reaching behind herself unsuccessfully. The car started the climb. The rumbling of the track shook them. Without her anchor in place, Dotty bounced around her seat. She finally found her feet and stood slightly, trying to reach back.

Then gravity took hold. The rise became too steep. Dotty fell back into her seat. They were getting close to the top.

"Lady, grab it," Nico yelled.

"I can't. I can't. Carl, help me!"

"I ain't got no fingers, baby," the man moaned from the front. "And I feel rotten. I think I need to take a dump or something," Carl said.

The man spoke with a slur as if drunk. He was a man in transition. Louis screamed about his need to escape the car. Dotty tried one more time to stand and grab her bar. Dotty managed the turn, but the steep angle caused her to fall into the seat, facing backward like Amelia before her. Dotty stared at the riders behind her, her hands reaching out to them for help. She could not push herself off the seating. The ride plateaued, then rocketed down the other side.

Dotty locked eyes with Nico right before the speed of the coaster ejected the woman. She flew out of the car and into a spin, her foot nearly kicking Nico in the face. He ducked just in time. Something popped into the car near their feet. A shoe. A woman's shoe. They came out of the freefall and rocketed into the first loop. When they turned upside down, the shoe fell out of the car. *Into the puke cage*, Nico thought.

A fresh scream drew their attention. Carl feasted on his best friend two cars up. Pops turned to Nico.

"The straightaway up top. It's the only chance to get off."

"What are you talking about?" Nico said, battling tears still, thinking of his poor friend.

"It slows just enough at the top. It's designed to do that for the view, and to build tension for the upcoming loop."

"The top? Like a million miles above earth?"

"It's climbable. Idiots do it all the time. You're smarter than them. There's too many waiting on the tracks below. We're not getting another go around this thing."

Nico had no time to argue. They were already reaching the highest point on the coaster. Why was everything moving so fast? They reached the stretch. They were at the top. Pops released the safety bar and Nico leaped out into a run, holding the side of the car to remain upright until he could find his footing. He stopped and windmilled his arm, almost falling off the ledge immediately. Fighting for control, he struggled to stand upright on the track. The car continued moving, picking up speed. Pops was nowhere to be found.

"Good luck, kid! Bum knee. I'll try to keep them busy until you get clear!"

Pops yelled over his shoulder and was gone. Nico stood above it all, towering over Clown Town at a height that made him dizzy. In the distance, he saw the defeated Ferris wheel. Everywhere he looked, clowns and patrons wandered, walking listlessly through the wreckage of the once vibrant Clown Town.

Nico understood he had to move fast. Pops was right. If the car came back around, there would be no safe climb. The car would surely hit him or dislodge his grip. He walked along the track to a spot where it dipped. From there, he watched the car heading back to the platform but could not see the platform itself. There were too many barriers in his way.

He lowered himself over the edge, grateful that he was just tall enough for his feet to reach each successive support beam. Maybe that was why one had to be a certain height for the ride, so they were tall enough to make the climb down if needed.

The wind was brisk and carried with it the stench of death. Whatever the black goo that afflicted the people, it emitted a foul smell of the first order, but an abundance of corpses proved even worse. Gripping tightly to avoid the wind saved his life. The structure shuddered, accompanied by screeching metal below, followed by shouts.

The car had stopped. Its crash proved powerful enough to shake the structure. Pops yelled defiantly down below for some time. Eventually, the man's hollering ceased. Soon there was nothing but the constant murmur of afflicted clowns gurgling and spitting and moaning. Their voices approached a collective wail, a cry of people mourning the loss of their former selves.

Nico eventually reached the lowest rung of the structure and dropped to the ground on all fours. It was time to go. He was in the safety of the puke catcher and made his way towards the opening that he and Humphrey had created. Then he would run to the next spot they cut in the fence and... What? Was everything limited to the fair, or had it spread everywhere?

He would worry later. It was time to escape. He reached the opening to the puke catcher fence, bent down to exit when a gloved hand grabbed his shoulder. A clown! He turned and punched. The clown's nose squeaked like a dog toy.

The clown grabbed her nose. "Hey kid, what'd you do that for?"

He stood there in shock, hands balled into fists, his face scrunched into defeat. Nico's eyes were wide. The boy focused on one thing on the clown's outfit.

"Oh, the blood? It's not mine. It's from my customers. No bites, see?"

She lifted her clown sleeves, which comically refused to stay up, and kept falling back into place. She repositioned her nose as if taking it off was not an option. Her large red feet were dirt covered and abraded from running. Sadie was the name on her badge.

"I run the game that shoots water into clown mouths."

Nico recognized her. "I like that game."

"I used water cannons to shoot at real clowns. Got some of them in the mouth. Their heads didn't explode, though. Except my customers did. Well, not exploded but had parts bit off. One clean off at the neck." She stared into distant space and tilted from side to side, lost in memory until refocusing on Nico. "Oh my gosh, you're just a kid and I'm talking like this."

"It's okay. I'm tall enough to ride the rides," Nico said.

"Still, how about I don't over-share, anyway?"

"That would be great," Nico agreed.

"Went for the fence to get away. Surprised to see you."

She held the cut fence open for him, then crawled through herself. They started toward the exterior fence and the parking spot beyond. Nico led her to the cut opening. She eyed him curiously as they navigated through the next opening.

"You wouldn't know anything about who cut these fences, would you?"

"A great friend told me about them," Nico said.

The tears started again but failed. He was cried out. The woman noticed.

"This is where we might part and go our separate ways, but I've got a car and don't really want to find out what's in town by myself. Need a ride?"

Nico nodded. The woman placed one of her hands out. Nico gripped it. Her oversized gloves comically swallowed his own hand, but he was happy to have someone to talk to. They walked toward the sea of cars which appeared free of the afflicted.

For a moment, Nico closed his eyes and imagined it was his mom still in his life, taking her son on a trip to the fair. In the vision, they were not poor, and it was only his mother. His father was nowhere to be seen. As they walked the concourse, he smelled the grease of fried dough, the sweetness of cotton candy, the milky notes of soft serve ice cream.

His mother would love the rides and be happy to take him on them. They would ride the Titty Twister together, though she would scold him for saying the ride's name. Nico would playfully laugh it off and maybe repeat the word through a fake sneeze. His mother would laugh, and they would ride together through both loops. And the rides would still be fun.

Except when he opened his eyes, he realized he no longer remembered what his mother looked like. And the idea of ever riding a coaster again made him sick. But for now, he had a clown, one who was not hungry. One who did not eat folks. She seemed nice, and that was enough.

As they wandered the cars, he realized that life itself was a ride. Wilder than any theme park. It was a ride that he wished to stay on as long as possible. For now, at least, it continued as if some dead arm had its hand on the controls, keeping it from stopping. This ride came without a safety bar, and he could only hope that while it lasted, no one would ever notice that he was not tall enough to ride.

CAFÉ DU MONDE, NEW ORLEANS, LOUISIANA

L IVING IN MOBILE, ALABAMA for three years had its perks. One of them was that I lived only two hours from one of the most exciting cities in the United States—New Orleans, Louisiana. Just being there, you're surrounded by a surreal amount of life and culture you can't find anywhere else. Before I made my move to Vermont, I traveled once more to the Big Easy, and took in all the sights and sounds that I could, and while sitting multiple mornings and evenings in the outside café at Café Du Monde, I thought about a ghost tour I'd taken where our guide talked about a resident of New Orleans named Jacques St. Germain. Legend suggested he was a vampire who escaped arrest right before the 1920s after attacking a sex worker and sucking her blood.

I sipped on coffee and ate beignets and listened to live jazz out on the street as I looked out over Jackson Square. I thought about vampires and what would happen if one brother was lost to the night. It also became a sort of metaphor for the relationship with one of my own brothers, who I've had a difficult relationship with.

Café Du Monde is an ancient café with a rich history, just like the city of New Orleans. If you find yourself there, please do yourself a favor and grab one table and get the beignets with your coffee or latte. If anyone compliments your shoes, just ignore them, because they're going to bet you they "know where you got 'em".

COFFEE RECOMMENDATION: New Orleans has a particular coffee blend which you can find everywhere and that's with Chicory. My recommendation, if you want to taste a little New Orleans culture, is to find yourself a Chicory coffee or hot latte. Just sit back and enjoy, preferably if you can find yourself a beignet

LOUISIANA JACK

Joseph Carro

E VERY TIME DANNY REYES stepped out into the sunlight, he wondered if his brother ever missed its warmth. Or missed him. Arthur was three years younger than Danny, which placed Arty at the ripe old age of thirty-eight. Danny imagined what Arty would look like had he lived a normal life. Maybe Arty would be a little heavier, with some of that happy relationship weight Danny heard about from other, happier people. Or he might have kids giving Danny nephews and nieces since there was now almost no chance of him having kids of his own. Maybe Arty would have sprouted a full beard and watched UFC fights at Buffalo Wild Wings and play fantasy football. It would have been nice to see Arty grow older like he had, but that wasn't possible, because Arty would forever be seventeen years old.

New Orleans was a city Danny wished he'd found when he was younger than forty-one. Now he was well beyond the bacchanalian call of the nightlife, and even if the urge struck, he was too busy hunting his brother cross country. It was no wonder Arty traveled sixteen hundred miles from Biddeford, Maine, to make this his base of operations. The city was a jazz-infused fever dream. The dream restarted every night on Bourbon Street where people drank Hand Grenades or Hurricanes while scantily clad shot girls enticed passersby into the dive bars for space on the balcony overlooking the debauchery on the streets below.

Flocks of sailors during Fleet Week roamed the city in their white and outdated-looking naval uniforms, making it look like a wartime musical from the fifties was being filmed there. Danny stood before a display case hanging on an exterior wall of LaFitte's Blacksmith Shop. The number of posters featuring missing men and women was staggering, hinting at the dangers in such a city. The display confirmed Danny had been correct about coming here to find Arty. It chilled Danny's blood to think the last thing some of the missing had seen was Arty's boyish face. Danny snapped a photo of the missing posters on his iPhone, shoved the phone into his pocket, and walked to his hotel room at the Astor Crowne Plaza.

He ignored the drunks splayed out on the sidewalks as the chemical truck made its rounds trying to cleanse Bourbon Street of its sins, its fan-shaped spray of chemical cleaner mingling with the ripe armpit smell of the French Quarter, creating a pungent bouquet singularly unique to New Orleans.

"Nice shoes," a staggering drunk with a SpongeBob tee mumbled to him.

"Thanks," he said, brushing by the man.

"I bet you I can tell you where you got 'em," he said, a grin spreading across his face.

"Yeah?"

"You got 'em right there on your feet."

Danny sighed and shook his head. The man held out his hand as if expecting payment. Danny kept walking and didn't look back.

"Motherfucker," SpongeBob tee guy called after him.

Danny dreamed of the day he lost Arty to the thing in the mill. It was less a dream and more a nightmare, and no matter how many times it visited him in sleep, it never terrified him any less.

The day had been cold, so when he and Arty approached the mill near the Saco River, the wind cut like a blade of ice through their denim jackets. It got so frigid that Danny couldn't feel his fingers anymore and his lip stuck to his zipper while trying to cover his face from the wind with the collar of his jacket. As they reached the mill, each of them shivering, the Saco River raged underneath. They stepped up to a broken-hinged door on the mill's side covered in graffiti depicting penises and boobs. Once they entered, the wind ceased, making the air tolerable. Danny could still see his breath and watched as Arty rubbed his hands together for warmth.

Danny and Arty had never been to that part of the mill before. There were so many abandoned buildings in Biddeford that it would take years to explore them all. Their mom hadn't been there when they'd gotten home from school. She was likely drinking at her friend's house across the city. With her not there to protest, the boys planned their trip to the massive structure.

Visiting the place brought some sense of excitement, if only because the place so worried their mother. She warned them not to hang around the mills, showing them newspaper clippings she'd saved of people going missing around Saco and Biddeford. THE CURSE OF THE SACO RIVER? One article read. Theories circulated, but most people, including Danny, assumed the missing were runaways. Once they neared the mill, they followed a stray dog they'd seen outside the entrance, but it took refuge inside, entering through a small hole near the door they used. The dog was gone by the time they were inside..

"I think I see a tunnel over here," Arty said. "He probably scampered down that way."

Danny warmed his hands with his breath and rubbed them together. He didn't respond but followed his brother, who moved confidently down the passage. As the *passage narrowed, Danny grew uneasy with the confined space. The walls were closing in on either side of them, and they each had to crouch to make any headway. Ahead of them, the old passage opened into what looked like a wider room. Danny could just make out heavy panting and whining somewhere in the darkness ahead. Arty was right.*

Danny emerged after Arty, who was already bent down trying to coax the dog. The place was an old warehouse or storage room. Old crates lay half-rotted and open, full of cobwebbed and mildewed sneakers.

"C'mon, boy," Arty said, whistling and making kissy sounds with his lips.

The dog whimpered and took a tentative step toward them. It looked like a boxer. The weathered floorboards were thin enough that they even creaked under the dog's paws. Cold air blew through the cavities in the floor's teeth, which were the floorboards. A rotten smile the place had which failed to mute the roar of the Saco river below.

"Careful," he said to Arty. "These boards are..."

Before Danny could finish, the boards broke, sending them both plunging. Danny landed on what felt like concrete. While immensely painful, it was better than the icy and turbulent Saco River. Danny struggled to breathe after having all the wind knocked out of his lungs. And struggled further to locate his brother, but his vision grew dim and soon he passed out.

It was the smell which woke Danny, the mill's own version of smelling salts. Fading slivers of sunlight filtered in from above where they'd fallen through the floor. Danny coughed, wanting to retch from the odor. His chest hurt. When he turned himself over, there was a sharp pain in his left elbow and wrist. (He found out later that he'd sprained his arm.)

He cried out for Arty, whom he couldn't see. The dog was nowhere to be seen, either. He didn't know where to go, but behind him there was a massive chamber where water churned violently. The dark seemed impenetrable, but Danny thought he glimpsed movement, so again called out for Arty. No answer. If something happened to Arty, he'd never forgive himself. I called out for Arty again and again until I heard a response just ahead.

"I'm in here, Danny. The dog hurt himself pretty bad."

Danny's heart pounded at the startling sound of a voice in the darkness, but discovering the voice belonged to Arty calmed him.

"Christ, Arty. What'd you leave me laying in there for?" Danny said, emerging into another small basement area. Arty was clutching the wounded boxer and petting him. The dog whimpered softly. Danny could see a gash on its side.

"You were fine. You just hit your head like me. The dog was whimpering and scared, man. I couldn't deal."

"Yeah, well, what if I was dead?"

"You're not, though."

Danny went to pet the boxer and the dog's ears raised in alert. The animal ceased whining and struggled from Arty's grasp.

"Aw, man, he doesn't like you," Arty said. "Stay away from him for a sec!"

Before Danny could respond, the dog burst through the space between his legs and back toward where they'd fallen through the floor, barking, howling, and gnashing its teeth. Its mouth foamed.

"Holy shit!" Danny said. "I think it's rabid!"

Arty pushed past Danny and gave chase. Danny hobbled along after them but slowed as the odor from earlier grew stronger in the direction they were heading. Even Arty covered his face with his denim jacket sleeve, suddenly aware of the toxic smell. Danny's mouth watered and his stomach turned somersaults. The dog no longer paid attention to Danny and Arty, too busy growling into darkness.

"This dog definitely has rabies," Danny said. "Look, he's crazy."

Arty pleaded with the dog, trying to coax him back, but a peculiar aggression and madness had overtaken it. Then something like a cacophony of bird wings sounded above, and a shroud of darkness fell over the dog. Danny stepped back. The dog was gone. Arty was still trying to coax it toward him, unaware that the dog had just vanished before their very eyes.

Danny felt water splash on his face from above. He quickly wiped at the drops, fearful it was viscous and toxic. It smelled strongly of copper. The dying light revealed the liquid to be red.

There was a horrific tearing sound and a harsh yelp overhead. Danny and Arty screamed as the torn carcass of the dog landed between them. Demonic red eyes glowed in the rafters of the building above. Danny and Arty ran as fast as they could. They ran in silence with no words needed to spur them on their terrifying retreat from whatever pursued them through the darkness.

The smell grew stronger, both rotten and sweet at the same time. It reminded Danny of a dead cat he once found in an alley. This was much stronger, like black licorice and oranges sitting in the scorching summer sun inside a bucket of dead fish. The odor made his eyes water, making it hard to see where he ran. Arty, who was right behind him, suddenly screamed.

That's when Danny saw the pile of bodies just ahead, near a small hole in the wall which looked big enough for Danny and Arty to fit through. The bodies were in various states of decay, their collective skin whiter than the snow outside the mill. In the dying light, one corpse appeared to stare at Danny with what remained of its eyes. The orbs were nothing more than milky white blobs, stained black, sitting awkwardly on the shallow, yellow-white bowls that were eye sockets. The corpse's skin sloughed off at the hands and partially on the face. Its mouth was open, as if designed to display what remained of a blackened and chewed tongue.

Danny screamed, but moved forward, scrambling for the opening. He assumed his brother's scream related to the corpse pile as well, but it struck Danny that he had not heard his brother since the scream. Danny was halfway through the escape hole when he pulled out to look for Arty. Danny spotted his brother and tremors wracked his body. Arty stood in the distance, standing still, with the creature's mouth wrapped around his throat in a grim embrace. Arty stared straight ahead in a kind of trance, a tear rolling down his cheek.

Danny screamed for his brother, damning the evil thing that looked to be killing him. The creature extended his hand, pointing at Danny, before disappearing into the shadows.

Danny woke with a start, as he always did after the nightmare, finding himself covered in more sweat than usual. It was the thick New Orleans humidity, which permeated the air even throughout the air-conditioned hotel lobby and up into his room. It seemed to soak into his very bones, and being from the north, he thought he might soon melt. He rolled out of bed, grabbing his iPhone from its charger. It was 9pm.

Time to get ready.

Danny pulled from his suitcase a blue suit, which he'd only worn once to a wedding, and left it on the chair while he got in the shower. He let the water flow against his muscles, ironing them out. After turning forty, everything hurts unless one takes care of themselves early on, and Danny had definitely not taken care of himself. Not in his twenties, and certainly not in his thirties. He wasn't exactly looking forward to wearing a suit in the New Orleans humidity, but he needed to stand out and look the part of the lost tourist. Not that he wasn't actually one, but he needed the outfit to be a better actor than he was.

After the shower, Danny dried off, put on the suit, and slicked his hair back with pomade. He ran beard balm through his beard and dabbed some cologne on his neck. Within the hour, he was already on Bourbon Street again, having left his hotel and ventured out into the night.

Bourbon Street was alive and bursting with activity. Throngs of people huddled close to the entrances to bars and chicken shacks. Some late dinner folks hustled out of creole restaurants, clutching their bellies in contentment. Danny walked among them, his eyes searching.

"Ay, man, I like your suit," said one man as he passed. "I bet I can tell you where you got your shoes," he said, following up.

Danny ignored him with a wave of his hand and headed to Lafitte's Blacksmith Shop. When he arrived, he stepped inside the crowded bar. Famous for being haunted, Lafitte's was purportedly the oldest continuously operating bar in the United States.

After ordering a Hurricane, (a strong alcoholic drink that tasted like purple cough medicine mixed with Kool-Aid) Danny exited the bar and walked toward the infamous LaLaurie Mansion. The Mansion was also said to be haunted. In his blue suit, holding a touristy drink, and stumbling in front of a tourist landmark, Danny looked like an easy mark. He walked up and down the street several times before noticing he had grown a tail. Three men, in their twenties. Danny moved onto a deserted side street.

The young men followed.

Danny continued on until he almost reached the end of the street.

"Hey, nice shoes, man." One of them finally said, trying to get his attention. Danny turned.

"I already know that one," Danny said. "I've got them on my feet."

The young men fanned out in a small crescent around him. To his left there was a tall skinny guy wearing a wife-beater and cargo shorts. He was bald and had tattoos on his neck. In front of him was a short, squat, muscular man with long red hair. To his right, and circling around toward his back, was an obese man with army fatigues and thick boots.

"Hey, that's what's up," said the redhead. "He heard that one, boys."

"Nice suit, man," said the bald one, no doubt trying to draw his attention from the big one circling around.

"I got it at Goodwill," Danny said. He hoped his plan was going to work. "You'd be surprised what you can find there."

"Deadass?" the bald one asked.

"Deadass." Danny said, prompting the two in front of him to laugh at his usage of the word. "In fact," Danny continued, "One time I found three uncut books there. You know what an uncut book is?"

Before the two men could respond, Danny felt wire-strong arms grab his own from behind. The big one. Within a second or two, the redhead came over and decked him in the stomach, knocking the wind from him. Then, the bald one punched him across the face and knocked him unconscious.

Danny dreamed he was back in college in Standish, Maine. They had given him a scholarship to attend Saint Joseph's College. His third year was almost over, and despite his issues growing up and his sadness and depression at losing Arty, he was excelling at his studies. He had a girlfriend, Kelly, and he was going to school to be a writer. Everything was looking up. But then, as he traveled back to Biddeford for a weekend to visit his mother, a deer leaped out in front of his car and smashed through the windshield. The impact caused Danny to lose consciousness, even though the vehicle never slowed.

A whoosh of frigid air woke Danny, and the intense pain wracking his body woke him further, but nothing made sense. Maybe he was unconscious in a hospital bed in a coma and was dreaming. He remembered the deer through the windshield and remembered the sound of the engine gunning where his foot involuntarily pressed against the gas, unable to move because of the weight of the deer pressed against him. Then blackness.

Now Danny stared at the ground, which was about sixty feet below. Something was carrying him! He looked up and saw the creature from the mills all those years ago. Blood ran down his side and his other arm dangled useless from his body. He couldn't move it.

Eventually, the flyer dumped Danny in a heap at the entrance to an old shed at the edge of the forest. He couldn't move, but he watched the creature clamber inside. Soon it returned with Arty in tow. Only Arty hadn't aged at all. Danny had aged since Arty had disappeared, had grown facial hair, and filled out some. But Arty looked the same as he had that day in the mill.

Then Danny shook. a cold overtook him, and he realized he was about to pass out again, but somehow knew it would be permanent. He felt his life fading as surely as the sight of his brother faded. He found some peace in knowing his brother's face was the last thing he saw. Then the world went dark.

Danny woke to blood and sucked in air, only to cough and spit the blood which had filled his mouth. It sprayed everywhere. The taste of blood in his mouth was strong.

"I'm sorry, Danny. I really am. It was the only way to save you."

Another man's voice called out from somewhere nearby. "After this, we head south. You've got 20 minutes."

Danny looked incredulously into the face of his brother.

"Arty?"

"Don't talk, Danny. You were almost dead. Jacques saved you. But you might be uncomfortable for a while."

Arty was correct. Danny screamed as he felt his veins boiling on the inside of his skin. His back arched in pain as the feeling returned to his arms and legs.

"Tell Mom I love her and miss her," Arty said.

As Danny screamed in pain, he watched Arty step over to the creature he'd seen in the mill. The creature appeared to be a man in his forties, slightly built, with sharp features, a few feet taller than Arty.

"I love you, too, Danny. You'll always be my big brother. Don't feel bad for me."

With that, Arty's eyes turned red, and the two burst into the sky and out of sight. Danny lost consciousness again. Danny woke again to find his wounds healed, though his clothes were blood drenched.

In his dream, time became disjointed, and he was suddenly in Gettysburg, Virginia, at Devil's Den when he'd turned thirty. He'd gone there on a weekend to get away from work and dig into some history. The park was closed, but he'd wanted to get some night photos. That's when he'd felt what seemed like ants crawling under his skin. The sensation startled him at first, and he slapped at his torso and arms, trying to bat away the insects swarming him, but he found none.

Turning as the sensation grew stronger, he saw Arty once again, standing before him in front of a rock formation where a mighty Civil War battle took place in the 1800s. He was less surprised this time, almost as if he knew it would happen. He thought maybe he'd hallucinated Arty back in college when he'd totaled his Volkswagen Jetta, but here he was again, looking exactly like he did back at the mill.

"Hi, Danny," Arty said. "You got old."

"You should be older, too, Arty. What happened to you? Are you a ghost?"

"No. I'm... something else. Remember Lost Boys?"

Danny said nothing, only stared in horror.

"Yeah, there's no easy way to say it. I guess I just can't help checking in every once in a while."

"I think I could feel you when you got close. Jesus, Arty, I'm so sorry. I thought you died. We all did."

"I did die. Now, listen, there are more of us out there. We drink blood, Danny. We have to. It was bad at first, and I felt horrible, but now it's just the way it is. But I don't want it to happen to you. Stay clear of New Orleans. Jacques is one of the last of the Old Ones. He didn't want to save you, but he owed me a favor. I know you've been trying to find me, just don't."

"You saved me in the cabin with blood. But I'm not a vampire?"

"No, thankfully you're not. But I guess the blood does more than just bring you back from death. I could feel you nearby, too. We all can. That means he can, too. Next time, he'll kill you. He wanted to before, after turning me back at the mill. He didn't want you to tell everyone what you saw. But you never really did, so he mostly left you alone. But I know he watched you and watched Mom. Just promise me you'll stay away from New Orleans?"

"Will I see you again?"

"Not if you follow through with your promise."

Danny said nothing. Arty moved in close as if he were going to hug his brother goodbye, but his mouth opened in a terrible gape and Danny saw Arty's eyes turn red and two glistening fangs extend down from the roof of his mouth. Danny took a few steps back reflexively.

Perhaps because of the look on Danny's face, Arty turned and flew off into the sky, soaring high above the Gettysburg Battlefield and into the night.

Danny woke to the sound of his own body being punched and kicked. His left eye swelled shut, and his ribs felt broken.

"This motherfucker don't have shit on him."

Another powerful kick landed square on his jaw, rocking his head back. Someone stomped on his left hand.

Despite his beating, Danny smiled and laughed. He grinned through bloody teeth.

"We gotta' go," said the big one. "He ain't got shit, and he's crazy. Look at him."

"Motherfucker, what are you smiling at?" asked the redhead.

The bald one kicked Danny in the face again, sending him sprawling and coughing up blood onto the New Orleans street. Danny could hear live music being played, jazz, and it was good. He could also feel what felt like spiders crawling under his skin.

Danny sat up, watching the three men retreat down the side street back where Danny had first lured them. That's when a lone figure entered, blocking their path. The men stopped in their tracks as the lone figure advanced. Then, almost imperceptibly, the figure ripped the head from the big one's shoulders, literally. The other two didn't know how to process what had happened, and within the blink of an eye, the bald one had an arm thrust through his rib cage. From where he was, Danny could see the silhouette of an arm come through the bald one's back.

The redhead pulled a gun from his waistband and emptied his clip into the figure. When the muzzle flashed, Danny saw Arty's face contorted and gruesome, but still Arty. The redhead stood no chance. Arty grabbed the man's lower jaw and ripped it off before stabbing him with his own jawbone. As the man fell, Arty cradled him in his arms, and Danny could hear awful slurping sounds as Arty drained the man of his blood.

Danny scrambled to his feet and found Arty standing before him, soaked in blood.

"I told you never to come here, Danny," Arty said.

"I had to," Danny said, spitting out blood. Danny noticed Arty's eyes following the red spit as it landed on the street.

"Why? I thought you understood."

"Mom died, Arty."

Arty stood for a moment, and his grotesque features faltered in the moonlight and softened. He turned his back to Danny.

"How'd she go?" Arty asked.

"Cancer."

"When?"

"Just a few weeks ago. I know what you said, but I had to tell you. You'll always be my little brother, Arty. You're all I've got."

"Leave here, Danny. I'm not the same anymore. It's different. Arty is dead. I'm dead. Death surrounds this place. I don't want you to die, too."

"Look at me, and look at you, Arty. I'm forty years old. You look like you're still a teenager. If you ever see me again, I'll probably be really old or maybe you won't ever see me again, but I had to tell you about Mom. She died missing you."

"I'm sorry, Danny, but you have to go. I can't protect you if Jacques finds you here."

"I'll leave," Danny said. "Don't worry."

As Danny walked by Arty, he wanted to hug his brother one last time, but couldn't bring himself to do it. He could feel the hunger in his brother, and each moment he stood by him was a moment he was risking death. Arty was gone. Most of him was, anyway.

A powerful hand gripped Danny's left shoulder. He felt its icy touch even through the sleeve of his blood-stained suit. Danny stopped.

"You'll always be my big brother," Arty said.

Taking a risk, Danny clasped his brother's hand that rested on his shoulder. His chest erupted in pain with the effort. Arty's hand did not feel like a corpse's hand; it felt like solid ice. Arty withdrew his hand.

Danny walked away from his brother, and when he did, he heard awful slurping sounds emanating from the deserted street directly behind him from Arty feeding on the corpses of the street thugs. The intense feeling of bugs under his skin waned as Danny reached his hotel. He'd ditched his bloody blazer in a dumpster behind a bar.

Though exhausted and needing sleep, Danny turned on his phone and looked at the missing posters he'd photographed earlier in the day. Danny had always wanted to see New Orleans. Now he knew he could never come back, or he'd end up on a poster, too. He knew that most likely, the thugs he'd encountered wouldn't warrant a missing poster themselves, and he wondered how many other wayward souls went missing in New Orleans that nobody ever looked for. Before he knew it, he was asleep despite the pain in his body.

Danny dreamed. And when he dreamed, he and Arty were on top of Rattlesnake Mountain in Casco, Maine, during a summer camping trip. The moon was full. The wind was chill, and the two of them sat side by side in the moon's glow. Beneath the cliff where they sat, the moon's reflection winked back from Sebago Lake and several other smaller lakes in the distance. The two boys had hiked up in the dark, with no flashlights, carrying knives strapped to their waists and pretending they were in the Lord of the Rings and traversing through the forests of Middle Earth.

"I'm glad you hiked up here with me, Arty," Danny said.

"Me, too, Danny."

"Isn't the moon cool? I don't think I've ever seen it so big."

"*Yeah, me neither. It looks super cool!*"

Arty shivered. Danny was kind of cold, too, but took his sweater off and handed it to Arty.

"*Here, put this on. I just want to sit up here a few more minutes and then we'll go back down.*"

"*Are we gonna' get in trouble?*"

"*Nah, we've just got to be quiet when we get back to camp.*"

"*I love you, Danny.*"

"*Love you, too, bro.*"

In his dream, Danny felt the pang of loss as he relived this moment, but he didn't want to wake up. He wanted to stay in this dream, and relive that moment when Arty was still Arty and Mom was still around, waiting for them to come back from camp at the end of summer.

"*You'll always be my big brother, Danny,*" *Arty said.*

When Danny woke to strange sounds, it did not surprise him to see his hotel room window open. It surprised him less to see Jacques' red eyes staring back at him from the darkness just above his face.

"You shouldn't have come to New Orleans, little one. But you've come full circle and come back to me."

Danny tried to think about that night with the moon as Jacques St. Germain, the legendary vampire of Louisiana, drained him of his life. But all he could think about was how he had flinched from his brother's hug back in Gettysburg a decade ago. He closed his eyes and let the darkness take him.

GLORIA JEAN'S COFFEES, PORTLAND, MAINE

T HIS WAS THE FIRST story ever written for The Little Coffee Shop of Horrors Anthology. Why is it only appearing now? Because I could not finish it then. It was too soon. I wrote this near the hotel I was staying at during my mother's funeral. And in her death, this series was born.

Before my mother had passed unexpectedly, I developed the idea for this series and planned to author these books. However, initially it was going to be only my stories unless I could convince a certain someone to write these with me. Joseph and I had attempted a writing project together years earlier but were at different places with our writing and that fell through.

When I flew home to Maine for the funeral, I reconnected with Joseph and pitched the idea. The answer was yes, and the series was born. Well, I was staying at a hotel next to the Maine Mall, which was a significant drive from where other family members were, so by the time I was back at the hotel alone, I had little to do. I was suffering through the loss, still shocked, saddened, and lost.

Writing in coffee shops was familiar and a comfort, so I lugged my laptop to the mall, which was walking distance. There I discovered Gloria Jean's coffees. The place deserves comment before I move on with this introduction, as things will soon get heavy.

What I found in Gloria Jean's Coffees was a staff who were amazingly friendly. They did not know I was suffering, no idea I was in mourning, so they did their thing, bouncing around, likely on their own caffeine highs.

I needed that, being around people who were celebrating life, not mourning a passing. They did not know my circumstance so treated me as a functioning member of society. If only they knew I was one wrong word away from crying in public.

They did not use the wrong words. They were friendly, funny, engaging, and full of life. Even better, they kept dueling tip jars at the counter. Each had a sign with a different way to perish in a zombie apocalypse. One could make their choice known via tipping. I knew then I was with my people. (Not just Mainers, but those appreciating horror.)

Their coffee was exceptional, which helped because I was eating and drinking very little. Besides one dinner out with my dad, I only ate Italian sandwiches and drank coffee. (There is a second coffee shop from Maine that will be in a future volume as I did a twofer while alone. That place remained open later, so when I could not sleep, I went there. Technically, two originated in Maine. Check out volume three in the future for that one.)

If ever I get back, I will visit and let them know how much they helped a lost soul get through a difficult time. Three years have passed now. I'm certain there are fresh faces, but I will be forever grateful to them and hope you all visit.

As for why I failed to finish this for the first volume, well, it came down to the sadness behind it, which kept me from looking at the pages at a certain point. Then there was the editing. Did I have time to get it right? Because if not, that would be a problem for my mother. One of the few fights we ever had was over my writing. I was away at college, where literature was my minor.

The professors were Machiavellian in their assignments. The short story output expected from a single semester produced enough pages for several novels. What it meant was one would always be writing without the luxury of time for editing. Stories were often handed in raw. There was no choice. Hand in what you had or fail.

My mom was a heavy reader, so when she discovered my stories after I came home that first summer, I came home one day to find she had edited one and added some stuff of her own. The act of doing so upset me greatly. (I know, don't judge, you had to be there.) Why it offended me was, I thought she figured that was the best I could do, that somehow, I was not ready for prime time. Meanwhile,

I had already started writing screenplays, the first of which would make it to the semi-finals in one of the biggest screenplay competitions in the country.

Those stories were not for public consumption. I did not mean them to be seen outside the classroom, and I got the understanding that she intended to submit one for publication once finished. Trust me, if I was going to send something out, it was not those stories. We argued and then we let it all drop. No more editing my school stuff.

I submitted only one story to a publication while in college. Though rejected, I received a very nice handwritten letter from someone well known in the horror industry, so I kept that. But never again. I wrote screenplays and moved to Los Angeles.

Years later, I finally wrote the horror stories I wanted to for my whole life. Ridiculous that I had put it off for so long. I just finished The House, my debut horror novel, and it was one edit pass and one week away from publication. Then I got the call.

Call home quick, it's bad.

My mother went to the hospital for a checkup and fell ill and could not breathe (this was 2019, pre-Covid). Doctors had intubated mom once before for a heart issue and she did not wish to go through that again, so she signed a DNR. I reached her on the phone, and nothing made sense. She sounded fine. She was my mom, and she was speaking to me. And finally, I had a book she could read and be proud of.

I was in public when I called her and so was walking down streets in Los Angeles talking to her, suffering through the situation out in the open. It made no sense. I was talking to her. Something in me jumped to the bargaining stage of grief.

I explained to her the book was about to come out and I would send it to her, so she had something to read in the hospital. It would give her something to do until I could get on a plane to see her. I wanted so much to see her, I just needed for her to hold on. Hold on mom!

"I'm not going to make it, Paul," she said, except she used a nickname for me instead.

It no longer mattered I was out in public. I broke down then and could barely speak. I wanted to talk to her forever, but I had a plane to catch. We said our goodbyes and told one another other how much we loved each other.

Twenty-five minutes later, mom was dead.

After going home and meeting up with Joseph, the anthology series was born. I started writing the following story but recently completed it in Los Angeles when I was better able to handle the emotions behind it.

It is not a story about a mother and son. Mom would have considered that too on the nose. Instead, the focus is on a couple. Because in the end, everyone faces loss, and must figure out how to go on.

I'd be proud today to have my mom critique anything, edit anything, submit away. I would give up all these stories to have her back, but that is not life. Life is living while you are here and celebrating those who are no longer with us.

In the end, this story is about loss. But it is also about carrying on. Because what else can we do?

COFFEE RECOMMENDATION: My mother enjoyed the simple things in life, so enjoy a regular cup of coffee with a little milk and a bit of sugar. Remember to tap that spoon on the cup after you stir. And if you could raise a toast to Gerri Carro before you sip, I would be grateful. Miss you, mom.

SHELLS

Paul Carro

"**Y**OU KNOW I LOVE you right?" Toby asked Baker.

"Since you are my best friend. It is a requirement. It's the deal in our unsigned contract," Baker said.

"Wren is way out of your league, no offense."

"I take offense. That is an objectively offensive statement."

The two friends smiled through the slam. Friends since childhood, the two men in their late twenties kept full balances in a joint bad blood bank account. With so much goodwill shared over the years and mutual support offered in the toughest situations, both were free to withdraw from the account as needed. Without such an agreement, certain statements could otherwise end the friendship.

Toby was head chef at a trendy restaurant. The duo's long-term plan involved Toby opening his own restaurant with Baker serving as a major investor. That was

Baker's deal, money. Baker was notoriously frugal and a homebody, so he rarely spent on frivolous things. That left plenty stashed away to assist his friend when the time came to open a place.

Baker mostly served as wingman to his pretty boy friend who snagged nearly every woman who caught his eye. Toby's hookups never went much beyond one month, and then it was on to the next adventure. Baker (Andrew by birth but nicknamed for burning down his sister's Easy Bake Oven as a kid) did okay with women but was more of a long-term guy. Problem was that the women he often dated had different relationship goals. Ones not so lengthy. Until he met Wren.

Baker decided Toby's assessment of Wren revolved around the way she shot Toby down. A rare strikeout for the home-run king. Baker did not hide the thought.

"Is this because she chose me over you?"

"Partly," Toby said. "But it's more than that. She hangs out at the Citadel. I'm a head chef and I have trouble getting into that club."

"She has boobs. Boobs help," Baker said.

"Yes, they do. But she never takes you along?" Toby asked.

"It's not my thing. You know that. I go to clubs to pick up women. I already have one, so why bother?"

"Who is she with when she goes there? Is she yachting?"

"You don't trust her?" Baker asked.

The smiles faded as the conversation turned heavy. Levity left the room. The two had a shorthand, and the shared look suggested it was time to get serious. Time for the conversation to get real.

"Wren is stupid hot. Of course, I went for her. Thing is, she did not blink. It was as if she looked through me," Toby said.

"I appreciate that about her. How many of my girlfriends have you slept with over the years?"

"Only the ones that broke up with you."

"They broke up with me to sleep with you. They all knew your rule. You would not cheat on someone with me, but once they were single again, fair game. That is a dance in semantics, my friend."

"I saved you from future heartbreak with each woman I stole."

"Look everyone. I have the most altruistic best friend in the world!" Baker raised himself off his barstool and raised his glass.

Toby shushed his friend. The pair occupied a corner of the restaurant bar where Toby had just ended his shift. The drinks were work comps but causing a scene could get them both kicked out. Baker simmered and settled back onto his stool.

"I've dealt my whole life liking girls who only had eyes for you. Now I have one who only wants me. You should be happy for me."

Toby sipped his martini. "I am. Would be, I mean, were there not something off about her. She could be a model on magazine covers and she has settled for someone who never wants to leave his apartment, only wants to play video games all day."

"Again, more to love about her. And magazines don't exist anymore. How can she be on the cover of any?"

"She travels."

"I am aware of what my girlfriend does."

"Like all the time. She says she wishes to experience everything the world offers. And she goes to all the places without you?"

"What am I going to do in a museum?" Baker asked.

Toby finished his drink. "Why does she never take you? Don't answer. It's because you don't want to go. You stay at home. It takes a Herculean effort to drag you anywhere. If we weren't best friends, I would have broken up with you long ago myself."

"You always have dates. I got used to staying at home while you went and had your fun," Baker said.

"Valid point. But she is your girlfriend. Why don't you ever accompany her?"

"I do. Sometimes. Look, you are correct about one thing. She wants to explore the world every second of every day. But she comes home to me and no offense, the sex is ridiculous. After a night with her, I don't have the energy left to even think of going out. Plus, I work remotely, and…"

"Stop the excuses. Do you trust her?"

The shorthand between them evolved once again. Another shared look and the two men went to the next level of conversation. Gut spilling time.

"I understand she might meet men in every crazy place she visits. But when am I ever going to have a girl like her again? If I were you, it would likely be next Tuesday. But for me? She's all I got, Toby. Can't I keep her for as long as I can?"

Toby nodded. "Sure, you can, pal. I probably read her all wrong. What the hell do I know about women?"

"Besides. We are taking a trip together next week," Baker said.

"Wow. Okay. Progress. Where to?"

"The desert," Baker said.

"What desert? We live in New York."

"In Utah."

"Utah? What's in Utah?"

"Desert. Weren't you listening?" Baker laughed over having ball-busted his friend. "Yeah, it is crazy, but I'm crazy in love. She wants me to go to a desert, then I'm going to a desert."

"Make sure you don't have a shovel in your trunk. If she asks you to buy one…"

"Why are we friends again?" Baker asked.

Toby raised a hand to his mouth and made a zip it motion. Then he patted his friend on the shoulder and they drank.

"Seashells? We came to a desert for seashells?" Baker asked Wren.

He was a confused boy, but her smile put him at ease. A double banquet table worth of shells stretched before them. Wren exhibited joy while lifting each one, searching for something he could not understand. The shells were the least strange part of the store's inventory where Baker was concerned.

They were on their fourth day of driving. They made good time and were already in Utah, well on their way to THE desert. They had driven through plenty of desert already, but Wren had a special section of sand in mind, apparently. The entire trip she remained elusive about their destination other than to say it was a festival of sorts.

The two of them did not enjoy the same musical tastes so he hoped whatever the music festival lineup was, it would have crossover potential. On their cross-country drive, Wren had directed Baker to make multiple strange and specific stops. The result was a circuitous route to Utah. They could have arrived a day earlier, but Wren's mysterious side trips delayed their arrival.

Maybe she planned it that way. No sense arriving at a festival early. It started when it started. He wished he had some idea when the event took place or where it was. Easy enough to plug the address into his GPS, but she gave him the weird destinations one at a time. Each time they stopped at some odd hole in the wall, she emerged with an object of some sort and then fed him new coordinates, leading them on one more detour.

The current one led them to where Wren lifted seashells, large ones, shaking each as she went. *Joe Bob's Curiosities and Wonders Bazaar* was the store's name, the one that had shells. It also had taxidermist birds hanging from fishing line from the ceiling, spread throughout the room so that one might feel they were in Hitchcock's *The Birds*. Birds were not the only dangling thing in the room. Crossed sticks wrapped with colorful yarns also dangled from the ceiling. God's eyes they were called, at least when he made them in Sunday school.

One section of the shop alongside the shells had lunchboxes form time gone by. Then in plastic cases locked by a cheap padlock were toys from an even earlier era. The metal toys included trucks, ray guns, robots, and spaceships. Baker felt a nostalgia for the items even though they were well before his time. His childhood leaned plastic and was mostly Star Wars based.

The strange place was of a type he would never set foot in on his own, but there he was, standing patiently by while a beautiful woman goofed around with seashells. There were so many. She found matching ones and placed one over each ear.

"Tell me, darlin', would you still be with me if I looked like this?" Wren asked.

"Sure, I've always had a Princess Leia fetish."

She laughed and set them down. "This will go faster if you help."

"Help you find a seashell? Isn't that more of a personal taste kind of item?"

"I'm not looking for one. I'm trying to find one. Big difference. Help me shake them."

"What are we looking for?"

He picked one up and shook it. Nothing. He shrugged in her direction.

"We're lookin' for a rattle."

"The snake section was downstairs, lest you forget." It was not a lie.

She laughed and set hers down before shaking one after another. She nodded her head to get him moving. Baker shook one like a cocktail mixer. He knew the move, saw Toby do it many a time. He sometimes helped behind the bar at the restaurant as well. Wren's eyes sparkled with joy. Her eyes were deep pools of violet. Technically, they were blue, but most days they leaned violet.

Her black hair ran shoulder length and flopped around when she gave over to fits of laughter. She laughed often, especially when he acted goofy. Baker considered himself the serious type, but she brought a jovial streak out in him. He set the shell down and grabbed another. She did the same, and it was game on.

Each of them grabbed and shook as if in a race. Wren laughed as they both impersonated bartenders, shaking shells in the desert in a curiosities shop. Baker figured if he could stop laughing, he might find the whole thing absurd. Strange at minimum.

The proprietor heard the commotion and stopped by. He simply rolled his eyes at the shenanigans and walked away. The appearance and exit brought a fresh round of laughter from Wren. Such joy was one of the many things he found attractive about her. And as he watched her goof, he felt his legs go weak.

Beautiful. Too beautiful. Too stunning. She had no right being with him. She wore a skimpy black tank top and denim cutoff shorts, leaving her plethora of tats on full display. The ink started just below her neck, on her chest, just out of reach of her enticing cleavage. It took the form of a butterfly with images built into its wings, as if the butterfly had its own tattoos.

The scoop neck and strap of her tank top framed the butterfly perfectly. From there, a patch of bare skin rode the cleft of her shoulders before the inked sleeves began, one covering each arm. Hidden under the denim was a hip tattoo he kissed often to drive her wild before moving further south.

Ink picked up below the frayed denim of her shorts, the ink covering her toned, long legs. A tapestry was how Wren described her near full body tattoos combined. Whatever the term, it excited him, even though he did not understand how the images fit together. The ink was her story and he had come late to the game.

Toby had asked Baker if he trusted Wren, and Baker did in one unique way. He trusted with one hundred percent certainty that Wren would indeed leave him at some point. It was a foregone conclusion. He understood the woman would eventually move on, but until then, Baker planned to enjoy time with her.

Such sober thoughts arrived with no sense of misery. He was too excited to be with her and treasured what time they had together. The world had gone through a pandemic and souls were battle scarred. Maybe that was why Wren found her way to him. Most people had reassessed what was important.

For Baker, he reveled in his private time, loved staying home, so years of lockdowns served him well. But doing so alone eventually wore on him. Usually there was a girl in his life, one who would eventually fall for Toby. Maybe that was why Baker was so ready to let go of Wren when the time came. He had lost plenty to his best friend, so losing Wren would be par for the course.

Wren bounced with joy and made an announcement. "This is the one!"

"The one? Are you sure? You're leaving a lot of shells on the table. How do you know you have the right one?"

She set it down, approached him, and wrapped her arms around his neck. She looked him in the eyes. "Sometimes you know when you have found the right one."

When she kissed him, he thought maybe he and Toby were both wrong. Maybe he was the one for her. Or maybe he was a fool.

"Are you fools going to buy anything? I'm about to lock up shop," the proprietor said, rolling his eyes at their kissing.

"Yes, fine sir, we are taking this shell," Wren said, holding it up.

"Yay, I can retire."

They followed him down to the cash register and he rang it up. The lower level had various planetary mobiles and spaceships dangling from the ceiling. The elderly man noticed Baker checking them out.

"Big event tonight," the proprietor said.

Baker lit up, wondering if the guy knew about the festival. "Tell me."

"Aurora Borealis. Right here in Utah. Rare this far south. Say it will be as brilliant as in 1989. I was around then. It was spectacular. Course I did drugs back then, so who knows, might have been a cosmic fart and my mind filled in the blanks."

Baker deflated. "Oh. I thought you meant a music festival."

The proprietor twiddled his beard in thought. White chest hairs jutted through the linen fabric of the man's shirt. If he was aware they existed, he had no shame. "No festival I can think of. Not out here. And you two were my only customers of the day. Make all my money from online orders nowadays. Rare are the couples like you who still travel together to uncharted territories."

"Sounds romantic when you say it like that," Wren said. "Do you have a missus?"

The man jerked upright. "You didn't notice her? Had her stuffed when she passed. She's over there in the corner."

The couple froze and looked out into the distance. The corner was dark. Was that a body? It could have been a lamp. Then the man bust out laughing.

"Nah. Left me long ago. I have my birds and shop. I'll be just fine. But you tire of him, then how about you look me up?" The man looked at Wren.

"Sorry. This one's a keeper," Wren said, and exited the store with her shell and her boyfriend.

The heat immediately dampened their clothes. Sweat dripped by the time they reached the vehicle. The handles proved so hot that Baker used the bottom of his tee to open her door, then his. Once inside, they did the butt shuffle as the heat of the seats cooked their collective asses.

Baker started the car and the air conditioner, but it would take some time to get air going in the heat. They pulled out of the lot and Baker dropped the sun visor. The sun was setting but in the direction in which they were driving, so its rays blinded him. They were the only ones on the road which he found peculiar if they were attending a music festival.

Wren upturned the shell and a folded piece of paper fell out. She giggled as it fell into her lap. Baker glanced over as she opened it, Numbers. A series of numbers. Wren retrieved her cell phone and entered the numbers on an app. She smiled and brought up her screen to show Baker.

"This is the next address. Last stop before our final destination," she said.

"Last one before the festival?"

Wren nodded noncommittally. Baker added the address into the GPS. It was a straight shot, no turnoffs. They would be there within an hour. Wherever there was. The trip was not what Toby suggested it would be. Baker and Wren laughed the entire trip and had a great time. Sex in different hotels each night was a plus. But how they were four days in without his knowing where they were going bothered him.

Baker knew there were scavenger hunts of a sort back in the city. People made stops at various businesses and purchased pre-arranged items. Each one led them to the next. Businesses took part because it provided them an income boost, and people gladly paid up for the items to receive the clue to an address for an exclusive party. Sometimes in a legit club, usually in a converted warehouse. It was a way to ensure an upscale crowd. Hosts looped in only the most exclusive people on the scavenger hunts.

Wren was one such a person. Her looks got her invited anywhere. Baker was never one of the cool kids, so was not in the loop. He was the dreaded plus one and grateful she brought him along but wished she would share details. He probed during their drive, but she always changed the subject.

She saw the look on his face so headed him off at the pass. She placed the shell on the dashboard. Dropping it in place where it would not slide around. It was large and the vagina like opening stared out at Baker as he drove them further into the desert.

"You know why I love shells?" Wren asked, answering the question before Baker could chime in. "They have nothing to do with the thing inside. How many shells looked identical when we searched them?"

"The Leia hair ones, for sure."

"Exactly. But sea snails wear conch shells. There are sixty different species of them. Sixty! Can you imagine? That alone shows you how different they can be from one another. Now isolate to one species and consider how different each individual mollusk is. Some like the surface. Others prefer the deep. Warm water or cold. Some might explore the entire ocean, or as much as they can in a lifetime, while others might remain in one place, hardly ever moving except with the tide."

"I can empathize with that slug," Baker joked, but Wren was on a roll.

She leaned forward as if doing so would get them to their destination that much quicker. "The shells left behind, as beautiful, or as chipped, or damaged as they may be, do not represent the creature that lived inside it. That is where the true beauty or beast lies. Within the shells. Do you understand?"

He did not understand, but like all things Wren, he played along. Baker went along for the ride, only physically in the driver's seat. He was not in control of the path they were on. The GPS announced the destination was coming up on their right. Wren's face grew morose as the destination came into view.

A gas station loomed. Baker slowed the car down, but something stood out immediately. Someone had cordoned the gas pumps off with yellow caution tape. Baker pulled into the lot close enough to read one of several handwritten signs attached to the tape.

The sign read: *Retrofitting gas pumps. Convenience open until five daily.*

It was already seven PM. Wren panicked while looking toward the convenience store. A mom-and-pop type, not a chain. She stepped out of the vehicle and stormed toward the place. Baker followed.

"No, no, no. We need this place to be open."

"That's okay. We will wait for tomorrow. There must be a hotel somewhere."

"The last piece of the puzzle is in there, and the event starts soon. Hello?"

Wren looked through the window and pounded on the small panes of glass rising from the door's center. Wren's sudden frantic nature shook Baker. Her actions were out of character for the normally laid-back woman. At least she confirmed they were on a quest for party directions.

She kept pounding despite no answer. He looked around the vast parking lot, feeling somewhat embarrassed. It was closed. What could they do? He noticed a pickup truck in the far corner of the lot. Its windshield caught the last rays of the sun. It was a long way away, but he did not see a driver. Maybe there was a worker still on the premises.

"I see them, they are right there," Wren said, frustration tinging her voice.

"What's right there?"

"Maps."

She took off toward the side of the building. Baker looked back to the distant pickup once more before following his girlfriend. She stormed along the side of the store where a particle board enclosure jutted out from the side of the building. It sat under a roaming tide of flies. The smell was awful. Garbage. Baker noted the lack of wheels on the container. No garbage pickup this far out. It meant they owners had to haul it to a landfill themselves.

Wren continued to the rear of the store and groaned. No back entrance. No emergency in case of a fire. They were in a different world, with different zoning codes. The whole place was one giant box. She continued around to the last side of the building and lowered her head with a sigh. Finally, an entry point.

Albeit a small one. A tiny window sat high on the otherwise solid wall. Probably ventilation for whatever hot foods the place offered. Wren reached for it but could not touch it.

"I'm going in," she said.

"What? Are you crazy? Breaking and entering? Who are you?"

"A desperate woman," she answered simply and looked him in the eyes.

Baker looked toward the truck in the distance once again, then up to the window. She could not reach if he did not give a hand. He chose not to give in so easily.

"It will have your prints. This is serious. And how will you get back out? If you need help to get in, how do you reverse engineer it without me there as well? I can't fit. You would be on your own."

"I'm not on my own. I'm with you, Andrew. And I am not worried about the consequences. Were you able to follow, I would urge you not to. Not yet. I hope you follow me elsewhere, but not here, not now. I'll let myself out the front if possible. And if not, I'll find something to climb on once inside."

She called him by his first name, another rarity. Andrew was Baker so long, he almost forgot about his birth name. He would do anything she asked, would have climbed in if he could. Baker would even smash through the door at the front if she asked, but he would not tell her that. He was not the felonious type, but for her, he would make the exception. He laced his fingers.

After giving him a quick kiss, she accepted the ride. He lifted her, and she slid the window open with ease. Unlocked! She dropped out of sight. There was a loud crash inside. Wren announced she was okay.

Baker headed to the front. By the time he got there, the world had gone gray. Much better environment for breaking and entering, he thought. There was still no traffic. They were in no-man's-land, apparently. The trip to the front brought him closer to the pickup. He squinted in the growing darkness but still saw no one. Maybe they used the vehicle for dump runs, he thought.

Approaching the store's front door to look for Wren, Baker found her, wincing at the sight. Wren stood behind the front counter, which made everything real. A quick glance toward the ceiling above her revealed no cameras, so maybe they were okay. What did Wren mean by following her somewhere else? He **wa**s following her. While he desperately loved her, Baker did not always understand her.

A large rack of road maps rose from behind the front counter. All folded into small rectangles, old school. Wren frantically opened each one and tossed them aside before grabbing the next. Her fingerprints would be everywhere. Why did she need a road map? They had GPS and their phones. A clue. Clearly, the last clue had to be on a map. That's why she was tearing through them with abandon.

Baker eyed the truck again, uncertain why it unnerved him so. He decided Wren would need more time, so he wandered over to the pickup. Dusk was in full swing, but they could still see as it was not fully dark yet. Upon arriving at the truck, he froze. The cab was empty, but a man slept in the truck's bed, head propped on a makeshift pillow. He wore a mechanic's onesie with the name Butch stitched on the pocket. He snored gently.

Walking backward, Baker spotted something startling in the cab. A revolver on the passenger seat, in full view. Was the man waiting for a client? Waiting for the owner? Sleeping off some beer? Baker had no answers about why the man would be there, but the gun concerned him.

Baker fast walked back to the storefront, as frantic as Wren was when she saw the store was closed. Once at the door, Baker tapped gently on the glass and made the universal gesture for *hurry your ass up*! Wren grabbed one more map in the sea of open paper around her and waved it. Eureka! She found what she was looking for. Baker glanced back to the truck, happy to see sleeping beauty remained so.

Wren approached the front door and opened it from the inside. The structure was that of a converted home versus a traditional business, so the front door was like many a home. Wren twisted the button as she exited and closed the door, testing it. She smiled at Baker.

"Locked, see? I got it. We're good, honey, we're good," she said.

"Not yet. We're not."

She stood before him, between him and the truck. Her position blocked his view, so he grabbed her shoulders and leaned her to one side. His eyes went wide. The man was sitting upright in the truck bed! It was getting too dark for Baker to make out anything more than the man's shadow, so he could not tell if the man was looking their way.

"Run!" Baker said.

Wren did, heading toward their vehicle. The sound of the truck door opening sounded off to the side. The man called out, angry, threatening. Had he seen them exit the store? If so, it would explain the man's anger.

Baker got in the driver's side, and they peeled out. He looked in the rearview. The pickup lights came into view. The man was on their tail! Baker looked for an escape route, but they rode a straightaway. Wren had fallen silent despite the chase. She simply opened the map and followed a line on it with her finger. Something already marked it in red with a sharpie.

"A gun. He had a gun in the truck," Baker said.

Wren remained lost in her paper. Even the mention of a gun did not shake her. Baker was in it for the ride with her, but he never expected something like this. His heart beat like a jackhammer. The truck flashed its lights behind them and honked the horn. The man was intent on getting them to stop.

"Maybe we offer to pay for the map, maybe tell him we meant no harm. We can pay for all the maps," Baker said, eyeing the shadow of the man behind the wheel in his rearview.

Closing in, it would not be long now. Wren stabbed the map with a finger. She searched the landscape across lanes to their left.

"Turn left. Turn!"

Baker eyed the stretch to their left. There was no turn. He yelled as much to his passenger. Nowhere to go. The truck closed in, almost on their bumper.

She reached over and jerked the wheel. Baker screamed as they shot into the opposite lane. The car swerved into what would have been oncoming traffic were any cars on the road. They drifted toward the sand beyond the opposite lane.

The world went bright as the pickup roared toward them from behind. Light filled the cabin of their vehicle. They had slowed during the wrestling of the wheel. The truck caught up and followed their desperate maneuver. Baker drove into the desert itself, onto the sand, but the truck stopped where it was.

Baker looked in the rearview. Through the dust, he saw the truck sitting across both lanes, a disaster if vehicles came from either direction. The truck engine roared in the night, gunning, as if eager to follow. Then, inexplicably, it backed up and returned from where it came. Back to the convenience store buried in maps.

Baker stopped the car and leaned his head on the wheel. Wren rubbed his shoulder.

"Are you okay?"

"No, Wren. No, I'm not. The man had a gun," Baker said, head still resting in place. He murmured, without anger.

"And the man is gone."

"He could have hurt you, Wren."

"Could have hurt us."

"Do you think I care about that?" He lifted his head, tears streaming down his face. "Nothing. Nothing matters to me, except you. My whole life, I've been wandering. I have a best friend who lives a life for me. I find little joy in things around me. Nothing makes sense anymore. Then you came along."

She smiled, meeting his gaze. She reached up and wiped the leakage from one of his eyes. He gripped her hand and held it to his face. Needed it there.

"How is it you mean so much to me? I already know you will leave me. Hell, you probably have other boyfriends."

"You believe that?"

He felt guilty saying it, especially in the face of how angrily she responded. But it was true. Baker feared losing her. He nodded, affirming the answer, disappointed at being so weak in front of her.

"I have been with many men, Andrew. And now. Now I am with you. I have never cheated on you and never considered it. The shells, Andrew. Remember them?" He nodded. "Yours contains something special inside. You are the only person I ever considered accompanying me on this journey. I only regret I never considered the consequences of it all."

"Your journey? Not ours?"

"It could be ours. That is your choice. I wish it was so. But yes, this is my journey."

"So, where are we going? To a festival?"

"Yes. To a festival and the show is about to begin. All we have to do is drive."

Baker looked ahead, realizing they were on a road, barely. Mostly windswept sand, but there was a semblance of a lane. He remained unaware of their destination but was ready to find out. Baker stepped on the gas.

Wren rolled down the window and stuck her feet out. It was a balmy night. Wind whipped into the vehicle. Her hair danced with abandon. She let it fly. Baker rolled his window down as well, gripped the wheel and breathed.

His buddy Toby mentioned how cross-country trips tested relationships. Well, Baker and Wren had been tested and they passed. Baker was more in love as they drove on a strange road than before they started. Not only had the couple faced adversity together, but Wren confirmed that there was no one else.

Baker eyed the shell on the dashboard and thought, *it's you and me, buddy. We passed some sort of test and now we get to ride out into the desert with one magnificent gal.*

Baker laughed at the thought. Wren did not ask what brought on the chuckle. She simply smiled and reached out to caress his leg. The sky was spectacular, sparkling like Wren's violet eyes. The moon hung perfectly framed in a sky of stars. It was a view impossible to find in the city. Back home, buildings stood as the center of the universe. It was easy to forget that man was part of something greater. Bigger. The sky threatened to swallow them whole.

After some time of driving in silence, Wren returned to the map and made an announcement.

"We're here."

Baker stopped. He looked around and stated the obvious. "In the middle of nowhere?"

"Yes. The map says this is the spot. So now, we wait."

The tiny lizard part of Baker's brain wondered if she had packed a shovel. Maybe one of those fold down military style in her bags. Then it hit him. Her bags. She had a simple backpack. She brought almost nothing with her.

Aware that such thoughts fell into stereotypes, he could not help but think how he packed more for their trip than she did. Only now, four days in, and in the middle of nowhere, did it hit him. No, she did not have a shovel packed because she had almost nothing packed.

And why did the man in the truck stop? He was armed. Did the man ever even notice they broke into the place? Did he see the couple exit the store? He must have, otherwise he would not have chased after them. Did he call the police? Would they be showing soon? If so, sitting still would be a bad idea.

Wren grabbed his face and turned it toward her own. She touched her forehead to his and locked eyes with the man. "I can see those wheels turning. I know as little as you do about what to expect. But we made it. We found it. And now, can't we just wait and see what the night holds for us?"

"You know me, I'm a planner."

"I know. I can see the stress on your face, poor thing. Can I change that?" She kissed him.

There was something there, something more than normal. It was passion without the promise of more passion. She was not trying to stir him up, she simply wanted the connection. He was fine with that. He kissed back. Finally, she pulled away. Despite his best efforts to remain cool, she had stirred him up.

"Better?" she asked.

He nodded and moved her hand to his crotch. "But I could feel even better."

"I'm sure you could."

She moved the hand, reached over him, and pulled a lever. His seat collapsed. It fell harder than expected so she dropped with him. They clacked heads but came up laughing. She slipped back into her seat and lowered it as well so that both sat reclined, side by side. Waiting.

They looked at the sky, and it began. Green. A flicker at first. A wave? It lined the sky in the distance, shimmering with a cascade of stars as a background. Baker sat up, leaning his head toward the windshield. Wren remained reclined, smiling knowingly. Then the green descended like a curtain in a movie theater. It overtook the sky in the near distance.

The cab of their vehicle filled with a green glow. Baker heard the door open, watched as Wren slid from her seat. He stepped out of the car as well. The green loomed as a shimmering wall before them, a stunning display.

"It's beautiful," Baker said. "Wait. Do you hear that?"

Was that music? Somewhere in the distance he heard it, strange sounds, beyond a hum. Music for certain. The festival. She said there would be a festival. But where? Wren walked toward the light, toward the green. Then a flash off to their right. Bright, still green, but brighter than the rest of the sky. It opened like a doorway and throngs of people emerged. Music followed their path.

The strange melody came from instruments Baker did not recognize. The tune was celebratory yet hauntingly beautiful. Hints of trumpets sounded within the score. There were figures, many, dancing in a line, waving hands and spinning as they moved forward. They were light on their feet, almost too light, as if they danced on air.

Wren approached the line of people. They moved across the desert, passing by the couple. Wren continued toward the celebratory procession. Baker thought of a rave in his younger days as he watched the throngs of people pass. As they moved closer, Baker finally glimpsed the participants. A strange bunch.

Baker could not see any faces. Not because of the darkness, as the stars, moon, and aurora borealis were plenty bright. The green offset the darkness, making their footpath a stage of sorts, one with its own light show. There were dozens of figures, yet not one face in the bunch.

The procession included individuals of different heights and builds, all celebrating with equal vigor. They strolled, danced, pranced, and waved hands. They occasionally took hands and spun one another, all while the music continued playing from an unseen band.

All the revelers wore strange masks, with variations of beaks. Plague masks. Having recently gone through a pandemic, Baker watched several documentaries involving plagues of years past. Plague masks contained long snouts. Originally made from leather or copper, the masks covered the entire face up to and including goggles. The plague mask wearers usually combined the face covering with head-to-toe clothing. Like robes or overcoats.

The people dancing in the green light wore similar outfits. Baker studied them further. The tallest near the head of the pack was skeletal thin, wearing a full leather overcoat that crested along the shoulders. His beak was long and studded and included thick goggles which hid the eyes within. Only green light reflected off the thick lenses.

Behind the leader was another who raised curled arms to her right and then to the left, never stopping, mimicking one of the dance moves from *Thriller*, only never getting to the rest of the dance, and moving forward the entire time. She (for somehow, he thought of it as she) wore head to toe leather over an androgynous form, along with a leather cape which danced in the wind. Her beak was bright yellow with white stripes slashed in spots along the top of the nose and studded with colorful jewels.

The line kept growing. All the celebrants were similar, but unique. Each celebrating some dress code unknown to him. Wren was close enough to join them. She moved within arm's reach of the crowd, which unnerved Baker. He rushed forward too late. She called to him as the crowd swept her up.

"It's my journey, remember? You must make your own choice," she yelled and then she was gone, lost in the crowd.

There was no fear on Wren's face as she vanished, only fear in Baker's heart. Not yet. He wasn't ready to lose her yet! Baker understood it was coming, but not so abruptly. He rushed forward, screaming her name. The crowd paid him no heed. He stayed beyond their reach but followed the line toward whatever destination they marched toward.

"Wren! Wren!"

She laughed somewhere in the crowd. Glorious, contagious. Her voice rose above the music that grew in his head like an earworm. Not unpleasant, but persistent. Magical in its tones. It made him wish to dance as well, but he was too busy searching the crowd for his love.

The diversity of the crowd grew. There were cloaks, tuxedoes, and beaded dresses that looked as if they were from the roaring twenties. But all wore the plague masks of different types, and none showed even an inch of skin. Wren appeared briefly, a bobbing head in the crowd. She yelled to Baker.

"It's beautiful, Andrew, so glorious. The world sings here!"

Wren crowd-surfed, not of her own volition. The people passed her along, hands lifting the woman in celebration, passing her along overhead, allowing her to ride the throng. He did not witness any groping hands, no malevolence from the throngs of people, only celebration.

They were human, right? The celebrants? Baker wondered for a moment as the nature of the instruments eluded him. The parade people were bipedal. Baker sensed some were male, some were female despite an overwhelming sense of androgyny. It was happening so fast. Baker ran tirelessly, worried he would lose her not just for the moment, but forever, if he slowed. He chased not just Wren but the idea of her.

The sand. The sand should have exhausted him. Never in the best of shape, running in a desert should have fatigued him immediately. Were they on a ridge? He could not spot the sand on which they stood. Below his feet, he saw only light, a world bathed in flickering green.

He had never been to New Orleans, but he imagined it to be close to what he experienced now. It looked like the many movies he had seen, minus parade goers flashing themselves to secure gaudy bead necklaces. Here the only beads were on masks, and dresses, even studded gloves, but there was no skin in sight. Except for Wren. Her tattoos took on a green hue as well, now part of the show in the desert. The festival she had promised him.

The joy of abandonment played out before his eyes. In that line, no one worried about pickup trucks with guns in them. (The guy was likely sleeping in the truck while waiting to watch the aurora borealis.) There were no break-ins at convenience stores with evidence left behind. There were now worries of a lover leaving.

Baker took a leap of faith and leaped into the crowd. He nearly stumbled over uncertain ground beneath his feet. Spongy. Soft. He literally bounced with every step. He felt drunk the way he stumbled about. A bouncy house. He had not been in one since childhood, but that was what it felt like. Walking around in a bouncy house. It made little sense.

And then he was no longer on his feet. The surrounding people lifted him until, like Wren, he crowd-surfed. The people happily welcomed him. Earlier, as he drew closer to the crowds, he felt his worries fading. Now in the hands of the celebrants, peace and joy overtook him. He was along for a ride. This might be Wren's journey, but he was riding shotgun.

He laughed uncontrollably, screaming out in bursts of excitement. It was then he noticed the music came from the beaks themselves. The people were singing. Or their beaks served as instruments of unknown origin. Their dance-like movements kept time with the music as they moved forward.

The green light deepened in the distance and took on form. (A square?) It appeared an opening in the green, a darker green framing the outer sides of the square. Those at the head of the line stepped through the square and vanished. For the first time since joining the party, Baker felt uneasy. Where were they going? Why could he not see past the square?

Wren's omni-present laughter ceased immediately as the group carried her through the green light. Baker twisted, trying to take control of his forward momentum, but there were too many people, too many hands. The square drew closer as they were about to step through. His section of the line advanced, and the light grew so bright it forced him to close his eyes. The world went from green to black.

Baker heard chirps and whistles as he struggled to regain his senses. He woke to delirious comfort, like sitting on a cloud. Never had he felt so comfortable. Waking in a bed curled in the blankets at the perfect temperature was a rare moment in his life. The feeling approximated that, but even more comfortable as he struggled to open his eyes.

The world was cotton candy. There was no need to ruin it by waking. Except he did. His eyes shot wide. Bright white circular lights lit a room with an antiseptic glow. The white circles were intensely bright but did not bother his eyes at all.

What bothered him was paralysis. He could not move! Only his head seemed mobile. Clearly, he was on a medical table, but it made little sense why he did not feel the chill of the metal surface. How could metal feel immensely comfortable? Cotton candy, warm, soft. He felt cradled in a place worth staying forever.

Still unable to move anything beyond his head, he looked down in search of what held him in place. He checked both his arms and legs. There were no restraints, but he remained flat on his back. How was he held down with no restraints? He attempted to lift one arm and felt resistance but saw nothing there.

The singing had stopped, replaced by odd chirps and squeaks. The beak people. He turned and saw Wren unconscious on a table a few feet to his right. Several of the plague masked people stood over her. He struggled to break free but could not defeat the invisible bonds.

One beaked figure noticed Baker and gestured to the largest bird, the same one who earlier led the crowd. That one turned to Baker. Minus the green lights, Baker finally glimpsed what lay beyond the goggles. Pools of universes. In each lens he saw not just blackness but infinity, endless stars sparkling where there should have been eyes.

The large being (man?) paid Baker little heed. There was work to do. Baker felt as if he interrupted a surgeon mid-operation. Except when this individual turned back to the operating table, there was no surgical mask, only a lengthy leather beak lined with metal studs. The nose extended so long it threatened to brush against Wren's chest. The being took hold of Wren's arm, lifting it and dropping it. Wren's limb drooped lifeless, unconscious for certain.

Baker planned to call out, to ask what was happening, but the words caught in his throat. His eyes shot wide in shock. A dream. It all had to be a dream. Or nightmare. It could not be happening. The beaked individual pulled Wren's arm again, and it came off!

There was no blood, no gristle left between arm and torso. The arm simply came off. What the being held could have been a mannequin arm. It ended in a nub of flesh at the shoulder. Wren's shoulder also appeared fleshy at the point of amputation. Blood should have poured, but it was as if they somehow clamped off an oil well with a fleshy sleeve.

Baker could not scream, too shocked at the sight of Wren on the table alongside him. Her chest moved, she still breathed, but she seemed unaware of the sudden amputation. The beak dropped the limb to the floor. It landed with a fleshy thud. Not a mannequin at all. The sound along with the view of Wren's nubby shoulder roiled Baker's stomach. He felt the gorge rise in his throat.

The individual moved to Wren's leg on the same side next, tracing hands down her calf, an intimate caress leading to her ankle. With a jerk, the plague doctor pulled off her foot! It looked so small in the man's gloved hand. So much skin showing on poor Wren, but none on the beaked crew surrounding her. The man dropped the foot to the floor and reached for her shin, detaching that next, leaving her thigh ending in a stump. Each detachment occurred minus the expected gore. Like doll pieces pulled away, everything ended in stubs of bloodless flesh. Somehow, they were pulling her apart.

Was he next? What was their plan for him? He did not care. Only Wren mattered. He finally found his voice. "No! Leave her alone. Take me. Take me!"

Suddenly, a beak was in his face. The metal point facing him was metallic and rust covered. Its tip touched his nose. There were no goggles on the figure, only a metal faceplate strapped to the skull above the beak. The sharp pointed nose dug into his own and he winced despite feeling no pain. His situation was nothing compared to Wren's.

Baker stopped yelling, and the beak immediately left his face. Silence. Baker realized if his cries drew attention, he could not watch what they were doing to Wren. He needed to remain silent. How else to watch and figure out a way to help her? He needed to help her! Why could he not move? Was this experience what people spoke of when claiming to be abducted by UFOs?

While distracted with a beak in his face, they had already done more damage. The being dropped her second leg on the floor in one large piece. Wren was losing the fight to remain a body. It was impossible to contextualize it in any other way. Wren was simply falling apart at the hands of madmen in beaks. Her other arm came next. There was only a torso now. What more could they do to her? Why would she not wake?

Then the worst, the unthinkable. Beaked bastards stood on either side of her torso, each placing gloved hands on her sternum. They pushed their hands through her chest until buried to their wrists. They yanked and Wren split in two! The action loosened something deep inside the woman, for her head lolled to one side and lazily fell off the table.

The head spun in place on the frictionless ground like a spun coin before finally settling into place. From where her head rested, she stared up at Baker. Wren! Wren was gone. Torn to shreds with no sign of blood. Baker felt madness rising in his brain. Nothing made sense any longer. He wished for them to take him in such a manner. For why not? He lost that which he held most dear, watched her torn from limb to limb. How could he ever go on?

The hands lifted from her chest, revealing a light so bright, Baker had to squint. Wren's two torn halves fell to the ground. Unlike the clean fleshy stubs at the points where they tore other limbs free, the halved sections of torso revealed internal organs split down the middle but held in place by transparent covering. She could have been a display in a human anatomy class.

The light in the hands of the figure was dazzling. Brilliant. Warm. The leader cupped his hands around the ball of light from Wren's chest, walked past Baker, making a show of the brilliant orb. Baker followed the individual's movements to a medical table on his opposite side that he never noticed. On it lay a pink plague mask at head height on the table below which rested an empty leather outfit.

The leader inserted the orb in the mask which glowed so brightly Baker had to look away. When he looked back, a figure filled out the previously empty leather outfit. Someone was inside! The individual sat up. She, for he understood now who it was, had round glass eyeholes cut into her mask. The glass was pink, of a shade less bright than the beak.

The outfit comprised a leather shawl over a leather dress. Wren was taller than before, her prominent breasts nowhere in sight. Androgynous like the others, yet beautiful. Stunning in her own way. She did not look like the others. She was, as always, Wren.

Wren stepped off the table and approached Baker, speaking in an unfamiliar voice, one fluctuating, searching for its new identity. "Oh Baker. My journey has begun. In our shells, we must roam only one place, one plane. Now I can finally live!"

Baker tried to speak but could not. A tear rolled down his face. Wren wiped it away. Her gloved hand was as warm as flesh. Maybe it was flesh.

"I will not remember your language much longer, will have no need for it. Now is your choice. You can join me, or you can return."

"I can leave?" He finally found his voice.

"I hoped you would stay, but I understand if you do not," she said, her voice fluttering into tweets.

"I love you Wren," he said, and she understood his answer.

"You were the best thing on my old journey, Andrew. I loved you, please never forget. It could take years in your time, but you know how to find us. You know how to join the festival if ever you change your mind."

Wren sang, and the song made Baker weep.

Baker found himself in the desert, blinded by light. The sun lingered high in the sky, the night and its green curtain of shimmering light had retired. He went to the car and took the driver's seat. Wren's scent lingered in the car.

He started the engine and drove back the way he came. He wondered if he would encounter the man in the truck. It did not matter. Such things meant little anymore.

Baker planned to start the search soon, look for the clues. It would be foolish to think the same places they visited would lead to the same spots. Somewhere in the heart of New York, at the trendiest locations, he would pull a thread when he was ready. Unravel it and follow the clues to lost love.

He turned on the radio where a DJ spoke of the spectacular light show from the night prior. If they only knew. Baker had a front-row seat where he experienced a world without blood or pain. It would have been so easy to stay there. So easy to give up. When he was ready, he would join the parade and rediscover his love.

Until then, there were things to experience. Baker changed the station to some good old rock and roll, then spun donuts in the sand until facing back the way he came. He drove off thinking a beer sounded good, along with some sloppy food.

No, Baker had not finished his journey, but he was ready for it to begin.

About the Author

Joseph Carro

Joseph Carro holds an MFA from Stonecoast at the University of Southern Maine. He is the co-author of The Little Coffee Shop of Horrors Anthology and has served as an editor/proofreader for the Glyphs Productions line of comic books since 2015. He has written for itcherMag and can generally be found engaging in some kind of geeky/nerdy activity throughout the day. Oh, and he was also in a movie with Kelsey Grammer (he's going to say that every chance he gets). He currently resides in Woodford, Vermont located within the infamous Bennington Triangle although he will always be a Mainer at heart.

About the Author
Paul Carro

Paul Carro was born in Maine and was published at the ripe old age of eleven (yep, fifth grade) in an anthology of Maine authors alongside one of his horror icons. Paul took a long break from publishing and moved to LA after college to toil in the film/TV industry writing and producing but not in the horror genre. A long time comic book and horror nerd, Paul finally got back to his literary roots and published books in the superhero and horror genres. His debut horror novel The House put him on the horror genre map and the book has had a highly successful run which continues to this day. He has followed up with more novels and has co-authored The Little Coffee Shop of Horrors Anthology series which is his love letter to the horror anthologies that inspired him from a young age. When not doing horror related things, Paul can be found hiking all over the state of California. He currently resides in Santa Monica, CA.

For updates check out: paulcarrohorror.com

ALSO BY PAUL CARRO & JOSEPH CARRO

The Little Coffee Shop of Horrors Anthology

Two generations of writers from one family get together for twelve terrifying tales. The writers visited twelve different coffee shops across the country to craft stories as dark as any drink served by a barista.

Stories include: *A killer who keeps his eyes on the prize. A divorced couple face unspeakable aquatic horror when they hand off their child for shared custody weekend. A creepy cafe customer gets as good as he gives when he picks on the wrong barista. A group of influencers learn the hard way what a side hustle really means.*

Read these and eight more shots of horror. Welcome to our coffee shop where the shaking does not come from the caffeine and the chills do not come from iced drinks but from the twelve tales of terror. You will never look at coffee shops the same again!

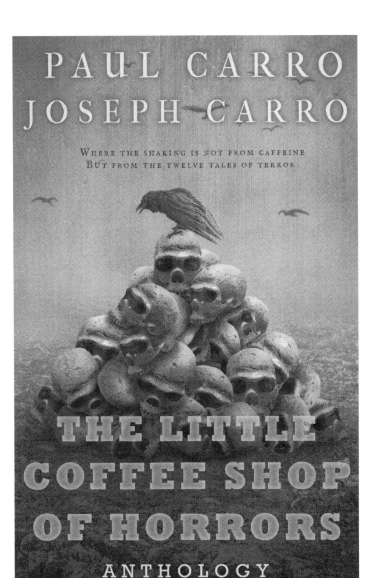

Also By Paul Carro

The House

The day began when Sheriff Frank Watkins found two bodies and three heads. Then things got strange.

Paranormal TV host Charlie "Thunder" Raines has spent a lifetime seeking answers to the unexplained. When he spots a woman no one else on his crew can see, it appears he will finally receive his answers but at what cost?

Yoga instructor Suzy Potter thought she left her past behind by moving cross country and changing her identity. When a door that previously did not exist creaks open in her studio, she discovers the past can never truly die.

Before the day is over more doors will open before slamming closed, trapping residents of Tether Falls, Maine in a place seemingly existing between two worlds. The mysterious event brings together nine strangers with nine secrets so dark they plan to take them to their graves, with one house willing to accommodate them all.

Welcome to The House–Where secrets go to die. Enter if you dare!

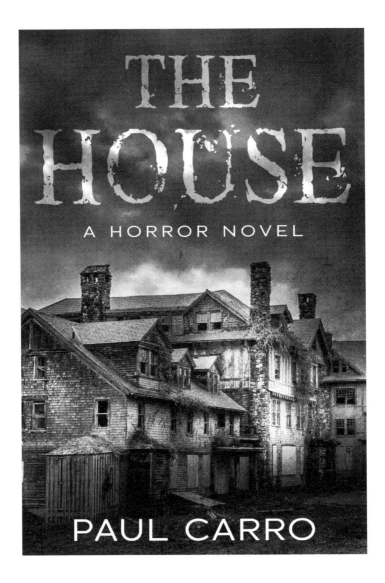

Also By Paul Carro

The Salem Legacy

Between 1692-1693, innocent women were hanged as witches in Salem under mysterious circumstances. Why did friend turn on friend? Why did crowds cheer the death of neighbors? And the biggest mystery, why did the executions finally stop?

Centuries later on the California coast, Linda Hunt became a teacher at the same orphanage she was raised in. Resigned to a life without family, her world turns upside down when a mother she never knew dies in a nearby nursing home leaving more questions than answers about her lineage.

Inheriting a deed to a house in Salem along with an antiquated key, Linda and her friends travel to the infamous town in search of her family name. But some mysteries were never meant to be solved, and some secrets were meant to stay buried.

With the aid of a local historian, Linda pulls at the threads of the past, waking ghosts of a tragic time. Soon the group is subjected to unspeakable terror as they find that uncovering the truth comes at a price.

As history reveals itself, Linda learns witches were not born in Salem, they were made.

In 1692 residents of Salem began a hunt for witches
In 1693 they found one

PAUL CARRO

THE SALEM LEGACY

A HORROR NOVEL

Made in the USA
Middletown, DE
06 May 2023